THE LAST IMPERATOR

M. L. TISHNER

M. L. Tishner
c/o AutorenServices.de
Birkenallee 24
36037 Fulda

For more information on Dissociative Identity Disorder, check out the following YouTubers for more information: DissociaDID, The Labyrinth System, & The Entropy System

Edited by Tiffany White at Writers Untapped.

For my husband, my parents, and Roxy.
And for my fans...

PART ONE
THE
PEACEMAKER

CHAPTER 1

REI'S HEART HAMMERED IN HER CHEST AS SHE TOOK her first steps onto the stage. The spotlight blinded her, yet the applause of the crowd reminded her she was not alone. She took a deep breath and wished giving speeches didn't make her so nervous.

"Good evening, people of the wonderful planet of Kapetyn II!" Manden's voice boomed next to her.

"It's a beautiful night for an election!" Rei followed.

She glanced up at the glass ceiling and the twinkling stars above. A deafening roar responded, and the stage shook beneath their feet. The crowded room smelled of sweat and sparkling wine.

Kapetyn II's polls predicted that Federation favorite Sariah Bray would win as representative of the planet, over-throwing the long-tenured Malachi Wayon of the Dominion. Inspired by Rei's actions back on Trappist V six months before, Sariah put down her Daer gladius and took up the mantle as a politician. Her credentials as a knight helped her rise in popularity over the last six months. It also didn't hurt that the media discovered she was the ex-girlfriend of the now famous Bronx Manca. They predicted tonight to go down in history: after over thirty years of Dominion major-ity, the star cluster would be in a deadlock. Sariah's win represented that change and was the very reason Urius sent the Volocio to make an appearance as the votes were counted.

"We are so happy to celebrate this evening with you! Aren't we?" Rei glanced behind her at Arram, Kaz, Crona, and Artema, who waved with enormous grins plastered on their faces. Bronx was the only one who didn't. His wide dark eyes and tall form shifted from side to side, his anxiety flickering around the edges of Rei's vision. It always presented itself over the last six months in the same golden yellow.

Ever since Bronx brought her back to life, she had been able to see his emotions as flickers of color. It still took some getting used to after all this time.

She wished Urius wouldn't force the reaper into the spotlight, but after the media released the video of him resurrecting Rei, suddenly the public wanted to see him. She interlaced her fingers with his and drew him to her side, giving a reassuring squeeze. His shoulders relaxed, he gave her a more genuine smile, and the color around the edges of her vision melted into bright green.

"Whatever happens tonight," Manden called, "just know that we have made it clear to the Dominion that the Federation is not a dead party—but alive and ready to return to glory." The crowd cheered.

"Sariah!" Rei said, looking back toward the large sign with the words *Sariah Bray for Kapetyn II: Change You Can Believe In.* "Come out and join the party. Your voters want to see you!"

The young politician appeared from behind the tall blue curtains. Her blue suit brought out the red in her strawberry blonde hair, and her light eyes glittered with excitement.

Sariah's fiancée followed closely behind with an impeccable smile. Elmessa Ettowa's dark skin glowed against the blue of her dress, and her darker eyes missed nothing as she took in the crowd.

Rei never forgot Arram's comment about their relatives

when they first arrived in the Federation six months before. Ettowas literally filled every crevice of the star cluster, especially in politics. Elmessa was one of many cousins they had met in the last several months, especially now that she was engaged to Sariah.

Sariah wasn't an innocent bystander either since her family, the Brays, had just as many entanglements as the Ettowas between the two political parties.

Rei, Bronx, and Manden drew back to allow the two their time in the spotlight and returned to the other Volocio upstage. Sariah and Elmessa stood before the adoring crowd in their matching colors of blue and silver—Federation colors—and waved vigorously before reaching out to take hands from those in the crowd. The image reminded Rei of what she did the first time she spoke in front of Federation supporters.

"I hope we win," whispered Crona.

"We will," answered Kaz. "We have to believe people want change."

"We should join the crowd," said Artema.

"She's right." Arram gently touched his sister's arm and led her to the steps of the stage. "People paid good money to shake our hands."

Crona straightened her coat as she followed. "Good to know my handshakes are worth a lot of money."

"The tickets for tonight cost over a hundred thousand prox a head," Arram added.

"Some people just have too much money," muttered Bronx at his sister's side.

The group split up and took their posts in various areas of the ballroom. Blue banners with the Federation star hung in several places between large screens currently showing videos of Sariah and Elmessa from the campaign. That same star decorated the high tables that Rei and the others had to weave through to reach the guests. The smell of cologne and hairspray hung in the air. Soft violin music filled the space between the murmur of conversation while servers fluttered about with trays of hors d'oeuvres. Rei grabbed a few to nibble on.

Bronx never ventured far from her as Crona's words remained ever present in both their minds:

He cannot hurt you as long as you're together.

Bronx took the warning more to heart since the last time they were separated Rei had died. He feared what would happen if he left Rei's side again. Fortunately, most patrons wanted to see them together, anyway. The heat from Bronx's hand warmed the small of her back.

"You make such a handsome couple," said one woman in a gold-sequined dress. The fluorescent lights in the room hit a sequin just right, sending a beam of blinding light into Rei's eyes.

Rei smiled as she took Bronx's arm. "Thank you. That's very kind of you to say so."

"I had hoped that Bernadette would also join you tonight."

"Her presence was required elsewhere." Rei gave the woman a tight smile.

"She has such a relaxing aura about her. Perhaps I will see her at another event."

"Perhaps."

"I have been meaning to ask," said a man in a suit that appeared a little too tight. Rei hoped the last button on his jacket would make it through the night. He pointed his half empty wine glass in Bronx's direction. "Are you related to

Yuri Manca? He was an air commodore in the early days of the rebellion against the Dominion. He has seemed to enjoy stepping back into the spotlight after that complete disaster on Wolf X."

"The Federation still won that election," the woman retorted.

Bronx gave the man a tight smile that didn't reach his eyes. "He's my half brother."

Rei raised an eyebrow. Bronx rarely acknowledged his relationship to the air commodore. She was shocked when Bronx first told her a few months before, but he and his brother had a strained relationship because Yuri blamed Bronx for their father's death. It wasn't a surprise the younger Manca refrained from acknowledging their relationship. But ever since the elections on Wolf X, Yuri had come back into the spotlight, and suddenly people all over the Tyre Star Cluster were interested in the connection between the air commodore and Bronx.

The man furrowed his eyebrows. "Brother? But surely Yuri is old enough to be your father."

"Don't tell him that."

"I thought Crona was your half sister." The woman pointed at his sister, whose laughter was easy to pick out in the crowd.

"Crona and I share the same mother. Yuri and I have the same father."

Bronx's posture went rigid, and the yellow aura returned. Rei's hand ran down Bronx's arm and took his hand, giving it a gentle squeeze.

"How complicated. Your parents never married?"

Bronx shook his head and met Rei's eyes.

"I see Sariah waving us over," Rei said, giving the

couple an enormous smile. "I am sure she needs us for something. Will you excuse us?"

"Of course," said the woman.

Bronx pulled Rei away before she could reply. "Thank you," he whispered after they disappeared into the crowd.

"You looked like you wanted to slink into the darkness and never come out."

"Only when people poke around my background. The media would love to know I am the product of an affair. I would much rather talk about what a handsome couple we make." He pulled Rei's hands to his lips.

"And we both know you're the prettiest of the two of us," Rei said with a smirk.

"I am so damned pretty."

They chuckled. Rei caught her breath as Bronx brushed a strand of hair behind her ear. His eyes softened. She loved the way he looked at her; it made her forget anyone else was in the room.

"Ugh, young love," said Manden with two glasses of sparkling wine, handing them to the couple. "Smile for the media, children, our faces need to stay the highest ranking on the Nexus." The redhead put an arm around Rei and Bronx, and they smiled as a few journalists scurried around behind flashes of light.

"And by the way," said Manden, letting them go, "I am the prettiest." He gave them a wink before shaking hands with more patrons. Rei and Bronx laughed, then continued their own salutations as more people gathered around them. The champagne tickled Rei's nose when she took a sip.

The peal of bells pierced through the raucous of the room. A hush fell over the crowd as eyes moved to the largest of the screens above them.

There were 497 districts along the La Silla archipelago of Kapetyn II, the only habitable part of the planet. Depending on the popular vote of the district, the winner got a point. The first to reach 249 points was then deemed the winner.

The screen displayed a topographical map image of the archipelago with each district in gray. The first of the final votes appeared, and a wash of blues and reds spread across the map.

Rei refused to look at the numbers. She watched as more silver-starred blue banners took over the islands. Pride bloomed in her chest—the Volocio helped the campaign where they could during the last few months, and they had really gotten through the otherwise staunch Dominion planet.

Rei caught Arram beaming out of the corner of her eye. He had been the one who organized most of their appearances and speeches. It was the first time Urius let Arram take the lead after her brother begged for an opportunity, and it appeared to be paying off. His violet eyes sparkled with delight.

A gasp escaped the crowd, bringing Rei's attention back to the screen. Red-flowered black banners bled across the islands, even a few that were previously blue.

"Did you see that?" she asked Bronx.

"Those were just blue. It's Wolf X all over again," he responded.

The Dominion votes had quickly reached and surpassed the stars, just barely reaching the 249 goal. Just like that it was over. Malachi was reelected.

Rei's stomach clenched, followed by a wave of nausea. She barely noticed that she let go of her empty glass as it clattered to the ground. Her other hand never let go of

Bronx's, and she squeezed it as a hush fell throughout the room.

"Well, shit," muttered the reaper as the people booed around them.

Rei rubbed her face, no longer caring that she smeared her heavy makeup. Sariah was sure to win, and Malachi was a known corrupt politician who had been lining his pockets from the coffer for years. Rei shouldn't have been surprised that such corruption could buy ballots. Roiling heat pooled in her belly as her blood pressure rose.

The image on the screen changed to the open-mouthed shocked faces of Sariah and Elmessa. The word "live" blinked above the image, indicating they were being broad-casted across the Nexus. Everyone quickly composed them-selves, but their carefree smiles were long gone.

"This has been a disappointing turn of events," began Sariah, her voice shaking ever so slightly. "I must congratu-late Malachi on his win." A half-hearted applause rolled across the room.

"Our god queen spoke true," Elmessa said. "Tonight we still made history. We may have lost, but by one district. That is a number the Dominion cannot ignore!" The crowd murmured in agreement.

"The Dominion will not ignore us," shouted Rei from her place in the audience. Several people turned to her. She knew she should let Sariah and Elmessa have their moment, but the rage humming in her veins gave her the push. "We may still be a technical minority, but we are closing in. Tonight we give to Malachi, but tomorrow we ensure the Dominion does not forget that even though they won, it was by a tiny margin. Soon Anekris Praymer will no longer enjoy the power he once wielded—and neither will his followers."

The crowd roared in agreement.

The Dominion sovereign deserved to be stripped of everything. He had already taken so much from Rei: her parents and her grandparents were murdered by either him or his Negander knights. Then she had discovered that he had captured her brother Niklaryn, allowing her to believe that he was dead for a decade. Since then she had thought of nothing else than making Praymer pay.

"Thank you, Sariah and Elmessa." Malachi's voice blared over the speakers. His face took up the large screen above the stage as he gave his acceptance speech. Apparently it was his turn to accept his win as the word "live" blinked across the top corner of the screen. "I want to thank my opponent for accepting her loss with grace. Sariah has campaigned well, and I recognize that if we are to continue to live in peace, we should work together. I do sorely wish our god queen was not so bloodthirsty. Perhaps if she had the grace you possess and tried to talk to our beloved sovereign, they may find common ground and end this squabble before it becomes a full out—" His head burst into a shower of red, splattering across the screen.

Rei let out a gasp and her chest tightened. Several people screamed, but all eyes remained on the screen as a gloved hand wiped some blood away from the lens and a new face appeared: a woman in blazing orange robes, a band across her forehead with the huge embroidered golden gryphon.

Over the last few months, as Rei's popularity as the god queen increased, a new group rose from the ashes of the attack on Kepler IV—where Bronx brought Rei back to life. There were people who grew tired of both parties and wanted something new, an alternative path. Under the sigil of the gryphon, the Path had been attacking the major players of both the Federation and Dominion since. So far, they had spared the Volocio, but it was only a matter of time before that changed.

"We are tired of the Dominion tampering with votes just as we are tired of the Federation's unwillingness to compromise. The time of the two parties is over. Even the god queen is not all powerful to stop what's coming." The woman's dark eyes stared into the camera, Malachi's blood still dripping from her chin. "Better run, Feds." Then the screen winked out.

Rei turned to Bronx, heart thrashing in her ears. The Volocio weren't safe from the Path; they were probably on the planet already. He pulled her close and dragged her through the surging crowd. People screamed and ran in several directions. Rei was grateful for Bronx's towering figure pushing against the tide. The crowd could have easily swept her away.

They joined the others on stage. Sariah yelled, directing nearby soldiers and Daer to usher people out of the building and hopefully to safety.

"We have to get off the planet now," Rei said to Sariah, pulling the politician away from the crowd.

"Do you think they'll attack this time?" Sariah asked.

Rei nodded.

The group ducked behind the curtain and to their shuttle parked outside. Kaz had made the group invisible, but it was all for naught: the hallway filled with more orange-robed warriors, guns ready.

There was no way they would have passed them unnoticed. Kaz dropped the illusion just as Rei and her brother came forward to face them.

"Stay back, Arram," Rei said. "I can handle them myself." Adrenaline flowed through her veins as she drew closer, electricity from her lightning fluttering about her hands. The hallway was too narrow for all of them to fight, but plenty of room for her alone. She had hoped to have at least one election day without running into them. But it wasn't meant to be.

CHAPTER 2

"The Path demands the god queen and her fake gods surrender," said the man in the front. "Come quietly and no one will get hurt."

Arram rolled his eyes. "That line is old. We would've taken you seriously if you didn't pull the same stunt on Wolf X. People died there."

Arram stretched out his fingers and called the particles in the surrounding air to charge. His sister could handle them alone, but he was going to help anyway. He was so grateful for all the training he and Rei had been doing the last six months.

Rei surged forward and threw her lightning; the first group of orange-robed fighters were thrown back in a flurry of smoke and sparks.

Arram followed close behind. He threw his hands forward and let the sparks fly, and the two of them worked together, pushing the group toward a room where the other Volocio had more space to fight.

Out of the corner of his eye, he caught Bronx with his gladius in hand to take care of stray bullets while Arram and Rei called their powers. No one yelled "Fire!" but the rain of bullets started. Bronx swung his weapon, and the bullets ricocheted off with little sparks.

The rest of the Volocio soon joined the attack. A gust of wind to surged by Arram, throwing several orange-clad figures about, banging them hard against the metal walls, followed by Artema who flicked her wrist and threw more about.

Arram pressed forward, calling more lightning. His hands shook as the energy fought his control. His heart raced as he willed the lightning to bend, and then he threw it at a group of three Path members. Two shuddered as lightning danced across their bodies before falling to the ground, yet one remained standing. Arram gritted his teeth as he called more lightning. A flurry of steel and vines shot past him, followed by Manden, who took the last Path member down.

"I had it!" Arram shouted.

"Come on!" Manden said, pulling the younger man down the hall.

Kaz and Crona flickered in and out of view as Kaz used an illusion to make him and Crona disappear before beginning their own attacks. Several of those in orange robes cried out in pain as some mystical force tore through their group, cutting and slicing.

Arram and Manden joined Rei and Bronx, who fought side by side. Together they surrounded Sariah, who had a hand on her gladius and another around Elmessa's shoulders as the Volocio forged their path to the exit.

Once through, they scrambled into the shuttle where Manden took control and flew them away. Tiny dinks of bullets hit the side of their vehicle as they increased in altitude. The shuttle lurched under their feet and Arram landed on the railing. The force pushed the air from his lungs and he spent several moments gasping. He always hated it when they had to make a quick getaway.

⁂

Arram rubbed his face as he looked in the mirror of the small bathroom of their current ship. Some blood splattered across his cheek; at least this time it wasn't his. He splashed some water on his face before pulling open the sliding door and entered the common area where the other Volocio were seated. Rei leaned against the wall outside the bathroom, pulling her hair from the tight braid she wore in her role as the god queen. Their eyes met as he closed the door.

"You did really well against those terrorists," she said with a smile. "Your powers were on form today."

"Thankfully. I'd just hoped we could have gone an election day without the Path."

Rei rolled her eyes. "I know."

The attack was too close this time. the Path had never attacked the Volocio before, usually preferring easier targets like innocent bystanders to make their point.

"How long until we reach the wedding venue on the *Liberty*?" Arram asked, watching his sister as she paced the room, a habit she picked up in times of stress. The shuttle was a typical model from the Ettowa Starline, filled with artistic silver-upholstered furniture that bordered on impractical, several plants, a stocked bar holding bottled water and a bottle of the best whiskey from Proxima Centauri II as well as floor-to-ceiling windows that boasted a view of the black outside; Kapetyn II's horizon was still visible on the bottom corner.

Manden, Kaz, Crona, and Artema had taken seats on the sofas while Elmessa sat on the arm of one next to Kaz. Sariah leaned against the far wall, drink in hand, her gaze remaining on the stars outside. Bronx stood close to Rei. He never strayed far from her.

"We'll be there in about eight hours," answered Elmessa. "Enough time to get some sleep before the big event." She groaned. "I really regret allowing our parents to plan the wedding. I would never have planned it so close to the election."

"I don't know how you can think about the wedding right now. We need to discuss what the fuck happened back there?" Sariah said, taking a swig of her drink.

Arram understood Sariah's sentiment. The joining of the two big houses, Ettowa and Bray—hailed across the Nexus as the social event of the season—was something he cared little about. He was grateful he was not in either of their positions, considering they were the ones getting married.

"How did we lose?" Sariah continued, but they already knew the answer to this question.

"Do we know what districts were the ones that suddenly changed?" asked Artema from her place on a nearby couch, swiping through her slate.

"I tried to find out who was in charge of the final votes," Arram said.

"And?" Rei asked, pacing back and forth.

"You'll never guess his registered party."

"Gods bless it," she growled.

"So what now?" Crona asked, leaning back against the plush sofa. "We saw that they changed the votes. Can we still win like on Wolf X?"

Elmessa shook her head. She approached the bar and took one of the bottled waters. "No. We can't prove it. Maybe if enough people saw it and rioted like on Wolf X, we could find out the real votes, but Kapetyn II is so small in comparison. I call the planet a loss." She broke open the bottle and took a long sip.

"Even though the candidate's blood painted the camera?" Crona asked.

"His running mate left the party before the attack. They still have a candidate," said Sariah.

"How do you know?" asked Rei.

"Even though you don't talk to anyone from the Dominion, Rei, I do. I know people who worked on that campaign."

Rei's shoulders hunched.

"Are your friends all right?" Kaz asked.

Sariah merely shrugged, but the furrowed brows made Arram believe that she was worried. He rubbed the infinity brand on his collar and scoffed. He didn't understand Sariah. He was surprised to learn she was also part of the queer community, but she had been privileged to not see the darker side of the Dominion and their views of people like him. She may have friends in the Dominion, but he could never see them as such.

"Why do they keep referring to Rei as bloodthirsty?" Bronx asked. "Last I checked, Rei didn't like the taste of blood."

"Too much copper," Rei muttered, having stopped pacing.

"It's a reference to Micaela," Manden said, pulling at a loose thread of his god king costume. "Her nickname was the blood empress."

"A nickname she earned from *your* people," Artema said, looking up from her slate at Manden. "She enjoyed facing you in battle over Earth, Manden, but otherwise war was never her first choice."

"Nor is it mine," Rei said, unbuttoning the high collar of her god queen costume and approached the bar for her own drink.

Arram furrowed his eyebrows. Artema and Manden had this annoying habit of dropping tidbits of their previous lives as if everyone in the room remembered it. One day he wanted one of them to just sit down and tell the complete story from start to finish.

"Between the rigged elections," Rei continued pouring a finger of whiskey, "and the Path attacks, I feel we are being backed into a corner, as though I am being pushed to take some kind of action." She drained the glass in one quick succession.

Arram had the same feeling. It wasn't enough that Rei was prophesied to be the god queen, the star cluster also expected her to call the "war to end all wars" or something equally hyperbolic. The longer Rei remained in the spotlight, the more people cried for her to fulfill the rest of the prophecy.

"Urius is on the line," Elmessa said. "We can take the call in the meeting room. But he only requested Rei, Arram, Sariah, Manden, and myself."

They followed Elmessa to a little room with sterile white walls, like the rest of the shuttle, with a few embedded screens displaying landscapes. A round wooden table sat in the middle with a large pot that smelled like coffee. Arram poured himself a cup. After all that excitement, he needed it. A larger screen on the far wall already showed Urius, Bernie, and Alma Canale waiting.

Arram was surprised to see Canale with Urius and Bernie. Ever since the disappearance of her daughter, Camila, on Trappist V—when Rei made her first appearance as the god queen—the representative had remained on her planet working hard to expel her home world of any Dominion supporters. She maintained a strong front after having won reelection, yet Arram knew she pleaded with Urius in private on numerous occasions to send the Volocio to save her daughter from the Dominion, who she accused of the kidnapping. Urius refused every time, causing a rift between the two.

"Glad to see you made it all safe," Urius said as the others took their seats.

Arram sank into the plush seat, its crushed velvet soft under his finger. His other hand held the steaming cup, just the right temperature. The coffee was a little too sweet for his liking, but free coffee was free coffee.

"We were always safe," Rei said. "We have managed to avoid the Path until today."

"Yet they attack others instead," Sariah said. "Remember Temple of Tasya on Kepler IV? The ones who helped you find Artema? They weren't so lucky."

Arram rubbed the infinity brand on his collarbone again, a gift from Infiernen years before. Turned out the Path also liked to brand their victims. From what Arram had seen on the information collected about this group, they used plenty of different symbols: infinity, circle, star, key— almost as though they used whatever they could find. There was no logic with this group. At least Infiernen was predictable.

No one had seen the Negander since Rei's resurrection on Kepler IV. This new group had taken the chaos Infiernen had left and increased it tenfold, on all planets. Neither party had found a way to deal with them, and the whole ordeal left an unpleasant taste in Arram's mouth. The Path had to be dealt with. In his mind that should be the Volocio's first priority.

"Sariah's correct," Bernie said. "The Path has also attacked the Holy Father of Sancta Sedes on Wolf X."

"What?" Rei and Arram chorused. The holy father was the top position of the organized Volocio religion, the very man who raised Kaz. Their cousin grew up knowing that he was a Volocio and would one day take up the mantle as the religious leader of the star cluster. But once Kaz discovered the Volocio weren't gods, he disappeared from the monastery and spent the next few years roaming the cluster until he finally joined the Federation. Kaz had long left his life as a monk behind, but Arram knew his cousin would not like the news.

"Is the holy father all right?" Manden asked.

"He's fine," Urius answered. "The temple suffered damage, and at least one monk lost his life, but the Daer were swift to protect them. Yuri Manca was also on hand to help."

Bronx's brother appeared very interested in meeting the Dominion sovereign on the battlefield. He had already offered Rei his own militia many times in case she needed them, but Rei still wanted to try diplomacy. Yuri believed the Path was a secret group within the Dominion tasked with pushing Rei to call for war. Arram hated that his sister was called a warmonger while these men who screamed for blood received less-threatening nicknames.

"I am sure the holy father was grateful for Yuri's help," Rei said. "Did the Path give a reason?"

Canale fidgeted with the sleeve of her jacket before speaking. "Same as before: both sovereign Praymer and the god queen are weak for not fighting a war as the prophecy states."

"They want you to start, Rei," Bernie said. "That's why they keep attacking those who helped you and now you directly. They want to prove the propaganda and the prophecy right."

Arram roll his eyes. He couldn't stand fanatics that demanded an outcome without a follow through. Rei calling for war was one thing, but being in a position to win was impossible at the moment.

"Even if we wanted to start the war," Sariah said. "The Federation army doesn't have the numbers. We can't fight the Path and the Dominion."

"But the Dominion is also fighting the Path," added Arram. "Remember? They first started attacking when Praymer started rolling back some of his more extreme practices."

Arram scar's on his collarbone prickled. Praymer had immediately requested the ceasing of branding of anyone from the queer community, and he lifted the ban on the worshiping of the Volocio. It was a tactic to make sure his party remained popular and was no longer seen as threatening. The Path took insult and vowed to continue the practices anyway, using the star cluster as their playground.

Arram wished the others would recognize that they had a common enemy with the Dominion. Arram had lost count of how many times Anekris Praymer had made a call on the Nexus to unite against this common adversary. But Rei couldn't be bothered to watch anything with Praymer's face —she claimed his voice was grating.

"What if Yuri's right and the Path is working for Praymer?" Elmessa asked. "It feels too convenient."

"I agree," Rei said.

"But the candidate on Kapetyn II was a favorite of Praymer's. I don't see him sacrificing Malachi to the Path." Arram sighed. "Every day, the Path is trying to push us all into a war we can't win—like Sariah said, we don't have the numbers."

"That is why Rei needs to bring the Volocio army to fight," Manden said.

"But that means Rei going to Tas'und'eash, and I can't

let her leave," Urius said. "She's too important to the cause at the moment to run off to a group of people who never gave a damn about us."

"They do care," Manden said. "But our seers have predicted that war will come when Micaela returns. That means she needs to come to Tas'und'eash."

"I have already told you I don't want to go," Rei said.

Arram knew what his sister was thinking: it was more than just leading an army—they expected her to take Micaela's throne. She only wanted revenge against the sovereign Anekris Praymer. She didn't sign up for a crown. Arram wouldn't have minded a crown, but no one asked his opinion on the matter.

Manden sighed. "You will have to eventually, Rei. I find this attempt at diplomacy to be a huge waste of time. I have done my part: I have brought you all together, and now you have to do your part and unite the Volocio army to join the war."

"I am needed here," Rei pressed.

"You don't need to go to this wedding. I don't need to go to this wedding. I want to go home. I have to go to . . ." Manden's voice faltered.

Arram knew the name Manden wouldn't utter. Hotara. His wife and queen and also the woman who raised Rei. Manden proceeding with phase two of his plan was more personal.

"I miss her too," Rei said. "I know you think war is the answer, but we are winning. We lost Kapetyn II this election, but we won Tau Ceti II, Trappist V, and Wolf X. Urius spent almost thirty years holding on to three planets for the Federation, and in the last six months we doubled that number."

"We barely won Wolf X, Rei," Sariah said. "They tried to rig that election, too, but failed."

"We still won." Rei tugged on her braid. "I believe in democracy. I believe that the people should decide their fate, and until they call for war, I still want to fight through the ballot box."

"I agree with my sister," Arram said. "We are winning slowly. Praymer has to realize that by now, which is why he has also gone a less violent route and has constantly made comments about joining forces."

Arram scanned the room. An idea had been brewing in his mind over the last few weeks, ever since he saw Praymer's first plea. Rei wouldn't like it, but something had to be done. Without an army to fight both sides, they would have to choose. Both he and Rei wanted to fight with votes, but people were still fickle.

"I have an idea," Arram said.

"Enough with your ideas," snapped Urius. "We tried following your lead with this campaign and see how that turned out?"

"That's unfair," Rei said. "You can't blame rigged elections on my brother. His ideas have always been good." She gave her brother a small smile. "What are you thinking?"

The answer had been staring everyone in the face for weeks and yet only Arram seemed interested.

The moment of truth. Arram took a deep breath. "I think it's time for Rei to take Praymer up on his offer and talk. I think she should unite the Federation with the Dominion to fight the Path. Only after that threat is eliminated can we continue to focus on defeating the Dominion."

Rei's eyes narrowed. The hair on the back of Arram's neck raised as he felt a charge in the air.

"Unite?" Her voice was dangerously low. "Maybe I'll take back what I said. That's a stupid idea. He may not hunt us anymore, Arram, but he's still dangerous. Why would I want to be in the same room as the man who murdered our parents and—" She stopped, but Arram knew what she meant: who enslaved Niklaryn. No one knew their brother was still alive, a fact the Volocio had kept among themselves.

Urius sighed. "I agree with Rei, Arram. But it looks like you'll get your wish. It was another reason I wanted to speak with you all immediately. I saw the completed guest list for Elmessa and Sariah's wedding. Praymer is also a guest."

CHAPTER 3

Rei was grateful she sat in a chair. Her legs turned to jelly upon hearing the news. She had been looking forward to a party with her family, but now—in a few precious hours—she had to rub elbows with the man who hunted her most of her life. Rei was the reincarnation of Praymer's wife, and his determination in finding her suggested that he wanted Micaela back. Her hatred of him was more than his actions towards their family, but also her safety.

The man had to ruin everything.

"This is why I hate having family in Dominion," growled Elmessa. "It's bad enough my parents voted for that man."

"You and me both, darling," said Sariah, running a hand through her strawberry blond hair.

Elmessa ground before placing her head in her hands. "Why did I allow my parents to have control over the guests list?"

Manden shook his head. "We should never have agreed to attend this wedding." His green eyes met Rei's. "We have to make our excuses. It's ridiculous that you should be put into danger like that. Hotara wouldn't want that for you."

Dread pooled in Rei's belly. She wanted to see her family, she wanted a night where she could be a normal person. She had dreamed of dancing with Bronx on the dance floor, of drinking with her cousins, of hugging her grandmother. All of those dreams came to a crashing halt at the thought of being in the same room as that monster.

Her gaze turned to Elmessa, whose lips had turned down into a frown. "We understand if you don't come, Rei. Unlike my parents, I do care what harm Praymer has done to our family."

Rei scanned the room as she contemplated her next move. It would be easy to simply not go to the wedding, despite how much it would break her heart to do so. But Arram always reminded her about making sure her actions were always a show in strength. She knew that if she refused to go because of wedding, the sovereign would technically win. She never backed down from a fight.

"I'm going."

"So you'll talk to him?" asked Arram.

"I didn't say that," she stared dagger at her brother and Arram's gaze returned to his coffee he had been sipping throughout the meeting.

"Despite Anekris Praymer's political history, I am sure it won't hurt to play nice at the wedding," said Canale. "Urius, you said many times before that you and Praymer were friends before the split between the Dominion and Federation. Maybe these first talks can help heal the rift between the two parties and perhaps give us answers that we need."

Rei knew what answer Canale wanted: the location of her daughter, Camila.

Bronx told her of the rumors surrounding Praymer's appetite for women sharing Rei's looks, mainly dark hair and green eyes. Frankly, Rei didn't want to know what happened to the young woman, especially if she was still alive. She hoped Camila wasn't—better dead than a toy for a monster's whims and appetite. The pounding in her ears was louder than her own thoughts.

"Anekris Praymer was a different man thirty years ago. I

don't know what to expect of him. I didn't think he was a Volocio who could live as long as Manden."

"He's not a Volocio," said Rei. The word "abomination" echoed in her mind. That's what Artema called him. He wasn't one of them, but something unnatural, but Artema never elaborated further.

"Fine," said Urius. "I didn't know he was a ... whatever he is. Manden, you claimed to have known Praymer. What do you think?"

The redhead shrugged. "I knew him when he was a child. I know he has a kind soul—or at least had. He wasn't someone who could murder people then, but a lot can change in a few thousand years. But he has shown himself to be a powerful ally when needed in the past."

"I understand Rei's concern for her safety," said Urius. "But at least it's a public event. She won't be alone."

"We will all be there," said Arram, reaching out to take her hand, but Rei pulled away. She was still angry with him for the very idea of talking to that monster. His face fell. "But if it makes Rei feel any better, I can talk to Praymer in her stead."

Urius shook his head. "No. The star cluster will want to see Rei and Praymer together. They are the two figure-heads. Rei will look weak otherwise."

Rei gritted her teeth. She hated people calling her weak because of what other people thought. She was anything but. She squeezed her hands into tight fists until her nails cut deep grooves into her palms. She didn't hear Urius ending the meeting, but returned to the present as the screen flickered off.

"Arram and I will join you in a second," said Rei as the group made their way to the door. Rei stayed in her seat and watched the others share a glance with her brother before leaving the room.

"What the fuck, Arram?" she asked once the door was closed, and they were alone. "Why would I ever want to speak to that man? Or did you forget all those years you spent on the run because of him or what he did to our brother? To our parents?"

Arram sighed. "I didn't forget. But unlike you, I didn't know Niklaryn or our parents. Call me heartless, but it's hard to dredge up feelings over murders of people I never knew." He rubbed his face. "I mean, you never cared who murdered our parents before. You only truly hate Praymer now because he killed them *and* enslaved Niklaryn. Admit it, you really care because of Niklaryn. I know I should hate Praymer more for what he did, but my focus is more on fighting The Path and then the Dominion. I am wiling to put aside my personal feelings. You should, too."

Rei shook her head but dared not meet him in the eye. "Praymer has hunted us our entire lives, Arram. He murdered our grandparents to get to us."

"And yet he doesn't hunt us now." He moved into her line of sight, forcing her to look at him. "We are out in the open, and he does nothing to us. The Federation may still be a minority, but that's a technicality. The Dominion is resorting to rigging elections now, because Praymer knows that you have started something. You were right: we're winning. We don't need the Volocio army. Democracy is on our side. People are voting because of the god queen. But I think we should approach Praymer and show him and the rest of the Tyre Star Cluster how little we fear him. Even after everything he did to us. And maybe gain an ally to get rid of The Path—at least long enough to get rid of them. He has just as much to gain from their removal as we do."

Rei held his gaze, but clenched her fists. She agreed, but determined to hold on to her anger. Arram reminded her he wished she would try to think of the big picture like he always did, but revenge has always been her primary drive.

"I hate that I have to speak to him. I don't want an opportunity to humanize him. I may not want a war, but I wish violence on him and cutting off the head of the Dominion may be our next course of action."

She walked towards the door to leave.

"And what about Niko?" Arram asked.

Rei stopped and slowly turned around. Her green eyes wide and she met her brother's gaze. "What about him?" she snarled. She didn't think Arram would bring Niko into this.

"Infiernen has been hiding since he accidentally killed you on Kepler IV, and the only other person who knows about our darling brother is Praymer. Maybe you don't have to talk about peace with the sovereign, but you know you want to find out about Niklaryn." He approached Rei and took her hand. "Talking to Praymer can work for you twofold. You might find out about our brother and appear to talk peace with him. It will weaken the argument that you're craving war if you start the conversation. Show the star cluster that you want to avoid violence."

Rei bit her lip, and she pulled her hand away from him. Arram was right. If Rei wanted to end this squabble between the two factions, eventually she would have to be in the same room as Praymer. But she wished Urius would let Arram talk to the sovereign and spare her the grief. But no one wanted that. Try as Arram might, the Federation only seemed to care about certain Ettowas. Niklaryn, Kaz, and Rei were always in the spotlight, while they forced Arram into the shadows.

"I'll start the conversation," she muttered.

"I can talk to him afterwards."

Rei shook her head. "I'll handle him myself. But thank you for offering. I don't care what Urius says. I will do the minimum to make the Federation look good, but only that. As much as I want to ask about Niko, it's not entirely enough to convince me to talk to him."

Arram's shoulders hunched. "You know I want to help you."

"I know you do." She gave her brother's shoulder a reassuring squeeze. "I am sorry Urius was an ass."

Arram shrugged, but he wouldn't meet her eyes. "It's okay. It's not your fault. He's right, you're the more famous of us. Of course, they would rather see you. I guess I need to come up with something to make me stand out. Maybe then people will want to hear what I have to say."

"They should have been listening to you to begin with."

Arram finally met her gaze. "We should get some sleep. If there's one thing I know, Crona will want a drinking buddy and I am going to need some shut eye if I am to keep up with her."

Rei chuckled, and the pressure in her chest lessened. "Good luck with that."

CHAPTER 4

Bronx watched Kapetyn II grow smaller as their shuttle floated away. The silver sofa squeaked as he shifted his weight to get more comfortable, not that it was possible— the sofa was too soft and his tall frame sank too deeply into the cushions.

His eyes kept flitting to the doors of the conference room, where Rei and the others still met with Urius. He had grown more anxious in the last months whenever Rei was not near him. He could never forgive himself for letting her leave him at that theater on Kepler IV, only to die alone in the snow afterwards. He knew she was just behind that door, yet his heart raced.

Crona offered him an apple from the basket of fruit from the small table in front of him, but he couldn't eat. Something was happening inside. He felt Rei's anger earlier as a fire in his chest, but a cooler pressure had replaced it. It was still disorienting knowing each other's feelings, but it was a small price to pay when he gave Rei a piece of his soul to bring her back to life.

Eventually the door opened, but only Elmessa, Sariah, and Manden left. Sariah snarled the name "Praymer," followed by other very colorful adjectives. It gave Bronx an idea of the root of Rei's anger earlier, but it was Manden who confirmed it: Anekris Praymer would also attend the wedding.

Bronx's veins went cold.

"Fuck," muttered Crona, voicing his own thoughts. She

sank into the sofa opposite Bronx and stared at the half eaten apple in her hand.

"We must be on high alert," Manden said from his post leaning against the wall next to Kaz, a half empty water bottle in his hands. The god king's green eyes met with Artema's dark one from her position near the bar. "Hotara spent most of Rei's life making sure he wouldn't find her, only to have that dumbass of a brother suggest they 'talk it out.'" The redhead shook his head.

"Arram suggested they meet?" Bronx asked.

"He did. I know it's not Arram's fault that Praymer happens to be a guest. I know he would rather talk to Praymer and leave Rei out of it, but Urius always wants Rei front and center, as if to show how he can command a god." He chewed on his thumbnail. "The whole situation is just shit."

Artema twirled a strand of her black hair. "I can imagine that's why Rei and Arram are still in the room."

"Arram will know what to say to calm her down." The coolness in Bronx's chest told him that. "Arram always knows what to say to his sister." Whether it was to piss her off or calm her down. He had to admit, he always felt wary of the youngest Ettowa and the influence he wielded over Rei. When Rei first discovered it was Praymer who had murdered her parents, she was ready to call for war and take on the whole Dominion herself, but Arram managed to calm her wrath and convince her otherwise.

Bronx had enough close calls with Praymer over the years to know that peace was never going to be an option, and yet Rei couldn't be convinced. The Ettowas were blindly loyal to each other. Such luxuries were never afforded him, especially where Yuri was concerned. But he stopped seeing Yuri as a brother a long time ago; Niklaryn was his only true brother.

He and Yuri had parted on bad terms when Bronx's powers manifested and his father became his first victim. Neither of them knew what Bronx was at the time, and Yuri threw the younger Manca out of the family home as a user of dark magic. But now that Bronx was a recognized Volocio, a reincarnated god, he had hoped Yuri would finally reach out and they could talk about what happened. Disappointment burned in his core when he realized that Yuri had only reached out to Rei and not him.

The door opened with a whoosh and both Rei and Arram returned to the common room. Arram gave his sister one last smile before heading down the hall, presumably to his room. Rei hardly seemed to notice. She stared at the wall in front of her.

Bronx touched her arm, and she flinched slightly as she came out of her reverie. She blinked a few times as her green eyes grew clear when they met his.

"I was so looking forward to the wedding," she whispered.

"I know." He gently cupped her face. He envied Rei's connection with her family. Over the last six months, several helped with the campaign, yet there was one member Rei had yet to meet: Aurelia Ettowa, her paternal grandmother. She was going to be at the wedding, and Rei had been looking forward to meeting the matriarch, but now . . .

"Are you okay?" he asked.

"I am still trying to wrap my head around how I feel about all of this." She removed the band holding her hair in the braid, and the waves came undone. He wanted to tug the rest of her locks free, but he had to wait until they were alone. "I thought I could have a break from being the god queen for an evening. I wanted to enjoy time with the family and then deal with Praymer. Not at the same time."

The wedding was only hours away.

Bronx didn't know what to do, and he hated not being able to help her. "You know I will be at your side the whole time. You won't have to face him alone."

She smirked. "I better not."

The two turned to the others still in the room. Lines of worry covered Kaz's face.

"I don't understand why it's a good idea to talk to Praymer," he muttered, pulling away from the wall and drawing closer to his cousin. He offered her an understanding nod.

"Arram made a good point," Rei said. "I have to at least make the first move, to help weaken the argument that I am desperate for war. Arram also thinks it's time we joined forces with the sovereign against the Path. They attacked the holy father on Wolf X."

Kaz took a step back, his hand pressed against his lips. "Is he all right?"

Rei nodded. "But now something has to be done, and we may need the Dominion to get rid of this mutual threat." She made a face.

"Do you want me to talk to Praymer?" Kaz asked. "I have spoken with him before."

"I can do it," she said. "Everyone expects me to play nice." She rolled her eyes.

"We will all have to work with him."

"Yet Praymer has only been interested in working with me," Rei countered.

"We must be careful." Artema rummaged through a nearby bar and produced a few empty glasses and a bottle of water. She filled a glass and handed it to Rei. "He was an excellent ally to Micaela when she needed an army, but his help always comes with a price."

"And what price was that?" Bronx asked. He couldn't imagine what deal could be sweet enough to entice someone to work with Praymer.

"Marriage."

Bronx swore he felt Rei's heart stop. At least now they knew why Micaela had hitched herself to that monster.

Manden held a finger in the air. "But to be fair, they were also good friends for several years before that."

"They were," Artema said. "I am sure she was happy with the arrangement in the beginning, but it always felt wrong to me. Then again, I wasn't the one who needed the army."

"What did she need an army for?" Rei held the empty glass tightly between her hands.

"Don't worry about that bit of history." Artema waved a hand dismissively. "It was a long time ago. That threat is long gone."

"I don't know about you, but I think it's time we get some sleep," Manden said. "Big day in a few hours."

Bronx put an arm around Rei's shoulders and with a quick "Good night," the two left and headed to a room on the ship.

The other Volocio were faster in claiming their rooms, but Bronx didn't care as long as there was a bed that could fit both him and Rei. The last remaining room was small, with another outrageously large window that filtered starlight into the dark room. There was barely space between the sides of the bed, but there was just enough room for the two of them to move around.

"You are too tall for this room," Rei muttered with a giggle.

He touched the ceiling, just a few inches above his head. She was right, and the thought made him smile.

Once inside, Bronx edged toward the large window at the surrounding stars. Somewhere out there was the super-secret wedding location. The threat of attack was always present as powerful political figures of both parties were also going to be in attendance. Because of this, the brides only gave the guests the location a few hours before their planned departure. The fewer who knew, the better chances of not being found by this organization. Even though it was the event of the year among the elite, both families decided to not allow over two hundred guests. Bronx was impressed. The last time a Bray got married, the guest list was over a thousand. He had attended it with Sariah back when they were still together. It felt like a lifetime ago.

He watched Rei get ready for bed and thought about what awaited them at the wedding destination. Meeting Praymer now felt real. In a few hours, they would be in the same room with the man who hunted the woman he loved. All because she was Praymer's wife in a previous life. The idea should sound preposterous, yet Bronx and Rei were lovers in that same lifetime, and the universe ensured their paths would cross again. He couldn't silence the little voice in his head that reminded him that something drew Micaela to Praymer to begin with. Manden's voice rang in his head. *Good friends.* Good enough to get married, apparently. What if it drew Rei to him now?

"You don't have to worry about him," Rei said, coming to his side.

"Excuse me?"

"Praymer."

"How do you know what I was thinking about?" He raised an eyebrow.

"The look on your face. Your mask is back up whenever something is troubling you, and I can't imagine what would trouble that pretty head of yours." She drew close and cupped his cheek. Her scent of vanilla and sandalwood washed over him.

"Ah, yet there's a lot going on in my pretty head."

"But I'm not wrong."

"No." He smiled. He knew he could no longer hide his feelings or thoughts from her; he and Rei had grown more in-sync with each other in recent months. "Are you okay with a public meeting?"

"There's not much of a choice." She sighed. "I didn't want to say in front of the others, but Arram made another good point. We have heard nothing from Infiernen since Kepler IV, and if I am going to help Niko, I have to get more information. Maybe I can get it from Praymer or something."

Bronx's heart skipped a beat at the mention of his mentor's name. He had hoped with the Negander missing, Rei would focus on defeating Praymer. But it was a fool's wish. She loved Niklaryn and would do anything for him. But there were things she didn't know, things he didn't want her to know. A secret that needed to remain between him, Urius, Skylar, and Artema—the only ones who knew the truth. A secret Niklaryn made him promise to keep the last time they spoke on Kepler IV. No one could know the connection between Niklaryn and Infiernen. Not yet.

"Be careful," he said. "Infiernen is probably hiding for a reason, and saying something to Praymer could jeopardize that. Maybe Praymer figured out that Infiernen was a double agent."

She tapped a finger to her lips as she thought. "You're right, but I don't plan on asking him directly." Her fingers moved to a strand of hair and she gave it a gentle tug. "I don't know how to go about it. But I have to do something."

Bronx wished she didn't. He was sure that Praymer also knew the truth about her brother. He could tell Rei, and the thought scared him. Of all people, she should hear it from Nik. Bronx wanted to tell her, but he had sworn not to, and honestly, he wasn't ready for her to know either. It meant admitting how much he had lied to her about her brother in the first place.

"Talk to Skylar at the wedding." He took her hands and rubbed her knuckles with his thumb. "Infiernen will probably communicate with her first." The two had been working together for years to feed Dominion information to the Federation. "Maybe you won't need to talk to Praymer for more than a quick photo."

She absentmindedly squeezed his hands before pulling away from him. "I have messaged her many times on the subject. She has heard nothing from him either." She growled with frustration. "I'll just wing it when we get there. I don't want to dwell on it more than I have to."

Bronx's shoulders relaxed. He joined her at their closet, where someone had already unpacked their things. This was something he was still trying to get used to.

"What would you rather talk about?" Bronx asked, folding a pair of trousers. It wasn't necessary, but he felt restless.

"Something your brother wrote in his recent message."

"Oh?"

"He wanted to know what I planned to do about the

Dominion's attempt at rigging the election. I think he expected me to smite his foes or something." She chuckled.

"Yuri wants war," Bronx said. "He knows what the Dominion is capable of. He is ready to fight again if he needs to."

"And what do you think?"

"I agree with him. There's a lot of pressure coming from all sides: Federation, Dominion, the Path. War is coming, and Urius is a fool to think we can do it alone. Manden is right. Eventually you may have to plead our case on Tas'und'eash."

Rei rolled her eyes. "I wouldn't plea." She opened the outer jacket of her god-queen costume revealing a thin, silk chamise underneath. "Manden thinks I need the Dinay crown, Micaela's crown. Apparently the Volocio will only go to war if a seer sees it, and they see Micaela returned to her throne." She pulled off the outer layer of her costume and let it fall to the floor. "Being the reincarnation of her is one thing, but I am no leader. What would I do with an empire?"

Bronx shrugged. "I don't know. But there's good you could do with power like that."

"I don't want it." She eyed him suspiciously. "What about you? You hate being in the public eye. My being empress would put you in the spotlight as well."

He thought for a moment before answering. "I was only thinking about the money. With you as empress, you can finally support me and the lavish lifestyle I've always wanted."

She snorted. "If we survive all of this."

"We will. And if not, our fates are sealed together anyway." He tried to smile, but it felt hollow. They rarely spoke about what happened in the Land of the Dead. They weren't entirely sure of the ramifications of Bronx breaking his soul into two in order to bring Rei back to life. However, Bronx had a sinking suspicion that if Rei were to die again, he could likely be snuffed out at the same time—a detail neither had acknowledged. He still wasn't sure if he enjoyed being so entwined with Rei, but if it meant her being alive, then so be it.

"We don't know if that's true, Bronx." She tugged on his Daer robes. "One of us could die and the other could still survive."

"I know. But I couldn't bear it if I lost you again." He kissed both her hands, inhaling the perfume she wore on her wrists: vanilla and sandalwood.

"And I you." She pulled him closer. "Watching Atrius die in a dream was hard enough. I don't think I could survive watching it happen for real."

"Then I guess we make sure we don't die then."

"It's as easy as that." She smirked. Her green eyes sparkled as they met his. She leaned in and brushed her lips against his, sending a current down his spine.

He wrapped his arms around her waist and drew her close until their bodies were flush. His eyes settled on the small scar on her collarbone, on the implant she had placed to keep from getting pregnant. As much as they had traveled over the last six months, it was the best way to keep their extra-curricular activities from producing more than pleasured exhaustion.

He never admitted out loud that he hoped to have a more of a normal life with her when this was all over: children, marriage, a house, and a garden. He never thought such a future was possible when his powers were out of control. Even now, he still wasn't sure if such a future was feasible. But he clung to it like he clung to Rei. He welcomed any future as long as she was in it, in whatever capacity she wanted it.

His heart hammered in his chest. He needed her, he always needed her. He returned the kiss and grabbed a fistful of her hair, enjoying how soft it felt between his fingers.

Her hands slid down his chest, and she opened the first layer of his Daer uniform, peeling it off him, letting it fall to the floor with a loud rustle.

"Shouldn't we get some sleep?" he whispered against her lips, knowing he would not stop anyway. "We'll have plenty of time to play later."

She nipped his lip and his knees grew weak. She pulled away the second layer, leaving his chest bare. "We can play again too." She gave him a gentle push, and he sat on the bed. "But I still want you now. Is that a problem?" She crawled onto his lap, leaving a trail of kisses up his neck to just below his ear. His trousers grew uncomfortably tight.

He chuckled and shook his head. "Never." He tugged on her costume, drawing the wrap back, and throwing the garment across their tiny room. He pulled the chamise over her head in one single motion and brushed the back of his hand against the curve of her breast. She leaned in, letting out just the hint of a sigh. "I want you," he whispered.

She pulled on the buttons of his trouser, giving him a brief reprieve before wrapping a hand around him. A ragged sound scraped out of his throat. Only she could coerce such sounds from him.

"Then let's dance," she whispered before claiming his mouth again.

CHAPTER 5

Bronx couldn't sleep. Too many thoughts and concerns ran through his head. Nightmares. Reliving Rei's death every night was the worst of it.

Rei snored softly next to him. She ran herself ragged with the campaign, and now she slept in a dreamless sleep. He was grateful to see her at peace. The exhaustion on her face became more visible each day. Although she and Praymer would meet in a few precious hours, she was out. Or perhaps she slept so soundly because he held all her worry through their bond.

If that were the case, then this sharing souls business was very inconvenient.

He slipped out of bed and pulled on a shirt and pants. The dim lights in the hallway kept too much light from spilling in and possibly waking Rei as Bronx slipped out. Once the door closed behind him, the corridor grew brighter. He followed the path before him until he ended up back in the common room. Stars flew by the large window and on one couch sat Artema.

"You too, eh?" he asked, taking a seat on the other couch. He sank into the plush of the cushions, silently cursing and wondering how he was going to get back out again.

"I'm just nervous seeing Anekris." She pulled at one of the loose threads on her nightgown. "The last time I saw him was when Mica, Atrius, and I fought him. I helped Atrius cut off his arm, and I am sure he hasn't forgiven that."

"I always wondered where he got that mechanical arm."

Bronx leaned back and rested his head on his hand. His gaze remained at the window as a cloudy nebula encapsulated the Alcubierre-Krasnikov tunnel that they traveled through. Wherever the wedding was taking place, it was far enough to require a tunnel that allowed them to travel faster than light.

His thoughts returned to Praymer's infamous arm. The metal appendage was a recognizable trait of the Dominion sovereign. It comforted Bronx to know that it was his previous self with Artema who had done the deed. Praymer deserved more than just losing an arm. Hopefully next time it would be Rei or Nik dealing the killing blow. Then his thoughts settled on his primary worry: Nik.

"What about you?" Artema asked.

"Arram almost had Rei convinced that she should talk to Praymer about Niklaryn—or at least Infiernen."

Artema watched him, her dark eyes trying to find his, but he refused to meet her gaze. "You still haven't told her the truth, have you?"

He continued staring out the window.

She wiped her face. "Bronx, I didn't think you would be this stupid. Does she at least know you've been in contact with him?"

He remained silent.

Artema let out an exasperated breath and leaned forward. "I have respected the fact that you want to let Nik tell her, but it will only hurt her more the longer we wait. She deserves to know the truth."

"I know," Bronx said, turning to face her. "I want to tell her. But Nik made me promise not to say anything. Not to her, not to anyone."

Artema closed her eyes and pinched the bridge of her

nose with her thumb and forefinger. "He made me promise too."

"See? You know it's more than just that. Infiernen has a part in all this. He needs to do more than pretend to play both teams to prove he's worth redeeming. Until then, Rei's not ready to learn the truth."

Artema rolled her eyes. "Bronx, this is getting out of hand. You know Infiernen has always been on our side. He has always been on Nik's side."

"Are we sure?" Bronx rubbed his face. "None of us know. Infiernen has done so many terrible things over the years in the name of being a double agent. That truth is hard enough to understand in the first place. But Rei can't know what Niklaryn did for the Dominion all these years, or worse, what he did to Arram—"

"You know it's more complicated than that."

"But that's all they're going to see." Bronx sighed and rested his head against the back of the couch. "As far as how it looks, Niklaryn has done some questionable things in the last decade—"

"Niklaryn is innocent." Artema's voice was dangerously low. "Infiernen made him do those things."

"I know, Artema," Bronx said. "But no one will buy it. I had lost hope for years. I thought Niklaryn had betrayed us too. You weren't there on the battlefield that day. Nik walked off that battlefield, and the Negander followed him like he was their leader and then he—"

"Infiernen attacked me." Artema's dark eyes challenged Bronx's. She dared him to utter the truth he didn't want to utter. "Not Niklaryn."

Bronx sighed. "Even if we can convince the others, they will ask why Nik didn't fight back all these years? Why did it take Rei's death for him to come back?"

Artema took Bronx's hand and gave it a tight squeeze. "You know it doesn't work that way."

Bronx shook his head and sighed. "I know." Niklaryn had suffered so much trauma as a child, his brain adapted in the only way it could to move on. Bronx understood on some level. When he was a combat medic, he helped other officers who suffered from PTSD. But his training didn't prepare him for Niklaryn. He wouldn't know how to help someone whose pain ran so deep and so far back in his history.

"I have experience in these matters." Artema's voice was low. "The fact that Niklaryn has made himself visible for the first time in almost a decade is proof enough that he is stronger now. It just frustrates me he is determined to fight alone and wants to keep Rei in the dark. She needs to learn the truth. What if Praymer tells her? How do you think that's going to look when she finds out that you also knew and didn't tell her? This man—this abomination—who will do anything to claim her could use this truth to drive a wedge between the two of you."

Bronx's attention returned to the stars. Artema was right. After Kepler IV, he finally felt hope for his mentor, but having to maintain this secret meant he was damned either way. The last thing he wanted to do was hurt Rei. Learning the truth about Niklaryn could go horribly wrong, but knowing that Bronx had kept the truth from her could be equally devastating. He should have told her months ago, but every time he came close, he remembered his promise to Nik. He cursed his mentor for putting him in this position.

"I have not made it a secret that my brother and I don't get along," Bronx said after a time. "When I was a child, I was desperate for his acceptance. I didn't meet Crona until I was an adult, and Yuri was all I had besides our father. But

Yuri was cruel. Father sent me to the Daer Academy as soon as possible to protect me from Yuri. I told myself for years that I didn't need him because I had my own brothers and sisters in the knighthood. But then I met Nik." Bronx whispered the last sentence. "He was the first to call me brother, he stood by me, he protected me. One time, I had done something incredibly stupid when I was his apprentice because I wanted Nik to like to me. I fell into the same trap when I wanted Yuri's approval, and it could have cost me the knighthood. Had it been Yuri, he would have turned his back on me, but not Nik. He stood by me and even took the blame so I could stay in the program. I can't betray that kind of loyalty, even for Rei." Bronx tugged at one of the plants next to the sofa. He pressed the waxy leaf between his fingers as he remembered the day Niklaryn became his brother.

"I can't betray Nik's trust. Only he can explain his choices, his relationship with Infiernen, and explain how he's been playing both sides all these years. It's not my story to tell, Artema. It's not yours either. I want to tell Rei, and I hate lying by omission, but I only know a small sliver of Nik's story. He has to come clean with his sister about his illness."

Infiernen had done atrocious things in the name of the Dominion, including taking part in kidnapping all those women so that the Dominion would continue to believe that he was on their side; Niklaryn played a part as well, even if indirectly. Bronx told himself that his mentor could have stopped Infiernen, yet he didn't. It made Nik look just as culpable.

It also didn't help that no one had seen neither Infiernen nor Niklaryn in the last six months, which left Bronx in doubt that Niklaryn was still in control. The fact that his mentor only ever responded with a cryptic message that ended with "trust me" did little to sway Bronx's opinion.

"Have you heard from him?" Bronx asked. "Has he contacted you?"

Artema's dark eyes watched a shooting star that flew by faster than their shuttle. "I did. He wrote to me shortly after Kepler IV. He was sorry for not being there for me all these years. He said he still loved me but needed to finish what he started. Only then could we be together again." She closed her eyes, and a tear rolled down her cheek.

Bronx knew in that moment how much Nik hurt her by pulling away. He wished he could shake some sense into Nik, but he was just as stubborn as his other siblings.

"Self-righteous ass," Bronx muttered, making Artema let out a soft chuckle. "He is so determined to take on Praymer himself."

"You can say that again."

"Self-righteous—"

"I didn't mean literally, smartass." Artema laughed a little louder. "But thank you. I hope we can get an idea of what his plans are. We all have the same goal. I hate not being able to help him."

"Me too." Bronx stood, groaning as he pulled himself out of the deep cushions. He should probably try to sleep again. He needed to be sharp when Praymer arrived. "If you could, what would you do for Nik?" he asked. "To help him?"

"I would drag him to Tas'und'eash myself. At least there, I know how to get him the help he needs."

Bronx chuckled. "I hope you get a chance to. I want to see the two of you together. For now, just let Rei believe Nik is the hero of the narrative."

"And Infiernen?"

"I won't throw Infiernen into the mix until we know more." Bronx gestured between them. "Until then, we keep it between us."

Artema pressed her lips together until there was nothing more than a line. "I hate this."

"Me too."

CHAPTER 6

Arram had seen nothing more beautiful in his life. The wedding venue was on the most famous ship of the Ettowa Starline, the *Queen's Pearl*. It floated in the middle of the stars, just outside their ship, with the perfect view of Orion Nebula.

The common room housed the biggest window, and the swirl of colors reached well beyond the edges of the glass.

Arram had fancied himself an amateur astronomer when he was younger. He didn't have many friends since they moved so much, but he had an array of hobbies. When he lived in Ballarat and had a decent enough camera, he obsessively took photos of the Orion Nebula. Even when zoomed in all the way, the nebula looked so small in photographs, but Arram couldn't get enough of the pinks and purples and the vibrant green in the center.

Now the nebula filled the window, its edges reaching beyond the limits of the thick glass that protected him from the openness of space. Even though there was no sound outside, the colors swirled in a way that made Arram swear he heard music.

Crona joined him at the window, dressed in a blue gown so pale it appeared silver. He had opted for a suit in a similar color. Neither wanted to go alone, and they figured since they were regular drinking buddies, they'd opt for matching outfits.

"Wow," she whispered. "The photos don't do it justice."

Arram nodded, his eyes never leaving the surrounding kaleidoscope. The swirl of gas and dust shone like a lighthouse, calling him home. He had to give his family credit; Ettowas knew the perfect place for a party.

A beep from the door brought Arram out of his head. It was Kaz, wearing a tunic in royal blue that he usually wore in his official role as a Volocio.

"We'll be docking in an hour and then heading to the champagne reception. Apparently, Nana Lia is champing at the bit to meet both you and Rei." Kaz winked.

"Nana Lia?" Arram asked. "Do we really call our grandmother that?"

"Not to her face." His cousin's smile widened. "She prefers Grandmamá Aurelia. I'm going to check if the others are ready." He disappeared down the hall.

A pain pinched in Arram's chest as he thought about the woman who raised him. He wished Virga could have seen him now. She always had impeccable taste. He still couldn't bring himself to forgive her and Sagitan for not telling him that Rei was his sister or that he was the younger brother of the famous Niklaryn Ettowa. But he still missed them dearly. He never had to compete for their attention; he was raised an only child, his grandparents' whole world. Despite that, he couldn't understand the love that pushed people to lie, or a justification strong enough to value a lie over the truth.

"Are you all right?" Crona asked.

He nodded. "Just nostalgic. I used to show photos of this nebula to my grandmother when I was younger. She had promised me one day we would see it together." His eyes pricked at the memory.

Crona linked arms with him and gave him a gentle squeeze.

"At least we can all see it together." Rei's voice rang out.

His sister entered with Bronx. She opted for a violet

dress that shimmered blue from a certain angle. Bronx wore a black-fitted jacket with a high neck, the button and border matching the shade of Rei's dress. She had spent most of the last six months wearing the same shade of god-queen-green, and she complained about it often. Arram understood the sentiment behind her fashion choice. Tonight she was not going as a Volocio on state business but as Rei attending her cousin's wedding.

Manden, Kaz, and Artema also joined, and the group watched as the ship crept closer to the hangar attached underneath the domed ship.

Sariah was the last to arrive.

"Elmessa?" Kaz asked.

"She's getting ready. Her parents will meet us at the hangar so they can bring her down the aisle later," Sariah said as she inspected her dress that was dark as night.

The ship shifted under their feet as they landed. They then made their way to the main hatch, which opened with a hiss. An older couple and a familiar face met them; the latter beamed as they walked down the ramp.

"Hello, everyone," Skylar said, pulling Rei in for a hug. "It's good to see you all again."

Arram couldn't help but notice the dark bags under his cousin's eyes as the knight continued her round of hugs.

"He's not here yet," Sky muttered loud enough for the group to hear, and Arram's shoulders relaxed. They didn't have to deal with Praymer yet.

The couple approached the group warily, but it was obvious who they were: Elmessa's parents, Jenson and Ildana Ettowa—or, technically, Arram's aunt and uncle. Even the words felt weird to say in his head since they were strangers to him.

"You even look like your father." The man extended a

hand to Arram, and he took it, yet his mouth hung open. Arram was about to say the same thing to Jenson. There were photos of his father, Jeanh Ettowa, all over the Nexus, and the man in front of him with the dark hair and sparkling blue eyes was a carbon copy.

"You're his twin," Crona blurted out from her position on Arram's arm.

Jenson smiled at both Arram and Crona. "Correct. And you are?"

"Crona Sandern."

"Sandern? Are you Riker Sandern's daughter? From Wolf X?"

Crona stood a little straighter. "I am."

"It's so wonderful to meet you both finally." Ildana towered over them, her midnight skin contrasted against a silvery gown that only further lent to her aura of authority.

"You have no idea how happy I am to finally meet you," Rei said, taking their aunt's hand. Ildana squeezed back and gave Rei a big smile.

"We miss your parents dearly," Ildana said, cupping Rei's face, and Arram swore his sister's heart was about to burst. "But we are together again and that's important."

"I agree," Rei whispered.

"Good. After the wedding, we should really talk about you finding a nice Dominion boy and not . . ." Ildana's dark eyes glanced in Bronx's direction. "A Manca." Ildana and Jenson then continued their way to the shuttle where their daughter waited.

Arram held back a laugh at the woman's gusto. But he had to use more strength to hold Crona back.

"That bi—" Arram cut Crona's comment off, holding a hand over her mouth. Luckily, he lifted her with ease and pulled her away from the ship. Arram's eyes met Kaz's and his cousin took the hint.

"Where's Nana Lia?" asked Kaz.

"This way." Sky's eyes were wide but refrained from saying anything more as she pointed down the hallway before heading in that direction.

Arram looked at his sister. Her eyebrows furrowed and her lips turned down into a frown. Bronx chuckled. At least he found it as amusing as Arram did.

"Don't be disappointed, sis," Arram said. "I told you the Ettowas only care about position and power. She's just upset because she can't manipulate you into a position that will benefit her."

Rei sighed. "It's just . . . I think I know which 'good Dominion boy' she's referring to."

Praymer.

Arram made a face. "Fair enough."

The group followed Skylar down the first hallway of many. Most of the ship comprised of rooms for all the guests along the outer rim, with an enormous hall and a glass-domed ceiling in the center where the ceremony would take place. A ring of Daer Knights stood at attention around the ballroom. Sariah and Bronx waved to a few of them.

The nebula filled every visible inch of the glass ceiling. The view was even more glorious than on their little shuttle. Arram could have stopped where he stood to admire the view, but Crona pulled him, and his attention immediately drew to the straight-backed older woman who stood among a group of people. All eyes were on her.

Arram didn't know what to expect, but once her eyes caught him and his sister, her lips upturned into something resembling a smile. The woman was likely out of practice.

He had a hard time imagining any of her grandchildren calling her "Nana Lia."

The older woman reached out to both Rei and Arram. He took her hand, but the gesture felt hollow. Just like his feelings for her. Her hands were dry, but her grip was firm. "It's a pity Niklaryn is no longer with us. It would have been lovely to have the three of you together with me." She tapped Rei lightly on the arm. "Sit up straighter, dear. You have the posture of a barmaid."

"Well, until six months ago, that's what I did for a living, and I enjoyed it," his sister responded with an equal bite, and Arram held in a smile.

"Oh, how middle class."

Rei glanced in Arram's direction. Aurelia patted Rei's hand again. "I apologize, Rei. I am not putting my best foot forward. I am sure you lived a lovely life in Ballarat. I simply wish that Niki had said something about where you were. It would have been nice to watch you both grow up." The older woman then turned to Arram. "You look so much like your father." She cupped his cheek. "Perhaps tomorrow, after the festivities have died down, we can sit and get to know each other. But until then, please come and let me show you off."

Arram had no idea how many people belonged to the Ettowa clan. He thought there would be under two hundred guests, and yet he stood in a throng of at least a thousand—and a good percentage were relatives. Arram had a sinking suspicion that his aunt and uncle had invited more guests to share in this exclusive event. More and more people arrived. Too many people. Arram wondered if their secret location was, in fact, a secret at all.

Bronx and the others had disappeared at some point, but the reaper returned with bottles of Black Phoenix, the popular beer on his home planet Wolf X. It was hard to find outside of the planet, and the joy on the reaper's face was infectious.

Eventually a herald announced that the wedding would begin shortly and that the guests should find their seats.

Rei, Arram, and Kaz took their seats in the front row next to the Ettowa matriarch. Manden also sat down next to them—the god king should sit near the queen. Aurelia's dry hands continued to hold Rei's and Arram's. Rei sniffled softly. His sister had waited for this moment for so long, but Arram had mixed feelings. Try as he might, he could not relate to these people. Rei was his sister, and that was enough for him. He didn't need the others, and he didn't need some old lady's hand. But the way she squeezed reminded him of Virga and how much he wished she and Sagitan were at his side. He told himself that for now he would close his eyes and pretend it was so. He could dream for a few moments that they were still alive and could almost hear his grandmother's laugh and the smell of the cedar wood cologne his grandfather wore.

The murmur of the crowd crescendoed as something new occurred further back, bringing him out of his head and out of his fantasy. Aurelia sighed. "Of course he had to make an entrance."

Arram twisted to get a better look. Several Negander knights with their blood red cloaks entered the room and lined up along the outside of the pews. He couldn't see, but Arram knew who it was.

Anekris Praymer walked down the aisle. His suit was a midnight blue that brought out the sapphire shade of his eyes.

His golden hair was slicked back in waves. His right hand was no longer flesh, but mechanical. He brushed back a stray lock in a motion that looked almost human. Arram knew it was all a facade; Praymer had the look of a man who could have a family slaughtered without a second thought.

Aurelia patted Rei's hand. "Don't worry, darling. You are safe with us." Their grandmother meant well, but Arram knew his sister didn't feel safe. Praymer's eyes scanned the aisle until he met Rei's, and he gave her a grin that reminded Arram of a hawk finally about to capture its prey.

CHAPTER 7

Anekris Praymer stood at the foot of the altar and watched Rei. It was clear he expected her to react. She hated him more for turning this event into something political. She also never backed down from a fight.

She stood, and the sound at her side told her Manden had as well. Her eyes never left Praymer's as she approached him. He wasn't as tall as Bronx, but she still had to look up to meet his gaze.

"It's nice to meet you, Praymer," she said, giving her best smile. It was the one from her years of working in a bar that warned of danger if she were crossed.

"The pleasure is mine, God Queen." His gaze shifted to Manden. "It has been many years, old friend."

"Anekris," growled Manden before giving the sovereign of the Dominion a deep bow, which Praymer returned.

Rei bit her lip, not sure what to do next.

"You should curtsy," whispered Manden.

"I'm not going to fucking curtsy," she returned.

A small smile crept over Praymer's face. Rei had the suspicion she was still expected to do something. So she did what felt more natural. She met his eyes again and extended a hand. A curtsy or bow felt like submission. A handshake meant they were equal. Praymer's smile widened as he reached for her with his mechanical hand, the low whir of the gears audible in the suspended silence of the room. His grip was gentle, and she briefly wondered if there were any synthetic nerve endings on the arm. She wasn't sure if he was capable of feeling, but the hand moved with a fluidity that resembled flesh.

Before she could pull away, he drew her fingers to his lips for a light kiss. She almost jerked her hand away but remembered she wanted to look like she was willing to meet for peace. She knew him for the monster he was and hoped he would instigate the war she was prophesied to end. That meant withstanding a gesture from him, even though her stomach roiled.

"I look forward to speaking with you again, Rei," he said before letting go. The way he said her name, as though he knew her, made the hairs on the back of her neck stand.

She wanted to respond, but her tongue remained stuck in her throat with the built-up bile. If she spoke, she was likely to throw up. She nodded and put an arm around Manden's as he led her back to her seat. She squeezed his arm tightly, hoping no one would notice how violently her hands shook. She didn't look back to see if Praymer took a seat or not; she didn't care.

"You did well." Manden's voice was low.

"I'm going to be sick."

"Me too."

Praymer didn't sit near her, and she assumed he was somewhere on the other side with Sariah's family.

A wave of murmurs swept about the crowd. Rei hated playing the part of wanting peace. She wanted nothing more than to wrap her hands around his neck and wring it until he apologized for everything he had done to her and her family. Electricity coursed through her veins and flashes of white flickered along the edges of her vision as she raged at the missed opportunity.

If Bronx were with her, he would remind her to breathe. She would get her opportunity. Revenge was sweeter when the timing worked, but she wanted it to work now. She took a deep breath and then another and another until the current under her skin dimmed.

Sariah and her best men and women appeared. She gave a tight smile as her eyes wandered to where Rei assumed Praymer was seated. She appeared just as happy with Praymer's presence as the god queen.

A singer approached the foot of the altar and sang as the lights dimmed, save for a shining glow from the entrance. Everyone stood and watched as Elmessa entered, holding what appeared to be a star in her hand.

Manden's arm snaked around Rei's shoulders and gave her a comforting embrace. Rei couldn't help but feel bad for her cousin. Elmessa and Sariah's day had now been overshadowed by what transpired between her and Praymer. Their meeting was a long time coming, but did it have to be today? Rei shouldn't have been surprised. Praymer was a man who started a war because his wife was screwing another man. Of course he would use someone else's wedding as a stage for his own selfish purposes.

Rei didn't care for the ceremony. She closed her eyes and tried to think of something else. Eventually her breathing slowed and her eyes reopened, just in time to watch Elmessa and Sariah cut their palms and hold their hands together as the officiant bound them together with ribbon. A few drops fell on Elmessa's rose-colored dress, but she didn't seem to care. Tears of joy streamed down her face as they then exchanged rings, their hands still red with blood.

The crowd stood and roared when the ceremony ended with a kiss from the couple. Elmessa and Sariah led the crowd toward the entrance, where they could line up and congratulate the newlyweds. Rei scanned the crowd, trying to find Bronx, who was seated with the others in a row not reserved for family. It was rather far back, but she had seen him before the ceremony started. She hoped he was somewhere finding her a stiff drink. She was going to need it.

"Looking for me?" Praymer asked, appearing at their side.

Rei flinched and glanced in the direction of Arram, who had never left her side. "Looking for Bronx, actually."

"Ah." Praymer's face fell. He quickly gave Rei another smile. "We can look for him together after we congratulate the lovely couple. I would like to extend my thanks to the man who brought you back to life."

All eyes in the immediate vicinity turned to Rei. She shook her head before taking his arm. There were too many people in the hall.

"What is it you hope to gain, Praymer?" Rei asked as they stood in line, inching forward toward the couple.

"I want peace in the star cluster, obviously." His piercing blue eyes rested on Rei's face. "Isn't that what you want? And please, call me Anekris."

"Praymer's fine, and of course we want peace," she muttered. They walked in silence for a few moments more before she continued. "Although it would have been nice to grow up without a target on our backs."

"Or maybe even grow up with parents," added Arram. "Instead, they were hunted down for hiding us."

"And who said they had to run?" Praymer asked. "I never understood what they were hiding you from. Certainly not me. I would never have harmed either of you. You are both far too precious."

Rei didn't like the way the sovereign drew out the word "precious."

Soon they arrived, and Elmessa's smile faded as

Praymer approached to offer his congratulations. She and Sariah received their well wishes, and Arram followed Rei and Praymer down the line of Brays and Ettowas. Aurelia scowled at Praymer.

"Aurelia, my old friend, it has been a long time." The sovereign offered Rei's grandmother a grand smile.

"Too long, Anekris. I believe you have forgotten what friendship means."

"How could I forget? You were once a powerful ally at my court."

"Ah, yes. I remember. But it's hard for courtiers to remain loyal when their sovereign slaughters a son and daughter-in-law and forces grandchildren into hiding." Aurelia lightly tugged on Rei's arm. "Come, you two. Help your grandmother find the refreshments. My throat is rather dry."

Praymer's grip on her arm tightened, and Rei's heart pounded. "But I wasn't finished talking to Rei. We are having a lively conversation."

"Lively indeed," muttered Arram, meeting his sister's eyes and obviously seeing the panic she felt.

"Any livelier and I am sure my granddaughter's eyes will pop out. Come, Rei."

"Yes, Grandmamá. We can speak later," Rei said, slipping out of Praymer's grasp. "My grandmother needs my help."

"I'll join you shortly," called Arram as she and Aurelia scurried away.

"Thank you," Rei said once they were well away.

"Go enjoy the festivities, my dear. I am sure he's not done with you. Take the time to regroup." Aurelia disappeared into the crowd.

Rei moved through the crowd quickly, the same way she

used to weave through the crowded bar on Ballarat: with purpose. Luckily, no one stopped her. She passed Bronx, who chatted with Crona. His eyebrows furrowed with concern, but Rei waved him away. She just needed to get away from the crowd.

A large window sat at one end of the ballroom with a spectacular view of the nebula. There were fewer people there, and getting away from the crowd was like a weight lifted from her lungs. She could breathe deeply for the first time in the last hour.

She tried to lose herself in the colors swirling outside, but the growing murmurs behind her indicated that her peace was short-lived. She had hoped Arram could keep the sovereign occupied longer when their grandmother came to her rescue, but Praymer was determined.

She spun around and found Anekris standing there, two glasses of a vibrant yellow drink in his hands. She knew this drink from her time on Kapetyn II. It tasted of lemon verbena and sugar to mask the taste of alcohol mixed in. She and Hotara used to spend many evenings sharing a bottle. The smell brought back happy memories.

Praymer's blue eyes studied her, and she took the glass from his hand and sniffed it. She dipped her finger in the drink and pressed the liquid to her tongue.

All her years working in a bar gave her an opportunity to study the different drugs used. She always wanted to make sure her patrons were safe in her bar. There were no traces of anything she knew, so it would appear that Praymer wanted to make her feel at ease. At least for now. She took a swig, then turned back to the stars as he joined her.

They watched the other ships float lazily, just barely out

of view, including the one Rei arrived on. She briefly wondered which one was Praymer's ship.

"I know you hate me," he said, his voice low. "And I am truly sorry for everything I have done to you and your family, Rei." He didn't bother looking at her this time; his eyes remained on the nebula outside. "To say I have anger issues would be an understatement. But I hope we can move past this and work toward peace."

She should take the higher road and work with Praymer. It's what the Federation council wanted; it was the right thing to do. But she hated the fact that everything hung on whether she and Praymer could get along. Politics should not be so simplified.

Unfortunately, Praymer liked his tight control of Dominion, and only he had the power to allow whatever he wanted from the Federation to filter through. To bridge the gap between the two political parties, Rei and the Federation had to go through the sovereign.

"For the sake of avoiding war, I may have to learn to forgive what you did. But I won't forget." She held his gaze. "You want to talk about peace. Then talk. Be grateful one of us will listen."

Praymer's eyebrows raised. "Grateful? It should be the other way around. My Dominion army outnumber the Federation by a significant number. I just think it's time we end the feud my ancestor started with the original god queen."

"I know how old you are, Praymer."

Praymer's lips turned down into a frown. "I guess I shouldn't be surprised. Manden must have told you." A waiter came by with a tray of crystal glasses partially filled with more of the intense yellow drink. Praymer drank the one in his hand in one gulp. He placed the glass on the tray and took another. Rei continued sipping the one she had. Praymer's blue eyes studied her as she drank.

"None of you are what I expected," Praymer said finally.

"Oh?"

"Take your brother. He looks like Maximilian. Exactly like him, but he seems less angry, less ambitious."

"Oh, he is plenty ambitious."

"Really?" Praymer's eyes glittered from the chandeliers hanging above them. "Then there's you. Now that we've finally met, I feel as though your passion is an act. Everything you do is for the pleasure of others. You're holding back because you fear people will see you as the blood empress. Micaela let no one tell her what to do; she usually did as she pleased and dealt with the consequences later."

Rei smirked as she took another sip. "So you want to talk about peace to show that you are merciful?" she asked. "You have the bigger army, why not take the Federation back by force?"

Praymer sighed and finished his drink. "At my age, I realize that I have made many mistakes. I should not have reacted with such violence when I first learned that my wife had made a cuckold of me with the reaper. I let my anger at Mica get the better of me concerning your parents." Praymer shook his head. "But that first time I saw you take that stage on Trappist V, the first time you made yourself known, I realized how wrong I was. You're not Micaela, although you have the same magnetism. Your ability to inspire people is not something that I can ignore. You're even popular within the Dominion. The Path has been leaking footage on my channels. They are determined to weaken my hold, even if it means making you look stronger." Praymer held his glass and tapped it with his mechanical hand. "Fighting a war with you would be political suicide for me. I could beat you in battle, but I would lose the support of the people."

Rei didn't believe for a moment that she had that much leverage. He wanted more, and she only hoped to keep him talking to find out what. "I have to admit, even coming here could also be suicide." She finished the rest of her drink. "Most of the people here vote Federation, and there's nothing stopping me from burning you where you stand. I am sure plenty would welcome it."

"Ah, there's that fire." He raised an eyebrow. "You could. But I am just a piece of a much bigger machine. Most of the Dominion likes things the way they are for their own perverted reasons. I am the only one who wants peace with the sway to convince my followers. If I die, you have guaranteed war. Do you want to be responsible for that?"

She didn't, and she hated to admit that he was right. The Dominion had been isolationists for years, and it had to mean something for him to reach out. He expected something out of it, Rei was sure of it. She had to play into his game and play dumb to find out what. Maybe she would finally get the proof she needed to justify killing him.

Her eyes wandered to the ships outside as she chose her next words carefully. But something wasn't right. Bright lights in space drew her attention, and they silently broke apart into several pieces. The other ships in the area quickly followed suit. Then two bright objects flew toward them.

"Shit," muttered Praymer. "They found us. Rei, get away—" The ground lurched beneath them and the lights winked out, plunging them into darkness. The room erupted in screams.

CHAPTER 8

Bronx pushed through the frantic crowd to where he saw Rei last. His heart hammered in his throat until his eyes adjusted to the glowing nebula above them. In the darkness, all he could see was Rei's face in the theater and the way she smiled before she ducked behind a curtain. He blinked as he staggered in the darkness, his mind filled with the image of Rei's lifeless body in the snow. His chest grew tight and his breathing labored. He had let her go again and now Rei was trapped somewhere in the darkness.

Finally, his eyes adjusted, and he discovered Praymer had caught Rei and helped her to her feet. His heartbeat finally slowed, but only slightly.

"Thank you," she said before pulling away.

"What was that?" Bronx asked.

"The Path," Praymer said. "Someone must have told them where we were."

The auxiliary lights flickered on, and a panicked voice rang through the speakers.

"Ladies and gentlemen. We have been boarded by the Path and they have destroyed the engine. Please do not panic and make your way to the nearest escape pod. They have destroyed all other ships in the vicinity."

Bronx met Rei's gaze. They were in the middle of nowhere; there was no place for the escape pod to go.

"My ship wasn't destroyed," Praymer said. "I purposefully hid it behind a moon in case I had to escape from the Path again."

"You expected them to attack?" Rei asked.

"I have been attacked by them enough to be prepared. You? Or did you really think you were untouchable?"

Bronx shook his head. They didn't. "Will the pods reach your ship then?"

"They are programmed to head for the closest signal. They'll make it."

"Then we fight the Path and allow everyone a chance at the pods," Rei said, quickly pulling off her heels, then flexing her fingers as lightning danced around them.

"Are there enough pods for all?" Praymer asked.

"There are enough for three times the number of people on this ship," Bronx replied. "Let's go, Rei."

"I'll help!" The sovereign motioned for his Negander to draw closer.

The group joined the other Volocio as panic ensued around them. People cried and screamed and pushed in all directions. Elmessa's and Sariah's voices echoed in the far corner. Pods were located everywhere to keep the mob from pooling in one area.

"Where do we start?" Crona asked. A flood of figures in orange and gold entering the ballroom from all sides answered her question.

Praymer rushed forward, sword in hand, and with incredible speed, a nameless member of the Path lost their head, which hit the wall with a wet spatter.

The group positioned themselves between guests and the Path. Rei brought down a number with a single bolt, and Arram followed with a wave of his own.

Manden's vines slithered around a few warriors, choking them until they crumpled to the ground. A few more vines held a few more Path terrorists down, burrowing into faces or torsos, leaving his victims writhing in pain as they slowly died.

Bronx tore through them with a light touch, plumes of smoke in his wake, taking whatever weapons he could and handing them to the other Volocio. The energy rushed through his veins like ice, waking up all of his senses.

One particular man in orange did not want to stay down. He swung his sword, grunting as Bronx easily deflected the blow and parried. Bronx regretted wearing his jacket as he started sweating.

He deflected, feigned, then thrust so hard that his attacker stepped back. This orange-robed man made a wide sweep of his sword, and Bronx took up the defensive. Bronx's thighs ached and sweat dripped into his eyes.

Then he struck quickly, causing his attacker to stagger back, fighting to keep his footing until Bronx could make the final blow with a swipe. A line blossomed from the attacker's neck, his life's blood spilling out and turning his robe from orange to red. The headband with the golden gryphon slid off and fell to the ground.

A glint of steel appeared out of the corner of his eye. Bronx turned to see another figure in orange approach, and before he could react, Rei appeared with a sword plunging deep into this attacker's side. The hood had fallen back to reveal a woman. Bronx cupped her cheek, and the plume of smoke appeared before the woman crumpled into a heap on the floor next to Bronx's other victim.

Energy raced through his veins and his heart pounded so loud he heard it in his ears. Rei wore a similar expression to how he felt as she put a hand to her chest. She felt it too. Through their bond, she felt the strength of all the lives he had.

"What a rush!" She flung her hands out and a larger bolt of lightning blasted through several orange figures.

Arram's bolt flew in Bronx's direction and he braced for

the impact, but Rei reached out and grabbed Bronx's hand as the lightning passed through him and hit a Path member behind him. He was grateful she was there. Lightning had hurt like a bitch the last time she wasn't there to help him.

"Arram, careful!" she yelled. "More control!"

"Sorry!"

A wave of red figures poured in and began attacking the others. The Negander had joined the fray to fight the Path. A third wave in black appeared as the Daer also arrived.

Rei gave Bronx one last grin before diving back in.

The Volocio and the sovereign continued to tear them down, but Bronx questioned who he was really fighting. His eyes must have been playing tricks on him. He swore he saw Niklaryn in the crowd, but it was another nameless Path member or Negander. The red and orange robes did not help, and it was hard to keep up at this point.

A Path member came for him, a man of similar build as Bronx. He swung his gladius, grunting as the orange figure easily deflected the blow and parried. The assailant came in for another attack, and Bronx brushed it aside with the side of his blade. The man's life force tugged at Bronx, and he knew the man was going to die. They danced further, Bronx's frustration getting the better of him as he tried to discover an opening but found none.

Then Kaz appeared out of thin air from behind the Path member and stabbed him between the ribs. Bronx touched the man's face, and the familiar plume of black smoke appeared and faded into the air.

"Thanks, Kaz," he breathed.

"My pleasure." The illusion Volocio disappeared again.

The energy surged through him, heightening the world around him. Bronx ducked as a blade aimed for his head. Everything slowed down. He swung his gladius at his attacker's legs, slicing through just under the knees. Bronx then used his body and slammed into the attacker, who fell away from his legs with a high-pitched scream.

Time continued to slow for Bronx as his eyes scanned the surrounding scene. Kaz made himself invisible and took down several as a deadly shadow. Artema threw several around with gusts of wind. Arram and Crona hacked through them. His sister's laughter bounced off the walls.

He found Rei and Praymer fighting side by side as more of the Path circled around them, and Bronx watched in horror as a figure in orange robes pointed a gun at Rei's back. Neither she nor Praymer appeared to have noticed the threat, and Bronx was too far away to help. His heart raced as all he could do was yell Rei's name as the cloaked figure fired.

CHAPTER 9

Praymer rammed his body into Rei's, knocking them both to the ground. Her heart leapt to her throat as he landed on top of her. Praymer pulled himself up, his blood splaying across her dress and chest. He groaned as he reached for his shoulder, his sword laying discarded between them.

A wall of vines crept around them, holding the Path away.

"You all right?" Manden's voice came from behind the crowd.

"For now, thanks!" Rei cried. She turned to Praymer, blood seeping between his mechanical fingers that held his wounded shoulder.

"We have to get out of here," Praymer growled, but Rei didn't respond.

A few of the Path members hacked at the vines protecting Rei and the sovereign. She grabbed Praymer's discarded blade. They had been conveniently backed toward an open pod, and Rei tried to maintain space from the Path by swinging her blade wildly, trying to charge the air with every swing. Yet they hardly paid attention to her as more Negander attacked the Path, coming for Rei and the sovereign. She briefly hesitated in using her lightning. But Negander were also her enemy, and she didn't care if they were collateral damage in her fight against the Path.

Rei threw her hands out, but no sparks flew. There was nothing where her powers were, only a gaping chasm. Her green eyes met Anekris's and panic raced through her heart.

Rage replaced the panic when a Path member punched her in the jaw and she fell to her knees.

The ground lurched again beneath them, and a roar from a beast slowly reached her ears. Someone had planted explosives.

She threw her hands out again, but all she felt was a chasm where her powers normally lay. It made little sense. She swung the sword and tried to find Bronx, her heart in her throat. The ship would break apart any moment, and she couldn't bear the thought of leaving without him.

"Rei!" cried Praymer. "We have to go!"

His metal arm wrapped around her waist and lifted her from the ground. Her pulled her away from the violence and toward a pod behind them.

"Wait!" she cried. "I have to find Bronx!"

"There's no time," he growled, throwing her into the pod. "I'm sure he'll find a way out," he continued, slamming the door shut. Their pod shot out into space, the force throwing Rei into the back wall.

CHAPTER 10

Praymer took Rei.

Bronx lost feeling in his limbs as he watched the sovereign drag Rei into a pod. A tightness grew in his chest, threatening to consume him entirely. Yet he couldn't stop the sovereign from taking her. He was too far away.

A bolt of lightning sped by Bronx's head to the Path member behind him, the heat of the bolt warming his cheek and pulling Bronx from his reverie.

Arram appeared a moment later at his side. Bronx clenched his fists at the thought of telling the younger Ettowa again to be careful.

"Where's Rei?" Arram asked.

"She's gone," Bronx responded. "Praymer got her into a pod, but we have to get off this ship."

"Not yet," the younger Ettowa muttered before disappearing again.

"Arram!" Rei would not be happy if something happened to her brother. Before he could follow, a beefy hand slapped Bronx on the shoulder, and he whirled around, gladius drawn. He came face-to-face with Niklaryn dressed as a member of the Path.

"You!" he cried.

"Get off the ship, Bronx!"

Bronx scanned the crowd to find the fighting had lessened. He wanted to demand Niklaryn tell him why he wore the robes of their attacker, but his head spun. The air thinned with every breath. Somewhere the ship had already fallen apart. They only had moments.

"I need to get the others off the ship," Bronx yelled over a monstrous roar that came from deep within the ship.

"I'll take care of it. Go!" Niklaryn shoved Bronx toward a nearby pod where Artema was already helping Manden inside.

"Nik!" his wife cried, stepping out.

"Praymer," Bronx said with a gasp, each breath growing more labored as the air thinned. "He took her."

"I know. We'll get her back. Just get off the ship. I'll find you later," Bronx's mentor said, slamming the door shut. Their pod shot out into space, and Bronx braced against the frame to keep the force from propelling him back.

CHAPTER 11

Arram fought against the powerful pair of hands that shoved him into the escape pod with Kaz and Crona. But once he confronted his rescuer, he was speechless.

"Niklaryn?" Arram asked. He barely felt their pod hurtle out of the ship and into the vastness of space. He couldn't believe it. He had to be hallucinating.

His brother dressed in the orange robes and golden gryphon of the Path looked at him with furrowed eyebrows, but the crease in Niklaryn's forehead disappeared when he saw Kaz.

"Cousin," he whispered, pulling the younger man into an embrace.

"Did you see the others?" Kaz asked. "Did they make it to the pods?"

Niklaryn nodded. "All the Volocio made it out. No need to worry."

Arram let out a sigh of relief. He knew Praymer had helped Rei onto a pod, and Bronx was moments away from getting into another.

"Nik," Kaz said, rubbing his chin. "Should I be worried about your outfit?"

"No. Trust me." Niklaryn's attention then turned to Crona.

"I'm Crona. Bronx's sister." She leaned back into her seat, her aquamarine eyes narrowing as she studied Arram's brother. Rightfully so. She had known Niklaryn was alive before the rest of the group. She told Arram later that she had seen a vision of Nik with a strange collar and Bronx punching him in the face. She discovered it was a vision of the future but wouldn't elaborate why Bronx would exact violence on his mentor.

"Bronx?" Niklaryn whispered. "Sister? You don't look related."

"I know. I am the better looking one of the two of us."

Niklaryn laughed. "It's a pleasure to meet you." He turned back to Arram again and the quizzical brow returned. "Your eyes."

Arram's cheeks burned. Violet eyes weren't normal, but it always made him uncomfortable when people pointed them out. He was well aware he had strange eyes.

"I'm Arram. Your brother." He felt ridiculous pointing out the obvious. They looked almost exactly alike save for the fact that Niklaryn's blue eyes didn't match his, and the faint lines around his eyes and mouth gave away the fact that Nik was about nine years older. A few strands of gray stuck out in Nik's brown hair and beard, even though the older Ettowa was just over thirty. Yet Arram had the feeling that Niklaryn didn't believe what he saw. He stared too long at Arram. "Do you remember me?"

Niklaryn smiled, but it didn't reach his eyes. "Of course I remember you. How could I forget my little brother?" He clapped Arram on the shoulder—almost too hard.

"You're a member of the Path?" Kaz asked, gesturing to Niklaryn's robes.

"Oh well, yes." Niklaryn pulled the robes open to reveal a black suit with blue paneling underneath.

The hair on the back of Arram's neck rose. "But your friends have been attacking us for months."

Niklaryn glanced in Arram's direction, then looked down at his scarred hands as he spoke. "They're not my friends. Trust me."

"You said that already."

"Did you masquerade as a guest?" Crona asked.

Niklaryn's eyes met hers. "We all did. Our aunt and uncle are terrible at vetting their guests. They were so concerned about making the wedding an exclusive event, they allowed anyone in who appeared to have an iota of influence."

"But you have a recognizable face," Kaz said. "How did they let you in without knowing you are Niklaryn Ettowa?"

"I have my ways." A hint of a smile spread across Niklaryn's lips.

"So why did you attack us?" Arram leaned forward, resting his forearms on his legs.

Niklaryn turned to Arram but didn't look directly at his younger brother. His blue eyes remained on the window and the stars behind him. "What? No! We were there to kill Praymer, or at least start a chain reaction to get the Path on his ship."

Arram clenched his jaw, unsure what made Nik adverse to acknowledging his own brother. But he didn't want to focus on it in case his instincts were right and his brother had truly forgotten him. Instead he focused on the rest of Niklaryn's actions. "You planned on blowing up the ship just so the Path could hide in escape pods and weasel their way onto the sovereign's ship?"

"Pretty much."

"But people could have died! Some may have!"

Niklaryn shook his head. "No. No one was supposed to die. The ones who attacked you recently—they were the ones attacking the Federation while posing as members of the Path."

"I'm so confused," muttered Crona.

Niklaryn rubbed his face. Then he leaned toward Crona and Kaz. "Okay. Let me start over. After Rei came back from the dead on Keppler IV, I created the Path and we began attacking Dominion. I let Infiernen dictate what I did for so long before, and I realized that it was time to fight back. We leaked the video footage of Rei and the rest of you within the Dominion to help grow support. However, someone has hired a group of Negander to pose as members and attack the Federation to ruin our reputation."

"They did a good job," Kaz said. "No one in the Federation will believe that you were on our side."

Niklaryn rolled his eyes. "I know. Infiernen fucked it up again."

Arram shook his head. Something didn't add up. He didn't understand what Infiernen had to do with this. But his limbs tingled at the mention of the Negander's name.

"And where is he now?" Arram's hand instinctively went to his stomach where Infiernen had shot him months before, almost killing him.

"Off sulking, I suppose." Niklaryn gestured to the stars outside. "Skylar helped me with this plan. Our aunt and uncle were planning on retiring the cruise ship soon anyway, so it was already scrap. We only shut down the engines to get people into the pods. It wasn't supposed to be destroyed. We set up explosives for afterward, once everyone escaped, but someone let them off early."

"Well, that was massive fuck up," Crona said.

"But we are here, heading to Praymer's ship." Niklaryn tugged at the collar of his suit.

"To kill him?" Crona crossed her arms.

"That's always been the plan. Infiernen doesn't believe it's possible. He seems to think Praymer is a Volocio and can't die."

"Artema says he's not a Volocio," Kaz said. "She called him an abomination."

Niklaryn ran a hand through his hair, a gesture Arram knew intimately. A frown appeared on his brother's lips. "Abomination, wow. I never understood why Infiernen thinks that Praymer is a Volocio."

"Praymer is the last emperor," Crona said. "That means he's old. Old enough to be mistaken for one of us, but with no gifts as far as we know."

"Were you never aware why Praymer hunted us?" Arram asked.

Again Niklaryn's eyes refused to meet his. "I knew." His voice grew quiet. "Rei is the god queen and Praymer saw her as a threat, obviously."

"It's more than that. Praymer was married to the original god queen. We think Praymer sees Rei as his dead wife, Mica."

"Gods." Niklaryn's entire body shook. "Infiernen," he growled. "Why didn't you tell me?" His attention returned to Crona and Kaz. "I have been rather out of it this last decade, but I plan on making it right."

"Whatever that means," Crona said.

"Look. Once we get on Praymer's ship, it's best that you forget you saw me. Praymer can never see me coming. So keep the fact that I am here a secret among yourselves. In fact, maybe keep the fact that I am here a secret from Rei."

"Why?" Kaz narrowed his eyes.

"Because Rei will always look for me," Niklaryn said with a scoff. "She needs to prepare. War is coming. Tension between the Dominion and the Federation are reaching a boiling point. There are rumors that Praymer is already getting his army ready on Wolf X. What better place to start a war than on the first planet to rebel? I don't want her to be distracted by me."

"Too late, cousin," Kaz said. "She has been searching for you since Bronx resurrected her and she realized you weren't dead. She will figure it out."

"Fine." Niklaryn's eyes softened. His shoulders relaxed and a full smile formed on his lips. "Then . . . tell her I love her and miss her fiercely, and I am doing what I can to make her safe, but not to look for me."

Kaz and Crona agreed, and Arram only nodded as disappointment pooled in his belly. He had expected more from meeting the great Niklaryn. He had hoped his brother was someone wiser and more calculating, like him. Someone who could better plan how to protect their sister from her recklessness. Instead, Niklaryn was no different than Rei. What hurt more was hearing how much he loved her, and yet he could barely look in Arram's direction, nonetheless meet his gaze. Niklaryn furrowed his eyebrows the same way Rei did, as if questioning the very blood he shared with Arram.

He never resented being raised by his grandparents until that moment. Growing up away from both Rei and Niklaryn gave him a disadvantage and made him an outsider to their little twosome.

The group sat in silence for most of the trip, and eventually a red swirling planet drew closer until the nose of a large ship peeked out from behind one of the planet's rings. Praymer's personal ship.

Niklaryn never dared look in Arram's direction again during the rest of the flight. Lines deepened in his older brother's brow as his blue eyes stared out the window.

Arram wished for more from Niklaryn, but it was as though he wanted to avoid his younger brother. At least that's what Arram assumed, and the thought hurt him more. He wanted Niklaryn's approval so much it hurt, but that would not happen as long as Niklaryn had forgotten he had a brother at all.

CHAPTER 12

Rei studied at Praymer sitting beside her in the pod. His messy blond hair stuck out in all directions, his skin pale. His cologne of roses and vervain filled the small pod, and he shifted in his seat. The blood stain on his jacket shone as he continued to bleed from his wound. Blood spatters dotted Rei's arm, a lot of it all over her dress. More dripped from under his wound onto his seat. The bullet nicked something.

Rei also shifted back and forth. His wound was her fault. She should have paid attention and could have dodged the bullet. She sighed, then tore several strips and applied them to the sovereign's wound, using the last piece to tie it down with her good hand and her teeth. He grunted as she tightened it.

"Why did you take the bullet for me?" she asked, laying back in her seat and lightly touching her jaw. There would likely be a bruise, but at least it wasn't broken.

"Why do you think?" He spoke with a low voice.

Rei stared daggers at him. "I'm not your wife. She's dead."

He sighed. "I know. But I can't help but see her when I see you. I was at her funeral, and it nearly destroyed me to see her lying there—to never see her smile again or to never look into those ravishing green eyes. I couldn't go through that again if something happened to you."

The words echoed what she and Bronx had often told each other. She faced the window of the pod and watched as the starship slowly broke apart. Rei hoped that there were other pods among the debris and that the others escaped. Bronx definitely survived; she was sure of it. She could reach out into the void and pick out exactly where he was.

She turned back to find Praymer watching her. A shiver ran down her spine. "Stop that," she said. "It's creepy when you look at me like that."

"Sorry," he murmured, and a small smile danced upon his lips, filling Rei with rage. She could finish him right now and no one would know. Well, there may be scorch marks. She reached deep into her well, only to find a block. No lightning. She slowed her breathing and reached again and . . . nothing. Maybe she was drained. She had used a lot of lightning against the Path. She just hoped she regained enough energy to finish Praymer before their pod arrived at his ship. But then she remembered his earlier comment: if he died, so would the chance for peace.

"I guess we might as well use this time," she said finally, "to get to know each other."

His breath hitched. "Are you sure?"

She shrugged. "Well, my other plans were canceled."

He chuckled. "All right. The best way to defeat an enemy is to make a friend of him—or her. I can't look at you without seeing Mica, so show me how you're different. Tell me about yourself."

She shivered and rubbed her arms. "I grew up on Earth. In a tiny village called Ballarat at the base of Panamint Mountains. It was not a palace, but a Volocio raised me, although I didn't know it. Hotara."

"Tara. I remember her. She and Mica were always thick as thieves if I recall."

"I guess. Hotara never told me. I found out later."

"Oh."

She turned to him. His face looked rather haggard and sweat beaded his brow. "Are you all right?"

"Yup," he whispered through gritted teeth.

Rei almost felt bad for his discomfort. Almost. "Tell me about yourself," she said.

"You're not finished."

"Fact for a fact. I tell you about me, you also spill. This is how we play the game."

"Oh, so it's a game?"

"You know what I mean. Tell me something, Praymer, before I die of boredom."

He chuckled. "I am the fifth son of a fifth son. I was never supposed to be the imperator."

Rei knew what he meant. In the myths surrounding the war of gods, Praymer was the last emperor. After the god queen died, the people assumed foul play and rose up to tear the imperator from his throne.

"Did you kill Micaela?"

Praymer sighed. "You first."

"But did you?"

"You tell me something, then I'll answer."

Rei's stomach turned to ice. Manden believed his friend was murdered, and there was no one with a bigger grudge. As much as she wanted Praymer dead, he could easily overpower her with that mechanical arm. She eyed it, grateful that it was far away from her.

"Hotara and I owned a bar," she continued. "It wasn't much, but it was enough to live off of. I used to be so bored living there, but now I wish I could go back, even just to visit. To remind myself to enjoy the simpler things in life."

They watched the nebula floating above them for several minutes before Praymer finally spoke. "I didn't kill her. I loved her too much. But . . . I started the war because of what she did and then she died, so . . . people made assumptions and it cost me my throne."

"What did you do for the last two thousand years before you became the sovereign?"

His eyes met hers, and he raised an eyebrow. It was her turn. A beam of sunlight shone through, illuminating the brilliant blue in his eyes and the light freckles across his nose. She wasn't surprised that Micaela may have found him attractive once, but he didn't murder her parents or enslave her brother.

Niklaryn.

This pod floated toward Praymer's personal ship. Rei wondered if her darling older brother was there, waiting to be rescued. His survival could be threatened if she didn't play this game with Praymer correctly. He continued to watch her with those blue eyes. She hated it—she hated the way they glowed when they met hers.

But she had to prove she wasn't the blood empress.

"I met a couple in Ballarat. They were the ones who raised Arram. They were loving people."

"Sagitan and Virga Bronto. I know."

"They were my grandparents. My mother's parents."

"Really?" He scoffed. "I didn't know that."

"Your turn."

"I lived a quiet life. Disappeared from the public eye. I wanted to regain my throne, but it had to be different and I had to reinvent myself, so to speak. So I waited until enough time had passed that the last emperor was a myth and I could pretend to be a descendant who happened to share the same name. It was easy to fake a family tree, and with my old money, no one questioned it."

Old money.

Her family also came from old money, and his words

reminded her of their traits: entitled, ambitious, and normal. She gritted her teeth; this was exactly the situation she wanted to avoid. She never wanted to humanize him. He was a monster, and she would be damned if she was going to let him get under her skin.

"I only found out that I was related to Sagitan and Virga after *your* Negander murdered them."

"Ah."

Rei would never get the image out of her mind of seeing Sagitan and Virga lying on the sandy ground outside of her bar. They died protecting Rei and Arram from Praymer, and he didn't even look remotely remorseful. She rubbed her face. "Honestly, Praymer. I don't know what you think will come of this. You murdered my parents and grandparents and enslaved Niko."

Praymer sighed, and his mechanical hand leaned against a window, lightly tapping it. "I was wondering when you were going to get to him. Arram told me you knew."

"How could you do that and hunt Arram and me and *still* expect me to be your ally?"

"Niklaryn came to me, Rei. Willingly. Although to be honest, my agreement was more with Infiernen than with your brother. Niklaryn simply tagged along."

"That makes no sense."

Praymer held her gaze and raised an eyebrow. "Then you don't know." He settled back into his seat. "Well, I won't spoil the punchline."

Infiernen had said the same thing to her the last time she saw him. She hated being kept in the dark; she hated that no one confided in her, whether it was about her identity or the fact that her brother had been alive all these years. "What's the fucking punchline?" she asked through gritted teeth, reaching for her lightning again, only to find her source still blocked.

"The real punchline is that I am the reason you can't reach your powers. I can dampen a Volocio's powers with my blood." A smile spread across his lips as he closed his eyes.

Rei's limbs went numb, the realization hitting her. She looked back at her blood-spattered arm and the deep crimson that stained her dress. She rubbed the stain, and some dried flecks flaked off. Artema's voice rang in her head, calling Praymer an abomination. "What the fuck are you?"

He half shrugged with his uninjured shoulder. "I wish I knew."

CHAPTER 13

Bronx scanned the debris floating among the slowly disintegrating ship. If there were any sound in space, he would have imagined it to be a deep rumble that shook him to his bones. He shook now. Somewhere out there, Rei floated alone with Praymer. Alone. If any harm came to her, he would make Praymer pay. But Praymer would likely protect her as fiercely as Bronx would. As much as he hated to admit, Rei was safe.

Yet Bronx knew about the other women. Women who looked like Rei who went missing after an attack from Infiernen and his Infinity Dogs. Rumors spread regarding what Praymer did to them, to satiate a hunger for his dead wife. It was what happened to Alma Canale's daughter, Camila. Bronx was sure of it. Rei was safe only until Praymer decided he wanted something else. Bronx clenched his fists until his nails bit into the palms of his hands. His head spun and his breathing grew labored as the thoughts swirled in his head. The collar of his shirt tightened around his neck so he tugged at the bottoms.

"Are we going to talk about the fact that Niklaryn was dressed as a member of the Path?" Manden asked, his voice rattling through Bronx's consciousness. He sat across the pod from Bronx, his suit disheveled and blood dotting his red hair. Bronx was quite sure the blood wasn't Manden's.

Artema met Bronx's gaze from her seat between the men, her gown torn in several places and her dark bruises spattering her skin. She held her head in her hands. "My darling husband said 'trust me.'" She shook her head. "This is probably what he meant."

"Well, at least we can finally tell Rei where her brother is."

"No," Bronx said, turning to the other two. "She has enough on her plate without worrying about what he's doing." He thought back to the messages he had received from Niklaryn. *Trust me* they said. But Bronx's trust hung by a thread after seeing Nik wearing orange and gold stained with blood. Niklaryn was supposed to be his brother, not fighting alongside people who would hurt Rei.

A little voice reminded Bronx that Niklaryn had taken a chance on him. Bronx had stolen classified information from Urius's office and the Federation leader was ready to brand Bronx a traitor and strip him of the opportunity to be knighted. Bronx had pilfered information on Praymer, in hopes of helping Niklaryn with his plan for revenge and also prove he could be loyal to his mentor. Niklaryn stood by his side, knowing that Bronx had put his reputation on the line for his mentor. Niklaryn deserved the same trust.

Bronx let out a resigned sigh. "No one can know what we saw. Not yet."

"But we know the truth," she whispered.

"I have to admit that Nik fighting along the Path is suspicious," Manden said.

"You're not helping, Manden," Artema snapped.

"Maybe I am, Arty." The redhead ran a hand through his hair, leaving it spiked in different directions. "Urius has hinted for years that not only was Nik alive, but fighting against us. Imagine what would happen if the Federation found out about their darling, and supposedly dead, Niklaryn. Maybe you're letting your love for Nik blind you to the truth."

Artema shook her head. "I am not blind. There's a lot under the surface we don't understand. I hate that you take everything you see at face value. You never bother to talk to Infiernen or Niklaryn. You would rather sit on your pedestal and judge."

Bronx winced. Talking to Infiernen was never something he wanted to do, but he could have used his connection to talk to Nik. A little voice in the back of his mind reminded him why he never asked: fear of being right. He was so convinced that Niklaryn was betraying the Federation all these years, and even though he knew the truth, the suspicion still lingered. Yes, he was being stubborn, but it was better to cling to the idea of being betrayed than hold out hope like Artema, only to be disappointed if he was wrong.

Yet he wanted Artema to be right.

"So what do you propose?" Bronx asked.

"Simple," Artema said. "We talk to Nik."

Bronx shook his head. "It can't be that simple."

"But it is—you just don't want to be wrong."

"I'd rather not get my hopes up."

"Let Nik prove you wrong. We talk to him."

Bronx didn't respond, not wanting to give Artema the satisfaction of thinking she was right. But she was.

Praymer's ship, a large vessel with green lights glowing from underneath the sheets of black metal, came into view, appearing like a predator swooping in for the kill. They were entering the belly of the beast, trapped with no way out. Bronx hoped the Federation would send help soon. All it would take was the wrong move to keep Rei imprisoned here. Regardless of how he felt about Niklaryn, his mentor's love for his sister was fierce. Niklaryn would also be on that ship, and Bronx could

count on his mentor to help carve a path for Rei to escape
Praymer if necessary.

CHAPTER 14

The pod landed with a hard jostle. Arram held onto the handle above him so as to not fall onto his brother.

"I could have done without that," muttered Crona, who landed on Kaz.

Several figures in red huddled around the pod as air released from the opened door.

"Remember," Niklaryn said, his voice low. "You never saw me." He was the first out after one last glance at his younger brother. Arram swore his eyes were deceiving him. He no longer saw Niklaryn, but another man with a heavy black beard who nimbly climbed out of the pod and disappeared into the crowd.

"Did you see?" Arram asked, pointing to where Niklaryn disappeared.

"See what?" Kaz joined Arram at the door and scanned the direction Arram had gestured.

Arram shook his head. He probably had low blood sugar. The little food he ate at the wedding wasn't enough. As much as his sister talked about Niklaryn, Rei never mentioned their brother having an ability like Kaz's.

"Never mind," he muttered, scrambling out of their pod.

Rows and rows of pristine aero fighters filled the massive hangar like predatory insects ready to attack. A few silvery shuttles lined the other side. Hopefully, they would fly to another planet and use one of the shuttles to return to the Federation when the time came—if they were allowed to leave. Arram shuddered at the thought.

More pods floated into the ship's hangar. Some held members of the Path, who weren't as clever with their costume changes. Negander dragged their prisoners and lined them along a far wall. One tried to run and was immediately shot. Arram flinched, and his heart sank at such rapid justice.

Several guests climbed out of their pods, looking out of place in their finery that contrasted with the unembellished black walls surrounding them, and Arram couldn't help but wonder who among them were members of the Path that blended in like Niklaryn—and which side they might be on.

Arram approached the prisoners, and Negander lined up along the far wall. Niklaryn had said someone else infiltrated the Path, maybe that someone would like to boast about this other leader.

"Arram?" Crona asked, coming to his side.

"I want to ask some questions."

At least four infiltrators kneeled with their hands bound behind their backs. More followed as the sound of others being captured and struggling against their Negander captors echoed in the large room.

Both Arram and Crona watched the four quietly until one decided to finally look up and acknowledge the Volocio. Only one bowed, while the other three stared in defiance.

Arram kneeled close to the one who bowed. He had dark skin, a shaved head, and dark eyes. His orange robes had the most rips compared to his compatriots.

"I only wish to help the Volocio," said the captive.

"Then tell me who you work for. Who is your leader?" Arram asked.

The captive gaze met Arram's, his jaw set. "A great Daer leads us. You know his name."

"Niklaryn?" Arram whispered. "My brother?"

The captive's eyes grew wide. "You know?"

Arram nodded. The hair on the back of his neck rose.

"Blasphemous," growled another captive next to the one Arram spoke with. "Infiernen is our glorious leader. Niklaryn is six feet under."

"You lie!" cried the first captive, throwing his body into the second one. The other two joined, and Arram had to scramble away before he was also drawn in. His muscles grew weak and his breath shaky.

"What happened?" Crona asked, helping Arram to his feet.

Arram's heart thrashed in his chest. "Infiernen," he whispered. "Infiernen is the other one leading the Path." His hand went to his stomach. He would never forget the way the bullet from Infiernen's pistol pierced through him. The Negander was supposed to be a double agent between the Dominion and Federation, but now he was working for the third, more dangerous group.

It was bad enough being trapped on the ship with no way out, but enemies surrounded them and the best they could do for now was cling together in case the Path made another violent appearance.

Arram grabbed Crona's hand and pulled her back toward Kaz, who stood with Skylar, Sariah, Aurelia, and Elmessa. He looked toward the opening of the hangar and hoped Rei was safe. He wished he believed in some higher being, then he might have prayed for her out there alone with Praymer in the vastness of space.

He had to tell his sister what he learned. Bronx had once said that Infiernen was on their side, but Arram was no longer sure.

"Ladies and Gentlemen," said a voice from an entrance at the far end. "My name is Dante. I want to be the first to welcome you to our ship, *The Sovereign's Blessing*. Unfortunately, our beloved sovereign is not here yet to welcome you, but he should be here shortly. Please follow me. The sovereign has already alerted me to the situation, and we have begun preparations for food and beverages."

A murmur rippled through the crowd, and Arram briefly wondered if the guests would take Dante up on his offer. They did. The majority were Federation loyalists now at the mercy of Praymer and his ship. But considering they never made it to the reception, Arram wasn't surprised when the group trickled behind the voice and slowly left the hangar.

"Are you coming?" Skylar asked with Sariah not too far behind.

Crona gestured to the incoming pods. "I want to make sure the others arrive safely."

Arram agreed.

"We'll join you as soon as the others arrive, Sky," Kaz said.

The Daer locked eyes with Arram briefly before she turned to leave. Arram grabbed Sky's arm. "Nik's on this ship," he whispered in her ear. "He's working with the Path, but I just learned that Infiernen has been leading them as well. Something isn't adding up."

Skylar gave Arram a slight nod. "I'll look for Infiernen."

Maybe being trapped on this ship wasn't a bad thing. It meant the sovereign didn't have many places to hide if Niklaryn was to succeed in his mission of killing Praymer. But it also meant that the Path had gathered, and if the sovereign and his sister joined forces, they could probably destroy the Path in one crushing blow—Infiernen included.

Arram continued watching as more people climbed out of the pods and followed the others out of the hangar. He made a list of what he wanted to learn about this place and how the Volocio could use this to their advantage. Trapped as they may be, he had a feeling he could make their situation beneficial.

CHAPTER 15

Rei and Praymer floated in silence. They hadn't spoken since the revelation of Praymer's blood abilities. Rei rubbed most of it off her skin, but plenty remained on her dress and continued to block her powers. She wanted to scream with frustration.

The merciless cold of space seeped through the windows and into their little haven until a shiver rippled through Rei, followed by another and another.

Praymer sat up and awkwardly removed his coat, handing it to Rei. Blood covered the coat. She still couldn't reach her powers, so more blood wouldn't have made a difference. She put the jacket on with a soft "Thank you," grateful for the warmth. His scent of roses and vervain hung on the fabric, overpowering the blood.

Praymer nodded and settled back into his seat. His skin was paler and his forehead coated in sweat. He was dying and was losing too much blood, but there was nothing she could do. Maybe her wish would be granted and he would die, but it wasn't a death he deserved. He shouldn't get a peaceful death in the arms of space with Rei at his side; it should be by her hand and violent.

"Gods bless it," she muttered, sitting up and inspecting his wound. It had soaked through the strips she made earlier. She fumbled around in the pod. There had to be a first aid kit in some compartment. She opened several small panels between the windows and their seats. Most had wires and numerous blinking lights. She found a kit with an antiseptic gel, bandages, glue, and a heat gun.

She turned on the gun and pushed against Praymer's shoulder.

"Lean on your other side," she commanded, pulling the strips away from his wound. The bullet had gone clean through Praymer's now-sodden back. She wiped what she could with the bandage and slathered gel on the exit wound. Praymer flinched and hissed, but Rei ignored him. The heat gun glowed red, pressed against his wound, and he let out an audible gasp.

"Be gentle, darling," he croaked.

"Call me darling again, I'll show you how rough I can really be." Rei slowed her breathing and tried not to think about the fact that their little pod now reeked of burned flesh. She did the same to the entry wound and pressed the gun a little too hard. Once finished, she wrapped his shoulder and wiped the sweat from her forehead.

"Thank you," he whispered.

"Don't thank me yet. You lost a lot of blood."

"I am grateful that you tried."

Rei shrugged. "I figured you didn't deserve a simple death."

He chuckled. "You're probably right."

She settled back into her seat next to him.

A red planet slowly inched across the window in front of them. A cluster of metal floated toward something behind it. She assumed it was the other pods.

"What could I do to make things okay between us?"

Rei furrowed her eyebrows and locked eyes with Praymer. "Okay? There's no okay." She scoffed. "But you could start by releasing my brother. I cannot believe that you are earnest if you insist on holding Niko hostage."

"I already told you, Rei. He came to me. Your brother is welcome to come and go as he pleases."

Niklaryn had told her he sold his soul to keep Rei safe. That didn't sound like freedom to her. Praymer must have recognized her silence as confusion.

"Perhaps the question you should ask is why would your brother work for me?"

"He said it was to protect me from you."

Praymer chuckled. "Protect you how? And from what? We are alone in space, and if you were in any danger, that time has long since passed. I don't want to hurt you anymore than I want to stop my own heart. Believe it or not, Rei, I am a good guy."

"A good guy with a vice-like grip on several planets. A good guy whose followers brand those from the queer community like my brother. A good guy who allows priests of your so-called god to murder innocent people because they won't follow your religion."

"A good guy who has surrounded himself with bad ones." He smiled, and Rei did not return the gesture. He ran the mechanical hand through his hair, no longer slicked back, and several ringlets fell across his brow. "Those were not my ideas. When I first ran for president, I took a lot of money from other lesser political parties and we pooled resources. Most had very zealous ideas, and I had to allow their platforms because they held the purse strings. I worked so hard to overturn those practices. Between you and me, I want to do away with a lot more, but I need someone like you to help me. You care about the people and they love you for it.

"Will you help me?" he asked.

"I should let you die. The way I see it, you're still the leader people rally behind to commit those atrocious acts."

"You know it's not that simple. Remember, most of the Dominion likes things the way they are, and I am the only one who can convince my followers otherwise. If you let me die, you have guaranteed war."

She hated to admit that he was right, but she still waited for the ultimatum. He had not made it clear what he wanted in return. It was all too simple.

"What do you get out of it?" she asked. "Why an alliance with me and not with Urius?"

"Micaela and I were friends before we married. We wanted what was best for each other. I don't think Urius and I could ever reach such an agreement for peace—there's too much bad blood between us."

"And there's no bad blood between us?" Rei said with a scoff. "Do I need to list what you've done to my family, or are you that stupid?"

Praymer growled in frustration. "And there's nothing in this lifetime I could do to make it up to you. If I could bring your parents back, I would do it. I have to live with that decision. I am sorry about your grandparents; I don't have complete control of my Negander, and I did not order their deaths. But the details don't matter because they died anyway."

Something in his voice made Rei look at him. Either he was a fantastic actor or he meant what he said. Regardless she knew his goal: to get close to her. As much as she hated feeling his warmth and his eyes when he watched her, she knew that he would likely do whatever it took to stay on her good side.

She could use this. She could use him to get what she wanted.

"All right," she said finally. "Let's just pray you make it to your ship, and then we'll talk about an alliance."

Praymer sighed. "Maybe your reaper can perform a miracle."

CHAPTER 16

Bronx scrambled out of the pod the moment it hit the floor. His eyes darted around the hangar, and he knew he wouldn't find who he was looking for. Her presence was still out in space, but she was close.

Dread filled his stomach as he saw the number of fighters and shuttles filling the hangar, more than he had ever seen in a Federation hangar. It reminded him how easily outnumbered they were against the Dominion and how much they lacked in resources. Hopefully, they could hold off war just a little longer.

"Bronx!" Crona cried from somewhere in the crowd. She appeared as if out of nowhere and threw her arms around him. Arram and Kaz weren't far behind.

"Rei hasn't arrived?" Manden asked as he stepped out of the pod and helped Artema to her feet.

"She's close," Bronx said, glancing at the hangar's opening as the remaining pods trickled in.

"Nik was with us," Kaz said.

"What?" Artema asked.

"Dressed as a member of the Path?" Bronx's skin tingled.

Arram nodded. "Apparently, there's a lot going on in the group. Nik is leading the faction to help us against the Dominion, and Infiernen is leading another group to hinder their efforts."

"There's infighting among the Path members," Crona confirmed.

Bronx locked eyes with Artema, and she merely

shrugged and shook her head. He shouldn't have been surprised that Infiernen was also involved, but he didn't understand why each man pulled the group in different directions.

"Where is Nik?" Bronx asked.

"He left our pod the minute it landed," Arram said, gesturing to the survivors trickling out of the hangar behind him.

"Wait, he was in the pod with you?"

Arram frowned. "Uh, yeah. How else do you think we found out everything about the Path?"

"Of course." Bronx breathed hard as his heart raced. There was no hiding the fact from Rei now.

"We need to find Nik," Artema said.

"He told us not to go after him." Crona shook her head.

"He doesn't want Praymer to see him coming. He plans on killing the sovereign," Kaz said.

"And yet he hasn't done it after all these years?" Manden asked. "I wonder why."

Arram rubbed his forehead. "Something doesn't add up."

Bronx barely heard the conversation. He glanced back at the opening of the hangar. Something else out there pulled at him. It reminded him of the call long ago that forced him to use his powers before he understood that he was helping a person die.

He followed the call, drawing away from the other Volocio. The stars glittered outside the hangar, but one little light blinked repeatedly as it drew closer. A pod floated into view; if there were others, he couldn't see them. He approached it as it landed with a soft thud. He was the first to pull on the latch and the door swung open. His vision filled with color as Rei leapt from the pod into his arms. Her ice-cold body shivered. He held her tight, willing her to warm up. His vision cleared as her green eyes came into view, and his heart clenched when he noticed her blue lips.

Rei touched his face, and he held her tighter before pressing his lips against hers. He felt whole again.

Yet the call screamed into every corner of his brain like a high-pitched alarm. He broke the kiss.

"Bronx, what's wrong?" she asked, but she sounded so far away.

He turned back toward the pod, where the call was at its loudest, demanding he use his powers. Praymer.

A few Negander arrived to pull the sovereign out of the pod. Anekris's pale face appeared, his shoulder wrapped in pieces of Rei's dress, blood seeping through and dripping onto the floor.

Bronx reached out to the sovereign and put a hand to the man's chest. Usually he needed skin contact, but this time it wasn't necessary. But no black smoke appeared; instead the energy was drawn from Bronx, even though he didn't have extra energy to give.

A sharp pain stabbed his shoulder, in the same place where Praymer was wounded. Bronx winced and tried to pull away, but the force kept his hand in place. He gasped as the pain grew more intense. This was not like other times, and while his heart should have raced from fear, it slowed down. It was too slow.

"Bronx?" Rei's voice echoed in his head, high with concern.

"I can't let go," he whispered. The colors in his vision faded away as darkness enveloped him. The last thing he remembered was Rei pulling him toward her, severing the link between him and the sovereign.

CHAPTER 17

Arram and Rei caught Bronx as he fell back. Arram took the brunt of the Daer's weight. They lowered him to the floor.

"Bronx!" Rei called, but he was unresponsive. She turned to Praymer, her green eyes sparkling dangerously. "What did you do to him?"

Arram glanced in Praymer's direction to find color had returned to the sovereign's cheeks, and he sat up with a groan. He used his mechanical arm to readjust his blood-sodden shirt and undo the few buttons around his neck. His deep blue eyes locked with Arram's before answering Rei.

"I did nothing. He saved my life. Isn't that what reapers do? They save those not meant to die yet."

"But passing out is not normal," Rei countered. "Not anymore."

Arram knew what Rei meant. Back when Bronx was still unsure of his powers, saving someone's life drained him too much. It happened when Bronx saved Arram's life after he was shot on Trappist V. Now the reaper was more conscious of how much energy was necessary without losing consciousness. Something told him that what happened between Praymer and Bronx was not normal. It felt wrong to hear Praymer speak of Bronx's abilities so matter-of-fact.

Praymer said nothing, but his attention turned to Arram, who flushed. The way the sovereign watched him unnerved him. He returned his attention to his sister. She grasped Bronx's hand as a Negander lifted him onto a stretcher to carry him out of the hangar. They brought a second one for Praymer. It was only then that he noticed she wore Praymer's jacket.

Arram wrapped an arm around Rei, her body like ice underneath the jacket. He had to get her to the medical wing. The fact that she was also barefoot didn't help matters. Rei would be useless if she suffered from hypothermia. Together they followed behind Bronx and Praymer as the Negander wheeled them out of the hangar.

The black and green exterior gave way to a deep gray metal hallway with gold paneling. The Volocio followed the Negander to what Arram assumed was the medical wing. They reached an area that split into several hallways. Praymer was wheeled into one while the Negander wheeled Bronx down a separate corridor.

"Where are you taking him?" Rei asked. She changed direction to follow, but two Negander blocked her view.

"They will run quick tests." Praymer's voice was strong considering how much of his blood pooled in the pod he shared with Rei. "You said what happened to him wasn't normal. We will make sure he wasn't harmed."

"I have to stay near him."

"There's no need, Rei," Praymer said with a dismissive wave of his hand.

Arram's sister swung around and met the sovereign's gaze. Her hands extended at her sides, half covered from the longer sleeves of Praymer's jacket. Arram knew she was calling her lightning, yet nothing came. Rei and Praymer stared at each other for several agonizing moments before she finally lowered her gaze and relaxed her shoulders.

Relief flooded Arram's veins. Rei didn't let her emotions take over. They couldn't afford a war right now.

"My medic is one of the best in the Dominion. We'll make sure nothing happens to your reaper."

Arram smelled the lie, and the way his sister narrowed her eyes told him she felt the same way. He wrapped an arm around her and she relaxed, yet her fists stayed clenched to the point that her knuckles were white.

Rei turned to Crona, who gave her a nod. "Kaz and I are on it."

The two slowed their pace and let the others walk past. When Arram looked back at them, Kaz had made them disappear.

Arram and the others continued down another hallway, and they heard voices as they passed a large room with gigantic floating chandeliers where the guests congregated.

"Artema and I will go to check on the other guests," Manden said. "I think we should try to find *him* and have a little chat."

"Good idea," Arram said as the two split off.

"Him?" Rei asked.

They entered a white room filled with instruments, beds, and beeping instruments, not unlike what they had in the medical wing of their own Underground. The smell of astringent burned Arram's nose.

"Nik's on the ship," Arram whispered in Rei's ear.

Her eyes grew wide. "Where?" She pulled away, but Arram squeezed her tighter and led her to a nearby bed.

"He disappeared. First, let's get you warmed up, then we'll find him."

Rei didn't fight him as a medic came and wrapped her in a space blanket, its reflective surface bringing color back to her cheeks almost immediately.

Arram and Rei watched as Praymer, surrounded by

several other medics, could sit upright and give orders and demand statuses.

"He could barely speak when we arrived," Rei whispered, pulling the blanket closer around her. "He did something to Bronx, something he couldn't control."

"I believe you," Arram responded. "Where do you think the Negander took him?"

"Wherever it is, I don't think it has anything to do with tests. But Crona will take care of it." Rei met his gaze, her green eyes bright. "Let's see if Manden and Artema had any luck with Niklaryn."

Arram wanted to tell his sister about what he learned concerning both Niklaryn and Infiernen. But not here, not with so many people around.

With all the medics scurrying around their sovereign, no one noticed Rei and Arram leaving the room. The blanket remained discarded on Rei's seat. They followed the echo of conversation and laughter that bounced off the eerily empty yet elaborately decorated walls.

It was abundantly clear Praymer had a particular aesthetic. Gold paneling gleamed everywhere, to the point it didn't look gold, but something burnished and fake. No one could accumulate that much of the precious metal. But something told Arram that Praymer had the funds. Every few feet they passed a painting of different lovely landscapes from each of the planets of the star cluster, including Earth.

Arram had expected to see Praymer to have paintings of himself. From their little interaction so far, he imagined the sovereign loving himself, but they had only seen one of him on a throne seated next to an empty one, save for a golden tiara. He appeared younger, with a sadness in his blue eyes that didn't fit a face so youthful. The painting captured the emotion so well. For a moment, Arram wondered the reason for such a deep frown.

"Tell me about Niko," Rei said, keeping her voice low. Despite being alone, Arram assumed there were cameras everywhere and kept his voice at the same volume when he answered.

"He pulled me into the pod right before the ship collapsed. I couldn't believe it."

"So he is no longer a captive of Praymer?"

Arram raised an eyebrow. "I guess not."

He recalled the moment he came face-to-face with his brother. They looked so similar Arram could have kicked himself for never having noticed it before, back before he knew of their familial connections. But he still couldn't forget the way Niklaryn looked at him. He had hoped to see his Niklaryn's relief when he learned that the brother lost in the confusion of their parents' deaths was, in fact, alive.

"But he doesn't remember me," Arram said, his voice squeaking at the end.

Rei tugged on his arm and stopped, forcing him to look at her. "What?" she asked.

"Nik didn't know who I was at first. But when I reminded him we're brothers, I swear for a moment he couldn't believe who I was. He doesn't remember having a brother." He continued walking toward the voices of the wedding guests. "It really hurt to see him looking at me like a stranger."

Rei wrapped an arm around Arram's and squeezed. "I'm sorry. I don't know what to say. It makes little sense."

Arram hugged her back. It felt good to be held, to be understood. "Nothing about him makes sense. I thought it odd enough that he was dressed as a Path member."

"A what?" she asked. "He was part of the attack?"

"No. Yes. I don't know. He said that he is part of the Path to help your cause, leaking footage of your speeches around the Dominion. But I talked to a few who had been captured, and apparently Infiernen has been leading another group that's causing havoc and branding people." At least Arram knew why the Path had continued the practice; Infiernen must've really loved the smell of burned flesh. Arram rubbed his chin. The whole situation was confusing and complicated. "The others don't know what to make of it all either."

"The others know?"

"We were talking about it right before you arrived."

"Oh." Rei stared at the empty corridor in front of them.

He wanted to know what she thought, but he had a guess: Niklaryn. So much of her motivation since joining the Federation had been about their brother.

"We should find him. Talk to him," she said finally.

"No. He told us not to look for him. He doesn't want Praymer to know he's coming for him."

"Why? That makes no sense."

"None of this does." Arram watched his sister out of the corner of his eye. She appeared so small, so lost. In some ways, she must have felt the rejection he felt from Nik. It made him feel better knowing he wasn't alone in the feeling, but he didn't like that it was at his sister's expense.

"What are we going to do with Infiernen?" she said after a time.

"You know I have never trusted him. I think this proves it."

"Artema told me I should, and he has never done anything to hurt me."

"Oh, no, not you. But he had no problem shooting me in the stomach."

Rei winced. "I'm sorry. I just wish I knew where he truly stood. Federation? Dominion? He always said he wasn't my enemy, so why do this?" Rei rolled her eyes and let out a low growl of frustration. "Let's just get back to the others."

They walked together in silence as the sound of the guests grew louder. Eventually they found the ballroom with several monstrously large chandeliers floating above a golden room with a large skylight where the red planet hung lazily. Laughter mixed with the chink of sparkling wine-filled glasses that floated around on golden platters. The smell of roasted meat hung in the air, but Arram had no appetite. He was still trying to recover from their adventure earlier.

Manden leaned against the frame of the entryway, and Artema stood next to him but facing the crowd.

"There you are," said the redhead. His eyes rested on Rei's face. "You feeling better? Blue lips don't suit you."

"Better."

"I told her about Nik," Arram said.

Artema turned upon hearing her husband's name. "I couldn't find him. I don't care what he said, we should help him. You saw what happened to Bronx; Anekris has to be stopped. We should kill him while he's still in his hospital bed."

"We can't," Rei said. Everyone turned to her.

They stood near the entrance, away from the other wedding guests. Aurelia, Ildana, and Jenson stood a few feet away and the Ettowa matriarch's sharp eyes darted in their direction. Arram gestured to the other Volocio to huddle closer; he didn't want a wayward relative to overhear.

"I thought you wanted revenge?" Arram asked.

"I do. But it's more complicated than that." Rei's voice shook.

"What happened in the pod?" Artema slipped her hand into Rei's. "Did he get to you?"

Arram had been relieved to find Rei unharmed when she came out of the pod. He didn't think Praymer would have hurt his sister, but he didn't expect her to change her stance on killing the sovereign so quickly. Then again, they were alone together in the pod for some time.

Rei shook her head. "No. Maybe. I don't know. But he made a good point: kill him and we have guaranteed a war with the Dominion. And it's a war we can't win right now. The time isn't right, and I know he wants to play a game. I'm just trying to figure out what it is." She opened Praymer's coat to show her dress soaked in blood. "We also need to contend with the fact that his blood suppresses our powers."

Arram's heart stopped. "What?" he heard himself say.

Manden turned to Artema. "Did you know about this? You called him an abomination before."

"Many times," Arram offered.

"I didn't know *that*." Artema played with one of her braids, her dark eyes wide as she pressed her lips together. "I just knew that he was human and he shouldn't have lived this long. There is something unnatural about him, but this just made it worse."

Rei closed Praymer's jacket around her again, arms crossed tight against her chest. "I think I need to shower. I need to feel my powers again. I don't feel right."

Arram gestured to the crowded room behind him. "Maybe we can find that Dante gentleman. He's been organizing everything for the guests."

"I saw him talking with Elmessa," Manden said. "Follow me."

They walked through the crowd. Some reached out to Rei, who offered them a smile. Some even reached out for Arram, but he could only respond with a tight smile. Music hung in the air, and off to the side, guests were dancing. So many of them could dismiss the attack and risk of their lives frivolously. But hearing "Thank you to our gracious sovereign" among the crowd showed that guests had their price.

All the while, Arram's mind continued to race with all this recent information. Praymer was more dangerous than they thought. Rei was so determined to see his end, and seeing her subdued after being alone with him for a few hours gave Arram a lot to think about.

Sure enough, Dante stood with Arram's cousin and her bride. He could finally put a face to the disembodied voice that rang in the hangar barely an hour before.

After a quick word with Elmessa and Sariah, Dante led Rei out of the room. Arram followed, wanting to ensure his sister's safety. Her silence made him nervous, and leaving her alone left him uneasy. They followed Dante through a labyrinth of gaudy gold corridors filled with doors and Negander on guard every few feet, a detail Arram noted.

They arrived at one door with red-lacquered paint. It opened with a hiss, and Dante left them alone without further comment. Rei passed the threshold before she faced her brother.

"Are you okay?" he asked.

She rubbed her face. Arram noticed that Praymer's blood ran up her arm. "Once I get this blood off of me, perhaps. Thanks for staying by my side."

"Of course. Do you need me to stay with you?"

Rei shook her head. "I'll be fine. But can you see if Crona and Kaz have returned with news of Bronx?"

Arram held back from making a face. There were more important things to think about than Bronx. He would have said so, but the tightness in her eyes kept the words from leaving his lips.

"I can do that."

He turned to leave.

"And Arram?" Something in Rei's voice made him meet her eyes. "I am sorry about Niko. I don't know what's going on with him, but know that I love you and I am grateful you came into my life when you did."

Arram's heart tugged at her words. It didn't make him feel that much better, but he believed her.

"Even though we always fought?" He gave her a small smile. They fought so much when they lived in Ballarat.

"It was a sign," she said with a laugh. "You wouldn't be a proper little brother if you weren't a pain in my ass."

A little pressure in his chest cringed at the word "little," but his sister meant well. "I love you too."

CHAPTER 18

Bronx fought hard to open his eyes. For a moment, he had forgotten what had happened with Praymer—why he had passed out. His heart raced as the memory flooded back.

His vision cleared and a white room came into focus, as did several faces covered with white surgical masks staring down at him. The smell of alcohol and rubber filled his nose.

He lifted his arm to find it strapped down with a thick band around his wrist. Its cool metal kissed his skin, but its corners bit as he tugged. The room around him spun as he realized he was separated from the others. Alone and trapped somewhere on Praymer's ship.

"Where am I?" he croaked.

"You had a seizure, just stay calm."

He didn't remember having a seizure, and as his mind sharpened, so did his doubt. He yanked harder at the metal band around his wrist.

A hand clamped around his arm, pressing it into the soft bed. He still wore his suit from the wedding. That likely meant that he was just recently brought in. "Please, stop doing that." The grip on his wrist was firm. "Remain calm or else we will have to sedate you."

Bronx relaxed his arm and continued staring at the faces whirling around him. His heart raced, and he tried to come up with a plan, but his mind remained in a fog. He had to get out of here. He had to find Rei and the others.

"We have it from here," one of the figures said, gesturing

to his colleague next to him. "You should probably go check on the sovereign."

"Who are you?" asked the one still holding Bronx's arm.

The other colleague held up a syringe with a bright green liquid inside. "We are here to make sure the sovereign's prize remains where he is."

Bronx didn't want to know what was in the syringe. Even bound, he was sure he could fight off the two if only they remained, but the weakness in his limbs reminded him that he just wasn't sure for how long. Hopefully someone was coming for him.

The other two medical technicians hesitated but appeared satisfied with the answer and eventually left with a nod.

Once they left, the remaining two removed their masks. Crona gave her brother a wink before pressing buttons at random below his bed. He chuckled in relief. The bands at his ankles opened and Kaz pried them open further. Crona helped with his wrists, and once free, Bronx sat up. The world lurched.

"Where's Rei?" he asked, rubbing his temple.

"She's with the others," Kaz said. "Shaken, but safe."

"What happened?" Bronx asked as he stood. He took several cleansing breaths and the world righted itself.

"You healed Praymer, and then you passed out," Kaz replied.

"They led us all away from the hangar toward the medical wing, but they took you in a different direction, so naturally we followed," Crona said. She pressed a button on the wall and the door slid open with a whoosh. She glanced outside. "The path is clear, let's go before those medics decide to return."

Bronx moved slowly, the dizziness continuing to abate,

but not quick enough. His mouth was dry and his head felt like it had been filled with cotton. He followed his sister and Kaz out the door to the empty metal hallway. Several other rooms lined the corridor, but most of their doors were closed. Bronx approached the one across the hall from his room to see if Praymer kept other "prizes." But before he could get closer, footsteps clicked from around the corner, and they retreated back into his room.

Bronx's heart continued to race as the footsteps drew nearer and the door slid open. Infiernen raised his eyebrows in surprise as he beheld the three Volocio.

Crona stood in front of Bronx, scalpel in hand, pointing it at the Negander. Kaz stood a few steps back, holding a tray and ready to swing it.

"Well, I guess someone else stole my idea," the Negander said with a smirk.

"You were coming for me?" Bronx asked.

"Of course. I am on your side."

"Our side?" hissed Crona. "You have been leading the Path and undermining our attempts at getting through this election cycle without violence."

"I'm playing a very dangerous game at the moment, Crona," Infiernen replied. "You have to trust me."

"Trust?" Kaz asked. "What's the point of playing such a game?"

"I do what I have to in order to stay close to Praymer. I have to undermine you because I can't let him think I am loyal to you." Infiernen met Bronx's gaze. "That I am truly loyal to Rei."

"So Praymer knows you run the Path?" Crona scoffed. "Of course he does. You have been at Praymer's side for years and haven't killed him. It shouldn't take so long."

"Praymer can't be killed, Crona."

The ground lurched under Bronx's feet. He wasn't sure if he was still dizzy from earlier or from what he just learned. He didn't want to believe it, yet the powers that forced Bronx to heal Praymer suggested otherwise.

"What about Niklaryn's plan?" Bronx asked. "He got his band of followers in the Path on this ship to do just that."

"Nik's a fucking fool." The Negander glared at Bronx, knowing what he was insinuating. Then his face relaxed and his mouth turned into a frown. "I saw what happened with you and Praymer. You felt it, didn't you?"

"What is he talking about?" Kaz asked.

Bronx thought back to that moment, the call in his head that controlled his actions, the way he healed Praymer and couldn't control it. He felt violated. "The pull," Bronx whispered. "Something forced me to heal Praymer, using my own energy to do it." He met Infiernen's gaze. "How do you know about it?"

"Why do you think I knew you could bring Rei back to life?"

"Shit," Crona muttered. "Wait, I thought Niklaryn told Bronx?"

"And I told Nik." Infiernen glanced at the hallway behind him. "Let's get you out of here. Praymer and Dante played their hand badly by trying to take you now. You should be safe as long as we get you back."

The Negander led the way through the sterile metal hallways. After turning a corner, Bronx's vision was assaulted by gold molding on the walls and the painting of the god queen by Benoit, the very one Rei's costume was based off of. Praymer owned the original, and seeing Rei's face on something in Praymer's possession left a bad taste in his mouth.

Infiernen's blue eyes stared at the painting with an

equal amount of disdain. Despite their differences, Infiernen's top priority was to make sure Niklaryn's sister was safe from Praymer.

"If Praymer can't be killed," Bronx began. "How do we kill him?"

"That's what I need you to find out," Infiernen said. "I only discovered he was doing this by accident a few years ago, and I watched a reaper die saving Praymer. No one else knows, except maybe Dante. But if we want to defeat him, we have to find out more about what he's doing."

"Do you think there is at least another reaper on this ship?" Bronx asked, his leg growing numb as he thought about another like him so close but also in terrible danger.

"Yes." Infiernen's voice rang in the empty hall. "But I don't know where."

"We need to figure out a way to learn the layout of the ship without being noticed," Kaz said.

"I think I have an idea," Crona responded with a smirk.

CHAPTER 19

Arram wandered back to the hallway where he thought the Negander had taken Bronx. He was grateful that Praymer had unique taste, and he remembered the intersection had a large painting of Praymer in robes and a crown with hands raised to the heaven, looking like he was the god king. He wondered if Manden had noticed his painting.

Voices echoed down the hall and sure enough, Bronx turned a corner, followed by Crona, Kaz, and Infiernen.

"Are you all right, Bronx?" Arram asked as the group approached. His eyes didn't leave Infiernen's face as the Negander drew near. Thankfully, he kept his distance from Arram. "Where did they take you?"

"Some room behind the medical center," said the reaper. "There is a lot about Praymer we didn't know before."

"You're telling me. Just wait until you find out what his blood can do," Arram said with a chuckle.

"His what?" Kaz asked.

"Oh, for fuck's sake," Crona muttered.

"Where's Rei?" Bronx asked. Arram wasn't surprised that the reaper's only concern was his sister.

"She's fine. Are you going to tell me what he's doing here?" Arram pointed at Infiernen.

"Not now, Arram. Where is your sister?"

Arram clenched his hands. Bronx could surely spare a moment to answer a question. He didn't understand the reaper's obsessive need to be at Rei's side. "Tell me why he's here. There are more important things to discuss than you canoodling with my sister."

"Arram, please."

The younger Ettowa sighed. "She has a room. She had firsthand experience with Praymer's blood and felt a deep cleansing was necessary. She's worried about you, too." Arram kept glancing at Infiernen, only to find the Negander quietly staring at the floor.

Bronx rocked in place and wrung his hands. "Where's her room?"

Arram wasn't going to get the answer he requested, so he gave Bronx directions. The reaper turned to leave but first turned his attention to the Negander.

"Infiernen," Bronx began. "I need to speak to Nik about Rei. Is there a way I can talk to him, or do I have to go through you again?"

"What about Nik and Rei?" Arram asked. "I think I should know too."

Both the Negander and reaper turned to Arram, and Bronx's eyebrows raised.

"He's right." Crona stepped in. "Arram should know, too, if it concerns his siblings."

Infiernen's gaze darted between the four Volocio before he shook his head. "No. Nik doesn't think it's a good idea, and I agree with him."

Arram locked eyes with Crona and Kaz. The blonde met his confusion with a frown while Kaz shook his head.

"It puts me in a bad position," Bronx continued. "She's going to find out sooner or later."

"And unless you say something, Manca, it will be later. I have a lot to repent for in order to encourage Rei to trust me. Once I have proven myself, then she can know."

And just like that, Arram was out of the loop again.

"And what about my trust?" asked Arram, but Infiernen didn't answer him. Bronx also ignored Arram, leaving the younger man seething with anger. This was not the first time Bronx put Arram on the sidelines while he worked his own plans.After they had discovered the stolen election on Wolf X, Arram set up meetings with the planet's parliament to introduce legislation and organized a public investigation about the validity of the elections. Bronx grew impatient and bulldozed past the idea by encouraging Rei and the other Volocio to amass a large protest. Millions of citizens marched around the governmental palace and the Wolf X government were forced to open an investigation. The re-elections took place and the Federation won, yet it was a blow to Arram's ego that Bronx's idea was the more efficient.

"What in the gods' name are you talking about, Bronx?" Kaz asked, pulling Arram out of his head.

Crona rolled her eyes. "It's not polite to keep secrets."

Bronx sighed and threw his hands in the air. "Then talk to her, Infiernen. If I don't trust you, then Rei probably won't either. I am done trying to appeal to you." Bronx's gaze returned to one of the paintings on the wall.

"Aren't you going to storm off, Manca?" Infiernen asked.

Bronx sighed. "Gods, this is embarrassing," he muttered to himself. "I was just kidnapped. Wandering alone on an enemy ship is not the smartest idea."

"I'll go with you," Kaz said. Both men turned to go, but Kaz wasn't finished with Infiernen. "I don't know what is going on between you, Nik, and Bronx, but your drama can wait. We need to work together." Both men turned a corner and were gone.

"Kaz is right," Crona said. "You may still have Praymer's favor, Infiernen, but we are technically his guests at the moment—although that can change at any time. No one knows what happened out here."

"Not necessarily," Infiernen said. "I helped Skylar transmit a message when we first arrived. Urius is aware of the situation and will send a transport to pick up the guests. He will make sure the Federation is aware. Even Praymer wants to avoid keeping the god queen as a hostage; there are a number of people within the Dominion who like her. It's in his best interest to make it clear that she's a guest and remains here willingly."

Crona narrowed her eyes. "I can't figure you out, Infiernen." She voiced Arram's thoughts. He gathered that Infiernen helped Bronx escape, but since no one bothered to clue Arram in, he could only assume. He clenched his jaw so hard it gave him a headache.

"Get in line, Crona." The Negander's blue eyes were hard. "You're not the only one."

"Crona, we should meet with Manden and Artema," Arram said. He was finished with the conversation and wanted to rejoin friendlier faces. "We should pool our information together and decide how we want to go forward until Urius is able to send help. They should still be in the ballroom." Arram jerked his head in the direction of where he last saw the redhead and his sister-in-law before leaving with Rei. Once in agreement, he and Crona headed in that direction while Infiernen never strayed from his post, his piercing blue eyes watching Arram.

Arram could never forget the feel of the bullet puncture his abdomen when Infiernen shot him six months earlier. Even after all this time, he knew Infiernen hated him, but he never figured out why. The way the Negander looked at him reminded Arram that the hatred had not abated.

"What, Infiernen?" Arram asked. Crona stopped mid-stride.

"I want you to stay away from Nik. Do you understand me?" Infiernen growled.

Arram furrowed his eyebrows. "Nik saved my life on that ship and we were trapped in the pod together. Maybe you should tell him to stay away from me."

Infiernen scoffed. "Easier said than done. I have worked hard to help Nik heal and forget his failures. It doesn't help to have you parading around as a living reminder."

"That's uncalled for, Infiernen!" Crona stepped between the two, nostrils flaring.

Arram took a step back. It never occurred to him that his brother felt remorse for only saving one sibling the day their parents died. Their brother was a child and could only do what he did in that moment. Arram survived and was raised by family. He had heard stories of people blocking out traumatic events to help with healing—perhaps that was the reason Nik didn't know who Arram was.

He refused to respond to Infiernen. He didn't care what the Negander thought; he wanted to find Nik and tell him he forgave his brother.

"Come," Crona said, putting an arm around Arram. "Let's go. Infiernen, you should decide which side you are really on before you alienate us. You want to work with Rei, but that also means working with us, and antagonizing your allies isn't going to help your cause."

Arram let her lead him away.

CHAPTER 20

Not too long after Arram left, a few servants came to Rei's room to draw a bath. She refused. She wanted to rinse the blood away, not steep in it. She preferred the steam shower over the bath and requested a few buckets of water to rinse off. She had spent enough time on Manden's *Luciernaga* to know that they had to be careful with water on the ship, and she wasn't familiar enough with Praymer's ship to know what was allowed and what wasn't. She opted for a more conservative choice.

While she waited for the servants to return, Rei wandered around the small room. An enormous bed took up most of the floor space, with a deep red and gold damask blanket that mirrored the tapestries on the wall. Fresh roses gathered into a vase on the nightstand next to the bed; the scent of the bouquet filled the room. The sovereign had to have a botanical garden on his ship. Praymer liked to flaunt his wealth. An enormous wardrobe stood tall on the other side of the room and inside were several items of clothing.

For a woman. About her size.

Rei shuddered. Unfortunately, she still needed to change out of her blood-soaked dress.

A few bottles of fragrant oils sat near the bathtub. One of them was lavender, reminding her of Bronx. She hoped he was all right. She took the lavender and held it to her chest as she continued to wait.

Once the servants returned with the water and a silk robe, they left Rei alone as she stripped the jacket and dress, letting them fall to the floor, and stepped into the shower.

She turned up the heat, let a few drops of lavender drip onto the floor, and stood in the steam as it fought the chill that had settled in her chest.

Rei grabbed a nearby cloth, dipped it into the nearest bucket, and scrubbed her skin vigorously, removing every inch of blood until she was raw. Yet the block on her powers remained. She used the same energy on her scalp before retuning to the mirror. Her tan skin was spotless, her powers still beyond her reach. She growled and returned to the shower. The steam opened all her pores and her skin burned from all the scrubbing. She took one bucket and doused herself, and like a floodgate, her powers returned. She almost wept with relief.

She lifted a hand to call the lightning forth, imagining each atom of air as a bead that charged while it moved along her skin. Laughter burst from her chest at the sparks dancing between her fingers. She never thought she could be so happy to see her powers.

Shades of red flickered along the edge of her vision, followed by a beep at her door, and she knew who it was. "Come in," she called, slipping a silk robe around her shoulders.

"Rei?" asked a familiar voice.

She jumped out of the bathroom to find Bronx standing in the room. His jacket was rumpled, and he swayed ever so slightly, but he was there and he was safe. She threw her arms around his neck and squeezed him tight. He hugged her right back, lifting her off the floor. His scent of lavender and sage enveloped her, and she felt whole.

When he finally lowered her, she pulled away and studied his face. Bags hung under his eyes, but he otherwise appeared all right. "Where did they take you?" she whispered.

"They took him to a medical wing." Kaz's voice pierced the room. Rei found her cousin at the door, but he didn't enter.

"Thank you for finding him," Rei said.

"We are in this together, cousin," Kaz said with a smile. "Enjoy, I'm going back to the others."

As Kaz left, the door closed with a hiss. Rei's attention returned to Bronx. His lips pressed against her forehead, and she closed her eyes, relishing the sensation.

"What did Praymer want with you?"

He said nothing for a while, and Rei feared that it was worse than she imagined. Then he said, "He has been using reapers to keep himself alive."

It was worse than she thought. Rei was grateful that his arms still encircled her as the strength left her legs. "His blood nullifies my powers." She pulled away and met his gaze.

His eyes grew wide as he and Rei both realized—Praymer was a bigger threat than they thought. "Are you alright?"

She nodded. "I washed it all off. My powers are back."

"Does he nullify yours or everyone's?"

A chill walked down her spine. She hadn't thought that far. She wondered if Praymer could use his powers to both nullify a reaper's ability and reverse it. "I don't know. How do you know he has been using reapers?"

"Infiernen told me."

"Infiernen?" Rei whispered.

Bronx then told her what happened, Crona and Kaz's involvement, as well as what Infiernen told them about his relationship with the Path. Then Bronx dropped the most important bit of information: Praymer couldn't die.

Rei lost feeling in her face. There were so many twists

and turns to this complicated knot, she wasn't sure she could ever untangle it.

"Praymer told me I shouldn't kill him because his death would guarantee a war. But it was a lie—he can't be killed anyway." Rei said this more to herself, staring at Bronx's jacket, which remained relatively clean compared to her blood-soaked gown now lying on the floor in the bathroom. She'd have to get one of the servants to take it away. She wanted to avoid coming into contact with Praymer's blood. She never wanted to feel that disconnect from her powers again.

"How are we going to stop him?" she asked, meeting Bronx's gaze again. He led her to the bed where they both sat. His arms moved from around her shoulders to her hands, giving them a reassuring squeeze.

"I don't know," he answered. "There has to be a way to stop him. But it does finally explain why Infiernen has been playing both sides for so long."

"Because he knew Niko couldn't kill Praymer, so they have been biding their time until they could find out how."

"Exactly."

"I need to talk to Infiernen," Rei said. "I understand doing what it takes to remain a double agent, but did he have to hurt so many people?"

Bronx said nothing as he stared at their hands. His thumb stroked Rei's knuckles as he appeared lost in thought. Rei wanted to know what he was thinking. Whenever Infiernen or Niklaryn were brought up, he always seemed lost, uncertain. The latter emotion appeared as a faint yellow off the corner of her eye. His eyebrows drew together in a frown. But she couldn't think about Infiernen now.

For so long, they had worried about what Praymer

would do if he ever captured Rei, but for the first time, she feared for Bronx. She touched his face, and he met her gaze. She didn't like the dark circles under his eyes; she swore they weren't there before. She stroked his cheek and drew close until they were a breath apart.

"We will make sure he doesn't hurt us. If playing his game keeps you safe, I will work with him," Rei whispered.

"I still worry what he could do to you. I was so afraid, thinking of you alone with him in the pod. You know I can't stand us being apart."

Her heart clenched at the quiver in his voice. She had lost count the times she held him at night when the nightmares were at its worst. He still blamed himself for her death, and she could only imagine the weight of his guilt for her being trapped with Praymer. She was still haunted by the dream of Atrius's death, but it must've paled in comparison to Bronx seeing Rei's lifeless body.

She nudged his nose with her own. "And I survived, darling. I think he's harmless. I can see him wanting a second chance, which I can use to ensure peace between the Federation and Dominion until we beat him with votes." She lightly pressed her lips against his. "He is more dangerous to you," she whispered into his lips. "But don't worry, I'll protect you."

His lips broke into the beautiful smile she loved so much. "We'll protect each other, my hero." He lightly touched his forehead against hers. "We should regroup with the others."

She moved onto his lap and tugged his jacket off. Her fingers worked the buttons of his shirt as his hands snaked inside her robes and pulled her closer to him. Their lips hovered a hair breadth apart. He exhaled and she inhaled. His hand rose, gripping the back of her head as though her pulling away, even a little, would be too much for him.

Rei shook her head. "There's so much noise out there." She breathed against his lips. "So much uncertainty and confusion. I can't handle any more of it tonight. I cannot imagine the thought of putting on my dress again or finding myself in the same room as *him*."

Rei kissed him deeply, giving him everything she had. "I just need to be with you. To feel you. To find that balance that I only find when we're together."

Bronx grinned against her lips. A tight flush spread all over her stomach, her skin on fire, heart hammering.

"What?" she whispered.

Her robe slipped off her shoulders and fell in a silent heap. His eyes darkened and Rei never felt more beautiful in her life.

"Rei," he purred into her neck. "I felt completely lost without you by my side." He left a trail of warm kisses down her throat.

She tugged at the last button of his shirt and reached for his trousers. She pulled at the hem of his shirt and pulled it over his head, mussing his dark hair.

His fingers tightened on her hips, pulling her closer.

"And now?" she asked, biting the sensitive spot where his neck met his shoulders.

He moaned in response, wrapping his arms around her waist and flipping her onto her back. "This," he whispered into her ear, hooking her bare leg around his waist. "I only feel at home with you. Anything else feels like only half a life. I promise to not let anyone separate us again."

It took little effort to remove the other scraps of clothing until nothing lay between them.

He kissed her, all teeth, tongue, and raw emotion. Their

hands scraped over each other, their bodies pulled together, determined to become one.

She dragged her hands against his powerful back and his grip tightened against her thighs.

The bed creaked as they moved together. Their movements were slow but urgent. Rei kept forgetting to breath for a second too long as if nothing else kept her alive. Eventually they were nothing more than a tangle of limbs and blankets and she cried his name as release blasted through her. Bronx kept moving, chasing each raw emotion as it came until he found his own release, groaning Rei's name into her lips before kissing her.

Rei understood Bronx's meaning. That same emptiness burned in her until he walked through the door. She hated being apart from him and only felt whole in moments like these where they joined in more than just bodies, but in their hearts and their shared soul.

That was just the beginning. He always left her wanting more. Several emotions played across his dark eyes, uninhibited, and she consumed them all.

"Show me you meant what you promised," she whispered as the waves of desire continued its ebb and flow. "Show me how much you don't want us apart."

He smiled then, the kind that reached his eyes, lighting his whole face, and set her heart on fire. "As you wish," he growled before spending the rest of the evening proving his promise.

CHAPTER 21

Despite the festivities happening around them, Arram and the other Volocio remained on edge. He sniffed the glass Crona handed him. The murky brown drink with green sparkling flecks swirled in circles and smelled like cinnamon and cloves. He sighed before pretending to take a big swig and joining Crona and Kaz as they met Manden, Artema, Sariah, and Skylar. The redhead appeared to be several drinks ahead of him with his boisterous laughter and reddened cheeks.

"So then I said to him, your beard tastes like glory. Glorious, glorious, glory," Manden slurred and was met with a roar of laughter.

Arram frowned and glanced around to the others hoping to garner an explanation. Once the others saw his expression, they laughed harder.

"I guess I missed the joke," he said with a smirk.

"You're not the only one." Crona swirled her bright yellow drink she held in her hand. The smell of lemon verbena wafted in Arram's direction. "We are trying to look like we're relaxed in case Praymer and his thugs are watching."

He chuckled. "Good idea," he muttered. But something told him that Manden didn't get that memo.

"Are you sure that's a good idea, Manden?" Kaz asked as the redhead drained the rest of his glass of wine.

Manden waved a hand dismissively. "I know pretty much everyone in this room. It's fine." Manden waved a hand dismissively.

"So what's the plan?" Sariah asked. "Some guests are feeling nervous about being here."

"Only some?" Sky asked. "I already received word from Urius. He wants to talk to the Volocio tomorrow, but he has already dispatched ships to pick us up."

"And what do we do in the meantime?" Sariah asked.

"We remain on guard," Artema said. "We are guests now, but we can become hostages very quickly if it's convenient for Praymer."

"I hate to be at the mercy of such a man," muttered Kaz.

"He wasn't always the big bad sovereign," Manden said, refilling his glass with a pitcher that appeared out of nowhere. He must've taken it from one of the servers. "I've known him since he was a child. In fact, he used to be quiet and shy."

"He and Micaela were friends for years before they got married," added Artema. "He was always a charmer. He knew what to say to get what he wanted, and he had been in love with Mica since the first time he saw her."

"I don't think that's changed," Kaz said. "I saw how he held Rei when our grandmother tried to end their conversation. He didn't plan on letting go."

"He didn't," Arram agreed. "But he couldn't do anything to her on that ship with so many people around. There are more Federation sympathizers than Dominion. None of them would be happy if something happened to their god queen."

"But things are different now that we are in his domain," Crona said, drawing close and speaking in a low voice. "We need to snoop around his ship, maybe get several people to ask this Dante about having a tour. Praymer strikes me as a man who would like to show off his toys."

Arram should have paid more attention to Crona's plan,

but his thoughts traveled elsewhere. He couldn't forget Infiernen's animosity or Niklaryn's apathy.

The lights from the chandeliers bounced off his face, suddenly too bright. The roar from the crowd pressed against his ears. He took a swig of his drink, but it tasted bitter. He needed to get out of the room.

"I need to go for a walk," he muttered to Manden, who patted him on the shoulder.

Arram pushed his way through the crowd, tugging at the collar of his suit. He was so close to the entryway when an arm lightly wrapped around him and tugged him away. It was Aunt Ildana, who pulled him toward a small group of relatives, including his father's twin and their grandmother, Aurelia.

"Tell me, darling," said Ildana. "What is the nature of your relationship with Riker Sandern's daughter? The two of you seem rather close, and your suit compliments her dress so well."

All eyes were on him, and it surprised him they brought the topic up.

"We're drinking buddies."

The group laughed, but Arram noticed the hint of disapproval in his grandmother's eyes. He had to admit that he rather enjoyed it.

"Come now, Arram," Aurelia said. "It is unkind to treat a woman like that. If you care for the woman, perhaps you should do more. She is quite a catch, the daughter of a popular mayor and with the beauty of her mother, Siba. It would be a wonderful match."

"I'm gay," Arram said.

Ildana made a face. "Oh, that's a shame."

Arram couldn't help but roll his eyes. Her own daughter was a lesbian, and Ildana still walked her down the aisle. Considering who his aunt voted for and the Dominion's views on those outside the hetero-normative sexuality, he shouldn't have been surprised. The brand on his collar itched in response, but he refused to move. His violet eyes matched Ildana's, challenging her to judge him.

"Then that means we must find a good man to match you with." Aurelia's voice cut through the tension. When Arram met her gaze, she responded with a smile, a genuine smile. "We'll find a good Federation boy for you."

"But, Mother," Jenson cut in, "you have already gotten your Federation match with our Rei. She and Bronx make quite the pair. From what I have heard, they are well received by Federation high society."

"Unless the rumors of his parentage are to be believed." Ildana's words caused Arram to sweat. They were treading into territory he was not comfortable talking about. This was Bronx's story, not his.

"What is his parentage?" asked Aurelia.

"I had to fight to get Sariah to tell me. If you recall, she was also attached to Bronx for years until that battle, the one where Niklaryn died."

Arram almost corrected his aunt, but the words died on his lips when he remembered that most of the star cluster believed his brother to be dead. It was such an odd feeling.

"Can we not talk about this?" Arram asked. "I don't like gossip, especially where my sister is concerned."

Aurelia put a hand on his arm as though to silence him. "Continue."

"He is the elder child of Siba," said Jenson. "But people forget that she was once married to Yuri Manca before he left for the civil war on Wolf X."

"While he was gone," Ildana continued, "she had an

affair with her father-in-law Patro, and . . . well . . . Bronx was the result."

Aurelia's hand brushed her lips as her mouth hung open. "The scandal."

Arram snorted, and three pairs of eyes turned to him. "What?" he asked, knowing that he didn't care if they answered or not. "It doesn't look good, I know. But my sister loves him, and what's between them runs deeper than any of us could know."

"But a bastard," said Aurelia. "Arram, surely she cares about her reputation."

"She doesn't and neither do I. Her position and influence derives from her being the god queen and not her lover's history. If you will excuse me."

Arram continued moving, ignoring any other attempts at gaining his attention until he stood back in the empty hallway. He took a few cleansing breaths and walked. He still held his drink and took a small sip. After dealing with those relatives, he needed something.

He wished he could talk to Rei, but if Bronx was in the room, then there was no point. He didn't feel like being ignored again.

He let his feet decide where they would go. He needed to get away from those people. He never really liked the Ettowas, and after this conversation, he liked them less. They had no right to meddle and use relatives for their own personal gains. How medieval. Unfortunately, some people still thought this way—as he had just witnessed—and while her relationship could hurt Rei's chances in certain demographics, Arram couldn't think of any other man who could offer Rei enough to leave her reaper.

If such a price ever existed.

Arram had been so lost in thought, he didn't realize that

his feet had led him to the medical wing. The doors slid open, the sound bringing him out of his head. Praymer sat alone in his bed, swiping through a slate. But he looked up, and Arram's skin tingled as he met Praymer's gaze.

"Is something wrong?" the sovereign asked, placing his slate in his lap.

Arram shook his head, taking a step further into the room. The doors closed behind him with a whoosh.

"Then why are you here?"

Arram wasn't sure, but he didn't like people seeing him caught off guard. There was no one else in the room; it would be a perfect opportunity to get to know the opposition. He took a few steps closer. "I am trying to process a lot of information right now and took a walk. Then I ended up here." He studied the sovereign with his ageless face, shining gold hair, and glittering blue eyes. He was very handsome, perfect almost. Aside from the mechanical right arm and rotting murderous heart.

"Sit with me." Praymer pointed to the empty chair next to his bed.

Arram hesitated. He preferred to stand. But such an action was a display of dominance and Rei had done enough of that. So he decided to take the seat, lifting his glass to take another swig, but thought better of it. The hair on the back of his neck stood as he felt the sovereign's eyes on him.

"I want to thank you for taking the bullet for my sister back on the ship," Arram said.

"I care about her welfare, despite what others may tell you. I care about yours as well, Arram. I was not pleased when I saw the footage of Infiernen shooting you on Trappist V."

Arram eyed the contents of his glass, its brown liquid

still swirling around. He wasn't sure if he believed Praymer, but deep down he appreciated the remark.

"I want us to work together, Arram," Praymer continued. "I am tired of this war that Urius so desperately wants."

"Are you also tired of rigging elections because you know you're losing?"

Praymer smiled and Arram's stomach fluttered. "You're just as clever as Max was. He always saw through my machinations as well."

"All the Volocio have seen through it."

"Most likely because you were the one to first point it out."

Praymer was right. Arram was the one who discovered something had gone wrong during the Wolf X elections and brought it to Urius's attention. The Volocio then brought the fact to the public, followed by the protests, and a recount was made, thus sealing the Federation's win.

"I was the one who pointed it out, yes."

Praymer scoffed. "And Urius is wasting your talents."

Arram's head jerked back. "Why do you say that?"

"You are never in the spotlight. It's always Rei, or Manden, or Kaz, or even . . . Bronx."

Arram took note of the way Praymer growled the last name. He had a feeling the sovereign would have rather called Bronx a different name.

"I am the unknown brother. It's hard to garner attention when you are competing against the ghost of the noble knight, Niklaryn, and the glory of Rei, our god queen."

"Yet you are also Jeanh Ettowa's son. Did you know he was the one who convinced me to come back into politics?"

Arram's chest grew heavy. He had tried to find information on his father over the last few months, but no records of

Jeanh Ettowa's deeds could be found in the Dominion, who did not like sharing information with the Federation. Skylar had told him once that their parents were also staunch Dominion supporters until Praymer hunted him. But even Skylar didn't remember her aunt and uncle enough to give Arram more information. Yet Praymer seemed willing to give it. "He did?" Arram feigned disinterest, but in reality, he wanted to hear more.

"Yes. Your father was an artist with politics. Your other relatives are amateurs in comparison. I am sure you inherited his calculating brain."

Arram smiled. He shouldn't have been surprised that his father was no less ambitious than the other vultures he spoke to earlier.

"If he was such an artist," Arram began, drawing closer to Praymer. "Why did you murder him along with my mother?"

Praymer's face relaxed. Arram knew he had him.

"Your parents betrayed me. I will admit, I let my temper and ego get the better of me, but not a day goes by without me wishing I could take it back. You three did not deserve to both lose your parents and be separated and scattered to the wind. You are too important."

Arram leaned back in his chair and finally finished his drink. He didn't believe the sovereign's words, but he had to admit Praymer was good.

"Well, Praymer, whether you think I am important is irrelevant if the rest of the star cluster doesn't agree. I have already accepted my place in the shadows of both Rei and Niklaryn."

"But you don't have to be happy about it."

Arram wasn't, but he didn't want to admit that to Praymer.

"Micaela and Maximilian were a team," the sovereign explained. "He was the brains, and she was the brawn. She was an empress, but he was her adviser, and she openly listened to his advice. They were always seen together because they worked together to rule. I don't see that between you and Rei."

"We are a team and she listens to me." Of course Praymer didn't see these things; Rei and Arram's conversations and plans happened behind closed doors. He had to admit, he wished he received more credit.

"Urius is the one who decides which of his pawns see the spotlight and which ones stay in the wings." Arram winced. He shouldn't have said that.

"Well," Praymer muttered, stroking his chin with his mechanical arm. The gesture seemed almost human. "It's good to know your thoughts don't completely align with his."

"What are you getting at? Just be direct."

Praymer shrugged. "Your sister and I had a moment in the pod. I think if she gave me a chance, we could work together to unite the Federation and Dominion. Urius, his cronies at the Federation council, and even that reaper want a war and so do my courtiers. But they aren't the ones who have the public support—Rei and I do. If only we can show the star cluster together."

"There's nothing stopping you two from showing a united front now. We are well away from Federation and Dominion. That was the reason you accepted the wedding invitation, right? You wanted to meet my sister in a public setting."

"That was the plan. Despite almost dying, I am glad that the Path attacked. Being stuck in that pod with your sister gave us an opportunity to talk." His human hand lightly touched the bandage on his shoulder. "She was determined to not give me the time of day otherwise."

Arram had to admit he respected Praymer's dedication to his lie of not being able to die. He bit his tongue, though, as much as he wanted to expose the sovereign's deceit.

"My sister knows what she wants. And I know she wants to avoid a war." Arram met Praymer's eyes—a brilliant shade of blue that still shone under the harsh lights of the medical wing. He broke eye contact. "She is aware of the prophecy—that she will bring about a war—and she doesn't want a future where people die for her."

A small smile crept across Praymer's face. "Good. Can you organize something then? I think with you working as a bridge between Rei and me, we can have a constructive conversation about how we can move forward. Perhaps we can start by doing something with those members of the Path we captured when we arrived on the ship?"

Arram stared at his empty glass. "You mean the members who work for Infiernen?"

Praymer chuckled. "You are thorough. I had Infiernen infiltrate the Path long ago to see what he could learn. He is a natural leader."

"And you want to make an example of the ones following a man under your orders?"

"The majority we captured admit following another, the real monster and true leader of the Path. I have to make an example of all so as to not compromise Infiernen. My hope is that your sister and I can send that message together. It wouldn't be as powerful if it were me alone. Strike once, strike hard."

Arram's head jerked back. Now he understood how Rei may have changed her mind about the sovereign. Praymer was calm, willing to listen, perhaps even genuine in wanting peace, as well as doing what was necessary. It was a good idea, but he wasn't comfortable enough to make this decision on his own. He never felt that Urius was as bloodthirsty for war as Praymer claimed, yet he wanted to show that he could be a more prominent player in this game.

"I'll see what I can do."

CHAPTER 22

The smell of enumerable spices filled Rei's nose, leaving her mouth watering. Rows of tables and booths with bright tablecloths and awnings lined the long cobble-stoned path. The hum of people talking surrounded her and the warmth of a bright red sun warmed her face. The market-place felt both alien and familiar. There was only one explanation for this.

This was a memory. She had not experienced one of Micaela's memories for some time, but she had seen this market before. It was on the Volocio home world.

But this time she wasn't alone.

Praymer stood next to her, a large smiled blooming across his face. He was younger, and the smile came more easily. He had two human hands, and one tugged on his light blue jacket. Several golden curls fell across his brow.

"This is beautiful," he said with a gasp.

"Just wait until you try the food," Micaela said, pointing to a booth just a few feet away.

Rei didn't like these memories; she sat in Micaela's consciousness but couldn't control her actions. She felt like a puppet with the original god queen pulling the strings.

An elderly woman stood next to a tall flame. A metal grate hung over the fire, covered in skewers of meat. She doused them with some sort of sauce that caused the flames to spring up to singe the meat, yet she remained unscathed.

Micaela ordered one and held it for Praymer to see, the stick still warm to the touch. "This is my favorite. It's traditionally from Munda."

Rei scanned Micaela's feelings that coursed through her: excitement, joy, and attraction. Micaela enjoyed the way a blonde curl fell across Praymer's brow.

If Rei could throw up in her dream, she would have.

"That's . . . Manden's kingdom, correct?" His voice was lighter. Praymer was so young, his blue eyes wide with curiosity.

"Correct." Micaela pulled off a piece of meat and popped it in her mouth. The flesh melted on her tongue. The skewers lay over the fire for a long time until the meat was tender.

She ripped off another piece and brought it to Praymer's lips, her fingers brushing against them as she placed the food in his mouth. A thrill trickled down Micaela's spine and a flood of desire bloomed in Rei's chest. But it wasn't the same uncontrollable passion she felt when she saw Bronx. This was much more subdued, controlled.

A beep pierced her thoughts.

His eyes closed as he savored the food. "Divine," he whispered. He opened his eyes again, and the way he looked at her was hardly different than the way Bronx did: with joy and admiration. "The next time you visit my empire, I want to show you my favorite places. If you will let me."

Micaela smiled. "I would like that very much."

Rei wanted this dream to end.

Another beep.

"Thank you, Mica, for showing me your lovely home. It's a shame I have to return to my star cluster tomorrow."

"It is a shame. You were just starting to get interesting."

Praymer blushed. "Unless you can give me a reason to stay?" He drew close, too close.

That infernal beep happened again.

Rei opened her eyes. She was still in her red damask room on the sovereign's ship. The beep came from her door.

Bronx lay at her side, exhaustion written on the reaper's sleeping face.

The beeping continued.

Rei groaned as she rose, grabbing the discarded robe from the floor and wrapping it around herself. Once she opened the door, she regretted it.

Rei did not expect Praymer to be up and about, nor did she like finding him at her door without a hint of his injuries. The shock removed the remaining cobwebs of Micaela's memory from her mind, but her gaze traveled to his lips and she still felt how soft they were under her fingers.

She shook her head, trying to rid herself of that last memory.

"Yes?" she asked once she recovered from her shock.

"Did you sleep well?" His blue eyes were soft as he studied her. She wore the robe she received the night before, and she didn't like how his gaze attempted to penetrate the thin silk fabric. She wrapped the robe tighter around her body.

"I did once Bronx returned to me. What did you do to him?"

His eyes moved from her face to Bronx's sleeping form in the bed behind her. "I did nothing. He saved my life."

Rei narrowed her eyes. "Is that why you had him taken to some secret room? So he could do it again when you needed it?"

"He was taken to the medical area for his safety. My medics told me he had a seizure. There was no secret room. It hurts me you think I would do something like that."

It wasn't a seizure, but Rei didn't feel like arguing. "Is that all you came for?"

"I wanted to ask about your health. I worried you might have hypothermia."

She studied his face. She saw shadows of the young man from the memory, but the years had hardened him. Lines surrounded his mouth and eyes; before he looked at Micaela with awe, but only a sliver of that remained in his gaze now. "I'm fine."

"Happy to hear it." Praymer's eyes remained on Rei's face, but she looked away. She wished he would stop looking at her like that.

"There's breakfast for guests in the hall," Praymer said finally. "But I also wanted to inform you that Urius wants the Volocio to take a call from him in an hour. I have a room set up for you and the others."

"Thank you."

He leaned against the door frame, close enough for Rei to smell his cologne, a mix of vervain and roses.

"I thought you and I made excellent progress in the pod, Rei. What happened?"

"I didn't outright kill you. I think that's progress enough."

"I told you, I'm one of the good guys. I only want what's best for the star cluster, and I think you can help me."

"But wasn't it just a few days ago that you stood on a podium and called me the blood empress? How can I be both good for the cluster and yet poised to bring about its destruction?"

"I have to appease my courtiers until I can align myself with someone with more pull. When we unite the Federation and Dominion, those holding my purse strings will find that they are grossly outnumbered." He leaned in closer.

"Arram told me how Urius tries to control the Volocio the same way. I am sure you are sick of playing his game as well. You must know what it is like to play a part even if you don't agree with the role."

Rei remembered how Urius didn't want her to meddle in the Trappist V election, and she did it anyway to the Federation's benefit. She hated to admit that the sovereign was right but didn't want to give him the satisfaction.

"Thank you for breakfast. We have to get ready." She let the door slide shut in Praymer's face.

She turned to find Bronx sitting up, worry lines spread across his forehead. "He certainly knows what to say," he muttered.

"I don't like that he's been talking to Arram. We can't let Praymer know our weaknesses."

Bronx nodded. "United front."

She joined him in bed and ran a hand through his hair, enjoying how soft it was between her fingers. "How are you feeling?"

"Better. Breakfast sounds glorious. I don't remember the last time we ate."

Rei wanted to tell him about Micaela's memory of Praymer, but she couldn't bring herself to do it. Her moments with Bronx gave her peace, and she didn't want to disturb that right now. Micaela's feelings lingered in the back of Rei's mind, and she wanted to scrub them away.

Bronx put on his suit, not having any other clothing options, while Rei looked at her wardrobe.

"Gods bless it, he has good taste," she growled, pulling out a red tunic with gold embroidery. It was the same wrap-cut style as her god-queen costume, but the fabric was softer. She had left her heels on the starship and they now were likely floating in space, but she found a matching pair of red silk slippers in her size.

She might as well accept his gifts since her gown still lay on the floor in the bathroom, where Bronx had pushed it with his shoe the night before.

"Isn't that always the worst kind of evil?" Bronx asked with a smirk. "The one who's a snappy dresser?"

"The absolute worst. You focus so much on how good they look that you don't see their true plan." She dropped her robe and pulled the tunic over her head.

"Smoke and mirrors, my darling," Bronx said, straightening his jacket and looking at himself in the mirror. "He dresses better than I do."

"Perhaps. But I prefer you without your clothes." Rei winked.

"True. I do my best work without the hindrance of clothing."

The look he gave her sent a rush of desire through her. She thought back to what they did to each other the night before, and if they weren't on an enemy ship, she would probably throw him on the bed and do it all over again. She knew then that whatever Micaela had felt for Praymer was nothing compared to the first memory Rei experienced of the god queen and Atrius on the balcony. The kiss, the lust, the way his hands on her body left currents across her skin. Praymer had always been eclipsed by the reaper.

"Best work? You know, some of those things you did are illegal on at least two planets in the star cluster," she teased.

"Yeah, the boring ones," he volleyed back, and they laughed.

Once ready, they met the other Volocio back in the ballroom where the guests had gathered the night before. Manden appeared the only one worse for wear, standing in line with the other guests, his dinner jacket open and his dress shirt not tucked into his trousers.

Rei and Bronx joined the others already in line with the redhead. Conversations from other guests hummed in the background along with scrape of chairs and silverware clinking against plates. Rei scanned the room for an empty table, while the smell of bacon left her mouth watering. She wished the line would move faster.

"Too much of that wine last night?" Crona asked with a giggle. Her blonde hair still wet from what Rei assumed to be a recent shower.

"A little, but I convinced Dante to agree to a brief tour after breakfast for anyone interested. Apparently, many of the guests have been making such a request for most of the evening."

"I wonder who gave them that idea?" Kaz asked, throwing a grin in Crona's direction. He also smelled of soap and aftershave.

Along one wall was a huge buffet with many available foods. Rei noticed many bright orange Gamba fruits from Kepler IV piled into a pyramid on one table and several rows of Black Phoenix beer from Wolf X. Rei found it too convenient the sovereign had plenty of the most popular products from the planets of Sariah and Elmessa.

"Beer for breakfast?" Artema asked, taking one.

"Not just any beer," said Bronx.

"The best beer," Crona said, grabbing a bottle for herself.

"And any other opinion is just wrong," said Kaz.

Rei held back a smile. Of course, all three were from Wolf X and were loyal to their brand.

"Thank you so much for the advertisement," Manden

said, grabbing a bottle. "I will admit, Black Phoenix is a good choice if you must have beer for breakfast."

"There you are," Arram said, joining the group. "It's almost time for the meeting. Take your breakfast and come."

The group quickly piled plates with food and followed Arram out of the ballroom and down the hall. The room had a deep red table with black grain that reflected the fluorescent lights above. Praymer stood at one end, flanked by Dante.

"I thought we had privacy," Rei said as the group chose their seats. Bronx was never far from her, and Rei felt Praymer's eyes follow them as they sat down.

"You will have it," Praymer said. "I would just like to send my regards personally to Urius."

Rei had managed a couple bites of toast and sausage before the screen on the far wall flickered on. After a trill of chimes, Urius's face appeared. His normal scowl loosened to a broad smile as he beheld the Volocio. Bernie's beaming face appeared above his right shoulder.

"Hello, gods and goddesses," Bernie purred. "I have never been happier to see all your beautiful faces."

"Indeed," added Urius. "Anekris, thank you for allowing the guests to take shelter on your ship."

"It's my pleasure to do so. In an attack like that, party lines shouldn't matter. Life does." Praymer looked to the other Volocio. "I just wanted to give you my quick greetings and I will leave you all to your meeting." He gave Rei and Manden nods before leaving the room, Dante following close like a shadow as the door closed behind them.

"Did anyone get hurt?" Urius asked.

Artema took a sip of beer. "Praymer took a bullet for Rei and almost died."

Bernie's and Urius's heads jerked back in surprise. "I

didn't expect that," said the Federation leader. "He looked to be in good health."

"Yes, by some unknown miracle." Crona tugged at her earring twice, meaning she was lying, before glancing in Bronx's direction.

Each Volocio had their own designated signals to let others know if they were about to lie or make a comment with a deeper meaning while speaking among potential enemies or strangers. For all they knew, Praymer was recording their conference, despite his promise of privacy. They could never be too careful.

"I see," Urius said. He glanced in the reaper's direction before turning to the redhead. "Do you fear Praymer will do anything rash?"

"He has been a gracious host." Manden laced his fingers together and touched both index fingers against his lips, indicating he was about to lie before he spoke again. "I do not think he has any further plans besides offering room and board until a Federation ship can pick us up."

"He has talked of an alliance," Rei said. "He told me he wants to unify the Federation and Dominion without bloodshed." Her mind returned to her conversation with Praymer in the pod. She believed his desire for an alliance, but until she knew the price, she said nothing more.

"He knows he is losing votes," added Arram. "I believe he is aware of how influential Rei is and wants to use it to his benefit. He asked me to organize something to show that he and the god queen can work together."

"Organize what, exactly?" Urius asked.

"Several members of the Path were captured when we arrived on Praymer's ship. I thought about organizing a live feed on the Nexus of the two sitting together for a trial, as well as having Rei and Praymer talk to each other. Show that they can work together to help ease the tension building up between the two parties."

Rei wrinkled her nose at the idea, but Arram had a point. They had to show they could work together, or at least Rei had to. It would help dispel the gossip that she would bring about the destruction of the star cluster with a war. But she didn't enjoy talking to Praymer more than she had to. She hated the way he looked at her when they talked. It was a knowing look, as though he knew all her deepest and darkest secrets.

At the moment, even if she did an interview, doing it on Praymer's ship may make her look weak. She couldn't afford that either. They had to look like equals, and that was hard as a "guest" on his ship.

"I don't agree with this idea," Urius barked. Even Bernadette raised her eyebrows in surprise, mimicking the reaction of everyone else in the room. "While I think joining forces in order to defeat the Path is a good idea, I don't believe it needs to be done on Praymer's ship. I think we should make a show on a Federation planet at a later time." Despite what he said, he placed a finger to the side of his nose which meant that rejected Arram's plan completely.

Arram gripped the arms of his seat so tightly Rei worried he would break it.

"And when would that happen?" Arram asked through gritted teeth. "If we want to avoid bloodshed and prove my sister doesn't want violence, shouldn't we want the more peaceful route as soon as possible?"

Rei tried to catch Arram's attention. She needed him to back down. Urius's jaw tightened, and he was obviously determined to dig his heels in further. Arram's lips pressed together until they were nothing but a line.

"Arram," she whispered.

Her brother's violet eyes snapped in her direction, a look of betrayal spreading across his face.

"You don't need to worry about Praymer," Rei said, turning back to Urius. "Honestly, I also agree that we should show a united front, but I think I would rather Arram organize an event somewhere more neutral at a much much later time. If only for my own safety."

"Agreed." The Federation leader's shoulders relaxed, as they did when he appeared to have won an argument. But Rei watched Bernie smirk silently behind her uncle. She always saw what her uncle could not. No matter what anyone said, Rei was still going to do what she wanted.

"Is there anything else we can do for you, gods and goddesses?" asked Bernie.

"Getting off this ship would be a good start, Bernie," Manden said.

"I have already sent several ships to pick you up."

Rei's eyes darted to Bernie's face, who dabbed her chin then tugged her right ear. Twelve hours. She just had to avoid Praymer until then, or at least minimize contact.

"How are the rest of the guests?" Bernie asked. "Sariah and Elmessa?"

"As well as can be," Crona said. "Plenty of people are on edge being on Praymer's ship."

"And with good reason," Kaz added. "Between being attacked by the Path and being a guest on a Dominion ship, there is a lot of tension in the air. Not all of the Path members were captured, and some must be masquerading as guests on the ship. Who knows if they'll attack us again?"

"I have reason to believe that we have an ally. They won't attack us," said Artema.

"Who's the ally?" Bernie asked.

Artema tucked on her braids behind her ears and let her hand rest there, reminding the group they were likely being listened to. "I think we can safely assume we know who it is."

Urius's mouth hung open. Of course he knew about Niklaryn. The Federation leader then nodded. "Bernadette and I must leave and meet with the council. Once we pick you up, your ship will take you to our rendezvous point for a further debriefing. Until then, try to stay out of trouble."

The group muttered a "yes" before the screen went black.

"What the fuck, Rei?" Arram yelled.

She almost jumped in her seat. Her brother rarely said anything to her with such a tone in front of the others.

"You know my idea for you and Praymer to talk is good!"

Bronx took Rei's hand and gave it a squeeze. "Why is it so important that you push your sister together with that man?"

"I just want you to try, Rei. Is that so hard to ask? If it comes to war in the end, so be it, but I want us to exhaust all options first. I am capable of coming up with good ideas." Arram's violet eyes dimmed, and Rei's heart clenched at the sight.

"No one is doubting that," she said. "None of us have said that your idea was bad. I just think we should be more calculating."

"Urius pretty much said it's a terrible idea," Arram muttered.

"Fuck what he thinks." Rei joined Arram on the other side of the table. She felt the others' eyes on her as she approached her brother. "Let's plan this, but we push for more neutral territory."

"Your sister's right," Bronx added. "At the moment, our position here on this ship can easily be construed as guests or prisoners, and if people consider us the latter, then they will assume we did this under duress and not sincerity."

Arram wrinkled his forehead as he glanced in Bronx's direction. Then he gave his sister a nod. "You're right. You're right." He scoffed. "I just let Urius get to me. It's so frustrating how dismissive he can be."

"He's that way with all of us," Crona said.

"You're right," repeated Arram. "I know we all want to avoid this war." He shook off Rei as she reached for him. "I need to calm down. Do you really think it's a good idea to work with Praymer?"

Rei bit her lip. Perhaps now was the time to come clean.

"I saw one of Micaela's memories this morning. She was with Praymer and . . . it was a good memory."

"What do you mean 'good?'" Bronx asked, his anxiety flickering yellow again.

"They were in a market in her empire, in Dinay." Rei looked to Manden and Artema. "You were right, they were friends. He was so different then, so hopeful."

"We have all changed in some ways since that time," Artema said.

Rei knew Artema was her sister-in-law's middle name, and only since Micaela's death had she stopped identifying by her first name, Tasya. Artema had yet to divulge why she changed her name, only that the decision was made two thousand years ago. Rei never questioned her. Manden had accepted it, since her also knew her as Tasya, but Rei didn't doubt the woman's meaning about change.

"The question is, has Praymer changed too much?" Rei said to herself. If there was still a sliver of that young man left, Rei could use it.

Praymer wanted her. She knew that with each of his glances. She remembered how he stared at her in the thin silk robe. He had been so close that he could have easily pulled it off. Dread pooled in her stomach at the thought.

"We need to go." Crona looked at her brother. "We don't want to be late for the tour."

"We should return to the ballroom," Kaz said to the rest of the group. "We need to alert the guests to be ready to leave."

Bronx never looked away from Rei. She had planned on going on the tour, but now she wasn't sure and Bronx sensed it. She knew he didn't want to leave her.

She took his hand and gave it a squeeze. "I am going to go with Kaz. I should make an appearance to the family."

Bronx hesitated.

"You'll live without my sister's presence," snapped Arram before rolling his eyes.

"I'll be fine," Rei said in a low voice.

"And if he comes to you while I am not there?"

"I won't be alone. You know I can handle him."

"I know. I was just hoping for front row seats when you decide to give him what he deserves." Bronx gave her a smile, but it looked forced.

His comment made her chuckle anyway. "I'll make sure to wait until you return before I give him a thrashing."

He nodded and followed his sister out.

She hated seeing him like that. She didn't know what more she could do to help him overcome this anxiety over her death, aside from simply being there for him when he needed it. But she didn't want to give the impression that too many of the Volocio were interested in this "tour." Yet Bronx needed to go. If there were another reaper on this ship, Bronx would sense them.

"Arram?" Manden asked as the others began filing out of the room. "You coming?"

Arram shook his head. "I want to walk and clear my head. I'm still annoyed with Urius, and I'm afraid I may say something regrettable."

"Be safe," said Rei.

"We're already safe."

Rei watched him leave, still trying to understand her brother's outburst earlier. He was normally so levelheaded. She was the one with the shorter fuse.

"But let's not say how long until the ships arrive," Rei said to Kaz as they left. "I don't want someone to accidentally tell Praymer. Let him think he has plenty of time with us. If he gets comfortable, maybe we can get a better read on him."

"That won't be necessary." Artema fidgeted with one of her dark braids while she shifted her weight from side to side. "We know what he wants. He hasn't changed."

"He wants war," Manden said. "The question is how is he setting up the pieces to get it?"

CHAPTER 23

Bronx was pathetic. He shouldn't have reacted like he did when it came to leaving Rei behind for the tour. But when the moment came, he froze, his body refusing to move. It was the worst feeling. He had willed his body to move, but it wouldn't, and a little voice in his head reminded him of the last time he left Rei alone.

"Are you alright, brother?" Crona asked.

"I'll be fine. Let's just focus on our mission."

Crona narrowed her eyes. He was quite sure she didn't believe him, but she didn't challenge him this time.

They arrived at the meeting place, and Bronx was surprised to find Sariah and Skylar there.

"Safety in numbers, brother," Crona said with a grin.

Bronx didn't recognize the others enough to tell which ones were Ettowas and which ones were Brays. He was grateful to find a rather large number of people who were also interested in the ship's layout.

Crona tugged Bronx's arm, drawing him to where Sariah and Skylar stood in the middle of the crowd to help them blend in more.

"Good of you to join," Sariah said.

"Wouldn't miss this opportunity," he muttered. He couldn't help but notice that several eyes glanced in his direction, and he shifted back and forth on his feet.

He met Sariah's eyes, and her lips turned down to a frown. His instincts told him she had something to do with it.

"I am so sorry, Bronx," she whispered. "I didn't think she would tell people."

"Who?" Crona asked.

"My aunt," Skylar said. "She found out about Bronx's parentage and now several of the guests are abuzz with the scandal."

Crona rolled her eyes. "Who cares?"

"Social climbers like the Ettowas and Brays," Sariah said. "Our families."

"Then why did you tell her?"

"We were talking, and it slipped out." Sariah touched Bronx's arm. "I'm so sorry."

Bronx rolled his eyes. He had enough to deal with besides getting strange looks from strangers. "It's fine," he said. "You know I never cared about these things." He didn't. Even when he studied in the Daer Academy, he was among plenty of people from various backgrounds, and no one cared that his parents weren't married or that his mother had an affair with her father-in-law while her husband was at war. All that mattered was him and his gladius.

Yet the buzz of the people talking around him was loud. Maybe it was because he was still on edge about leaving Rei, maybe a part of him did care what people thought, or maybe this was because of Rei's recent revelation about Micaela's memory of Praymer. The latter left him feeling sick. Regardless, the noise filled his head to where it left little else.

He caught the eye of a pair of older ladies staring at him.

"Yes, I'm a bastard and I don't fucking care."

The ladies flinched, then averted their eyes. Crona giggled.

"Tell them how you really feel," his sister said with a snort.

Bronx scanned the crowd that continued to grow in number, guests in their evening gowns and dinner jackets in every color imaginable. He wondered who would be the one to give the tour—if it ever started. Certainly not Praymer, the sovereign was likely busy with his plans for Rei. He gritted his teeth at the thought.

Sariah placed a hand on his arm and gave it a gentle squeeze. "Are you okay, Bronx?"

"I'm fine, drop it."

He didn't bother to see how the others reacted, but he did wonder why this tour hadn't started yet.

Ildana's words to Rei before the wedding floated in his consciousness. *A nice Dominion boy.* Now people may deem him unsuitable, and he worried that more than just Praymer would try to set up a union between the sovereign and Rei. And now that Rei had a memory of a "hopeful" Praymer . . .

Urius's ships couldn't come soon enough.

"I saw your aunt talking to Arram last night. If she can't get a match with Rei, maybe she'll succeed with Arram." A hint of a smile spread across Skylar's lips.

Crona laughed. "She's in for a surprise. Arram is just as averse to being manipulated as his sister."

"Ladies and gentlemen," Dante said after the chatter grew to a roar. "If you will follow me, please, the tour is starting." Dante stood off to one side, his shoulders slumped, a bored expression on his face.

The other guests clustered in different groups, chatting away. Bronx heard a few remarks attempting to guess what they would see.

"What do you think Praymer has to show off?" Skylar asked.

"Fifty prox says there will be a painting of him with Micaela," Crona replied as the group followed Dante down the hall that led to the medical center.

Bronx said nothing. His sister was likely right: aside from Benoit, Praymer would have at least one painting of him and his dead wife. He remembered that morning when the sovereign arrived at their room. From his position on the bed, he saw the way Praymer leaned in close to Rei, a hungry look in his eyes. Now that Bronx knew about Rei's memory, he tried to remember how she responded to Praymer.

He shook his head. "Get it together," he muttered to himself. "You are getting worked up over nothing."

Yet he still couldn't convince himself.

Dante informed the guests about the medical center in case anyone needed help, but Bronx only half listened. Once past it, they continued onto the bridge. All the officers inside stood and saluted as Dante entered. It was clear the man was also the captain of the ship. Made sense.

Dante continued their tour of the engine room, the armory, the brig, the communications room—where the Volocio spoke with Urius only hours before—the shuttle bay, recreational facilities, and the archive vault.

A painting hung on the far wall of the archive vault. Guests wandered the archives for a time, allowing Bronx a closer inspection. Praymer and Micaela sat on matching golden thrones. Praymer wore that ugly smug that Bronx hated while Micaela stared determined, her lips pressed together in a line. What alarmed Bronx more was her dress: red with gold embroidery, the same style Rei wore.

Goosebumps ran along his arms. Praymer knew Rei

would pick this dress. Bronx shouldn't have been surprised that certain tastes carried over from Micaela to Rei, but the little voice reminded him that Micaela still married Praymer over Atrius, and the thought gave him pause. He worried that despite everything, Praymer could still weasel himself into Rei's good graces.

The ship's pathway sloped up to the left as they continued spiraling up toward the top. There were fewer officers and more Negander and servants.

They continued to the top toward the upper observation dome, where a pair of large doors stood. Unlike others that were metal, these were thick and wooden, with a series of old-fashioned locks down the middle. Bronx had to admit the style was odd, but the older locks were harder to unlock since people weren't as used to them anymore. Good thing Crona had plenty of practice.

"This is the entrance to the sovereign's botanical gardens that pumps oxygen throughout the ship, but only he may enjoy sitting in the greenery," Dante said.

The group continued on, but Bronx didn't move. The scent of lavender filled his nose, and the sound of leaves rustling in the trees echoed in his mind. He heard the call from just the other side of the doors. He recognized the presence from his time in Hamastagan, the Land of the Dead. If Praymer was hiding anyone, it was behind those doors.

He quickly returned to his spot in the middle of the crowd but noted the path as they returned to the ballroom. He knew where they had to go. Now it was a matter of planning when to get in.

CHAPTER 24

Arram walked in circles for several minutes, quickly realizing that the hallways spiraled up. Eventually the corridor opened up to his left to reveal several twisting hallways reaching up into the top of the ship, with a large pillar and a glass elevator in the middle. He heard several voices bouncing off the walls, but he couldn't tell from where. One lone voice talked about the ship having been manufactured by the Ettowa Starline, and he knew it was the tour Bronx and Crona had taken part in.

He didn't understand why he let Urius get to him. Normally he could brush off the leader's dismissive comments, but today they got under his skin. He shook his head. There was no point in dwelling on this. He laid his arms on the balcony and stared at the cascading chandelier hanging above him that threw a kaleidoscope of color around the area.

"Are you lost?" asked a young woman.

Arram turned and his jaw dropped.

"Camila?" he whispered. Alma Canale's daughter, who was captured by Negander during the attack on Trappist V. They had assumed the worst, yet here she was in a lovely silver gown and jewels. They dressed her like a queen.

"Do I know you?"

"We met briefly on Trappist V. My sister is the god queen, Rei."

She showed little emotion on her face, but her green eyes widened just enough to indicate surprise. "Of course," Camila said with a smile. "Is she here?"

"Yes. All of us are here."

"Oh." Her smile faded.

"We were so worried about you." Arram leaned in closer. "Are you alright? Are they treating you well?"

Camila's lips parted, but she remained silent. Her green eyes darted away from Arram's face. "I'm fine. They treat me well."

"I see you have found one of my esteemed guests." Praymer's voice echoed in the hall. The sovereign's footsteps clicked behind Arram.

Arram turned to Praymer. "Why is she here?"

"I saved her from the Infinity Dogs after they attacked you on Trappist V. I would have made sure she returned to the Federation, but she wanted to stay."

Arram's eyes returned to Camila, whose smile returned. "Are you happy here?" he asked.

Camila nodded, her eyes remaining on Praymer's face. "Thrilled."

"You could have written to your mother," countered Arram. "She's been worried sick about you."

"I am fine. She did not need to worry."

Praymer's human arm snaked around Camila's shoulders. "You can tell Alma yourself. As you can see, she's very happy here."

Arram furrowed his eyebrows. He felt as though he was missing something but couldn't figure out exactly what.

"I'll tell her, but I think it would be better if you did, Camila."

She said nothing, a smile still plastered on her face.

"How was meeting with Urius?" Praymer asked.

Arram knew he shouldn't say anything. They used their signals for a reason, but his pride still stung from Urius's dismissal. It was petty, but he wanted to lash out.

"He was against the idea of you and my sister talking."

Praymer shrugged. "I'm not surprised. What did your sister say?"

There was no reason to trust Praymer, but his sister's revelation about Micaela's memory carried weight. She seemed open to the idea of working together but was still hesitant. Arram wished he knew more about the memory, but it confirmed what Manden and Artema had said before: Micaela and the sovereign were friends, and Arram could tap into that.

If Arram pushed, then perhaps he could make it happen soon. He didn't want anyone else to feel the same torture he had endured—the Path needed to be destroyed, and quickly. "She feels such a meeting should take place on more neutral territory. She thinks doing it here would weaken her position." Technically Bronx was the one who said it, but those two always stayed on the same side. They were already connected before Bronx shared his soul, but part of him worried that Bronx's influence over his sister deepened because of it.

Praymer's golden eyebrows drew together as he frowned. "That makes little sense. How could talking to me on my ship make her look weak?"

Arram shrugged. "We are already at your mercy by being on this ship, far away from any help should we require it. For all anybody knows, you could be forcing Rei or any of us to talk to you and appear to want peace."

Praymer chuckled, then reached out to pick off something on Arram's jacket. The sovereign leaned in close, and Arram caught the whiff of aftershave, roses, and vervain. The effect was dizzying. "Do I look like someone who could force you to do something?" His blue eyes sparkled. "I know you are someone who will do as he wishes, regardless what anyone thinks."

Arram's cheeks warmed. Praymer was right. "Runs in the family, I guess," he said to himself.

"Ah yes, your sister also strikes me as the rebellious type." Praymer's mechanical hand tugged on the sleeve of his jacket. "It's a shame she doesn't feel that her reputation is strong enough to be seen on camera with me on my ship. I'm surprised you couldn't convince her. I assumed she usually heeded your advice."

Arram leaned in closer to Praymer. "She didn't disagree. She wants a more neutral place. You have to see it from our perspective."

"Our perspective?" Praymer's voice was soft. "You keep talking about her perspective and saying it's 'ours,' but does everyone truly feel that way? Do you feel that she would be weak by being seen with me?"

The sovereign was so close Arram saw the lights reflected in his blue eyes. He looked away. He didn't like how unraveled he felt around Praymer. "I think my sister's reputation is strong enough to handle any criticism. I think she doesn't believe it herself."

Praymer said nothing, but Arram knew those eyes kept watching him. He finally met the sovereign's gaze, and the older man's face broke into a lovely smile. "I think your love for her is beautiful. You are a genuine believer of her cause."

Arram returned the gesture. "I believe in what she's capable of. I feel like it's my job to help her reach her full potential."

"Then show her. I think it's best she listens to her family and not her lover. Families have a bond that don't need a trip to the Land of the Dead to tie together. That bond is there from birth. I am sure you will know what to do."

Praymer left, arm tightly wound around Camila's shoulders.

Arram decided he would do what it took to convince Rei. Praymer would work for peace in a heartbeat. Soon they would take care of the Path, and if things went well, maybe Rei and Praymer could even find a way to garner peace between the political parties. Well, maybe the last part was too ambitious, but it didn't feel impossible, and it would be because of him.

Arram heard the distant echo of the tour continuing. He hoped Crona took good notes. He was very interested in the ship's layout.

He wanted to clear his head after the meeting with Urius, but now his thoughts were further muddled. Praymer's scent lingered in the air, and Arram cursed himself for noticing.

He turned to head back to the ballroom where his sister likely was, only to barrel face first into a slightly taller figure.

"Sorry," said a familiar voice.

"Nik," Arram whispered. "What are you doing? What if Praymer sees you?"

His brother pointed to the golden paneling on the wall. Arram saw his reflection, but the man standing next to him was not his brother, although they did share dark hair and the same nose shape.

"Are you a Volocio?"

Nik shook his head. "No. There's a secret to our family's success that neither you nor Rei are aware of."

"That being?"

"We are descendants of Hugh Ettowa, an illusion

Volocio. I don't know how far back, but once in a while someone in the family inherits an affinity for illusion. We have used it for our advantage since."

Arram took a step back as the ground lurched beneath him. He thought the Volocio were special, and yet plenty hid in the background. He shouldn't have been surprised that the secret to his family's success did not differ from Arram and the other so-called "gods." However, he was interested in learning how the Ettowa family used illusion for their benefit.

"How does that make you different from the Volocio? Does that mean anyone else in the family could have posed as Kaz all this time?"

Nik sighed. "No. What we can do with illusion is a mere fraction of what Kaz is capable of. I can change my appearance, but certain aspects, and not all at once. I usually keep the same hair color and eye color because changing other aspects of my face is hard enough."

"And I can see your true face now because . . ."

"Because I want you to."

Nik watched him, an eyebrow raised. Arram still could not believe how much they looked alike. He waited for his older brother to say something, yet his lips never moved.

"What's wrong?" Arram finally asked.

Nik ran a hand through his hair, a gesture Arram knew well. "I'm just trying to look at you, really look at you. You're real and not a figment of my imagination."

"You don't believe I'm real?" Arram furrowed his eyebrows. "Are you trying to logic your way around the fact that you forgot you have a brother?"

Nik took a step back. "I'm so sorry, Arram. Since I met you yesterday, I have spent all night awake trying to remember you."

Arram had wanted to forgive his brother, more so now that his brother had admitted a family secret. In a way, he felt closer to Nik, yet somehow the words stung like fresh wounds. The distance between them widened once more.

"Am I so forgettable? Is that why you left me behind when you chose to save Rei the day our parents died?"

Niklaryn winced. "No. It couldn't have been that. I saved Rei because she was important. She was prophesied to bring about the war to end all wars. She can stop Praymer." Nik shook his head. "My brain is wired differently, and I think the trauma of witnessing our parents' deaths caused me to block out a lot of details."

Arram didn't know whether to believe his brother or laugh at such an absurd theory. Trauma could erase details to protect the individual, but erase a whole relative?

"I would not have chosen to forget you," Niklaryn said. "Especially with those violet eyes." Niklaryn's face went slack as he locked eyes with his brother. His blue eyes squeezed shut and his hands pressed into his temples.

"I'm sorry," he murmured.

Arram watched, unsure what was happening. "Uh, Nik?" he gently touched his older brother's shoulder, only for the Daer to flinch and pull back.

Niklaryn's face shot up. "Please tell Rei I love her more than anything." He refused to meet Arram's gaze.

He then turned on his heels and disappeared around the corner, just as Arram asked, "What the fuck?"

Just like that, the euphoria from his visit with Praymer had completely dissipated. But that wasn't the worst of it. He was once again the third wheel in the little club Nik and Rei were part of. Jealousy hummed in his veins as he saw the love between his siblings like a glowing cord that connected them at the heart. Was there any left for him?

"Nik?" Artema's voice appeared before she did. Her shoulders slumped as she saw Arram.

"You just missed him."

She growled with frustration. "I always said I needed to put a bell on that man." She spun on her heels and disappeared, leaving Arram alone with his thoughts.

CHAPTER 25

BRONX CAME FACE-TO-FACE WITH INFIERNEN AS THE Negander appeared from around the corner. The two men stared at each other as Crona and the other tour guests passed. Most gave Infiernen a wide berth, but Crona stayed at her brother's side. Sariah paused briefly before joining the others. Skylar was the only one who didn't fear him. Of course she didn't—she had been working with him for years.

The Negander acknowledged Sky before she followed the others into the ballroom.

"Nik?" Artema's voice rang in the hall and she, too, appeared from the direction Infiernen had entered. She stopped and stared at the group gathered before her.

"Where did you come from?" Crona asked.

"I was following Niklaryn. I heard him talking to Arram," Artema said. "He disappeared."

Bronx glanced in Infiernen's direction, and the Negander merely shrugged.

"How was the tour?" Artema asked.

"Apparently there's a lovely botanical garden that's conveniently off limits to everyone but Praymer," Crona said.

Bronx couldn't ignore Infiernen in the area. He wasn't sure if it was the appropriate to discuss their plan with the Negander present. But they were going to need help; they needed someone on the inside, and if Infiernen was genuine in his claim to be loyal to Rei, now would be the time to prove it.

"The other reaper has to be in there," Bronx said. "I felt

death behind those wooden doors. Am I right?" The reaper gave the Negander a challenging look.

"I believe you're right."

Crona opened her mouth to speak, but nothing came out. Her light eyes kept darting in the Negander's direction until Bronx gave her a nod of encouragement. They should try and trust Infiernen. "So how do we get in?" Crona asked. "There are guards everywhere. We'll need a diversion to pull them away."

"What is the importance of this, reaper?" Artema asked.

"Infiernen told us that Praymer can't die. We don't know why, but a reaper should know. Hopefully this person has more experience with powers like mine and can help us."

Artema pressed her lips together. Then she nodded. "We'll need to talk with the others," she said. "We should meet somewhere more private."

"What about cameras?" Infiernen asked.

"Kaz," said the other three Volocio at once.

Infiernen scratched his jaw. "And the doors?"

"My specialty," answered Crona with a smirk.

"Looks like you barely need a plan," Infiernen said. "But may I make a suggestion? Let Kaz masquerade as Bronx. Praymer gets distracted seeing you and Rei together. He'll be less likely to think something is amiss if he's focused on you two."

Bronx frowned. "But that doesn't help us with the cameras."

Infiernen smiled. "I will take care of that. I am sure I can get Nik to help. He's always looking for an opportunity to do so."

"Infiernen, I need to talk to Nik," Artema said.

"Shut up, woman," Infiernen barked.

Artema drew close to Infiernen and lifted a finger to his face. "You will not speak to me like that again. Do you understand me, Infiernen?"

Her dark eyes hinted a murderous intent. Bronx had seen her in battle and would never want to be on her bad side. The look on Infiernen's face indicated the same sentiment. But his own blue eyes simmered with what Bronx could only assume was hatred. The Negander nodded and Artema lowered her finger.

Bronx hated the way Infiernen looked at Artema. Infiernen made it so hard to believe he was on their side with his treatment of her. So much disdain rippled from the Negander's blue eyes. Infiernen always felt that Artema came between Nik and himself, and it was jealousy that made him act out, but Bronx wished the Negander would stop this behavior. He wished Nik were here for his wife, but he wasn't. Not with Infiernen around.

"We also need to figure out our timing," Crona said. "I can see us getting inside, but after that I just see red. Red like blood. Something is blocking me from seeing more. I have tried visions of us going in at different times and it's always the same. The same block."

The timing would have to coincide with the arrival of the Federation ships. That way, if they could free whoever was being held behind those doors, they could hopefully get lost in the crowd as they simply walked off the ship and into the sanctuary.

"I have a plan," Bronx said. "Have the others meet in Rei's and my room after lunch. We have much to plan, and little time to do it."

A sharp pain panged in his chest, followed by the deep ache of disappointment. Bronx looked in the ballroom's direction. He couldn't see her, but he knew exactly where

Rei stood in the crowd. She was trapped among several loud voices, each trying to dictate her decisions. He assumed it was about him. Her family must be showing their true colors to her now that his background was common knowledge, meaning the family could insert themselves into their relationship. While he trusted Rei's love for him, a little voice whispered that her family could convince her otherwise. She cared for them and their opinions, but now they were set against him. He would not let her family come between them without a fight.

CHAPTER 26

Rei saw Crona and Artema out of the corner of her eye as they entered the ballroom. Thank the gods, she needed backup.

Her eyes rose to take in the vaulted glass above them with the golden metal molding holding it in place, framing the red planet above them. Somewhere in the crowd was the orchestra from the *Liberty*, their instruments harmonized with the murmur of man voices. The tapping of heels from the dancing guests on the hard floor matched the rhythm of the music. Her grandmother's perfume stood out among the rest, making Rei's eyes water.

"Rei, must you associate yourself with him?" Aurelia's blue eyes pleaded with Rei as did the solid grip of her wrinkled hands.

When her grandmother had pulled her aside for a "chat," she had not expected that it would be an intervention about the dangers of being in a relationship with someone with such a "colorful history." Had she known, she would have avoided the ballroom completely.

Rei sighed. "Would you believe that Bronx makes me happy?"

"But you are an Ettowa. You deserve the best." Aurelia gestured to the lavish chandelier hanging above them. "You deserve something like this. You are the god queen. Surround yourself with riches. What can a poor knight offer you?"

"He gave me my life."

"Nana Lia," Skylar said. "Can we get through a family event without talking about business?"

"Sky, darling, you know I hate that nickname." Aurelia wagged a finger in front of Skylar's nose. "Besides, Rei is old enough to pull her weight."

"I am sure being the god queen is weight enough," muttered Sariah to Elmessa, snaking an arm around her bride's waist, but Aurelia didn't hear.

"How long do you think we have to wait until the ships come?" asked Elmessa. "This ship puts me ill at ease."

"Soon," Rei answered. "Although, honestly, not soon enough." No matter where she stood, she felt Praymer's eyes on her, forever watching. She had not seen the sovereign since breakfast, and yet she felt as though she had not escaped him. It could easily be in her mind, but something told her that Praymer made sure Rei was watched.

A hand touched her waist, and she jumped. Bronx appeared with a smile before pressing his lips to her forehead.

Elmessa leaned in closer. "How was the tour?"

"I had a feeling Praymer was wealthy, but what the man possesses is just obscene." Bronx chuckled. He met Rei's eyes and held them. There was more. That's what his look told her, followed by a blue haze along the edges of her vision. However, it was likely something he didn't want to share in front of the brides.

"There's nothing wrong with wealth, young man," Aurelia said. "I wonder what sort of financial stability you can provide for my granddaughter?"

Rei fought the urge to roll her eyes. Instead, she pulled Bronx to her, threw her arms around his neck, and pressed her lips against his. She was tired of judgment, tired of everyone's opinions, and tired of the idea that he wasn't good enough. He laughed lightly against her lips, understanding what she wanted, and dipped her for a deep kiss. Rei swore she heard hollering of approval from the crowd.

When they came for air, Rei met her grandmother's gaze, whose expression remained neutral. "Reckless like your mother," was the only comment she made.

Dante had appeared and whispered something in Aurelia's ear. She gave the gentleman a quick nod. "If you'll excuse me, dears, Anekris would like to speak with me." She followed Dante into the crowd, and Rei felt as though she could breathe again.

"If you'll excuse us," Rei said. "The air is rather stifling." She gently tugged on Bronx's arm. "I want to head to the hallway."

"Of course, and well done with Nana Lia," Elmessa said with a wink. "Skylar, could you join us, please?" Her attention was already being pulled by another guest.

Rei led Bronx out of the ballroom, gripping his hand tightly as though afraid she would lose him if she let go. He returned the squeeze, and warm assurance spread through her. Once away from the crowd, Rei waited for Bronx to speak.

"Well?" she asked after several moments of silence.

"He has a painting of himself and Micaela on thrones. She wore a red dress with gold embroidery." His dark eyes glanced down at the tunic Rei wore.

Her hand lightly touched the embroidery along her collarbone. She hated moments like these. Little reminders of how much she and Micaela were alike. It was more than just her face, her lightning, and even her relationship with Bronx. Most of the time, the similarities didn't bother her. She knew she was no more Micaela than anyone else in the star cluster. But first the memory, and now this tunic had been placed in her room as though Praymer knew she would choose it.

"The two of you are inseparable." Praymer's voice came from behind her. "The color suits you."

Rei whirled around and came face-to-face with Praymer and a wide-eyed Camila at his side. Rei's concern about the dress paled in comparison to seeing someone she thought had been lost to them.

"Miss Canale," Rei said. "How are you? Your mother has been worried sick!"

"Your brother said the same thing to me." Camila gave Rei a smile, but her eyes showed no expression.

Rei first thought Camila meant Niklaryn, but of course she was referring to Arram. Niklaryn had yet to make himself visible to Rei, and it bothered her. She also hadn't seen her younger brother since his outburst during breakfast and hoped she could see him soon and talk to him. She didn't like this distance between her and her brothers.

Rei turned back to Praymer to find him watching her.

A small smile crept across his face. "It disappointed me to hear you didn't want to do a live feed on the Nexus with me. I think we can change a lot of minds."

"I never said no. But it would look better if we met somewhere neutral. Earth, perhaps? I am more than happy to show a united front, but it has to be an equal one too."

"Do you think you have the time to wait for another opportunity?"

"What do you mean?"

"You haven't heard the news?" Praymer pulled out his slate from his pocket and swiped a few times to find what he was looking for. Once satisfied, he handed it to Rei.

The Path had once again attacked the capital of Wolf X, including the Temple of Aladonis, the holy seat of the

Volocio religion; Escalante, the Volocio holy city on Earth; as well as the Dominion capital on Corincancha. Rei's face had gone numb, her eyes quickly scanning to see if the Holy Father of Sancta Sedes had survived, but nothing had been reported.

"Those damned terrorists," muttered Praymer. Rei narrowed her eyes as she looked up at the sovereign, who was now much closer to her than before. His coat lightly brushed against her shoulder, his cologne stifling.

"Their attacks are more fervent. My courtiers are calling for war. They think the Path is working for the Federation to undermine us. We need to stop this before more fights break out. We need to take the ones we have and make an example of them."

Rei couldn't help but notice his emphasis on the word "we." "And how do you propose we do it?"

"Public execution. Show them that neither the Federation nor the Dominion will tolerate this behavior. Then we join forces and attack them where it hurts. I have sources who know where their base is."

"How convenient," Bronx muttered.

Rei scanned the rest of the news to see Yuri Manca in front of the Temple of Aladonis. Only a tower had toppled, and smoke still rose from the ruins. She didn't need to read the article to know what Yuri wanted.

"Yuri Manca also demands blood," she said, handing the slate back to Praymer. "He has always blamed you for this. And he's not alone, there are plenty in the Federation who believe the Path works for you."

"Both sides are wrong. The Path just wants war, and we shouldn't give it to them. Instead we should smite them as quickly as possible, show a united front before our parties attack each other instead of the real enemy: the Path."

Yet Niklaryn fought with the Path. She was missing something; it was just beyond her reach.

"I can make it worth your while, Rei," whispered Praymer, drawing ever closer. "If you join forces with me, no one would dare contradict us. No one would stand against us."

Rei stared at him. She was close to figuring out his game, she just needed to know his last piece.

"I will let Niklaryn go if you do this favor for me."

Rei's heart leapt to her throat, and her limbs tingled. That was it. Niklaryn fought for the Path, yet Praymer claimed to still have leverage over her brother. "You said he was free to leave," she whispered, her voice and resolve failing her. He was hiding on this ship, but she had thought that he had gotten away somehow.

"That was before your brother betrayed me with the Path. I also know he's hiding on my ship and has been allowed to do so at my mercy. But I will give you my word that when the Federation comes, he may leave with the rest of the guests. But only if you do this. Help me show the star cluster what a team we can make, and I will release the hold I have on your precious Niklaryn. Do it for him."

Rei slowly drew away from Praymer and returned to Bronx's side. Bronx's distrust hummed around the edges of her vision in a shimmery silver. But Praymer had her. By admitting his own hold on her brother, he proved Niklaryn's innocence in his years of working for the Dominion. Niko had told her he sold his soul to Praymer to keep her safe. But now it was her turn to save him, and saving Niko was always a simple choice to make.

"Fine. We'll work together." Rei held out a hand. "Let's see how this works. But first, we won't publicly execute the Path prisoners. I have a better plan for them, but we need to show that we are merciful. I am not the blood empress, and I do not want our unified front to be one of violence."

Praymer smiled and gently took her hand with his mechanical one. The other lay on top of their joined hands, his thumb gently caressing her knuckles, and a chill trickled down her spine.

"You won't regret this." Praymer's smile made him look boyish. "I have a dress that is perfect for you. The god queen should also look the part."

He then left, tugging Camila to follow. That's when she saw it, confirming Camila's body language. The neck of the young woman's gown pulled to the side, revealing a deep purple bruise on her collarbone.

Rei once had a customer that frequented the bar on Ballarat. The woman was a piece of work who could never hold her liquor. Her partner usually tried to convince the woman to stop, but he always flinched when she swung her arm, raising her drink too quickly. He also had bruises, always in places normally covered with clothing.

Rei glanced in Bronx's direction, and by the wide-eyed expression on his face, she knew he had seen them too.

"We need to meet with the others," he said.

CHAPTER 27

Bronx and Rei wasted no time rallying the other Volocio to their room.

Dread pooled in his belly when he discovered a black box with a red ribbon waiting on their bed. Rei tugged on the ribbon and it fell away. She pulled the lid off to reveal a deep green fabric with silver lightning bolts embroidered across its length. Rei pulled it out, and it unraveled to a floor-length gown. The top appeared to have the same wrap-around cut as her god-queen costume.

Bronx held the fabric between his fingers as the rest of it tumbled to the floor like a silver waterfall.

It was better quality than the costume Rei wore; it was fit for a queen. But Bronx always thought Rei could make rags look regal.

He hated the way Praymer watched Rei. It was possessive and triumphant. Praymer had no right, and Bronx wanted nothing more than to punch that smirk off the sovereign's face.

"What is that?" asked Manden, being the first Volocio to arrive.

"It was a gift from Praymer," Bronx said, not taking his eye off the dress. "Rei is going to show a united front with him."

"I thought you wanted to wait," Artema said as she arrived, entering the room.

"We may not have the time." Rei put the dress onto the bed. "The Path have attacked the Holy Father of Sancta Sedes, Escalante, and the Dominion capital."

"My half brother is looking for a reason to start a war," Bronx said. "And the Dominion is apparently also preparing."

"We need to deal with the Path and show the star cluster that this group doesn't belong to either party." Rei met Bronx's eyes. He knew she didn't want to mention Praymer's promise concerning Niklaryn. At least not yet.

"Is that why we're meeting?" Kaz asked with Crona in tow. Arram was the last of the Volocio to arrive, with Skylar and Sariah at his side.

"So you'll do it?" Arram asked. "You'll work with him?"

Rei nodded. "If I want to avoid war. We have to try diplomacy. We can't wait."

Arram's face broke into a smile. "Thank you, Rei."

"Is that all we're here for?" Crona asked, picking up the dress to inspect it further. "Besides showing off this utterly gorgeous dress?"

"Not just that," Bronx said. "We have the distraction we'll need so Crona and I can hopefully break into the botanical garden and find whomever Praymer's keeping captive."

Rei raised her eyebrows. He hadn't had a chance to reveal his plan to her, but after his behavior today at the tour, he knew he couldn't let his separation anxiety get in the way of what needed to be done.

"Wait, what distraction?" Arram asked, but Bronx didn't want to answer.

"And then what?" Manden asked. "How do you get them off the ship?"

"Time it with the arrival of our pickup." Bronx pulled his slate out of his jacket pocket. "The ship should arrive in about eight hours. That's enough time to put our pieces in place."

"I will do a live feed with Praymer," Rei said. "We make a show with the prisoners. Invite the guests to partake. More people will require more guards, hopefully enough to draw most of the attention to us and less to the entrance."

"Even so, won't you need me to cloak your presence?" Kaz asked.

"Infiernen said he could help us with the cameras," Bronx replied. "But we need you to do something else."

"Can we trust him?" Manden shifted his weight and crossed his arms.

"We can," Sky said.

"He wants me to find a way to kill Praymer, which is why he is helping me find this other reaper. He's already saved me from getting captured, he'll do it again if necessary," added Bronx. Infiernen coming to his aid the day before was proof enough. "Crona will then pick the lock. Hopefully, if we discover what he has done to his prisoners, we can get further into Praymer's mind or at least show his true nature."

"True nature?" Arram asked. He turned to his sister. "Are you only joining forces with Praymer so your lover can get dirt on him? I thought you wanted peace."

"I do want peace," Rei answered. "But he has made it clear that he will not avoid resorting to using whatever leverage he can to ensure he gets his way." Rei glared down at her brother with an equally challenging stare.

"What leverage?" asked Artema.

Rei briefly glanced in Bronx. He knew what she was about to say. "Niko."

Artema's hand rose to her lips. "What does he have on Nik?"

"He said if I did this, he would let Niko leave with us."

Artema cursed. "Did he say Nik only or was Infiernen also mentioned?"

"Only Niko, why?"

"Nik goes where Infiernen goes."

Rei furrowed her eyebrows. "Does this have to do with whatever hold Infiernen has over our brother?"

Artema turned to Bronx. Now would be the time to tell the truth, to finally admit the connection between Infiernen and Niklaryn. But not here—not in front of everyone.

"I don't know," Bronx finally said. "I honestly don't know if Praymer is true to his word. But he's determined that Rei work with him now to campaign for peace. Hopefully getting what he wants will make him lower his guard."

Artema let out a growl of frustration. "I don't like this," she said. "Rei, Praymer could have brought up Niklaryn at any time and he didn't. He has always played the long game, planning several steps ahead, further than any of us could see. There has to be a reason he wants the talks to happen now."

"I'll do that talk with you," Manden said. "We should do this together."

"No, Manden, I can handle Praymer myself," Rei said.

"I would prefer you not deal with him alone," Bronx said.

"Agreed," added the redhead.

Rei shook her head. "Trust me. He relaxes when it's just me. I need him off his guard."

Bronx's heart rate elevated. The idea of her facing Praymer alone did not help with his anxiety. "Rei, please."

"Kaz will be floating around, so I won't be completely alone. It'll be fine."

"Then that means the talk and rescue should happen as close to the pickup as possible," Skylar said.

"We can alert the guests at least an hour beforehand. Once the ship is here, we should move quickly," added Sariah from her position leaning against the large wardrobe.

"I don't understand the mistrust," Arram said. "He has been nothing more than a kind and generous host."

"He murdered your parents," Bronx said with a scoff. Arram's cheeks flushed when Bronx mentioned the sovereign. There was no way Arram had a crush on Praymer, yet Bronx continued to watch the younger Ettowa with suspicion.

"Let's not forget Camila," Rei said. "She's on this ship."

Half the room let out an audible gasp.

"And Praymer has treated her as an honored guest," said Arram.

Bronx's chest tightened; nothing about Camila's behavior made him think she was a guest, nonetheless an honored one.

"There were bruises on her body," Rei clapped back.

Arram narrowed his violet eyes. "I didn't see any bruises."

"They're hidden under her clothes. If Camila was a guest she would have at least sent a message to her mother."

"She said she had her reasons."

Rei rolled her eyes. "I don't believe them."

"Regardless," Artema said, coming between them, "we should get her away from him, to be sure. Then we can give her the option to come with us."

"Fine," Arram said. "But we should be careful. We have a great opportunity here with Praymer. We should attempt to at least try to work with him—personal feelings aside."

Arram had a point. Bronx didn't want to return to the battlefield unless given no other choice. They had to try.

Just like the old saying: keep your friends close and your enemies closer. But the real question was what price would Rei have to pay to deal with the devil?

CHAPTER 28

"Crona, will you walk with me?" Arram asked as the group slowly trickled out of the room with the plan to reconvene in the ballroom.

The blonde shook her head. "I'm worried about you, Arram. This isn't like you."

"What isn't 'like me?' I have always been willing to put aside personal feelings for the greater good."

Crona narrowed her eyes. "Are we talking about the same personal feelings? Just really think about what you're trying to achieve and if it's worth getting too close to the enemy."

Arram didn't bother giving Crona a response and took a different route than the others, wanting time to clear his head. He was glad Rei would join forces with Praymer, but his pride suffered a blow upon hearing she did it for Niklaryn, not because it was the right move.

He should hate the sovereign—he murdered their parents—yet he didn't remember them. None of the Ettowas felt like family to him, especially the way they looked at him: like some pawn to be moved at their convenience. They were no better than Urius and his machinations. None of them ever felt real to him, not the same way his grandparents were. They were his actual parents.

Sagitan and Virga were critical of both the Federation and the Dominion and their platforms, but they believed in diplomacy above violence. They taught him to achieve the former first, no matter the cost.

He wasn't ready to face the other Volocio yet; he

preferred seeing a more friendly face. He wandered the halls until he found Praymer standing in front of a painting.

It was of an old man with a narrow nose, a full head of white hair, and sapphire eyes that mirrored Praymer's as he gazed, transfixed.

Praymer's eyes flickered briefly in Arram's direction as the younger man approached.

"He was my grandfather, Tynan Praymer." The sovereign's eyes had returned to the portrait. "He was the first Praymer Imperator. He captured Micaela and Manden when they first squabbled over squatter's rights on Earth all those years ago."

Jealousy hummed through Arram's veins at the way Praymer said Micaela's name. The sovereign's voice dropped a few notes, and her name floated on his lips like a lover's caress.

"Tell me about Maximilian." The words burst out of Arram's mouth before he could react. He never asked Manden or Artema about his previous counterpart. Part of him was afraid of what he would hear. There was no logical explanation he could give for his apprehension. While the other Volocio never hesitated to ask about their former lives, Arram feared the truth. He feared knowing he was like his previous self. If he were truly a copy of Maximilian, then it would mean that he had no control over his own destiny.

But now he wanted to know. He liked the way Praymer looked at him—the way Anekris looked at him—and he wanted to hear at least one of his names on the sovereign's lips.

Anekris's eyes sparkled as he beheld Arram.

"Max had a brilliant mind. He was a master player at manipulation and politics." Anekris smiled as he grew lost in thought. "I see some of him in you. I see what carried over from your previous life. Just like I see some of your father in you. You are destined for the same greatness as your siblings."

Arram's heart thudded in his chest. He had expected to feel dread about his similarities to Max. Instead, he felt a twinge of pride.

"How did my father betray you?" Arram asked. "What did he do to make you decide his death was necessary?"

"I wanted you," Anekris said, and Arram's heart thudded in his chest. "I wanted to raise both you and your sister in my palace to be my heirs, take over the Dominion when I died. I knew what you both were capable of—I had seen glimpses of it in Mica and Max, but they never achieved it. I wanted that for you and Rei."

Arram could have grown up with Rei, they could have been true siblings. He could have had what she and Niklaryn had.

"But did my parents have to die because you couldn't take no for an answer?"

Anekris sighed. "It's more complicated than that, but that's how it started. We fought for three years until the situation boiled into violence. I have regretted that day ever since because it was the day I lost everything: my friend and my chance."

Arram pitied him. He pitied the future that was lost. Maybe he would never have been branded; maybe he would have had a more stable upbringing, no running, no fear.

He wanted to ask another question but was afraid of hearing the answer. He met Anekris's sapphire gaze and briefly lost himself.

"Are you attracted to my sister?" Arram finally asked.

Anekris's face softened. His human hand squeezed

Arram's arm gently, and he felt Anekris's thumb through the fabric of his jacket. "To be honest, I was."

Arram's heart sank, and Anekris gave him a small smile.

"But not anymore. She lacks the grace and finesse that Micaela had."

"She's worried that you are."

Anekris shrugged. "I am interested in what her influence can do for the star cluster, but I only want a union of friendship." He leaned in close and his scent of roses and vervain wafted through Arram's nose. "But let's keep that between you and me. I think she's more amiable if she thinks I want more than just friendship."

Arram couldn't help but laugh. "Flirt with her and she will flirt back. She knows how to work a crowd and she shines when people love her."

It relieved him to hear how Anekris truly felt. It meant Rei wasn't truly in any real danger, and it allowed him to read Anekris's actions through a different lens. Rei had claimed the memory she witnessed showed that Anekris and Micaela had a friendship. A true one.

The sovereign's eyes remained on Arram's face and his cheeks burned.

"How far do you think your sister will go to ensure peace?" the sovereign asked. "How much do you think that reaper has poisoned her mind against our union?"

"His influence is powerful, but she'll do what it takes. She doesn't want war. You apply the right pressure, she'll bend." Arram didn't understand why he said that, but it was true. He loved Rei, but her weaknesses were very clear: Nik and Bronx.

He hated what Bronx had planned. The reaper could easily unravel the goodwill Anekris had for Arram and his sister. He hated that his sister went along with it. He could tell Anekris of Bronx's plan, but he hesitated. He remembered the look of fear on Bronx's face as Anekris did his magic to use the reaper to heal him. As much as Bronx annoyed him, the reaper didn't deserve that kind of punishment.

Anekris smiled at him, and Arram realized he would do anything for another smile. What the fuck was wrong with him?

CHAPTER 29

Rei stared at herself in the mirror. The dress Praymer gave her made her god-queen costume look like rags. She had found a tiara underneath the dress in a velvet bag. Now it was on her head, where it glittered in her dark hair.

She cursed the sovereign's good taste, but she enjoyed Bronx's eyes sparkling with desire as he watched her.

He swept her hair behind her shoulder and kissed the skin below her ear.

"Be careful," he whispered.

"*You* be careful." She turned to face him. He wore the red robes of a Negander. Infiernen had been surprisingly helpful in supplying them to both the reaper and Crona. But she had yet to see the Negander to thank him—or to warn him if he failed. She worried Infiernen acted too reckless in helping them, and she shuddered at the thought of what would happen if Praymer found out. "If you get caught, you could disappear without me knowing. At least I will be in the public eye."

"I'll be safe. Between Crona and even Infiernen, Praymer won't know we are there, and Crona will see if there's a trap. She must have had an entire pot of Star of Saskia over the last few hours." He gave a soft chuckle.

Rei still felt uneasy, but having another reaper with them in the Federation, if that's who Praymer kept captive, could be the key not only to defeating Praymer but also to understanding Bronx's abilities. He still knew only a fraction of his capabilities, and Rei wanted to see his full potential.

"I didn't get to tell you that I'm proud of you," Rei said, gently tugging on his robes to adjust them. "I know how you feel when we're not together."

"I hate feeling like this."

"You'll get through it. I have faith." Rei cupped his cheek. "It's also natural for us to want to be together. We are a team. We have each other's backs. Don't beat yourself up."

A beep broke the silence, announcing they had a visitor. Rei found Manden on the other side of the door in a magnificent gold tunic with a crown peeking out of his copper locks. Kaz stood not too far behind, leaning against the wall wearing Bronx's suit. Just to the other side of Rei's cousin stood Infiernen.

It was the first time she had been face-to-face with Niklaryn's so-called best friend since right before her death on Kepler IV. A jolt of fear ran through her, but something in his presence was comforting, familiar.

"It's show time," the redhead said with a fake smile.

"It is," Rei said, drawing closer to Infiernen. "I am trusting you with the lives of Bronx and Crona."

Infiernen's blue eyes showed not a hint of emotion. "Don't you worry, Rei. I have always been on your side. You want Bronx to save this reaper, so I will gladly help."

Rei believed him. She couldn't put her finger on why, but she did. She wished Niklaryn was here instead, but something told her that Infiernen was a good replacement.

"I'll see you soon," Bronx said, giving Rei a last kiss before disappearing out the door and down the hall with Infiernen.

"Are you ready?" Rei asked, taking Manden's arm. She

glanced at Kaz, only to find he was already wearing Bronx's face.

"It'll be fine. Just smile pretty and soon we will be on a ship flying far, far away from here."

"What do you think Hotara would say if she saw us now?" Rei asked. Hotara had spent most of Rei's life protecting her from Praymer and here was Rei walking toward him, to work with him. Whatever it took to protect Niklaryn.

"I don't even want to think of the string of curse words she would yell if she found out," Manden said with a laugh, but Rei knew it was forced.

"Don't forget," added Rei. "I do the talking. I can handle him."

They met Praymer just outside the ballroom. The sovereign wore a midnight black suit with crimson trim and a blood red cape. His handsome face broke into a smile once he caught sight of Rei. Just behind him was a camera crew and Dante, who studied the group intently before also smiling.

"The god king and queen look magnificent," Praymer said. "Bronx, good of you to join us."

"I wanted to make sure I had a splendid view of this momentous occasion."

Rei held back a smile. Even though Kaz used Bronx's voice, he was still off. She stole a glance behind her to where Kaz stood. He tried his best to imitate Bronx, but his posture was too straight and he smiled way too much. Surely no one would notice those details.

"Shall we begin?" Praymer asked, bringing her out of her head.

"Let's," Manden said and drew nearer to Rei.

The three stood close together as the camera crew

pointed and adjusted their devices while Kaz stood off to the side next to Dante. Rei gave the cameras a wide smile until her cheeks hurt. One camera gave off a tiny red flickering light.

"Hello members of the Federation and Dominion," Praymer began. "Tonight I am joined by these honored guests: your god king and queen."

"That's correct," cut in Rei, not wanting Praymer to completely control the narrative. "While celebrating my darling cousin Elmessa's marriage to the courageous Sariah Bray, the sovereign, god king, and I have used this opportunity to talk without the eyes of the council or courtiers."

The murmurs of guests standing at the entrance to the ballroom remained low, but Rei was sure the microphones on the cameras picked up every whisper. Aurelia stood front and center, and the look of approval in her eyes at seeing Rei at Praymer's side set Rei's teeth on edge.

"It was certainly eye opening," Manden said with a smirk. "We want to thank Praymer for allowing us shelter after those pesky devils from the Path attacked the party."

"We have found common interests," continued Praymer. "The most important of them being peace in the star cluster. So we have worked together."

Rei stared into the blinding ring light to the camera in the center. The heat from the lights made her sweat. "The Path comes from neither party, and it pains us to see finger pointing. We don't want war, despite what other people in our respective parties believe." Rei hoped Yuri was watching.

"We want to be allies," Manden agreed. "We will put aside differences for the sake of the star cluster."

Rei glanced in Praymer's direction. "People shouldn't go to war for another's ideals."

"Well said, my god queen," Praymer said, taking Rei's hand and holding it up so it was visible by the camera. She wanted to pull away, but the star cluster was watching.

"We are finding a union that will benefit both parties. We need to discuss this further, but I know how the Dominion would accept the god queen as an ally." His eyes remained on their joined hands. Then his sapphire gaze reached her face, and he winked.

Shit. She knew what kind of union he wanted.

Marriage.

"But first, we wanted to show our dedication to peace by presenting you with those of the Path we have captured after the attack." Praymer pointed to the line of prisoners as Negander led them down the hall. His other hand still held Rei's in a tight grip.

"I think the best way to show our dedication is to give them mercy," Rei said. "I propose we create a tribunal of Dominion and Federation to show them the justice they deserve. We should trust those who have studied the law to best decide how to punish those who break it."

Praymer smiled. "That's a wonderful idea, God Queen. Take them back to their cells. We will meet with the Federation council and my Dominion courtiers to decide who should make up the tribunal." He leaned in close. "You and I work so well together."

Rei dared not meet his eyes—instead she looked at her hand still in his. "I think it's time we joined the party," she said, her face numb. "I am sure the sovereign would love to dance."

Praymer looked as though his dreams had come true as he smiled with no restraint.

"I would gladly take the offer, my god queen."

She noticed that he emphasized the word, "my."

"What are you doing, Rei?" Manden asked in Castelan. They spoke the Volocio language often when they wanted to avoid being overheard.

"Just trust me," she responded in the same language. "I think I know his plan."

She pulled the sovereign's hand and together they entered the room. The cameramen followed. Her heart hammered in her chest as they walked through the parting crowd.

Praymer wanted her. She always knew that, and his orchestration of this moment was just as obvious. She wondered how many people in this room knew of his plan. How many approved? Knowing the Ettowas and the Brays? Enough to pressure her.

Once on the dance floor, Praymer's mechanical hand snaked around her waist, drawing her to him. His left hand held her right. The lighting in the ballroom grew a little dimmer, and the music changed to a slower beat.

All eyes stared at the couple as Praymer pulled her across the dance floor. His eyes stared into her as his thumb stroked hers.

"The union we spoke of," Rei said after a time, her voice low enough for only them to hear.

"We will be unstoppable, Rei. Together we can rule the star cluster."

"Rule as husband and wife, you mean." She swore Praymer's eyes grew dark at the words. "I won't marry you. We're not in some medieval story. Unions can be done with treaties—not marriage."

"Ah, but that's where you're wrong." Praymer dipped her, his mechanical arm digging into her back. He leaned in close, his scent of vervain and roses stuck in her throat.

"Did you forget that we're still married, Micaela?"

CHAPTER 30

THE HALLWAYS WERE EMPTY SAVE FOR A FEW carefully placed Negander. But Bronx and his sister could easily avoid their attention. They climbed the spiraling hallway with ease, keeping against the wall in case someone else happened to be around. He expected to hear voices or smell the same expensive perfume that pervaded the ballroom, but the halls were silent. It wasn't a good sign; it wasn't possible for everyone to be in the ballroom.

They made it to the top but remained at the side when Crona pointed out the first camera. They waited and Bronx watched as the cameras moved just enough to the side to where he and his sister were no longer in the line of sight. Infiernen would appear to be as good as his word. For now, at least.

As Crona crouched in front of the door, Bronx stared at the glass dome above him. The red planet continued to hang in the air. They were close enough to see its gaseous storms roll across the planet's surface.

Crona opened the door easily, and they slid through. Bronx didn't think there could be more gold decoration, yet the shine of the metal in every corner almost blinded him.

The two walked down the short hall and found only two doors, one closed and another open. The smell of wet earth wafted through Bronx's nose.

Crona was the first through, disappearing before he could shout a warning to her.

"Come see this!" Her voice rang from the other side.

Bronx followed and discovered the source of the scent:

the botanical garden was larger than he expected, with a calm bubbling fountain and thick foliage that filled the air with a perfumed scent of roses.

But that's not what drew Bronx's attention. Holographic candles filled every free space in the garden, their little flames flickering from an invisible wind. In the center stood a tall marble statue with flowing robes that fell to reveal smooth shoulders and a sparkling crown. Rows and rows of blood red roses covered the base of the statue. The smell clung to the back of Bronx's throat.

It was a statue of Micaela.

It was an altar to her.

His heart thudded quickly in his chest. "We need to be quick," Bronx said, venturing further into the garden. "I should get back to her," he said the last more to himself.

They wandered through the foliage for a time. Too long. He made his way down a marble path between the plethora of plants that grew on either side. The air was thick with humidity, causing the red robes to stick to his skin as he sweated. Then he saw it. His heart rose to his throat, and the ground lurched under his feet as he approached the raised platform to the large marble form on top. Another statue lay on top of it, but her face was still the same. Then there was the size of the marble, just enough to fit a body inside, and her name engraved onto the side that confirmed it.

It was a tomb. Micaela's tomb.

"I found them!" cried Crona from somewhere in the garden.

"Them?" His voice cracked. He shook his head and stepped away from the coffin. He could do nothing for Micaela. She was dead. Unlike Rei. "Keep talking," he said, pushing his way through the greenery. But she didn't respond. "Crona?" He shoved the wet plants aside, panic rising with bile in his throat.

The leaves were so thick and wet he didn't see his sister until he was practically on top of her. She stood staring at two figures lying on the other side of a small pond. Smears of red streaked her face.

He looked down at his hands, still wet from the leaves. It wasn't water, as he originally assumed. It was blood. He quickly scanned to see where the blood came from, but it wasn't from the leaves. Someone had sprayed the leaves, but why?

He returned to the figures his sister found, and a chill tricked down his spine.

One of the figures was a young man, bald, thin to the point his clavicles poked out of his rags. Drops of red hung from his lips. Bronx and Crona both jumped into the pond to reach the couple on the other side, the water barely reaching their knees. Bronx wiped off the blood where he could, but the red made his skin crawl. This was not a normal botanical garden.

Crona approached the man who wheezed over the splash of water. She wiped the stranger's mouth to find the red was not blood.

"It's a Star of Saskia." Crona leaned in further. "I think he overdosed."

The other figure lay obscured in the shadow, but Bronx knew who the figure was. The scent of lavender was strong.

Bronx laid a hand on the other person's shoulder and turned her to face him. His eyes grew wide, and he jerked back. He recognized her. She was in Hamastagan when he brought Rei back to life.

She was one of the reapers who led the way. Her skin was tight and her dark eyes sunk deep into her skull. Her hair was dark when he last saw her—now it was bone white.

"Kill me, Atrius," she whispered. "He'll take you too." Her voice broke. She touched Bronx's face, her fingers wet with blood.

"Praymer," she continued, her voice as cracked as her lips. "His blood. You can't see."

His blood. The blood that nullifies. Yet he didn't know what he couldn't see.

The reaper's clothes fell off her thin shoulder, revealing an infinity brand, just like Arram's. He glanced at his sister and the man she held. His exposed shoulder also had a visible brand.

"She can't see." The reaper pointed at his sister and the blood streak on her face. Then he realized.

Praymer's blood. The blood from Crona's vision. She couldn't see the future. She couldn't see a trap if something had changed.

"Crona," he whispered. "We can't save them. We have to go now."

But it was too late.

"They're here!" called a voice. Bronx expected Negander but was shocked to find the Path, the very ones who had been prisoners just minutes before.

"Careful with them," said a woman's voice, but Bronx couldn't see her face. "Praymer wants them alive."

PART TWO
THE
WARMONGER

CHAPTER 31

REI PULLED AWAY, BUT PRAYMER'S METAL FINGERS DUG into her back as he held her in the dip.

"I'm not Micaela," she whispered.

"You are. But you're also something better." He leaned in closer and she arched away. He brought her back up to her feet. "Having you in my arms again is better than all the riches this cluster can provide."

"Ew." The words shot out of her mouth faster than she could react. She tried to pull away again.

"Be careful, darling. The cameras are still on us. You don't want everyone to know there's trouble."

"This is not what I signed up for when I said I would be your ally."

"How else was this going to play out? You know how much I loved my wife, and here you are."

"This did not go well for you the last time. Why do you think it will be any different?"

"Because you met the reaper first? Doesn't matter anyway. I figured out your little plan, and I have already taken care of him and the seer."

Rei's blood ran cold. He knew.

Praymer smiled as though he had noticed her distress. "Let's go somewhere private," he said. "I had hoped to propose tonight, but it would appear you need more convincing." He broke their dance but not his hold. This time his mechanical arm grabbed her wrist and squeezed hard. She gasped, but he put a finger to her lips. "Shush, darling." He turned to the cameras. "We are looking forward to our peaceful future together, and while we would like to celebrate properly, there is still much to discuss." He pulled her off the dance floor.

Rei looked for Kaz, who still wore Bronx's face, but he was nowhere to be found. She caught Manden's eye. He stepped in front of them. "Surely you need me if you wish to talk to the god queen."

Rei held her breath as Praymer bit his lip, calculating his next move.

"You're right. Come along and tell Kaz he can drop the illusion. I know he's not the reaper."

Manden followed them as Praymer guided Rei out of the ballroom. She saw her grandmother, who simply smiled as Rei walked with Praymer. Ildana and Jenson also watched with shining eyes. No one seemed to notice his painful grip on her.

They left the ballroom and entered a smaller room. The door closed behind them and two gigantic figures in orange stood in front of it. The gryphon sigil on their foreheads told Rei everything she needed to know.

The Path.

It was also the moment Rei realized that Manden wasn't the one who followed. It was Dante.

"But where's . . .?" Rei asked, but the man's smile said enough. He could also wield illusion. He was probably the reason Praymer knew Kaz wasn't Bronx.

She was trapped. Alone. At the mercy of Praymer. Her pulse raced as she turned back to face him.

"I have tried to be nice, Rei." Praymer ran his human hand through his hair. A few golden strands fell across his eyes. "If only I had raised you like I'd planned. You would have accepted this truth," he muttered.

"If you had what?" Rei growled. Adrenaline rushed through her body as the pounding in her ears increased.

"Never mind."

"No." She got in his face. "We are going to finish this bullshit now. You have me alone, so stop this dance." She stared him hard in the face. "Let's lay this out in the open. You think I am your dead wife and your marriage to her is still valid. That's what this entire game was about? Get on my good side, get on my family's good side, and get the parties on board hoping I would choose you over Bronx?" She laughed hard.

"You will choose me. You chose me before."

"How can you be this stupid? I am NOT Micaela."

"Yet you all repeat the same choices as before. Your brother is still ambitious for power and recognition, not to mention he is attracted to me. He will betray you the same way Max betrayed Mica. Kaz is still the spineless idiot who believes in diplomacy. Crona sounds just as weak without a mind of her own; I predict she will be an addled junkie like her previous counterpart. And you . . ." He walked around her. "You, my darling, are still ambitious and powerful and destined for greatness, yet you waste your time fucking that reaper."

That's what bothered him. Rei didn't know what made Micaela marry him—that young man from the memory was gone; only a jaded older man remained. She could never have loved this man, even if the universe hadn't put Bronx in her path.

"And I enjoy fucking that reaper," she growled. She didn't care about diplomacy, not now. "He's the best lover I've ever had."

Praymer's mechanical hand punched her in the stomach faster than she could blink. Air rushed out of her lungs, and she stumbled from the blow, landing on her knees and gasping for breath.

"You shut your whore mouth," he snarled. "If you open your legs for him, you'll probably open them for anyone." He knelt next to her and grabbed her, bringing his face a hair's breadth away from hers. "As your husband, I have a right to take you even now," he whispered. Her heart raced as he stared. "But I won't." His grip on her loosened. "I would rather have your consent."

"You throw this childish tantrum all because I still choose another man?" she snarled, shoving him away from her before rising to her feet.

"And you question my intelligence, you little tart? I can give you an empire, riches, status, everything important and yet you choose a bastard?"

"You talk to me like this and expect me to fall in love with you because some dumb bitch said yes before?"

The mechanical hand wrapped around her neck and shoved her against the back wall. She tried to draw more breath, but little came.

"Do it," she gasped. "I dare you. I am sure you did the same to her."

"I did. I made her suffer." He stared daggers at her, and for a moment, she worried he would kill her.

Darkness ebbed at the edges of her vision. She couldn't pass out and leave herself further at his mercy. Her vision flickered and another took hold. She sat in a dark room with a rope around her neck, a younger Praymer standing above her with the same murderous intent.

He had murdered Micaela.

Anger charged through her veins and lightning followed. She grabbed his mechanical arm and sparks flew.

He yelped and released her. She sank to her knees, gasping for breath.

"Fine. You want violence? Bring him in!"

Dante appeared at Rei's side and grabbed her arms as a Negander entered the room with a wide-eyed Arram. "What's happening?" her brother asked.

The Negander threw Arram to the ground, but it was Praymer who grabbed a handful of her brother's dark hair and jerked his head back, exposing his neck. Praymer's other hand held a blade that kissed her brother's skin.

"Don't!" started Rei, but Dante's grip on her remained firm. "There's no need to resort to this."

"Do you know how much effort it took to have you brought here, Rei?"

Rei's face tingled. "Brought here?" Her voice was at least an octave higher.

Praymer waved the knife around, but it rarely strayed from her brother's neck. "That attack at the wedding wasn't on accident. It was the only way to get you on my ship. Then it was a matter of convincing both parties to work together and for your family to want it. Urius's ships will be here soon, but you won't be joining them."

Rei's heart raced. Artema was right: Praymer planned the long game. "Of course I will leave."

"Yet you televised your intent to work with me. All I have to say is that you wish for more time and decided to stay behind. Some of your relatives will do the same and no one will question it."

Rei inched closer to Praymer. She had to keep him talking; perhaps she could find the opportunity to wrangle the knife from his hands. They had to get out of this room. Arram said nothing, but his violet eyes widened with fear.

"Is that why you had Infiernen work for the Path? To maneuver them as well?"

Praymer's eyes sparkled. "You don't see it? I created the Path. The whole plan to blow up the ship to trick you into seeking refuge with me was Infiernen's brilliant idea. He and I have been planning this meeting for a long time, Rei darling. I had hoped that the spark between Micaela and me would rekindle, but I see I need more time. I am done with diplomacy, love. I will get what I want and that's you by my side."

Infiernen betrayed her. Rei's knees threatened to buckle, but she remained upright. The Negander had sworn he was on her side, and yet he was the reason for all of this. More white flashes continued to flicker along the edge of her vision.

"But it won't be real," she said, holding up her hands in surrender. But they itched. They tickled the same way when one of Kaz's illusions touched her. She stared at her brother, and he trembled.

"It will be enough for me. In time you will love me again."

"You're sick," Rei said. "You're a sick, sick man."

Praymer gripped Arram tighter. Rei's heart leapt to her throat. She had to have faith that he wouldn't kill Arram—his only ally of the Volocio.

"You wouldn't dare," she whispered. "You wouldn't kill Arram."

Praymer smiled. "How did you think Max died?" He dragged the knife across Arram's neck and a thin ribbon of red bubbled out.

"Arram!" she cried, reaching for him, but a Negander and Dante were at her side pulling her away as her brother grasped at his throat.

"NO!" she cried as his life's blood poured down his front. Her arms burned as Dante held her fast.

Tears blurred her vision, and Arram gave one last breath. She screamed as white light flickered around the edge of her vision. Electricity answered her call and filled her veins. She breathed deep and tasted ozone. Sparks fluttered about her body.

She released just enough to throw Dante off of her. Tears fell, and when she looked at her brother again, she gasped and dropped her hold on her lightning. It wasn't Arram's body—another young man with dark hair lay dead on the floor.

"Say you'll join me or I'll do it again to Niklaryn. Then I'll torture your lover in front of you," Praymer said with a triumphant smile.

Rei stared at the body of the nameless boy whose features melted away from Arram's with every passing second. It was an illusion. She was right, Praymer had limits. She rubbed her face, still wet with tears. Her hands still itched as the rest of the illusion faded away. But there was no time to dwell. Lightning flicked white around the edges of her vision again, anger building within.

"Fuck. You," she yelled between heaving breaths. "Where's Arram?"

Praymer's face fell. "Shit. You can see through the illusion. Collar her. Make sure she doesn't get on the ship with the others."

Before she could react, Rei turned to see Dante swinging the hilt of his gladius at her head. Everything went black.

CHAPTER 32

Jealousy hummed through Arram's core as he watched Rei dance with Anekris. Rei's smile was for show; he had seen it plenty during their months on tour. Anekris's smile also appeared for show; it didn't have that veil of secrecy like when he and Arram were alone. Anekris had already admitted to not being attracted to Rei, so it was the only way to explain the smile. At least that's what Arram told himself. Yet seeing his sister in the man's arms stung.

"I think Rei and Anekris look lovely together," Ildana said at Arram's side as his sister and the sovereign left the ballroom. "They would make a powerful match."

Arram rubbed the base of his neck. "But she's with Bronx."

Ildana waved her hand. "A slight detour to greatness, I assure you."

His uncle Jenson remained quiet at his wife's side.

"I still don't understand how you support a man who murdered your twin brother?" Arram asked.

"Anekris has been good for the Starline. He kept us afloat during those rough years when the Federation came into back into power and liberated planets." Arram sensed sarcasm at Jenson's use of the word "liberated." "You're certainly one to talk, nephew. I have seen you and Anekris speak more than once, and you look as though you could hang on the sovereign's every word."

Arram blushed. He didn't think his feelings were so obvious.

On his other side, Aurelia's long fingernails tapped her champagne glass as she observed.

"And you?" Arram asked her. "You usually have a comment. I thought you didn't want Rei with someone from the Dominion."

Aurelia shrugged. "I talked with Anekris. He assured me that your father's and mother's deaths were uncalled for and that he would honor their memory in repentance."

"So now you support the Dominion." It wasn't a question.

Aurelia shook her head. "No, dear. I want peace. I am tired of spending my twilight years seeing my children and grandchildren fight each other. I would like to leave this life knowing my descendants will have peace."

"Is that your way of saying you want to see my sister with Anekris?"

Aurelia smiled. "Making her his equal in power would be a start in his road to seek my forgiveness."

Arram chuckled, but he didn't find any of it humorous. His grandmother had a price and Anekris paid it. He didn't appreciate the way they wanted Anekris and Rei together. Aurelia's comment simply stoked the fires of Arram's jealousy.

"Ladies and gentleman." Anekris's voice could be heard across the crowd. Arram's eyes traveled to where the sovereign stood off to the side of the dance floor. "The god queen has retired for the evening. We have made significant progress, but she would like solitude so she can meditate on what else we can do to heal the star cluster." Anekris gestured for the cameramen to turn off their devices, and the flickering red lights went dark.

Arram was relieved to hear the talks went well but didn't like that his sister wanted to be alone. He wanted to talk to her and learn the details of what happened between them. He had to help her decide what else they could do to keep the Federation and Dominion from going to war. Anekris locked eyes with Arram and approached.

"I need to talk to you." His blue eyes were bright and his golden hair mussed. The sovereign pulled him gently through the crowd, hand on his arm.

"How did it go?" Arram asked, following Praymer to the edge of the ballroom, toward one of the large windows looking out into the stars.

"She didn't want to talk. She felt that she had done her five minutes of niceties and left when I tried to talk more details with her. I think she's cooling off somewhere. I didn't realize the temper she has."

Arram let out a sigh of frustration. "She only did this for Niklaryn. He is one of her greatest weaknesses. Perhaps you said something to antagonize her."

Anekris watched him. Arram desperately wanted to know what went on behind those blue eyes. He wished Anekris could trust him enough to get close.

"This had nothing to do with Niklaryn. But you are right. Your sister cares very much for her brother, more than you are aware." The sovereign's voice was soft, but the words hurt. He was well aware how Rei loved Nik more than him. "But it got heated between us," the sovereign continued. "I have always tried to be a gentleman to her, but she can say such horrible things. Though I was no better. I truly regret what I did to her."

Arram chuckled. "She does that. What did you say to her?"

Anekris shook his head. "I don't want to talk about it. I feel so ashamed. I didn't want to anger her or push her away." He sighed, his blue eyes staring at the stars outside.

"It doesn't matter what I do. She refuses to see me in any other way than a villain. Not like you. You see me as a person."

"Let me talk to her," Arram said, moving away from Praymer. Yet the sovereign's hand held Arram's, and he couldn't will himself to move further.

"Why don't you stay?" Praymer asked. "With me. Stay with me. Don't leave with the Federation when they come. Be my ally. I know your sister respects you, and maybe staying will be the push she needs to see that we can achieve peace."

Arram hesitated. He didn't want to be separated from the group if they all returned to the Federation. But if they all left, then peace may not get a fighting chance. Between Bronx and his half brother, Rei could be easily swayed into war. Maybe Praymer was right.

Arram didn't answer, but his gaze turned to the space as several large vessels floated into view. The Federation was here, and Arram needed to decide now. He looked down at his hand, still in Praymer's.

"I'll stay," Arram said. "We'll get her to change her mind. My father wanted this until he was too weak to take that last leap. I am not afraid."

Praymer smiled. "Excellent."

CHAPTER 33

Bronx stared helplessly as a figure in orange held a gun to Crona's head.

"One move, reaper, and we blow the blonde's head off."

"You just said you need us both," Bronx muttered.

"She's not entirely necessary; seers are easier to find than reapers."

Crona faced her brother, her aquamarine eyes wide.

"Stay calm," Bronx whispered. "I'll get us out of this."

Two Path members grabbed Bronx on either side and yanked him to his feet. There had to be at least a dozen. Two had their hands on his sister, but the rest were for him. More than he could handle alone.

They were dragged to another part of the botanical garden. The dying reaper and strung-out seer were left behind. He feared he would have to see Micaela's tomb again, and he couldn't face it, not in this state. Luckily they didn't pass it.

Pressure wrapped around his neck and he gasped. Something squeezed his throat, yet there was nothing there. Praymer's face flashed before him, and he realized the fear was not completely his. Something was happening to Rei. He struggled against the hands holding him until he watched one of the members pull Crona's head back by her hair, a gleaming knife held against her throat.

"Keep struggling, reaper," said the woman, the leader. Her dark eyes stared into Bronx's. "I dare you."

He relaxed, and the hands pulled him forward again.

They continued. They came upon one of the large windows looking out into space.

Crona fell into another pond, but the Negander yanked her out. The remnants of the blood fell from her face.

One of the Path members pulled out a small metal rod and flipped a switch, and its tip glowed red.

"Hold him," said the female Path member holding the rod.

Hands held him fast, another pulled his head back by his hair, and one more pair pulled his robes back and shirt open, exposing his collar. Bronx saw what awaited him: an infinity brand.

"No!" cried Crona. "Stop!"

Bronx's heart leapt to his throat. "You won't get away with this."

"Shut up, freak. You belong to Praymer now," the woman said as she pressed the brand on his collar. Pain exploded in his shoulder and the smell of burned flesh filled his nose.

He clenched his teeth. He wanted to scream, but he didn't want to give the Path member the pleasure. White filled his vision as anger boiled in his veins and the air crackled around him. He wanted to throw everything at the Path, everything at Praymer, everything at the whole Dominion, but the pain rattled his mind with little white flashes and he couldn't maintain focus.

It was Crona who screamed. Her voice vibrated in his head, piercing through the pain. He fought the hands holding him, but they were stronger than him. He squeezed his eyes shut and told himself it would be over soon.

Crona's voice still echoed in the garden, taking a more electronic tone.

Bronx opened his eyes to find the rod removed. He couldn't see his new mark, but his nerves remained on fire.

His eyes then turned to his sister, her face red and stained with tears.

"I will fucking destroy you!" she screamed, and Bronx swore the surrounding garden closed in.

Then he realized he wasn't seeing things. The plants reached for his sister as her rage increased.

It had to be the pain playing tricks with his mind. Yet several vines shot out from several directions, slamming into each of the orange figures and pinning them down.

A blur of movement tore through his attackers, and within moments, a dozen Path members were covered in cuts with surgical precision and wrapped in vines. Bronx only saw the silhouette of their savior.

"Are you all right?" Bronx didn't expect Infiernen's voice. "Is Manden nearby? I didn't see him with you." It was natural to think the redhead had to be nearby to manipulate the garden, but Bronx knew what he saw.

"I did it," Crona said, rubbing her face. "Or at least I think I did. I wanted to hurt them, to destroy them."

Infiernen drew closer to Bronx to inspect his wound. "I watched the camera feed and saw Dante free those Path prisoners and send them for you. I had to help. I promised Rei."

"What about her?" Bronx asked. "I felt fear. Rei's fear."

"She's still in the ballroom dancing with Praymer."

"Are you sure?"

"Ladies and gentlemen." Praymer's voice came over the speakers throughout the ship. "Your ride has arrived. Federation ships are approaching. Please make your way to the hangar. Thank you for letting me host you after such a troublesome time. My best to Elmessa and Sariah."

"We go now," Crona said, disappearing into the foliage again.

"Where are you going?" Infiernen asked, following her.

"To help the reaper and seer. We can get them off the ship now."

Bronx stood slowly, pain tearing through his shoulder. He pulled the red robe over his wound. It wasn't the best idea, but he didn't want anyone else to see what had been done to him yet. He followed slowly until he reached his sister and Infiernen. Crona pressed the seer's eyes closed while Infiernen examined the reaper and scooped her up. "She's fading. Come on."

They left the room, and after a few turns in different hallways, saw the river of guests making their way to the hangar. Elmessa, Sariah, and Skylar guided the crowd, reminding everyone to keep calm.

Bronx saw Artema first, but Kaz and Manden weren't far behind.

"Where's Rei?" Bronx asked.

"She went somewhere with Praymer. I swear I took my eyes off of her for only a moment," Manden said. "Arram has also disappeared."

Bronx didn't hear the last sentence. He flexed his fingers before balling them into a fist. Blood rushed in his ears as did the revelation that by leaving Rei alone, she was at the mercy of Praymer. And Bronx was too far away to help.

"Who's that?" Kaz asked, pointing to the unconscious reaper.

"Not now," Infiernen said.

"I saw them," Sariah said. "Praymer led her into a room with whom I thought was Manden." She pointed to the redhead beside her. "Obviously that was not the case."

Bronx remembered the vision he saw of Praymer with his filthy hands around Rei's neck. He knew what happened, and his chest tightened at the thought of her falling into further harm.

"It had to be Dante masquerading as Manden," Infiernen said. "He's an illusion Volocio and not the only one in Praymer's employment."

Bronx's eyes flicked to the Negander, knowing full well who else he meant.

"I think I know into which room he took her. It has its own security system. He had hoped to keep her on board." Infiernen handed the reaper to Manden, her white hair almost getting tangled in the god king's arms. "Get her on the ship, I will help the others find Rei."

"Hoped?" Bronx roared. "You knew this was Praymer's plan?"

"I did, but that's why I was working with you. I needed you to work against Praymer to keep Rei from him. I fear Praymer saw through my own plan as well."

Bronx wanted to swing for Infiernen in that moment, but he couldn't focus on that. He had to find Rei.

"What about Arram?" Kaz asked.

"If we find him, then we do," Bronx said. "But I only care about Rei."

"I am coming with you." Artema jerked her chin in the Negander's direction. "You and I should have a chat, Infiernen."

"First let's worry about Rei." The Negander refused to meet Artema's eyes.

"You can chat later," Crona said. "Manden, can you make sure the ship doesn't leave until we're on?"

"Of course. Good luck." Kaz, Sariah, and Manden

carried the white-haired reaper and rejoined the guests continuing toward the hangar.

"This way," Infiernen said, leading Bronx, Crona, and Artema against the tide of people.

Bronx's heart hammered in his chest. He couldn't leave Rei behind. He tried to find her through their bond but only saw darkness. He feared the worst. If they hurt her, he would bring down the star cluster on Praymer. He would tear that mechanical arm off and beat the sovereign with it.

Praymer wanted war, and if Rei would not start it, then Bronx might.

CHAPTER 34

Rei's head throbbed as she finally came to. Muffled voices filled her head. She wasn't sure if she had a concussion or the voices were far away.

She reached behind her head where she had been struck and found only a bump, no blood, but it was tender. Her hand slipped down to her neck where a collar rested, its cool metal kissing her skin. She felt around and found no clasp, no way to take it off. Panic bubbled in her stomach as well as a dizziness as she rose to her feet.

She lay in the little golden side room, but she was alone, save for the puddle of blood from the victim Praymer tried to masquerade as Arram. Next to it was a discarded orange robe.

The Path. They were Praymer's lackeys the whole time. They were led by Infiernen, her false ally. She moaned, her thoughts still muddled, and she couldn't focus.

Rei stumbled to the door and found it locked. She gritted her teeth as she pulled at the brass handles. She let out a yell and banged at the door. The ballroom was just on the other side. Maybe someone heard. But she was met with silence. She couldn't be left behind on this ship. What of Bronx and Crona? Praymer was aware of what they were trying to do. They may need her help.

She needed to open that door.

She tried to call her lightning, but nothing came. Once again that void remained where her lightning should be. Her hand grazed the collar, the only thing that had changed since she could last use her gifts.

She pulled at the collar, but it didn't budge. She pulled harder; the metal dug into her fingers. It was useless, but not being able to reach her lightning was like not breathing—and she was suffocating. She fell to her knees and let out another scream.

"Rei?" a faint voice called from the other side of the door.

"Bronx?" she returned.

She was answered with a bang at the door, causing her to take several steps back. Then another bang and the door caved in slightly, and another and another until the door opened. Bronx, Crona, Artema, and Infiernen stood in the doorway.

Rei only saw the Negander. She clenched her teeth and her body tensed. She took several steps toward him, but Bronx was the first to her side and wrapped his arms around her as she clawed at her collar. "You did this to me, you asshole!" she roared at Infiernen. She wanted to hit him, but Bronx's arms held her firm. "I can't feel my powers," she choked. "Praymer wants to keep me here," she continued. "He's trying to keep me here and that asshole planned the whole thing."

"It's okay," Bronx whispered, but she saw his helplessness as a pale yellow haze. She didn't understand how Bronx wasn't angry, but then flecks of red flashed in the yellow. He was holding back to keep her calm. He pulled away and gingerly touched the collar at her neck. He took her hands in his, tugging them away from the collar, and kissed them.

"He has Arram and Niklaryn," she sobbed. "We have to save them."

"Can we get the collar off?" asked Crona, her eyes never straying from the abomination around Rei's neck.

"I think I can. The clasp should be hidden in the back," Infiernen said. He drew closer to Rei, but she flinched.

"Don't you fucking come near me."

Infiernen let out a heavy sigh. "Please believe me, helping you has always been my priority. I have seen plans for this before. Some of Praymer's blood is mixed into the metal. I didn't realize he had already made them."

Praymer had found a way to weaponize his blood. Rei shuddered at the thought of Praymer having a way to subdue her. He knew she would fight him. His treatment of her had been a ruse. He had planned several steps ahead. She wanted to deny Infiernen, but her need to feel her powers again outweighed her need to punch the Negander in the throat.

"Do it," Rei said, turning around, holding Bronx's hands, her breathing hard. His ripped robes revealed a deep red on his chest. "What happened?" she asked. But he didn't respond. His eyes were on Infiernen as the Negander worked to free Rei.

"Holy shit," Crona said. "I have seen this all before."

Rei turned to see what the seer referred to, but Bronx touched her chin and locked eyes with her. "I'm so sorry," he whispered. "I love you."

"Sorry for what?" she asked as the collar fell away from her neck and her lightning rushed back like a flood. She turned around to find the collar was blood red. Then her gaze moved to the Negander. Her head spun and her heart grew heavy in her chest. She couldn't believe what she was seeing. The floor lurched beneath her as she came to the realization that it wasn't the Negander holding the collar.

It was Niklaryn.

Her insides turned to ice as everything finally fell into place. Niko had once said he sold his soul, and now she knew how. He became Infiernen and committed all those atrocities across the star cluster.

Now she understood why he was always on her side.

But he also tried to kill Arram.

He was working for the Path.

For Praymer.

He betrayed her.

Ice turned into fire and lightning danced around her fingertips in response.

"What the fuck?" she yelled and lunged, but Bronx and Artema held her back. Bronx grunted as he held her, whatever happened to him hurt, but she didn't care. She shoved both of them off of her. Her eyes never left her brother.

She hadn't seen him since her dying moments on Kepler IV, and he was just as she remembered him. Tall, handsome, full beard, and his beautiful blue eyes red-rimmed with tears.

"You're Infiernen?" she whispered.

"It's complicated." His voice was no louder than hers.

"That's not an answer."

"We don't have time." Niklaryn walked over to a wall and tapped four times. It clicked open to reveal a machine with several blinking lights. He pulled out a large drive and shut the wall again. "This should have the contents of what happened in this room between Rei and Praymer. Get it to Felix Royalt. He's the one who has helped me blast information across the Dominion." He handed the drive to Artema, then sighed and put the collar around his neck. "I still have to pretend I am loyal to Praymer. Bronx, make it look real."

"What?" Artema asked. "No, you're coming with me. I am not losing you again."

"You're not, darling," Niklaryn said, pulling her close.

"Arram is still in trouble, even though he doesn't know it yet. I will stay so I can protect him and get him out."

"No," whispered Artema. "It's too dangerous. He can't be killed."

"I will find a way. Infiernen and I have worked too hard to get this close to Praymer, and I can't give up now."

Rei seethed with anger. Artema knew. Artema knew her husband was Infiernen and said nothing. Rei then turned to Bronx, who merely stared at her with a pained expression on his face. He had betrayed her too.

Artema let her husband go, and before Bronx could react, Rei punched Niklaryn in the face. Niklaryn took the blow, but despite Rei's strength, he didn't stumble. "You find Arram and bring him back to me. But then you and I are done. Do you understand, Infiernen? Fucking done." Artema touched Rei's arm, but she shrugged it off. "You don't get to show sympathy. You're just as much to blame."

She wanted to cry, to scream, to blow up this ship. Her brother. Her darling brother was the one wreaking havoc across the star cluster. He was the one who shot his own brother and tried to kill Bronx, yet the reaper appeared to not want revenge. The red in her vision flashed hotly. She was wrong, he was angry.

Bronx took Rei's place and knocked Niklaryn to the ground and landed more blows on his mentor's face until Crona pulled him off. "That's enough," she whispered, pulling her brother to his feet.

Rei didn't stay to see more. She turned on her heels and left the room. A few guests were still trickling out. Not everyone made it to the ship yet. She followed them.

"Rei!" cried Arram.

Rei almost cried in relief as she threw her arms around him. "Thank the gods, you're safe."

"Of course I am." His violet eyes shone as his eyebrows furrowed. "What happened?"

"I can't do it, Arram. I can't work with Praymer. He's sick."

"He said things got heated, but he didn't give me details."

"I'll tell you all about it later." She took his hand and tugged. "Let's go. We have to get off this ship."

"I'm staying," Arram said, letting go.

Rei's face went numb, and a coldness hit her core. "What?"

"We are close to preventing this war. I know you still don't trust him and you have some anger you need to work through. But we can work past what happened today. We have to find a way for the greater good."

Rei's hand went to her stomach, right where Praymer had struck her when he called her a whore. He hit her where no one else could see the bruises. "Work past? There's nothing to work past. The man is crazy!"

Arram let out a growl of frustration. "Just give him a chance. He told me he was sorry for what happened. He sounded like he meant it. You just got under his skin." He smiled. "You know you have that way with people."

"No!" she screamed. She couldn't understand how he didn't see her pain or the marks on her neck and her wrist. Praymer was rough with her. Some evidence had to be visible. She didn't understand what hold the sovereign had on both of her brothers. She never thought her relatives were so easily bought.

Out of the corner of her eye, she saw that Ildana, Jenson, and Aurelia stood with other guests who appeared to be happy to stay with the sovereign.

Aurelia approached, her blue eyes full of concern. "Rei, darling, what happened?"

Rei looked at her brother and grandmother. "He hurt me."

"Come now," Aurelia muttered with a wave of her hand. "Your brother said that you have a nasty temper. Perhaps you should have watched your tongue instead of acting like an uneducated barmaid."

Rei's mouth hung open. "Did you say that, Arram?"

Arram's lips pressed together in a line. "You have a nasty temper, but I can't imagine what Praymer could have done to you. You're the strongest woman I know. You wouldn't have let him touch you unless you wanted it."

Rei couldn't feel her legs and the dizziness returned, but it wasn't from being struck. Her family truly had a price to overlook murdered relatives and assault. She couldn't do it anymore. She was finished with the lot.

"I'm done. You stay, Arram. You and Niko can take turns worshiping Praymer. I don't know what either of you see in that man, but you are welcome to it. But don't be surprised when he hurts you too."

Arram's head flinched back slightly. "He won't. You don't have to worry."

Rei scoffed. "I don't worry because I don't give a fuck what happens to those who betray me." Rei walked away. She heard the others behind her, but she didn't wait for them to catch up. She had to get off this ship. Tears filled her vision until everything was a blur. She blinked them away to find Crona at her side, putting an arm around her in an awkward hug. They continued until they arrived on the shuttle.

Manden waited at the hangar next to Praymer, who bid

farewell to the guests. The redhead's forehead creased with worry, but relief was visible in his eyes as Rei approached.

Praymer couldn't prevent her from getting on the ship this time, not in front of everyone. She stared daggers at the sovereign who, in return, pressed his lips together. He knew he could do nothing this time.

Rei grabbed Manden's hand and marched up the hatch to find Camila talking to Kaz and Elmessa. Skylar and Sariah were also not far off. Rei was relieved to find Camila had joined them. At least someone could escape that monster's clutches. Camila saw the others approach and threw her arms around Rei's shoulders.

"Thank you," she whispered. "I was so afraid I would never get out."

Rei returned the hug as tightly as the pressure in her chest. She only dealt with Praymer's roughness for a mere moment, but Camila withstood it for months. He would pay for what he did to her. The star cluster needed to learn what he was capable of, and between the two of them, they could show them.

CHAPTER 35

"BETRAY YOU?" ARRAM WHISPERED AS HE WATCHED HIS sister storm off. "I would never betray you. I love you." It hurt when she said it, but she was in pain. He didn't know what happened. Anekris had to have said something to anger his sister. He expected as much. She just needed to cool off.

Her hand had gone to her neck as she spoke; it was red, but he didn't see marks. Maybe Praymer did put his hand on her. The thought sent a chill down his spine.

Crona had given him a pained look before running after Rei; her look stung as well. The reaper remained behind as the other Volocio left, if only for a moment. His dark eyes studied Arram.

"Yes, Bronx?"

"You are playing a very dangerous game, kid. Staying with Praymer is not worth alienating your sister."

"I am doing what she couldn't. I am staying for her. I want her to see reason. She needs to let go of her ego and her thirst for revenge so we can fight the Path together. She and Anekris have to work together."

"So it's Anekris now?" Bronx whispered before shaking his head. "You are so blind." The reaper leaned in close. "There will be no peace between them. I can promise you that." He left, and Arram felt as though he could breathe again.

Curse that reaper and his influence. Bronx was such a jealous man that he assumed Anekris wanted more from his sister than peace. Idiot. It didn't help the reaper was obsessed with staying close to Rei, as though his sister was incapable of being without him. Bronx would make sure Rei wouldn't listen to Anekris. Arram rubbed his face as he debated his next plan.

He wanted to find Anekris and talk to him, but he conveniently was nowhere to be found. The sovereign lied when he said nothing happened between him and Rei. His sister had a temper, but only when properly provoked.

Arram turned to his grandmother.

"Dramatic. Just like her mother," Aurelia said before returning to Ildana and Jenson.

"And don't forget Yuri's younger brother," Jenson said. "He's not a good influence on Rei. She should be brought into the fold as soon as possible."

"Agreed." Ildana continued to stare in the direction where Rei had stormed out.

Arram couldn't stand their manipulations anymore. Every step they took was to further themselves and their own gains. He wanted peace . . . and perhaps some recognition.

He drew away from the group and saw an opening to a room he didn't know was there. Remnants of a wooden door were strewn about the floor. Naturally it had the same golden walls as the rest of the ship, but something sticky and red pooled on the floor. A groan caught his attention, and Arram gasped as he saw Niklaryn lying on the floor.

"Nik?" Arram asked, rushing to his brother's side.

Niklaryn didn't look at him right away, appearing dazed from the blows to his face. His left eye had swollen shut.

Arram grabbed Niklaryn's beefy arm and helped him to his feet.

"Infiernen?" Anekris's voice came from outside the door. The sovereign's face fell as he beheld Niklaryn.

"Niklaryn?" Anekris asked, cautiously moving toward the Daer.

His brother pulled at his collar. "He's under control. Rei and the reaper overtook me and left me in this collar and gave me a souvenir." He pointed to his eye.

"What?" Arram asked, looking from his brother to the sovereign. "Under control?"

"So Rei knows the truth?" Anekris asked.

"The truth?" No one listened to Arram.

Praymer unlocked the collar and pulled it away from Nik's neck and handed it to Arram. As his hands curled around the cool blood red metal, a hole formed in his chest where his powers normally rested. His stomach roiled and it felt like he lost a limb, yet the shadow of his powers still remained to taunt him. He yelped at the unnatural feeling, letting the collar drop to the floor with a metal clang.

Dread pooled in his belly as Niklaryn changed his face to Infiernen's. Arram's heart thrashed in his chest.

"You're . . ." Arram whispered. "You're Infiernen?"

The older Ettowa stood a little straighter.

The universe hummed around Arram as the last piece of the puzzle fell into place. Now it made sense why Niklaryn was so cold to him when they first met. This was the man who tried to murder Arram on Trappist V, and seeing that failure still walking about must have made him angry. Arram didn't understand what he had done to deserve this. He wanted nothing more than to be loved by his family, only to be rejected by his sister and shot at by his brother.

The shock quickly subsided. Anger pulsed through him and lightning danced along his hands. He yelled and brought his hands forward. A huge bolt jumped from his fingertips and landed square in the middle of Niklaryn's chest, throwing the Daer against the wall, where he crumpled to the ground with a thud.

The sovereign said nothing, his face remaining neutral as he turned to the younger Ettowa. "Are you all right?"

"I have a shit family." A traitorous tear rolled down his cheek.

"What do you want to do about it?"

Arram wiped his face and dried his hands on his trousers. "Niklaryn and I need to have a heart-to-heart first. Then I'll think about what I am going to do next."

Praymer gave Arram a tight smile and rested a hand on his shoulder. "You do what you need to do to heal. I'll be at your side."

CHAPTER 36

Bronx wanted nothing more than to disappear into the circuits of the shuttle that brought them from Praymer's ship to one of the three Federation ones that floated outside of firing range.

The Federation ships were quick to take an Alcubierre-Krasnikov tunnel out of the immediate area. The Volocio weren't the only ones who wanted to get as far away from the sovereign's ship as possible.

Rei rarely looked at Bronx, but when she did, he swore lightning dancing behind her eyes waiting to be unleashed.

"Now that vision I had on Kepler IV makes sense," Crona said. "I couldn't imagine what would make you want to punch Niklaryn with such anger."

Crona had that vision when they were looking for Artema. She knew Niklaryn had some connection with the Dominion and that he was alive, but she didn't know more, and Bronx refused to divulge. He couldn't afford for more people to know. It was such a hard secret to maintain that he shouldn't have tried.

Artema had told him this would blow up in his face. Her voice echoed "I told you so" repeatedly in his head. Seeing Rei angry at him was nothing compared to the heartbreak written across her face. Her heroic brother was—for all intents and purposes—Infiernen, and that truth hurt more than not telling her. He had wanted to spare her that.

He knew the look, the hope fading from her eyes. The same thing happened to him that day on the battlefield when Niklaryn came to his rescue against Riodan. But then his mentor's face melted into someone else just as he struck the final blow against the Negander, and it was another man who hacked at Riodan's face. He didn't believe in Volocio then; he didn't believe in that kind of magic, but he saw the stuff of nightmares with his mentor in the center of it.

Bronx was grateful to finally get away from all that gold on the ship and be back inside the clean white walls of a Federation ship. Bernie greeted them, immediately sensing something was wrong, but no one was in the mood to answer her questions. Instead Rei demanded a private room. There were things that needed discussing.

He dreaded the conversation.

"Well?" Rei asked once Artema closed the door to the conference room. It was only the three of them. "How long have you known about Niko and Infiernen? Who else knows?" she asked both of them, but her sparkling green eyes stared into Bronx's dark ones.

"The Battle of the Fortress of Riodan." Bronx's voice was barely above a whisper. "Niklaryn came to save me but turned into Infiernen to finish the job."

"How did I not know my brother was an illusion Volocio?"

"He's not," Artema said. "He isn't one of us, and that's why we didn't know. We didn't expect it. The members of the Ettowa family are descendants of a powerful illusion Volocio named Hugh Ettowa, who was a legend, even on Tas'und'eash. Nik's powers are not as strong as a true Volocio like Kaz. Nik could only change parts of his appearance to become Infiernen."

Bronx had faced Infiernen numerous times on the battlefield and still saw Niklaryn's face. It was a wonder no one else figured it out.

Rei shook her head. "You said they had walked off the

battlefield together. You were always so careful with your words, Bronx, making it sound like they are two people."

"But they are," Artema said.

"How?" Rei's voice almost squeaked. "You saw! It's Nik using his gifts to change his face."

"Infiernen is not Nik. They share a body, but they are not the same person. They suffer from dissociative identity disorder. Nik and Infiernen are part of a system with Nik as the primary host and Infiernen as one of his alters."

Rei looked as though her heart had stopped. "One of his . . ." she said to herself. Her eyes never left Bronx's face. "Alters?"

"Alternate state of consciousness," Artema said.

"I didn't know," he said. "I didn't know about his mental illness until Artema joined our group. I thought Nik did this of his own volition and was only using Infiernen as an alias to perform these horrible deeds. After the battle, I told Urius what had happened, and he said that if anyone else knew the truth about Nik, it would destroy morale for the Federation. Better to have him as a martyr than a traitor. I didn't want you to think ill of your brother or to know the complications and be burdened with the truth like me. So I said nothing."

"But that was before Artema joined," Rei countered. "What happened afterward?"

Bronx closed his eyes. "I didn't believe his illness, I'm ashamed to admit. All I had to go off of was over a decade of experience of Infiernen trying to kill me, and I never saw Nik in all that time. I thought he was gone for good. Until this . . ." Bronx pulled out his slate from his pocket and found the video he wanted to show, sliding it toward the projector on the table in the middle of the room. It sprang to life, throwing images on the opposite wall that Rei took when she fought Infiernen on Kepler IV. He had watched the video so many times after Artema told him the truth, and yet he still couldn't comprehend it.

Rei fought Infiernen before the poison from Infiernen's blade took effect. She screamed as she fell to the ground. Bronx hated that part, knowing he was so far away from her when it happened. He breathed hard as dizziness settled in. He had left her alone again, left her at the mercy of Praymer. If anything had happened to her, he would never have forgiven himself.

Rei fell to the ground and Infiernen disappeared. Niklaryn caught her. His first appearance in almost ten years. The camera didn't pick up what they said to each other, but eventually Rei relaxed in his arms.

Niklaryn laid her gently onto the ground and let out a piercing wail, beating his chest as his cry reached the heavens. Then he turned toward something—Bronx coming for Rei. Niklaryn stumbled to his feet and trudged through the snow to the tree where the camera sat waiting. The video stopped on Niklaryn's face as he shut the camera off.

"That was the first time Nik fronted in almost a decade. Infiernen had taken control, but seeing you made your brother want control again. Nik gave me your camera and told me you couldn't know the truth. I didn't fully understand why until Artema explained."

Rei said nothing. She backed away from both Bronx and Artema, putting distance between them until she stood against the far wall. "You still could have told me." Her voice was almost inaudible.

He could have. He should have. His heart ached as he watched the pain written on her face. "I don't know what your brother has been planning. Perhaps he wanted to control Infiernen before allowing you to know the truth."

"Or maybe he didn't want me to know he was working for Praymer with the Path."

Bronx sighed. That could have also been a reason. He still didn't understand Nik's motives. "I wanted to tell you, but I also wanted to respect his wishes. Even when I didn't believe that he had an alter, I still took his word without question. I didn't know where your brother stood in terms of Federation or Dominion, but I knew I would do as he asked because despite all Infiernen or your brother has done these past years, I am still loyal to him. He is my brother too."

His voice broke. He took a calming breath and willed his heart to stop racing, yet his eyes remained on Rei's beautiful face, and he prayed that that his words were enough.

"This is Nik we're talking about. He's the man who gave you up to hunt Praymer so you could be safe. I know how much that cost him; he made it plain every day. He wanted family so much, he adopted whoever he could, including me." Bronx rubbed his face. He was rambling now, but he couldn't stop. "He and I went through so much together, it didn't feel right betraying his trust. But I also hated him for it because I love you with every fiber of my being and keeping this from you felt equally wrong."

Rei turned back to the video as it remained frozen on Niklaryn's face. She remained silent, but through their bond, he felt her myriad of emotions: pain, disappointment, confusion, anger, all of it. Each one throbbed in his chest. He wished he could take it away, but all that was left was for her to ride through each of them.

"I need to be alone," she said finally. "I need to work through this."

"If you want to talk about it," Artema said. "I am here to listen."

"Honestly, if I feel like talking, it won't be with either of you."

Artema's face fell, but she straightened and left the room.

Bronx hoped Rei would turn and look at him, but her eyes remained on Niklaryn's face on the wall. He placed his slate on the table and slid it in her direction. "Watch the video as much as you like. I know I can't give you a good excuse. I just didn't want to cause you this pain."

"You still did." Her words were a punch in the gut.

"I know."

Her eyes remained on the screen, and Bronx left the room without another word. He swore he heard Rei cry as the door shut with a whoosh.

He leaned back against the wall and ran a hand through his hair.

"That went exactly as I imagined it would," Artema said.

"I never wanted to see that look on her face." He opened his eyes and looked at Artema. "I could literally kill Niklaryn for putting Rei through this."

"Well, you certainly made that clear with your fist."

Bronx winced. He only saw red when Nik asked him to do the deed. His mentor had betrayed him as well. He had hoped that his lying for Nik would have amounted to something. Instead, he only helped enable his mentor stay close to a man who could not be killed and helped deliver Rei into Praymer's hands. Niklaryn was an idiot. "I'm sorry for hitting your husband."

Artema shook her head. "If you hadn't, I would have. He's so desperate to be the hero he doesn't see the destruction he leaves behind in his pursuits. Infiernen is certainly no better."

He really admired Artema. He saw how much it pained her to leave Niklaryn behind— it pained him too. They both wanted to help Nik, but Bronx didn't know where to start.

He knew from their talks before about Nik's DID that his illness was exacerbated by his abandonment of Arram all those years ago. In order to heal, Nik would have to confront that part of his past and perhaps saving Arram could help set Nik on the right path.

A sharp pain in his shoulder reminded him he still had not taken care of the brand. He tried to ignore the pain, but he needed to attend to it before it became infected.

"I need to go to the medical wing," he muttered, pointing to his shoulder. "Did my sister talk to you about the plants in the botanical garden?"

"She mentioned it, but I told her it was a conversation best saved for the Volocio together." Artema's eyes remained on the door. She wanted Rei to be there too.

"Okay." He was tempted to reach through the bond, but he wasn't sure he could handle feeling Rei's emotions right now.

He wandered through the hall. Most of the guests stayed on a different ship heading to the Federation capital Madu on the planet Proxima Centauri II, Sariah, Skylar, and Elmessa included. He was grateful. After the last twenty-four hours among a throng of people, he needed the silence.

He passed Camila and Bernie, deep in quiet conversation in the ship's lounge. He heard them talking about "showing the star cluster" and "Praymer must pay." They were making plans, and he wouldn't be surprised if Rei wanted to take part in whatever they were plotting.

Crona, Manden, and Kaz were in the medical wing. His sister had a few cuts on her face, but the medic was busy with the white-haired reaper they had saved from Praymer.

"How is she?" Bronx asked. The medic was a young woman with dark skin and black tresses that fell over her white coat.

"She needs rest," said the medic. "I don't know what she went through, but it aged her unnaturally." The medic gestured for Crona to come to her for treatment.

Bronx knew exactly what happened but said nothing as he approached the bed. The woman was awake, surrounded by several bags of vitamins and nutrients being pumped via IV to help her regain her strength.

Her dark eyes met his, and her eyebrows raised. "Atrius," she whispered.

She called him that when he was in Hamastagan and had brought Rei back to life.

The reaper gave him a weak smile. "Sorry. I know you're not him. I still find it uncanny that you look just like him."

Bronx shrugged. "I get that a lot." He took her hand in his and she squeezed, her grip firm. "My name is Bronx. What's yours? We didn't have the chance for introductions the last time we met."

"Ananiel. Ana," she whispered. "Did you find her? The woman you searched for?"

Bronx nodded. "I found Rei. Cesar helped me and I brought her back."

Ana smiled. "Then you are as powerful as Atrius. I could never bring a loved one back. I wonder if you have his other abilities." Her voice grew stronger with every sentence.

"Other abilities?" Manden drew closer.

"Reapers are vessels of pure energy. We can learn from

other Volocio, manipulate energy from the dead, even mimic the other Volocio powers."

"Mimic?" Crona asked from her seat.

"Like an illusion?" asked Kaz.

Ana shook her head. "When a reaper has helped a Volocio pass on to Hamastagan, they can temporarily exhibit the gifts of that Volocio." She locked eyes with Bronx. "But when Atrius learned to do it once, he could do it forever."

All eyes turned to Bronx. He wondered if they expected him to suddenly start showing all of his new powers, which didn't exist. "No. I can't do that. But then again, I have never been around another reaper to teach me."

"I can teach you," said Ana.

"You have that ability," Crona added. "I saw it."

Bronx furrowed his eyebrows. "When? I would have known if I could do something."

"At the botanical garden, when they were branding you. I saw lightning form in your hands."

That couldn't be true. He would have known, but all he could remember was the pain. Then he remembered his vision filled with white and the pain appearing as flashes. Maybe it wasn't the pain he saw, but the lightning fluttering at his sides. He looked down at his hands, covered in scars from his years as a knight. He didn't think these hands were capable of any more. Yet that wasn't the case.

"But that would mean I would have come across another lightning Volocio and helped them into the after-life." Bronx shook his head. "The only lightning Volocio I know are Rei and Arram, and they are still alive."

"But you and Rei are connected." Manden leaned against Ana's bed, positioning himself between the reapers. "Maybe that bond allows you access to her abilities."

"How are you connected?" Ana asked.

"I broke my soul in half to bring her back." It was the first time he wondered if it was the right answer. He did whatever it took to bring Rei back. Being able to feel Rei's emotions was a side effect, and he had hoped that was it. But the way Ana studied him, he was no longer so sure.

"You are bonded then?"

Bronx nodded.

"Then you can siphon energy from her."

The floor of the ship lurched under his feet. He was just as guilty as Praymer, who had done the same thing to him. It was wrong. It was all wrong. He wondered if Rei was aware of what had happened—she probably wasn't; she was at the mercy of Praymer at that same moment, and if he had done anything to jeopardize her further, he would have proven he was no better than the sovereign.

They had to talk, but she was still angry about Niklaryn. Learning that he was taking lightning from her may not help in the road to forgiveness, but he couldn't afford to lie.

Never again.

CHAPTER 37

Rei cried when Bronx left the room. She didn't want either him or Artema to see her break. Between everything that had happened . . . It was too much. She couldn't hold it in any longer. She was overwhelmed and the pain in her heart only grew.

When Bronx left, she took his slate and logged in to play the video again from the beginning. Then she watched it again. And then again. And then a few more times.

She tried to piece together everything she knew about Infiernen. He said in their first meeting that he wasn't her enemy. During this fight, it was always her attacking him. He remained on the defensive. He didn't want to fight her. That much rang true concerning him being Niklaryn. However, he antagonized Bronx, Arram, and Artema. She didn't understand why Niklaryn would want to kill those he loved. Yet Niko didn't remember Arram. Maybe because of symptoms of DID. So many holes remained that simply saying her brother suffered from a mental illness was not enough.

Then she realized another piece of the puzzle: Skylar. She had been working with Infiernen for years, and now Rei understood why.

She quickly rang her cousin, silently kicking herself for not realizing it sooner and talking to Sky before they departed on different ships.

"Bronx?" Skylar's head flinched back slightly when she answered.

Rei only then remembered that she still had Bronx's slate in her hand as she dialed.

"Rei," Skylar said, recognizing what had happened.

"You knew, didn't you? You knew about Niko and Infiernen."

Skylar's face fell. She tugged at a strand of her long black hair before she answered. "Yes. How did you find out?"

"I saw it. I am trying to shuffle through it all and accept the fact that you, Artema, and Bronx have lied to me about it."

"Can you blame us, Rei? You only saw Infiernen as an irredeemable monster. Imagine what would have happened if you had hunted Infiernen only to find out that you also killed Nik? That's why I tried to get you two to meet. Infiernen was sure he could change your mind about him, and I had faith in him. I needed you to see Infiernen as an ally so when you discovered the truth, it would be easier to see that Infiernen's motivations have always been for Nik."

She was right. Infiernen may have helped Praymer with his plan, but he spent the rest of his time helping Rei and the others. Infiernen was so adamant that they were on the same side. Regardless if Infiernen and Niklaryn were separate or not, that truth unified them. It was a thread of faith, and it was all she had left.

They chatted a little while longer, but eventually Sariah called Skylar away and the slate went silent.

Rei watched the video one more time before turning it off and left the room, only to find Artema waiting outside.

Neither said a word at first. Artema took Rei's hand and gave it a squeeze. She knew what her sister-in-law meant: they could talk about Niko whenever Rei was ready.

The gesture reminded Rei of Hotara. She missed her

adopted mother fiercely and wished she were here to help her through this. But then she remembered how Hotara had also lied. She knew Rei was the god queen and kept that vital piece of information quiet. She also held back the fact that she was married. Rei could never forget the look of pain on Hotara's face when she revealed that Manden was her husband. She never spoke of him because she wanted to focus on the present, not on a man who was not there.

Rei could imagine it was the same for Artema. She couldn't ignore the connection between Artema and her brother, and she could only imagine the pain Artema felt when he wasn't there. There was also the fact that Infiernen had attacked Artema all those years ago. Artema surely had her own conflicting feelings about Infiernen and Niklaryn, yet her love for Rei's brother was unmistakable.

Most of the anger died out and left Rei tired. She didn't know what she would have done in their position. She didn't know if she could tell such a shattering truth, especially if it caused someone she loved this amount of pain.

But she wasn't ready to think more on her brother right now. There was something else she wanted to learn more about.

"You said once that you grew up with Micaela," Rei said.

"I did. Hotara and I grew up in the Dinay court."

"Could Micaela see through illusions?"

Artema's lips tugged at a hint of a smile. "You can. When did it happen?"

Rei wasn't ready to talk about what happened in the room with Praymer. "It doesn't matter when. I've noticed it for a while. My hands would itch around Kaz's illusions, but I didn't think much of it until . . ." she saw Arram clawing at his own throat; the illusion was too good.

"Until what?"

Rei shook her head. "I don't want to talk about *that* yet. But today was the first time I finally realized that my hands itched because of an illusion, and once I gave into it, I saw through it. Is it because Micaela and Kaz are related?"

Artema nodded. "Kaz and Micaela share the same grandparents: Lucas and Oksana. Lucas is an ambitious lightning Volocio, and Oksana comes from an old illusion family. Volocio powers exhibit in people in terms of dominant traits and recessive ones. Lightning is your dominant form, but because of Micaela's bloodline, she sees illusions, and Max could manipulate a brief illusion. Kaz can actually withstand lightning strikes."

"What about the others?"

"I think we should go talk with Crona. She also has the same questions." Artema hooked arms with Rei and pulled her down the hall. "Besides, we should have a medic look at those bruises on your neck. They're really pronounced now."

The other Volocio were in the medical wing. Kaz and Manden sat together on one of the empty beds. The redhead chewed mindlessly on a protein bar. A woman with long white hair and dark eyes that followed Rei sat on a bed near Crona. Her friend had a few cuts on her face that were being patched up by a medic, and Bronx had removed his shirt while he applied a gel on a horrific infinity mark burned into his fair skin.

Rei gasped when she saw it, drawing Bronx's attention. Praymer knew what Bronx and Crona were up to, and in her rage and fear concerning Niko, she didn't notice what wounds they had escaped with. So much had happened.

Bronx's face screwed up in pain, and it broke her heart to see it. It was then she knew she couldn't stay mad at him.

She knew how much Niklaryn meant to him; she knew how much Yuri's rejecting Bronx had pained him. He always tried to make light of it, but it was an act.

The first time Yuri contacted her, she also hesitated to tell Bronx. The reaper had hoped that his brother would contact him first to finally tell Bronx he understood that what happened to their father was an accident. Bronx didn't know how to control his powers then; he didn't know that he would kill his father with a touch. But that call from Yuri never came.

She finally told him, but only after hiding it for several days. Worse, it was right before a Federation council meeting where Urius wanted to know what Yuri had said to Rei. She understood what Bronx had tried to do. She would do anything to keep him from experiencing pain, from seeing that look in his eyes again. And that's exactly what he did. It may not have been the right decision, but she understood his motivation.

"Rei, this is Ananiel or Ana," Manden said, gesturing to the white-haired woman. "She's the reaper Praymer held captive."

Rei's heart sank as she drew closer. The woman's white hair was brittle, but her eyes showed youthfulness. This aging wasn't natural, and she knew this resulted from whatever Praymer did to her. She only hoped the effects weren't permanent, for Bronx's sake.

"Hello, Ana." Rei approached the bed. "I am so glad to have you with us."

"I am grateful to be out of that infernal garden." Ana sighed and tried to sit up. Rei tried to help her, but the reaper waved her away. "But enough about me, there's a lot more that needs to be discussed."

Rei looked back at Artema, assuming Ana referred to what she was discussing before with Rei's sister-in-law.

"Tell Rei what you told me," Artema said, just as Crona finished and the medic left the group alone in the room.

Crona's eyes flicked in her brother's direction. "They caught us in the botanical garden, and when that bitch from the Path branded my brother, I got angry. Somehow through my anger, the plants reacted and knocked all our attackers down, leaving Infiernen the opening he needed to kill them and save us."

So it was true. Everything Artema had explained was true.

Manden whistled. "Do you remember, Artema, when we placed bets on who Alexia's father was?"

It always unnerved Rei to hear Manden and Artema talk about the previous versions of the rest of the group as though they were still here. Yet it was Crona, not Alexia, who sat in the room.

Artema smiled. "I told you a plant Volocio was possible. Alexia was always tight-lipped about anything personal, including her parentage."

"It looks like I owe you money. How much was it again?" Manden ran a hand through his disheveled red locks.

"I think we wagered a hundred gold intis. I figured you had to be good for your country's currency." Artema chuckled.

"Remind me that next time we're back on Tas'und'eash."

Artema and Manden laughed.

"You never knew?" Kaz asked.

"No," Artema said. "The seers took lovers to parent children. Almost all seers know who their mothers are, but they usually keep the father's identity a secret. Seers use their gifts to foresee the best match for children. They either become seers themselves or are at least gifted with enough foresight to work their way into positions of power."

"Or become reapers," Bronx said. Crona and his previous selves, Alexia and Atrius, shared the same mother.

Rei felt his eyes on her, looking for a response. She met his gaze and gave him a small nod. She saw his relief in a shade of blue. He handed her a salve, for the bruises most likely. His eyes moved to her neck, anger brewing.

She strode to a nearby mirror and finally saw what Praymer's mechanical hand had done. A deep purple handprint spread across her skin. She took the salve and was about to apply it but stopped. Everyone needed to see what he had done to her. Those marks couldn't go away just yet, but she could at least take care of her wrist. She dabbed the gel on the mark, and its cooling relief seeped into her skin and around her wrist.

"So what do we do now?" Rei asked with more bite than she intended. "Jokes aside, where do we go from here? We have to figure out what we're going to do about Praymer. Working with him under his terms is out of the question, and I am worried he will want war in its stead."

"What happened when you were with him?" Kaz asked. "What does he want?"

Now she had to talk about it. There was no escaping it. "He believes his marriage to Micaela is valid with me. His idea of peace is us ruling together as husband and wife under a Dominion banner." The last words left a bitter taste in her mouth.

"I assume he put his hands on you to make you say yes?" Bronx asked through gritted teeth.

"He did until my lightning made his arm malfunction.

Then he brought in Arram." She couldn't look at the others as she explained the next part. "He threatened to slit my brother's throat if I said no. I thought he was bluffing, and then he did it. He even said it was how Max died. It was awful," she whispered. "It was then I discovered it was an illusion and Arram wasn't truly there. I think my brothers are both worth too much alive. I was ready to smite Praymer right there until he collared me. He had hoped I would get left behind."

"So you had no problem with your lightning?" Bronx asked. Something in his voice made her look at him.

She shook her head. "No problem at all. Why?"

He nodded. "I need to talk to you about something that happened. But one thing at a time."

Rei studied Bronx as though she could force him to say more. Her eyes then flicked to the horrendous brand on Bronx's collar. Arram had a similar mark. She wished she understood the motivation behind inflicting such pain.

"Praymer wants both Bronx and me as his property as well," Crona said. "He not only had a reaper, but he had a seer who was overdosing on Star of Saskia." She shuddered. "Definitely makes me rethink ever taking that flower again."

"A seer?" Artema asked. "I guess that explains how he can plan so far ahead of us."

"What happened to the seer?" Kaz readjusted his dinner jacket, having not yet changed from Bronx's clothes, and tugged at his shirt collar.

"He died," Bronx said. "There was no time to save him. But at least we could save Ana."

Rei looked back at Ana and her frail form. She thought back to Camila and her eyes filled with tears. Rei couldn't imagine what Camila had suffered in those months with

Praymer. He was always the monster she thought he was, and she was tired of taking the high road.

"Praymer is an animal. We have to tell the star cluster," Rei said, looking over to Manden. "We have to show them what he's capable of. What he did to me. To Camila." She looked in Bronx's direction. "To you. How the Path is actually working for him. It's all been a game to bring me to him. I don't think there was ever going to be peace. But we can still hurt him without violence. Infiernen gave us that footage of what happened between us so we can broadcast it across all planets. And he mentioned a name."

"Felix Royalt. Yes. I have worked with him before, I know who Infiernen meant," said the redhead. "Let's get this video to him so we can start working against Praymer."

"Once the video is broadcasted, then I think we should go into hiding," Crona said.

"Agreed." Artema tugged at one of her dark braids. "Praymer will not like the cluster seeing him for the man he really is."

"What about Nik and Arram?" Kaz asked. "Are we sure Praymer won't do something to them to retaliate?"

Rei regretted what she said to Arram. She was angry at Niko and took it out on her younger brother. She practically handed Praymer leverage against her. "Niko has played a dangerous game with Praymer this whole time, and Arram seems smitten. Like I said, I think they're more useful to him alive. Praymer knows they're my weakness, but killing them outright won't do anything. Chances are, he will try to turn them against me. That'll be the actual weapon."

CHAPTER 38

Arram grew impatient waiting for his brother to wake before finally pouring water over him. Niklaryn gasped as he snapped awake, quickly realizing that someone had tied him to a chair.

"What the . . ." Niklaryn found Arram watching him from another chair in front of him. They were still in the small golden room just outside the ballroom. "Arram, what is this?"

"You and I are going to have a little chat, Infiernen."

Niklaryn's face fell. "Arram, it's not what you think—"

"Shut up. I'm talking." Anekris had warned him that Niklaryn could spread lies, so he had to choose his words carefully, take emotion out of the equation. But pain and anger coursed through him.

"Why did you try to kill me? Why did you shoot me on Trappist V?"

Niklaryn's bottom lip trembled. "It wasn't me," he whispered. "I would never do that to you. It was Infiernen."

Arram didn't think his brother would lie so easily or think his brother was so stupid. "But you are Infiernen."

Niklaryn shook his head. "No. Arram, I have dissociative identity disorder. Infiernen is one of my alters, he is a separate person."

Arram leaned back in his seat. He clasped his hands so tightly he was sure his knuckles were white. "I didn't expect this sort of tall tale." He stood up and leaned forward.

"It's not a tale, brother, I promise you."

"I don't believe you. You wanted me dead because I

would find out you're Infiernen, the man who branded me, shot me in the stomach, hunted me down for years, had your Dogs kill our grandparents." Arram stopped to take a few calming breaths, but blood rushed to his ears as the rage continued to build. "What I want to know is why? Why, Niklaryn?"

Niklaryn gasped, trying to get the words out but failed until his eyes rolled into the back of his head and he passed out.

Arram scoffed and stood. "Well, that was disappointing," he muttered. He slapped Niklaryn's face. "Wake up. I'm not done with you yet."

Niklaryn's appearance rippled and blurred until he was no longer Arram's brother. Infiernen now sat in the chair and his eyes snapped open.

"That was unnecessary, Arram." The voice was distinct. Infiernen's was deeper, and the way his blue eyes watched Arram was more predator-like. Niklaryn was so wide-eyed before.

Arram didn't want to believe that his brother had an alter, but seeing a switch weakened his resolve.

"Nik will not answer your questions because he doesn't know."

Arram furrowed his eyebrows. "Explain."

"When Anekris wanted your sister and your father refused to deliver her, the family went on the run. There were many near misses, and Nik dealt with a lot of trauma."

"I knew our parents were on the run, but DID stems from ongoing trauma. Years of trauma. I thought we were on the run for a few months."

"Your parents were on the run for three years. I stepped up to protect Nik whenever I could. Nik doesn't remember a lot of those three years because of it, and since you were born in that time, it's why he doesn't remember you. But I do."

Arram's face tingled. His eyes burned as tears threatened to form. "But that's unfair."

"It is, but the brain does what it needs to in order to survive. The day your parents died, Niklaryn had to make a choice, save Rei or save you. I made sure he didn't see you so he could do what was more important: save your sister. Some part of him always knew he had made that choice, and it manifested in different ways. I also deal with those emotions, especially his distress over the color purple. Your eyes. A reminder of his failure as a brother."

Arram remembered how Nik first looked at him. The first words his brother spoke were "your eyes."

"Then why did you try to kill me?"

Infiernen's eyes softened. "I knew Nik didn't remember you, and I was worried how he would react if he did. I wanted to spare him the grief, so I thought taking you out would be best for him. But now I'm not so sure."

"Because Nik is curious about me."

Infiernen nodded. "I want to protect Nik from any pain. But maybe your forgiveness is what he needs more."

Arram didn't know what to think. His skin tingled and a heavy feeling sat in his core. Too many emotions ran through him: relief, sadness, confusion, bitterness, and a little empathy. Part of him wanted to forgive his brother, but that meant forgiving Infiernen, and the memory of the bullet tearing through his stomach and the brand on his collar kept those words from passing across his lips.

"So how is working for our parents' killer protecting Nik?"

Infiernen's eyes glowed as though warning Arram not to push the subject further.

"I would ask the same of you, kid. I knew getting close to Praymer meant doing unspeakable things to gain his trust. I didn't want Niklaryn to be the one to do the deeds. I was happy to be painted the monster to keep Nik's reputation safe."

Infiernen was the reason Arram suffered for so many years, being on the run, the loneliness, the feeling of being on the outside of Nik and Rei's little club, almost dying. Nik's sin was not being there, but Infiernen's sin was worse: he knew what he did was wrong and yet his thirst for revenge outweighed his morality.

"He's not the only one who needs my forgiveness."

Arram spun on his heels to leave the room.

"Where are you going?" Infiernen's voice echoed behind him.

"You need some time to think about where you stand. If you want my trust, you need to think about how you're gonna earn it. You've done a shitty job until now."

He returned to the ballroom and wanted to scream. But Aurelia, Ildana, Jenson, and the other guests stood there studying him. He had to maintain his composure.

Anekris was also in the crowd. He had changed into a deep blue suit that made his eyes glow. The sovereign's gaze softened, as though he sensed Arram's distress. Within moments he was at Arram's side, his human hand gently touching the younger Ettowa's shoulder.

"What wrong?"

Arram held his chin up. He refused to let the Negander's words hurt more than they did. "Infiernen said that Nik forgot about me because of his trauma, and he wanted me dead to protect my brother from the guilt of remembering his failure."

Anekris's eyes grew wide. "Wow," he whispered. "To be honest, I never knew that. How are you feeling?"

"Betrayed. I know it's not the right feeling. I shouldn't blame my brother or Infiernen—if this illness is to be believed—because trauma can really mess with someone. It's just unfair that remembering me was the cost of his surviving three years on the run."

"It doesn't make it right. Infiernen did Niklaryn a disservice by doing that."

"Infiernen believes that my forgiveness can help my brother."

"And do you want to forgive him?"

Arram was still reeling from watching Niklaryn turn into Infiernen. A small part of him wanted to dismiss what he saw as an act. But he had a feeling that Nik was just like Rei, lacking the finesse for such a performance. They were both too honest and straightforward for such elaborate lies. He almost felt pity for his brother and his mental illness. Almost.

"I don't know. I'm still trying to process all of this. I was on the run for so many years because of Infiernen, because he wanted me dead. Niklaryn allowed it. Even if I wasn't his brother, he could have stopped Infiernen from hunting down an innocent young boy. But he didn't."

Anekris pressed his lips together. "I think you're right. Perhaps Niklaryn doesn't deserve your forgiveness. But there's no need to decide that right now. Why don't you go to your room and take some time to reflect? I will keep your family company."

Arram nodded. He needed time alone to think, and the lights in the ballroom were too bright to even hear his thoughts.

"I am going to untie Infiernen now," Anekris said. "Unless you are still worried about your safety?"

Arram shook his head. "You can let him go. He's no longer a threat to me." His eyes traveled to Anekris's hands and his thoughts went to the red marks on his sister's neck. Anekris had claimed that he wanted peace, but Arram knew the sovereign was also prone to violence.

"Anekris, did you put a hand on my sister's neck?"

The sovereign's face fell, his blue eyes dimming. "I told you I was ashamed about what transpired between us. I want to work with your sister, but she can say such ugly things."

Arram rolled his eyes. "I can't take you seriously if you threaten the one person who can help us guarantee the peace we want."

"I know. I know. I promise I will never do it again. That's why I need you, Arram. You are just like your father. Jeanh never feared telling me when I was wrong. I have been surrounded by too many yes men who would rather agree with me than make sure I'm on the right path."

Arram let out a sigh. "No wonder she was so angry." The betrayed look on her face flashed in his mind. Between his sister and the sovereign, Anekris was still the more dangerous threat. He needed Arram to stay on the right path and to make sure he didn't decide to use his massive army to wipe out the Federation before Arram could do any good.

"You have to promise me that you are committed to peace with the Federation, Anekris."

The sovereign shook his head vigorously. "I am fully committed. We can't afford to have any threats to us if we want this to work."

Anekris's blue eyes were wide and his lips trembled

ever so slightly. Arram believed him; he believed that Anekris didn't mean to hurt Rei. But Anekris was human and stumbled along the way.

Arram thought back to Infiernen, still tied in the back room. After everything he had learned, the Negander was still a wild card, and Arram wasn't sure they could afford that. "Before I go . . . Infiernen. If I may be honest, I question his allegiance to the Dominion."

Anekris tilted his head. "What makes you say that? Did he say something to you?"

Arram shrugged. "No. I don't know what all he has done over the years to prove his loyalty to you. He knows you killed our parents but doesn't seem fazed by it. But I have a strong feeling that after all of this, he is still loyal only to Nik."

A slow smile crept across Anekris's lips. "I will monitor him. Thank you for your observation."

CHAPTER 39

BRONX FOLLOWED REI OUT OF THE MEDICAL BAY TO AN empty hallway. He wanted to talk to her; he wanted to ask for her forgiveness; he wanted to explain his ability to channel her lightning, but he also didn't want to talk about any of these topics in front of everyone.

"Rei?" His voice was soft, but it was enough to make her turn.

Her eyes still dazzled with lightning brimming underneath, her anger visible.

"Can we talk about Nik?" he asked, but she raised a hand to silence him.

"Not yet. I need to focus on getting this message out at the moment. I can't think about him right now."

"Of course."

He expected her to leave, but her eyes remained on his face. "But I want to know about my lightning. What were you talking about?" she asked.

"Ana told me that reapers can manipulate energy from Volocio they have helped die. Apparently, Atrius could mimic any Volocio ability."

Her lips fell open. "Wow. I'm actually rather jealous that your abilities may outshine mine." She laughed, and it was a beautiful sound.

He smiled, and the pressure in his chest lessened. "While I was being branded, Crona says she saw lightning around my hands."

"So you must have helped a lightning Volocio die, right?"

Bronx shook his head. "Ana thinks it's from you."

"Me?"

"Our bond. She thinks I siphoned the energy from you."

She took a step back, and the pressure in his chest returned.

He took her hands and held them to his chest against his racing heart. "I didn't do it on purpose. I'm not like Praymer; I would never do anything like that to hurt you. I was so worried that if I kept you from using your powers when you needed them the most . . . I . . . I don't know what I would do."

Rei chewed on her lip, and he felt several of her emotions at once until they faded to calm. She squeezed his hands. "I know. I can see how much this worries you, and I know you would never do anything to hurt me. You are not Praymer. That was always obvious." She sighed. "This bond is a nuisance. You feel my emotions and I see yours. Now it turns out you can use my powers? I don't know what to make of that."

"I don't like it either. Part of me wonders if Atrius did something similar to Praymer, allowing him to siphon from other reapers, which is how he has lived for so long."

"Yet if there is a bond, that would mean Atrius is alive. I saw Micaela's memory, he died a horrendous death." Her eyes glazed over and she grew lost in the memory.

Bronx touched her cheek, and she focused on his face again. "You're right. What we have is different. Annoying as it is, I would rather have this than see you lifeless again."

Rei nodded. "I do prefer being alive." She chuckled. "And Ana seems to know what you need. I'm relieved that we have someone to show you what you're capable of."

Bronx smiled. "Yes. Maybe as a reaper there's a way I

can kill him. We are the key to him living this long, maybe we are the way to end it."

"Especially because he can nullify all of us, apparently. We will figure it out together, just like we always do." She tugged on his hand. "We need to talk to Camila and see if she's willing to also condemn Praymer on camera."

He followed Rei, wondering if he should also make a statement. He hated being in front of the camera, but he would do it if Rei asked. Unfortunately, he was attacked by the Path and not Praymer directly. They had no other proof that this terrorist group was in cahoots with Praymer, and telling the star cluster that Praymer could use Bronx as his own personal rechargeable battery was also something he didn't want people to know about.

They found Camila still in talks with Bernie in the lounge where Bronx had passed by earlier. Rei sat next to the young woman while he sat next to Bernie. Camila's face was red and her eyes were full of tears. He remembered the bruises on her collarbone as part of her dress fell to the side and how Praymer had wrapped his arm tighter around the woman as he pulled her away.

His eyes returned to the purple marks around Rei's neck, and Bronx clenched his jaw. If he had been in that room, he would have torn Praymer into pieces for raising a hand to her. She was lucky she had her powers to protect her in that moment before he collared her, but knowing how easy it was to render her vulnerable made his stomach turn.

"She doesn't want to be on camera," Bernie said.

More tears filled Camila's eyes, and she shook her head. "I can't do it. I tried so hard to not encourage his wrath. He will be so angry." Camila whispered the last sentence.

Rei's arm circled around the younger woman's narrow

shoulders. "You don't have to do anything you don't want to."

Tears rolled down Camila's cheek onto her dress, leaving spots on the fine fabric.

"You are safe with us," Bronx said. "No matter what happens, he can't touch you."

"But I am still afraid of what he would do if I denounced him so publicly."

Bronx shook his head. "I didn't mean it like that. Your job is to heal. Nothing more."

"We do need to file a report," Bernie said. "Maybe we can somehow bring him to justice. Would you be willing to do at least that?"

Camila nodded. "I can do that." She wiped her eyes, leaving long streaks of black mascara down her cheeks.

"Then we should get everything ready," Rei said. "If I am doing this myself, I want it over with."

BRONX POINTED THE CAMERA IN REI'S DIRECTION. He tried to catch her eye, but she didn't meet his gaze. Her lips moved silently, and he assumed she was practicing what she had planned to say. Her green eyes focused on Crona, who helped with lighting.

"Too bright?" his sister asked.

Rei pointed to the dark purple mark on her neck. "I want the marks visible on camera."

Once everything was in place, Rei finally looked at Bronx. "Are we ready?"

Bronx nodded. Manden had already contacted this Felix and received the location of where to send the feed for

Felix to forward it to the rest of the Dominion. They set the camera up, and it was ready to go. He pressed the record button, the red light blinking.

"People of Federation and Dominion," Rei began. "Earlier this evening, Anekris Praymer, the god king, and I stood together in unity, hoping to ease the tension between our parties. Praymer's idea of unity is marriage, but I do not agree. We are a modern society where treaties form stronger alliances than this archaic practice. Much to my disappointment, Praymer did not like my decision and attacked me. Unfortunately, there were no Federation witnesses as Praymer tricked me into entering a room by myself, but there is video footage, which I will show.

"I ask that you decide based on the facts I present to you. Take those facts and use your voice, your vote, to help weaken his power. This is a man who can't be trusted to check his temper when he doesn't get his way. Why should he keep such power when he obviously abuses it?" Rei's hand moved up to her neck and her eyes glazed over as she appeared lost in memory.

Bronx's heart raced. He knew that look. He lost himself many times remembering the horrors he had witnessed on the battlefield. He wished he could do something to wipe the memories away, but he couldn't.

"I'm sorry," Rei continued. "After what happened, I knew I had to tell you. You should know what kind of man Praymer truly is. Show the film."

Bronx pressed the button again and her camera turned off. Behind him, Manden sat at a panel where he changed the feed from camera to the video that played across the wall.

Bronx's breathing quickened as he watched Rei enter

the room, presumably with Praymer and Manden. Yet the redhead was not there, and Dante's change of his appearance proved it. Other figures stood in the room, all of them wearing that same nightmarish orange of the Path.

His heart thudded in his ears and he could hardly hear what was being said, but a few phrases filtered through.

"You shut your whore mouth!" Praymer struck Rei, and she stumbled onto her knees. Everyone in the room gasped and Bronx flinched. Praymer's filthy hand eventually wrapped around Rei's neck. The action was hard enough to shove Rei against the wall.

Bronx turned to her and found her shaking. Her eyes remained glued to the screen, determined to face what she had experienced. Crona's arms were already hugging Rei's shoulders, but her hands were free and trembling. He took one of her hands and gave it a gentle squeeze. Rei returned the gesture tightly.

"Thank you both," she whispered.

Bronx returned to the video as it continued. Rei used her lightning to throw Praymer off of her. Then they brought Arram in. Rei and Praymer yelled at each other, but Bronx only heard his breathing. Praymer slit Arram's throat and Rei screamed. Dante and another Negander held her back as she reached for her brother.

Bronx breathed hard, and Rei's hand tightened in his. What he wouldn't give to have been in that room. He would've torn Praymer apart. He would have destroyed everyone in that room for making Rei suffer such a nightmare, even if it was just an illusion.

Rei's eyes glowed white and lightning danced around her body. A flash of light filled the room, and it threw the men off of her.

"Oh shit," Artema said from somewhere in the room.

"Say you'll join me or I'll do it again with Niklaryn. Then I'll torture your lover in front of you," said Praymer with a triumphant smile.

Bronx's heart sank. He didn't realize the implication of showing the video: the star cluster now knew Niklaryn was alive.

Rei said nothing as she stared at Arram's dead body, lightning still flickering across her body. "Fuck. You," she yelled between heaving breaths. Her voice was no longer her own. It took on a tritone quality not unlike Crona when she called the plants in the botanical garden. "Where's Arram?" Her eyes shone white again, and the lightning returned with a vengeance.

Praymer's face fell. "Shit. You can see through the illusion. Collar her. Make sure she doesn't get on the ship with the others."

Bronx closed his eyes as Dante swung something at Rei's head. He couldn't watch, but he heard the thud and the sound of her body crumpling to the ground. When he opened his eyes again, the screen had gone black.

"I knew Praymer killed Micaela," Manden said, breathing hard. "And he killed Max. That monster."

"I cannot imagine how anyone can support someone like him." Kaz ran a hand through his dark hair. "He admitted to creating the Path."

"Ask my brothers," Rei said, letting go of Bronx's hand and gently pulling Crona's arm off her shoulder.

Bronx couldn't imagine what Rei felt. But his hand grew cold after her warmth left it.

"What I want to know is about Rei's eyes," Artema said. "They glowed white. How long has she been able to do that?"

"She has always done that." Manden shrugged. "The first time she used her lightning was to destroy Negander in her village when they burned it and killed her grandparents."

"That's not lightning," Artema whispered.

CHAPTER 40

EVERYONE IN THE ROOM LOOKED TO REI, WHOSE mouth hung open. The words echoed in her head: *not lightning*. It never occurred to her she had wielded anything else. Her eyes sometimes turned white, but she had assumed it happened when she wielded more energy.

"Then what is it?" Rei asked.

"The Fire of St. Erasmus," answered Artema. "Not all lightning Volocio can wield it. Micaela could, as well as her father and other members of the Roya family. It's why that family and the Idamas were always the ones in power. They were known for being able to wield it—but it comes with a price."

Rei's hands tingled and her breathing became more labored. "What price?" she asked.

"What happened after you used the fire? Did you pass out?"

Rei nodded. "I guess. I never realized what I was doing. There have only been a few times I've seen white in my vision before throwing lightning. I only passed out when I used a lot." She pointed to the black screen. "When I used my powers with Praymer, when I thought he had killed Arram, I felt weak afterward, but not enough to pass out."

"It's much stronger than lightning. It's unpredictable and more energy than most Volocio can handle at once. Eventually everyone who can wield it succumbs to it by burning from the inside out. You need to be careful." Artema looked to Manden. "I think it's another reason Rei should go to Tas'und'eash. She should get proper training."

Rei pinched the bridge of her nose with her thumb and forefinger, as if she needed more reason to be wary of her powers. The timing wasn't ideal; there were other issues she needed to focus on. She couldn't stand hearing another reason she needed to go to the Volocio home world.

"I am not going," Rei said. "I just won't use the fire. Simple. I can't afford to leave. I can't leave the cluster just so Praymer can swoop in and take over." She lied through her teeth. She had no idea what she was doing regarding the fire, but it wasn't simple. She was needed here. Only she could keep the star cluster from going to war, and now that she knew about this level of power she possessed, she was the only one who could protect everyone.

The Volocio slowly filtered out of the room, Bronx being the last one, a haze of red surrounding him. "Bronx?" she called out, but he didn't respond. He barely looked in her direction.

She understood his sentiment. Even if she didn't leave for more training, she would be useless to the Federation if she destroyed herself, if she kept using the fire. He wouldn't survive watching her die again. There may come a time where they would need to go to the Volocio planet, but she was still needed here. How would it look if she ran now?

"Are you all right?" asked Crona, who never left Rei's side.

"I'm getting whiplash from these revelations."

"I hear you."

Rei met Crona's aquamarine eyes and thought about the blonde's revelation. She could do more than see the future, she could weaponize plants the same way Manden did. "What about you? How are you feeling about your new gifts?"

Crona gave Rei an impish grin. "It felt great to take

down those Path members with the plants in the botanical garden. It was as though the plants were an extension of myself." She sighed. "I enjoy being able to see the future, but I want to do more on the battlefield. Now I have the tools to do some actual damage." Her grin grew larger. "I will be glorious."

Rei chuckled. "You have always been a force to be reckoned with."

"All will fear me," Crona purred.

They both laughed.

"Honestly, I am glad. We are going to need all the help we can get in the days ahead," Rei said. But that was only if it came to war. Rei was determined to not let that happen. "It would be nice to use the fire. That power is also rather intoxicating."

"I'm sure. But I don't want anything to happen to you either. I would also be tempted if I had access to that kind of power, but a life is a high cost to pay."

Crona was right. Rei needed to make sure she didn't use the fire again. She went in search of Bronx but didn't find him right away. When she finally did, the ship's captain had announced their arrival.

Most of the ships had taken the guests either to Wolf X or Proxima Centauri II, but the ship that held Rei and others went to Gliese VI, back to the Underground.

Urius Boyard and Alma Canale were already at the hangar as Rei, with Camila at her side, descended the ramp. Camila ran to her mother, and the women embraced with tears of joy. Urius only watched as the other Volocio trailed behind.

"I told you talking with Praymer was a terrible idea," Urius said with a smirk. "Next time you should listen to me."

She couldn't believe the nerve of that man. She had let the entire star cluster see her get assaulted by Praymer, and all Urius cared about was that he was right. She clenched her fists until her nails bit into her palms. "You know what else was a terrible idea?" Rei snapped back. "Not telling me my brother is also Infiernen."

Urius's face fell, his hazel eyes snapping in Bronx's direction as the reaper approached. "I told you not to say anything, Manca."

"It wasn't him. Niko told me." Rei put herself between Urius and Bronx. "I understand not wanting the rest of the Federation to know, but I should have known."

"And now, thanks to your little stunt, the whole star cluster knows that your brother is alive."

Rei froze. Praymer had threatened to torture Niklaryn. "And we can tell them that he was a prisoner all these years. He'll remain your little martyr until we can free him."

Urius sighed. "And how long do you think it will take before some hot head like you decides they are going to free their beloved Niklaryn only to discover the truth? Don't you ever think about the repercussions of your actions?"

"I would've had a better idea if you were more forthcoming with me," Rei said. "You should have told me from the beginning why I shouldn't go after Infiernen. You can't only give us half the information and expect us not to question the rest. Had I known then, I wouldn't have risked everyone when we snuck out and flew to Trappist V. Arram wouldn't have been shot. I would have tried a different tactic."

"What kind of tactic? There's nothing you could have done. Your brother is still the enemy. Whether or not his mental illness is real, he still needs to be neutralized."

Rei realized then that Urius didn't believe what

Niklaryn suffered from was real. She shouldn't have been surprised, but perhaps that meant many would see Niklaryn and Infiernen the same way. Rei remembered that Urius didn't know Infiernen was also their ally. She had to pivot quickly. "Fine. But while you have kept this secret because you thought you were doing what's best for the Federation, my actions today were for the same reason. Thanks to me, everyone knows that I don't want to start a war and that Praymer is a violent and petulant child who should have never been given power."

Urius stared at her silently for a few moments. Then he leaned in. "Many already know of his violent tendencies and gladly gave him that power. While you have helped your reputation, you have done little to further sully his." He gestured to Camila and her daughter, and they left the hangar.

Bernie looked around the room. "Shit the bed, Rei, you always know how to antagonize my uncle." A smile broke across her face. "Keep doing it. It's good for him." She then gestured to one of the few remaining vehicles in the hangar. "Shall we head to the Underground? There's hot food waiting for you in the mess hall. What do we do with the white-haired beauty over there?" Bernie pointed to Ana, who slowly made her way out of the ship. Rei was surprised to see the woman bounce back so quickly. She walked, her movements rather slow. Two corpsmen rushed to her side and guided her to the medical bay in the hangar.

"I think she's in excellent hands. You guys go," Rei said before looking at Bronx. "I need to be outside for now."

"Be safe," Bernie said before ushering the others onto the vehicle. They drove away, leaving Rei and Bronx alone.

They stared at each other for what felt like an eternity. There was hardly another sound in the hangar aside from a few faraway voices and the occasional clank of tools being used. They had yet to talk about Niklaryn, Praymer, any of it. Rei wanted them to have privacy, and they would find none in the Underground. They had already worked past what happened on Praymer's ship, but Rei had yet to say the words. A part of her felt that they couldn't truly move on until the words finally passed through her lips.

"I forgive you for not telling me," she said finally.

Bronx's shoulders relaxed. "I should have told you anyway." He took a step closer to her.

"I get it. I would tear the universe apart to keep you from feeling pain. I shouldn't be surprised about the lengths you would go to keep me from feeling it too." She also drew closer to him.

"I hate myself for keeping it from you."

"Don't. I still love you."

His face broke into that beautiful smile she loved so much. Then he raised an eyebrow. "The best lover you've ever had, eh?"

Rei laughed. He at least heard her announce that in the video with Praymer. "Indeed. But you already knew we make a great team in all things. The tart and the bastard."

"I can hear the ballads about us now."

They chuckled. She threw her arms around his neck, and his arms wrapped around her waist. They held each other for a long time, and it felt so good to be in his arms again. His scent of lavender and sage washed over her, and she felt safe.

Urius may be right—perhaps her actions did little to further their cause. If seeing Praymer for what he truly was still didn't sway voters, then they had to find another way to take him down.

"Where do you want to go?" Bronx asked.

"Let's go to our place," she said, pulling back. "I need to get away from everyone else and just be with you."

CHAPTER 41

Arram had taken a long nap in his room and woke feeling refreshed. Infiernen's words no longer stung like before. In fact, he didn't really care what he or Niklaryn had to say. Niklaryn didn't feel like a sibling to him, not the way Rei was. His mood darkened again. He missed her. He wished he could talk to her, but she was hurt by him not returning with her to the Federation. He was sure once he could assure peace, everything would return to normal.

Arram's room had sea green damask walls and wooden furniture with beautiful designs carved into the frames, the wood stained a deep brown with hints of red. After years of being on the run with his grandparents and spending the last six months campaigning, he longed to be in a place that claimed stability. His grandparents could never have afforded such beautiful furniture. It was too expensive to move about. Their campaigning lodging also held an air of temporary minimalist furniture in white, lacking color and personality.

He could get used to this kind of wealth.

Arram's suit was wrinkled. It was the same pale blue that Crona had worn to the wedding. He missed her too. She was more set in her ways than his sister. Maybe once things worked out with his sister, she could help him with Crona. He didn't like the way she looked at him before she left, as though she didn't recognize him.

He ruffled through the nearby wardrobe and found a black suit that shared a similar pattern to what Anekris wore earlier. He quickly changed and stepped out of his room to find Infiernen—or Niklaryn—leaning against the opposite wall.

"Which one are you?" Arram asked.

"Infiernen."

"Does Niklaryn not want to talk to me?"

The Negander shook his head. "After you yelled at him? I don't think it's a good idea. He's not in a good place right now."

"*He's* not in a good place? What about me? What about making sure I am also in a good place?"

"My job is to take care of Nik. Honestly, I don't care how you are dealing with it."

Infiernen's words echoed Rei's just before she left the ship. He didn't care. Naturally.

"Of course not." Arram turned on his heels and strode down the hallway. The echoing click on the metal floors indicated that Infiernen wasn't far behind.

"So why are you here, Infiernen?"

"You sister uploaded something on the Nexus you need to see. Praymer sent me to fetch you and bring you to the bridge."

This was it. He was already too late and Rei had said something that could damage what goodwill Anekris may have felt toward his sister.

Arram and Infiernen entered the ship's bridge to find an angry Anekris stringing a slew of curse words together that would have made even Rei blush.

"What happened?" Arram asked, approaching the sovereign, who stared murderously at the screen.

"Play the video so Arram can watch," Anekris said with a wave of his hand.

Arram felt Dante's presence before he saw the manservant appear in the corner of his eye. Dante brushed some lint off of Arram's shoulder, then gently squeezed Arram's arm before approaching a panel to start the video. He almost pulled away, but he didn't.

The screen in front of him flickered on, and Rei's face appeared front and center. She looked haggard, her lips pressed together until there was nothing more than a line, and deep shadows appeared below her eyes.

"People of Federation and Dominion," Rei began, "earlier this evening, Anekris Praymer, the god king, and I stood together in unity, hoping to ease the tension between our parties." The video glitched. "But I do not agree. We are a modern society where treaties form stronger alliances than this archaic practice. Much to my disappointment, Praymer did not like my decision and attacked me. Unfortunately, there were no Federation witnesses as Praymer tricked me into entering a room by myself.

"I ask that you decide based on the facts I present to you. Take those facts and use your voice, your vote, to help weaken his power. This is a man who can't be trusted to check his temper when he doesn't get his way. Why should he keep such power when he obviously abuses it?" Rei's hand moved up to her neck to the purple shadows on her skin.

"I'm sorry," Rei continued. "After what happened, I knew I had to tell you. You should know what kind of man Praymer truly is."

The screen went black. He didn't notice the purple on her neck before. It was red when he last saw her.

Arram let out a growl of frustration and turned to Anekris. "Well done. Your moment of weakness has given my sister the fuel she needed to tell the star cluster."

Arram's eyes then caught Infiernen, who remained

staring at the screen. The Negander's jaw clenched in anger, yet the screen remained black.

"Infiernen?" Arram asked. "What are you looking at?"

Infiernen shook his head. "Can't you see?"

Arram was confused, and Infiernen appeared to give him the same look. His blue eyes darted to Dante and then to the sovereign.

"What are you looking at, Infiernen?" Anekris's voice was dangerously low.

Both men stared at each other. Arram didn't understand completely, but he understood the body language enough to know that the sovereign was testing Infiernen. Something the Negander did made Anekris doubt him. It would appear Anekris listened to Arram.

"Nothing," said Infiernen finally.

"Good," snapped Anekris. "Dante, make sure we find out where the video is being fed from and block it. No one else on this ship should see it either. What's important is that Rei is determined to remain my enemy. I tried talking to her, but she won't listen. She listens to you. You had her convinced before."

"I know. We also know what changed." If only Arram had reached out to Rei before to at least send her a message and remind her to stay calm and not lash out. He had an uphill battle if he didn't want either party to start escalating the situation.

Anekris shook his head. "She said very hurtful things to me. And I also apologized."

But Arram didn't apologize to his sister. He remembered their fight, the moment before Rei left him on the ship. His sister could be cruel. She knew what words did the most damage. He was going to have to do some damage control before Rei would even listen to him, nonetheless Anekris.

His thoughts returned to the purple marks around her neck. They looked like a handprint. He remembered her neck being red, so whatever Anekris did, it wasn't that terrible. Perhaps she painted her neck to make it look worse. She had a tendency to blow things out of proportion.

Right after her resurrection on Kepler IV Rei discovered that Anekris was the one who murdered her parents, and she went on a tirade. She was ready to bring the whole star cluster down on the man. Her eyes turned white, and she wanted to blast a hole into the first object she could find. It took Arram a long time to calm her down. She wanted war, she wanted to use everyone to get what she wanted, but Arram had to remind her that this was bigger than her, than their family. People didn't deserve to die in her war for vengeance. It took even longer after that to convince her that diplomacy and stripping Anekris of his power was the better, bloodless route. He feared everything that transpired between Rei and Praymer set her several steps back again.

"She needs time to cool off. She's likely in the Underground—" Arram stopped. He hadn't meant to say that out loud.

"The Underground," Anekris repeated, his voice growing soft. "So it exists?" Anekris drew closer to Arram, his mouth turned down into a frown. "I don't need to know where it is. I can give you a ship and you can talk to her. I am still so distressed with how things ended between your sister and me. We need to try again so she can apologize for saying these awful things. My courtiers will not like Rei's actions and will consider it an act of war. We need to act quickly."

Arram was frustrated. He had to clean up both of their

messes because neither could control their tempers. "Sure. But give me a small shuttle. If I show up in one of your ships, they could blast me out of the sky before I have time to talk to her."

"You'll need a slightly bigger ship than a shuttle to get you there quickly. I can make sure the ship stays outside of range, and you can take a shuttle down."

Arram nodded. Anekris was right, they may not have enough time.

"I'll go with you," Infiernen said.

"I don't think that's necessary." Anekris waved a hand dismissively. "We need to reunite your Infinity Dogs. I have a job for them coming up."

"I should get going," Arram said. "It will take me a few hours to get there, and I don't want to waste any more time."

CHAPTER 42

Bronx drove Rei to Yticol in one of the vehicles from the hangar. They sat in silence as they journeyed under the stars. It had to be close to midnight.

Rei opened her window, and the night air blew in, tugging at her brown locks.

"Storm's coming," she said after a time, a small smile growing on her lips. "It should be here by morning."

He parked the car outside the village and they crossed the bridge hand in hand to the old city floating in the middle of the lake. Its twinkling lights welcomed them home.

All the while, Bronx thought about his next steps. After learning about Rei's ability with this "fire" and the fact that she was still not convinced to go to Tas'und'eash, his anxiety grew. There were so many things piling against them both, he had to figure out a solution to at least one of their problems.

Before their ship landed on the planet, he went to Ana to ask her if she knew how to stop Praymer. Or if she even knew where Praymer learned his abilities to siphon energy from reapers.

"I don't know," she said.

"Is there a way to kill Praymer?"

Ana frowned. "We are trying to find out how."

"Do you think Cesar may have a better idea?"

Her eyebrows furrowed. "You could always ask him. He has more knowledge of a reaper's abilities than anyone."

"Is Cesar in the star cluster?"

Ana shook her head. "No. He is in the Land of the Dead. He no longer walks among the living like we do. If you want to talk to him, meet him in Hamastagan."

Bronx winced. He had not tried to return to the Land of the Dead since he brought Rei back to life. He knew he should if he wanted to learn more about his abilities, but until recently, there wasn't a reason to do more. At least that's what he told himself. Truth was he wasn't sure if he could return. He didn't know how he got there to begin with, other than in his desperation to save Rei.

Ana seemed to sense his dilemma. She leaned in and said, "Star of Saskia can help you reach the meditative state necessary to reach the Land of the Dead."

Luckily, Crona always had plenty.

Bronx and Rei arrived at the Rose House Inn, where they had a standing room whenever they wanted privacy away from the Underground. The energy was calmer than the frenzy of the hidden base.

The front desk was still open and one of the owner's, Kirsty, greeted the pair with a smile and the key to their room.

There was even a message for Rei. "Can you hold it until tomorrow? We've had a long day, and I just want to get into our room."

She gave Bronx a look that promised what they would do when they finally got into said room.

Everything was just as they left it. They had taped photographs on the full-length mirror. Rei's staff leaned against it. Their pile of clothes remained unmoved on one of the chairs.

Rei opened the window to watch the harbor, the lion, and the lighthouse in full view. Despite the late hour, voices of the people walking the boardwalk reached their room.

Bronx joined her, wrapping his arms around her, and she leaned back against his chest. They wouldn't be able to stay long, not with Praymer most likely wanting to hunt both of them. But he wanted to enjoy the stillness now, to have the memory and hold it tight for the time to come.

He buried his nose in her hair, taking in her scent of vanilla and sandalwood. Her sweet scent settled into his brain, leaving room for little else but the thought of her. She twisted in his grasp and found his lips with hers. How he loved the way her soft curves fit against his body. She was made for him, the universe made sure of it. How else were they able to find each other in multiple lifetimes if they weren't already two pieces of a perfect puzzle?

"Rei," he whispered into her mouth and she responded with a light nip of his lower lip.

Her hands wove into his hair, giving it a playful tug. A moan escaped him as she arched against him. She was lightning incarnate. The touch of her skin was electric, sending currents through him, violent and sudden. He could never get enough of her, could never satiate his need for her.

He gently peeled off her layers of her top and she reciprocated. Her fingers shook in the same way his knees felt.

"I can't bear it if something happened to you." He needed more, he always needed more. Desire coursed through him as he watched gooseflesh prickle across her breasts.

"Nothing is going to happen to me. We will get through this."

He took her face in both hands and kissed her. Rough, deep, messy, breathless. Her hands pull on the loops of his trousers, unbuttoning them, freeing him. Their kiss deepened, his tongue in her mouth, his teeth on her lips.

She pulled away ever so slightly. "But let's not focus on

what we just went through and what awaits us tomorrow," she continued. "I just need to lose myself with you."

He led her towards the bed, his hands tugging on the clasp of her trousers. He lowered her onto the mattress with careful tenderness yet removed the rest of her clothes with feral abandon.

They started gentle but it didn't last long. He grew tired of his restraint and lifted her, pressing her against the wall. She met his rhythm, calling his name. Her voice cast a spell over him whenever she did. Then she gave another cry as she came apart around him. He took her in several more places in the room before allowing his own release. He needed to feel alive, to feel safe, to lay himself completely bare for her.

He never forgot those years he receded from human touch for fear of killing those he loved. He never wanted to feel that emptiness again. It was likely why he always struggled to stop. He couldn't get enough of the taste of her, the feel of her skin against his. He could never gain back those years, but having Rei in his arms more than made up for them.

They fell asleep, her head on his chest. Her favorite place, she called it. It was his as well.

But sleep never came. He worried too much. Praymer was bound to search the cluster to find him or Rei at whatever cost, and he couldn't help but worry what Arram would tell him. He worried about Rei's welfare, but he feared for his own. He never wanted to experience that feeling of having his energy pulled from him, especially from Praymer. He needed answers, and no one alive had any.

Eventually Rei rolled over to her other side, freeing him. He stood quietly and opened his bag. His sister was kind enough to give him a few buds from her Star of Saskia stash.

Taking a whole bud was out of the question. Watching his sister the first time she did that was warning enough. On the far side of the room sat a small table with a pitcher of water. It wasn't hot, but hopefully the flower would steep. An icy breeze trailed in through the window. He quickly shut the blinds, plunging the room further into darkness.

He returned to the bed and drank the water. It probably wasn't enough, but he was too wary to do more with the flower for now. Once he drained the cup, he laid back down next to Rei and tried to meditate. His eyelids grew heavy.

He fell into a deep sleep, the smell of lavender tickling his nose. He floated weightlessly as he dipped further into slumber. Then he slammed onto the ground and his eyes sprang open.

It worked—he had returned to the golden forest of Hamastagan, and the black earth had taken the brunt of his fall.

He scrambled to his feet and scanned the area, but not a reaper could be found, not even the white-cloaked dead were in the vicinity.

"Cesar?" he called, but no answer came.

He wandered down the path, toward what he assumed to be the river and boat. He didn't know how long he walked; the path stretched on forever. He recalled running down this path, running toward Rei to bring her back to life.

"Hello?" he called again. The forest absorbed his voice, as though preventing it from traveling further.

Bronx wandered more until he finally reached the riverbank. The empty boat floated lazily, gently bumping into the pier.

"Gods dammit," he muttered. He was probably just

dreaming then, and he didn't take enough of the flower. His heart raced at the thought of having failed.

"Bronx?" Cesar appeared at his side, startling him.

"Am I dreaming?"

"Not entirely. You're not fully corporeal in Hamastagan."

Bronx scanned the area again. The emptiness was too unnerving. "Is that why I can only see you?"

"Yes. What's wrong?"

"Did you know that Anekris Praymer has been using reapers to keep himself alive?"

Cesar's face fell. His dark eyes watched the boat that bobbed slightly on the riverbank. "I feared so when I couldn't contact Ananiel."

"She's with us. We found her on Praymer's ship."

Cesar exhaled. "She is alright then?"

"As well as she can be. She's still rather weak. Her hair is white and her body has aged."

Cesar pressed his lips together. "I don't know how Anekris does it," he said. "Blood magic is a powerful way to manipulate energy. I don't know how to stop Anekris, but I know Atrius had something to do with it."

Blood magic. It was Praymer's blood that could negate any power of the Volocio. He wondered if it negated a reaper's powers as well.

"How do you know it was Atrius?"

"He was powerful and knew how to manipulate energy in ways no other reaper could, in ways no other Volocio could. He also knew the amplifying properties of blood magic. It's no surprise that you have the same potential. Only Atrius would have had the power to break his soul into two and give it to another."

"Do you think Atrius did for Praymer what I did for Rei?"

Cesar shook his head. "No. He tied Praymer to this place and allowed that man access to regenerate himself."

"How did he tie Praymer to Hamastagan?"

"Through a talisman. Atrius had to use an object to connect them, but I don't know what it is or where it is."

"And you have been searching for it?"

"Of course. Unfortunately, this forest is vast, and I am bound to it. However, the other reapers you've met are still alive in both Tyre and Tas'und'eash. They are also searching, but without Atrius, there's no way to know."

A voice whispered his name, a man's voice. It was faint and Bronx wasn't sure if he actually heard it. He looked out at the river toward the mist beyond. Something called to him and he shuddered. He took a step toward the water, toward the mist, toward the voice that sounded so familiar. His eyes rested on a small canoe at the edge of the river. For a moment, he considered taking it to follow the voice, but he couldn't. Not yet.

"Do you know where I can find the other reapers? Would Ana know?"

Cesar shook his head. "They move about a lot. It's hard to pinpoint where they are at any given moment. But you'll know when you see them."

Bronx gasped as fear shot through his heart.

"What's wrong?" Cesar asked.

Bronx looked at the golden sky, where he had fallen from. Rei's voice was faint in the wind, but he heard it. Her yells were growing louder. Something was wrong.

"I have to go," Bronx said and disappeared.

CHAPTER 43

It started with a pop, then another, and another, gently waking Rei. More came, and at first, she assumed it was hail; she knew a storm was coming. She tried to focus on returning to sleep, but the popping kept increasing in intensity. Her heartbeat also increased. It wasn't a storm.

Rei turned in bed to find Bronx still asleep. She touched his shoulder to wake him, but he didn't respond. Just beyond, Rei noticed the blinds had been closed, but a dim red light still filtered through. Rei approached the window and opened the blinds, her heart hammering in her chest. They swung open, revealing several buildings across the waterfront on fire. The popping came from the thin stone walls that exploded from the heat. The screams from the streets were louder, and through the roar of the blaze, Rei heard gunshots.

Rei watched in horror as a battleship hovered over the lake like a proud predator that had found its prey.

"Bronx!" she shouted. "They found us!" She whirled around and found he still hadn't moved. "Bronx?" She grabbed his shoulders and gently shook him, only then noticing the mug on his nightstand and the smell of Stars of Saskia on his lips.

His eyes fluttered open, but he was alert once he met Rei's face. "What happened?" he asked.

"The Dominion. They're here."

"The Underground!" He quickly rose, and they threw on clothes and packed what they could. Rei grabbed her staff and followed him out of the hotel and into the street.

Yticol erupted in a panic, people screaming and running combined with the rat-tat-tat of gunfire and the deep rumble of thunder. Several people fell as the bullets found their targets. The coppery smell of blood and ash filled her nose.

One man held his son and ran past Rei and Bronx through the streets. They sought refuge in a building across the harbor, only to have it burst into a pillar of flame as a bomb fell on top. The roar pounded in Rei's ears even from the distance, and the heat burned her cheeks.

Bronx and Rei made their way out of the city and across the little bridge to the mainland where they had left their vehicle. Several others ran around them, also trying to flee the city. Burn marks covered some, and several were crying. Yticol burned in a fiery blaze behind them.

Rei rushed to the passenger side just as Bronx reached over to unlock the door for her. She hopped in and shut the door as the first bomb fell, followed by the sound of buildings in the town crumbling and more screams.

Bronx put the truck in first gear, and they roared through the country road. Another bomb fell right where the truck stood moments before. Debris flew and crashed into the back window of the truck. Bronx never moved his eyes off the road, but Rei looked through the open top of their vehicle to find a Dominion aero fighter following them. Another bomb dropped to their right, almost flipping the truck on its side. The mansion that led to the Underground drew closer. They were almost there, but then what? The fighter could still fire upon them.

Just on the other side of the lake flames engulfed several other villages. Even from the distance, Rei heard the cries of despair as their homes succumbed to the destruction. More bombs fell, shaking the ground beneath them. This was more than personal, it was pure chaos for the sake of violence.

An enormous bolt of lightning fell from the sky, striking the fighter above them. The fighter wavered in the air for a moment before crashing into the lake on their left. This gave Rei an idea.

Bronx pulled the truck up to the entrance of the mansion and stopped. The couple piled out and ran up the steps. Rei stopped at the top and turned to face the battleship, which remained above the lake.

"What are you doing?" Bronx asked.

"Just wait," she said calmly, closing her eyes. The air was alive with electric currents, more so than she had ever felt before. It was like holding her staff, which remained inconveniently in the vehicle.

Rei brought her hand straight in the air above her head, then down in front of her. She aimed her hand like a gun, two fingers pointing at the battleship in front of her. Rei waited, expecting a gigantic bolt of lightning to fall from the sky like the finger of a god to strike down the evil battleship. What she received was the lightning bolt; however, it struck an old tree to her right. Sparks flew, showering her until Bronx grabbed her and pulled her into the doorway.

"What was that?" he asked.

An experiment gone wrong, thought Rei. Before she could say the thought out loud, the battleship dropped one, two, three bombs on various places on the lake, followed by a frightening moment of silence as the world slowed down.

A roar reverberated from the lake and the ground lurched violently beneath them. The couple held each other tight as the ground moved. Suddenly it stopped; however, the roar continued. Bronx looked at Rei and by the look in his eyes she knew he was asking the same question: *Where did it come from?*

Rei and Bronx looked back out toward the lake. They approached the shore for a closer look and found the source of the sound. The bomb had hit its mark and plunged beneath the water, passing the layer of earth that protected the Underworld from the outside. Roaring water gushed into the secret base.

"Crona!" Bronx cried, turning to rush into the mansion to enter the Underground. Rei followed, but another explosion leveled the mansion, throwing the two back.

"No!" cried Bronx, climbing to his feet. He tried to rush back into the crumbled, smoking building, but Rei's arm wrapped around his waist, holding him back.

"We can't get in from here," she called. "They would go to the hangar. They'll meet us there."

"Are you sure?" He turned and looked at her, his dark eyes wild with fear.

"She had to have seen this coming." Rei prayed she was right.

He led her back to the truck. "Let's go to the hangar, quickly, before another aero tries to find us."

Sure enough, another fighter flew lazily above them.

Bronx drove away from the mansion into the forest that surrounded it. Neither of them had traveled to the hangar above the surface before, but they knew which direction to take. Mount Environ loomed ahead of them, guiding them to the hangar hidden at the base.

Rei looked through the hole in the truck's top to see that Dominion fighter still following them. The thick trees masked the fighter, but that also meant that they could not be seen. Rei looked ahead. The trees quickly thinned and soon the forest would end, leaving nothing to hide them.

"Just keep driving; I've got another idea," Rei said, standing in the truck, a foot in her seat and the other on the dashboard for support. Rei stuck her upper body through the hole in the top just as the trees cleared away. She stuck her hand out to the side, dragging it through the air and charging the surrounding energy. Then she threw the hand up, aimed at the fighter above them, and fired. A bolt of lightning shot from her fingertips and struck the fighter. She watched as sparks danced around the fighter, but it still flew.

Rei brought her hand to the side again and gathered more energy. She raised her hand once more and shot lightning at the fighter. This time smoke spewed from the engine, and soon the fighter fell.

"Drive faster!" Rei cried to Bronx. "I think it's going to fall on top of us!" The fighter fell further, inching closer and closer to their truck.

"I got it!" Bronx yelled. "Hold on," he said before making a hard left.

It crashed in a blaze of fire. The heat reddened Rei's cheeks. No one else followed them as they made their way to the hangar.

Manden was already there. The wrench in his hand revealed he was working on the *Luciernaga*.

"You guys are all right!" The redhead gasped as he hugged each. "The others?"

"The Dominion destroyed the Underground," Rei said.

"Fuck!" Manden yelled.

Rei turned to the tunnel. They were the only ones in the area. No one came from the tunnel by way of the Underground. Rei shook with anger. If the others didn't make it, she would rain hellfire on the Dominion. Visions flooded her mind of her hometown going up in flames. It was no different than Yticol in flames. It was Ballarat all over again. Flickers of white hummed along the edges of her vision.

A rumble echoed in the tunnel, and Rei could have sworn it sounded like an engine. Bronx ran toward the sound. Once inside, he turned the corner and disappeared. Rei and Manden waited in silence, save for the distant sounds of Yticol being destroyed. Then Bronx returned. A look of relief shone in his dark eyes. Shortly afterward, the transport vehicle from the Underground arrived with water dripping down the sides. Crona was behind the wheel and Artema sat at her side. Kaz and Bernie sat on the bed in the back, sopping wet. They were alive.

Crona jumped out of the vehicle and into her brother's arms. Kaz and Artema ran to Rei for a group hug.

"I wanna join!" Manden said, throwing his arms around the group.

"Urius?" Bronx asked. He was no longer hugging his sister, but still kept an arm around her shoulders.

"He's gone." Bernie's voice trembled, her eyes red. "I was in his office earlier, before the Underground was hit. We were discussing the future and . . . and . . . and I left and ran into the Volocio." She let out a shaky sigh. "There was no way he or anyone else could have survived it. We only survived because Crona saw it." Bernie rubbed her cheeks furiously as fresh tears streamed down her face.

"We should keep moving," Manden said. "The Dominion will probably find the hangar soon. We should get out of the atmosphere before they notice us."

"Don't forget Ana," Bronx said. "She's likely still in the medical area here."

The Volocio made their way up the ramp of the *Lucier-naga*, while Bernie went to fetch the reaper. Only Rei stood still, her throat dry from rushed breathing. She gripped her staff tightly until her knuckles ached. Everyone else was gone, not just Urius. Camila and Alma—they just had their reunion only to drown. The Volocio may be alive, but who else must pay for Praymer's madness?

He had wanted to push her to start a war. He got it.

"Rei?" Bronx appeared in the corner of her eye as more white spots clouded her vision.

She approached the wide opening of the hangar. Her eyes focused on the ship that hung above the remains of the lake, now much smaller than before. Yticol continued to burn off to the left. Praymer had come for her home. Had come for her. He was going to pay.

"Rei?" The concern in Bronx's voice was almost palpable, but she couldn't focus on him. She could only see the ship.

She took a deep breath and screamed. She screamed and screamed, her voice unearthly and powerful, taking on a strange tone. The sound echoed from some unknown place, then multiplied, taking on the form of all the victims who died in the Underground. She cried harder and harder, straining her lungs. She raised her staff in the air, calling on the heavens to aid her.

As she felt the end of her breath, she threw her hand up and shoved it through the air. In response, the air crackled as she surrounded herself in the white light.

Then lightning struck her staff, filling her with power. That intoxicating energy that filled her when she laid waste to those Negander on Ballarat filled her. She felt a taste for it again when she confronted Praymer. The delicious electricity tore through her veins, threatening to burn away her name, her sense of self. She would have welcomed it to become one with this force. But she couldn't—she wanted to destroy that ship.

Rei threw her hands forward. Lightning came flying toward the ship above, slicing through the beast straight down the middle, and the whole broke into two in an explosion of lightning and fire. The pieces tumbled to the ground, but Rei didn't see where they landed. Instead, her eyes rolled in the back of her head and her knees buckled. She was vaguely aware of hands catching her before everything went dark.

CHAPTER 44

Arram watched in horror as Yticol burned below him. He raced to a nearby screen to get a closer look. Sure enough, figures in orange robes ran through the streets of the city, gunning down anyone crossing their path.

The Path had decided their next target. Yticol was Urius's hometown. Maybe they didn't know the Underground also resided here.

He had to move quickly; Rei could be in danger.

"How long until my shuttle is ready?" Arram asked the captain of the ship.

"It should be ready to go, sir. I suggest you make haste."

Arram was already out of the bridge, running as fast as he could to the hangar. The ship lurched slightly under his feet, but he didn't falter.

He made it to the smaller shuttle and gave the pilot a quick nod as the door closed. His heart raced as he willed the shuttle to move faster.

The shuttle left the dock just as a gigantic bolt of lightning exploded through the middle of the ship. The shock wave threw Arram and his shuttle to the side. Thankfully, the Negander driving the shuttle kept them from spiraling.

Arram watched as one half of the ship fell into the lake, toward the Underground, while the other half fell on Yticol. It landed on the burning city in a plume of blaze and smoke. His heart hammered in his chest and he lost feelings in his legs. He grabbed the chair next to his pilot and sat down before he collapsed.

Only one person could wield that much lightning.

"She . . ." the rest of the words died on Arram's lips. She was safe, that much was certain. He didn't understand why Rei would do that. She was likely spooked by a Dominion ship, but he had sent a message to her in the Underground. He sent it to that hotel she and Bronx frequented. He shook his head. There was no way she could possibly still be mad at him. The Path must've fueled her anger.

Arram closed his eyes and covered his face with both hands. Her anger created so much power.

Several Federation fighters appeared in the air, as did those from the Dominion, and a firefight broke out where the ship floated earlier. Arram growled in frustration as the fight erupted in the sky.

"We have to get out of here," the Negander said.

"Agreed."

There was no point in trying to talk to Rei now, and the thought made him sad. Even among the blasts and fire in the sky, Arram was sure he saw the *Luciernaga* flying off and out of the atmosphere.

He would have to find another way to communicate with Rei.

Arram switched on the communication screen at the back of the shuttle, and Anekris's face appeared after a few moments of Arram tapping his foot impatiently. Anekris must've noticed Arram's expression.

"What happened?" the sovereign asked.

"Rei . . ." Arram's voice failed him. "She destroyed the ship. Broke it in two. I've never seen lightning do that."

A wrinkle appeared on Anekris's forehead, and he chewed his lip before answering. "Are you sure about what you saw?"

Arram nodded, but he felt disjointed from his body. "Not everything. I was getting onto the shuttle as everything went down, but as soon as it left the dock, I saw the lightning split the ship in two and it fell onto the planet. Half of the ship fell on the lake." The hair on the back of Arram's neck rose and he came to the realization: right on top of the Underground. Arram shuddered at the thought of something happening to those people in the base. They wouldn't know what hit them until it was too late. "I can't believe my sister is capable of such power."

Anekris sighed. "Micaela could do that. It's what made her dangerous. Too dangerous. I worried that your sister would dabble in the same darkness as my Micaela." He shook his head. "I fear the power will go to her head and she'll call for war."

Arram gasped. "She wouldn't. She doesn't want war. I know her."

"Do you? You only met her less than a year ago, and a Volocio raised her with the expectation of ruling."

Arram looked out the window of his shuttle at the burning city below. Rei had loved this city so much, yet she dropped a ship on it.

He hadn't liked her when they first met. She was haughty and proud, which he didn't understand. She grew up in a one-horse town and had no remarkable education to speak of. He originally assumed she was the product of incest like the other slack-jawed yokels in Ballarat.

Once they were thrown into the Federation together and got to know each other, his opinion of her had changed. He wondered if his initial instinct about her was right. Not the incest, naturally, but that she lacked the finesse of an effective political leader. It was why she always came to Arram. She needed him and he needed her. She was the reason he improved and became more confident with his powers. He thought they were really bonding over the last six months.

Dread pooled in his stomach as the truth finally dawned on him: he would never matter to her as much as Nik.

Maybe Anekris was right, and he didn't know his sister at all.

"How bad is the carnage?" Anekris asked.

"The Path had arrived and wreaked havoc on the city. I think Rei was already backed into a corner, and seeing a Dominion ship made it worse. I watched one half fall on what was left of Yticol."

Anekris cursed. "Of course. The Path attacked just as we arrived. She's going to think we did this."

Arram's jaw hung open. "You're right." His eyes turned to the fiery pandemonium below. The pillar of smoke that rose from the city skewed part of his view. Then he scanned the lake above the Underground. The water level looked much lower than before. He prayed the people of the Underground were safe, but he didn't know the damage a fallen ship could cause.

"Come back to me." Anekris's voice brought Arram out of his reverie. He met the sovereign's sapphire gaze. "We need to take stock with this recent development," Anekris continued, "and figure out what our next step is going to be."

Arram's heart skipped a beat as Anekris said to come back. He wanted to return, but he didn't want to leave any loose ends.

"But what about my sister? I still need to talk to her."

Anekris shook his head. "I don't think she's in a talking mood right now. Not if she did that. Come back and we'll ride the storm together. I'll come to you."

Together. He liked how that sounded, to be a part of something and not in the shadow of it.

"After what I saw, I am going to need a drink." Arram ran a hand through his hair.

Anekris smiled. "Me too, friend."

CHAPTER 45

Bronx caught Rei as she fainted. His arms wrapped around her shoulders and under her knees as he lifted her. Her smoking staff clattered to the ground, but Artema was nearby to scoop it up. The two watched as the ship above broke into two pieces and plunged in a shower of smoke and fire.

"We have to get on the *Luciernaga* now," Artema said.

Bronx said nothing as he followed her, carrying Rei into the ship. The hatch closed quickly behind them and Artema called to Manden in the cockpit that they should leave.

Bronx took Rei to the infirmary in the back and gently laid her on one of the beds. He grabbed a health scanner and looked her over. It was the same as when she was first brought to him, when they first met. This "fire" had left her unconscious again.

"Shit the bed," Bernie said, leaning against the doorframe. "It's just like Ballarat. I didn't think I would see her go full god-mode again unless we were at war." Bronx turned to the woman to find her eyes still red. Her blonde curls tore free from their tie, making her look like a cornered wild animal. They were all feeling cornered.

"Are you all right?" he asked.

Bernie shook her head and wiped her face vigorously. "I don't want to talk about it. Did you know she could break ships in half?"

Bronx's gaze returned to Rei's face. "No. Turns out she can wield some kind of fire lightning."

"It's not normal lightning?"

"No. It's called the Fire of St. Erasmus. There are some lightning Volocio who can wield it, and it's dangerous. Artema says many succumb to it."

Bernie drew nearer and stood across from Bronx, Rei lying between them. "And here I was hoping I could have her use her powers to destroy Praymer's ship with him in it. He has to pay for what he's done."

"You know Rei would do it. I just don't want it at the expense of her life."

"I know."

Bronx thought about what he saw. Rei's eyes had gone white, and the lightning struck her staff, filling her with a godlike light. He understood how the presence of the Volocio created the religion all those thousands of years ago. They probably appeared equally godlike among the humans as Rei did in that moment.

He didn't want to leave Rei, but he followed Bernie up the metal stairs to the cockpit where Manden, Crona, Artema, Ana, and Kaz were waiting. A video played just above Manden's controls, a Federation news channel showing clips from another burning city. Just outside the ship, Bronx saw they had already entered the Alcubierre-Krasnikov tunnel. It's nebulous form with a bright light at the end was all that filled the ship's window.

"The Path has attacked the capital," said Kaz through gritted teeth. "The Federation council is gone."

"The Path did it? Fuck," muttered Bernie, pinching her nose with her thumb and forefinger. "I was so sure it was the Dominion."

"It was," Crona said. "The Path has been working for Praymer the whole time."

Bernie responded with even more colorful curse words. "Did you find proof while you were on Praymer's ship?"

"They were on that video of Praymer hurting Rei," Manden said.

Bronx winced at the memory of her alone, surrounded by Praymer and those orange-robed fools, but he noticed the convenient detail that no one wore the gryphon band across their forehead. His jaw clenched as he remembered Praymer calling Rei a whore.

"I have a feeling Praymer is going to fight to have that video suppressed in the Dominion." Bronx rolled his eyes. He hoped enough people saw it.

"How did they know where the Underground was?" Kaz asked, running a hand through his tousled dark hair.

Bronx had a hunch, but he dared not utter it out loud. In all the years the Underground remained hidden, there had been one thing that changed: Arram. He was in Praymer's thrall, Bronx knew that much. Gods knew what the sovereign had said to make Arram give up the location so easily. He wasn't ready to crucify another brother of Rei.

"Praymer is getting his war," Artema said. "At least Rei didn't start it."

"Technically she will." Crona crossed her arms. "The prophecy is rather exact. It says that she will do it. Praymer has been using the Path to put that pressure on her, but after today Rei will demand blood."

"Then where do we go?" Manden asked, turning off the screen. "The star cluster isn't safe. I propose we go to Tas'und'eash. We need an army."

"We go to Wolf X." Bronx chewed on a thumbnail. They would end up there eventually and his brother would finally get his wish. "Yuri has an army. He can protect us."

Manden's face fell. Bronx knew Rei would have to go to Tas'und'eash, but not yet.

"His army isn't enough," the redhead said. "We need the Volocio army."

"And that will take time," Bronx replied. "Rei needs to call for war. Urius and the others are dead, and the Federation will look to her anyway. Let her fulfill this prophecy so my brother and the others can finally have their games. Then while they are keeping the Dominion occupied, we will go to Tas'und'eash so she can work on the next prophecy."

"The Volocio really like their prophecies," muttered Bernie.

"We have a country full of seers on Tas'und'eash," Artema said. "There are literally prophecies for everything."

Bernie scoffed. "Is there even such a thing as free choice among your people?"

"There is," Artema said with a chuckle. "Prophecies tell us when we need to act to ensure the outcome we want. Rei has to call war so we can end it. She has to appear to the Volocio in a certain way so they know that she is truly Micaela reincarnate. The prophecy is there to help her—to give her the tool she needs to convince the Volocio to follow her. Otherwise, why would they? She is foreign born and a stranger."

It would only be an uphill battle for Rei once she reached Tas'und'eash. Although Manden had assured them long ago that plenty of Volocio waited for her return. They were ready to go to war for Rei, and all she had to do was come to the planet. To be honest, Bronx was skeptical. He believed they had some allies on the Volocio planet, but it was likely a smaller number than Manden boasted.

Now was not the time to focus on Tas'und'eash.

"I'll call Yuri." Bronx took his slate out of his pocket. "I'll be back."

He left the cockpit and went to the men's bunk. He didn't want the others in the room when he contacted his half brother. He hadn't spoken to Yuri since their father's death all those years ago, back when Bronx's powers manifested and their father died in his arms. He didn't know how the conversation was going to transpire, but he didn't want an audience. His heart pounded as he tapped his brother's name on his slate.

Yuri's face appeared almost immediately. Bronx then swiped the video and transferred it to one of the other screens in the room.

"Hello, brother," Bronx said.

"Bronx." Yuri's lips shifted into a sneer. "I must say, I am relieved to see you're alive. The god queen?"

"Indisposed at the moment. I am calling to let you know we are coming to you. It's time to call the troops."

A smile crept across Yuri's lips, but the expression didn't reach his eyes. "While I am glad to hear you're finally accepting what I have been asking for, had your little goddess called for war earlier, Urius and the others would still be alive."

Bronx's jaw clenched at Yuri referring to Rei as a "little goddess." There was nothing little about her, not after she tore a ship in half. "That's her call to make. Not mine."

"But she's your woman. I was under the impression she would listen to you."

"Listening is not the same as doing what I say. No one controls her."

"Spirited. I can work with that. If she wants to win this war, she better listen to me."

Bronx raised an eyebrow and hid a smile. Urius may be dead, but Yuri was not much better. His brother would soon learn what it was like to work with the god queen, and Bronx looked forward to seeing Yuri realize it. "If you were so certain she would listen to me, why did you never call me? Why not use your brother to get what you wanted?"

"You know there's bad blood between us."

Bronx scoffed as his heart sank. "Still?"

"You killed my father."

"*Our* father, Yuri, and I didn't kill him."

"Oh, reaper? Then what did you do?"

Yuri was being difficult. Bronx normally avoided interviews, but he had done an in-depth one at the beginning of their campaigning explicitly describing what he was capable of. He had done it in hopes his family would see it and finally understand that Bronx's past actions were not out of malice. "I eased his death. He would have died if I was there or not, but my being there ensured his death was peaceful."

Yuri chewed his lip as he stared at his brother. "And what about bringing people back to life? Can you do that?"

The answer was in the same damned interview. "It was a one-time thing."

"For her?"

Bronx nodded. "It's not something I can replicate." More like *wouldn't* replicate, but Yuri didn't need to know the details.

"I would have expected more from you than just being her arm candy."

Bronx rolled his eyes. He had a similar conversation numerous times with Urius when he was a child, and he hated it. "I have never wanted the spotlight. I am happy to do my part in taking down the Dominion, but I do it because it's right, not for the attention."

"If I had any control over your upbringing, I would have made you more ambitious."

Years ago, he would have cowered at Yuri's comments. But so much had happened over the years that he saw Yuri as nothing more than a whiny child. Bronx pointed a finger at his brother on the screen. "You had a choice, Yuri. Our father was too old to raise me, which is why he shipped me off to the Daer Academy as soon as he could. But you were there the whole time and were nothing but a fucking asshole to me. I was a child, I didn't deserve it. The problem was—and still is—that you look at me and see the product of your ex-wife's infidelity with your father. This has always been about your anger toward her, and I should not have to suffer for it."

Yuri's head jerked back. "You little brat," he growled.

"You know it's true. You knew how much I wanted your acceptance and you made sure to keep me at arm's length. Admit it."

Yuri stared silently while his mouth hung open. "You were right, Bronx." His voice had an edge Bronx had never heard before. "I am still bitter. You should have been my son. Seeing you work hard for your accomplishments should have also been my joy."

Bronx clenched his jaw. He couldn't understand the depth of this man's ego. There was no way they could have been brothers. Their father, Patro, was a kind and quiet man who gained recognition for his studies in early Earth anthropology, but he never wanted recognition or celebrity. He did his job because it brought him happiness. They were the same values instilled in Bronx.

"Ugh, do you actually think about what you say or are

you really this narcissistic?" Bronx growled. "You need to get over it. My accomplishments are mine alone. I already have the love and acceptance from people who matter. It's never been about you."

Yuri opened his mouth to speak, but closed it. Bronx had never seen the man speechless. A vein throbbed in his brother's forehead.

Bronx's heart raced as he waited for Yuri to finally retort.

Instead the older man sighed before saying, "Fine. Meet us at the port at Medeina. We'll make sure the god queen's first appearance takes place at the Temple of Aladonis, with the Holy Father of Sancta Sedes."

Bronx nodded as the tension in his chest eased. He felt lighter than he had in ages. He should have called Yuri to tell him off years ago. "Good plan. We will see you in a few hours."

CHAPTER 46

Rei woke up alone in the medical bay. She was on the *Luciernaga* and hopefully far away from the destruction Praymer left behind. Her throat screamed for water while her stomach rumbled. She didn't feel as drained as the last time the lightning made her faint, or the Fire of St. Erasmus, or whatever-the-gods-called that she had wielded.

She swung her legs over and off the bed and stood, only to plummet to the floor. She may not have felt weak, but her legs obviously thought otherwise.

"Damnit," she yelped as she banged her elbow from the fall. Her heart raced as she wondered why her legs didn't work. She used the fire again, and a worrying thought crossing her mind: what if the fire caused nerve damage?

She pulled herself up to a sitting position, surprised to find no one had come to her aid. They were probably all upstairs. Hopefully, someone was near. She didn't want to remain on the floor.

"Hello?" she called through the opened door of the bay. "Little help?"

"Rei?" Crona's voice responded.

"I need some help."

The seer appeared with Artema at her side and both helped Rei back onto the bed.

"What happened?" Artema asked.

"My legs gave out." Rei slapped her legs, relieved to feel the strike. No nerve damage.

"No. The fire. Why did you use the fire?"

Rei stared at her hands, remembering the surge of

power rushing through them. It differed from her lightning; it was more. It heightened her senses: the colors were brighter and the scents stronger. She even saw the electric currents and connected everything. It was beautiful. "I was angry."

"That's putting it mildly."

"It was awesome," Crona said.

"You're not helping," Artema snapped.

"I know. It was still awesome until half of the ship fell on what remained of Yticol."

Rei winced. It was not surprising that she let her anger get the better of her, and she became reckless with her powers because of it. She had tried to reassure everyone that she knew what she was doing. But there was no point in hiding that now. "I can't control if I shoot fire or lightning."

"That's why you need to go to Tas'und'eash," said Rei's sister-in-law. "There are lightning Volocio there who can teach you how to wield it properly."

"As well as obtaining that army Manden is so desperate for you to bring," added Crona.

Rei's resolve wavered. Not controlling a power that could kill her was a lot harder than she expected. "But I can't," whispered Rei. "I can't run. Praymer has to pay for what he's done."

"And there are plenty in the Federation who will help you make him pay." Crona took Rei's hand and gave it a squeeze.

"Like Yuri?"

Crona nodded. "I was actually referring to myself, but sure. Speaking of . . . Bronx is talking to Yuri right now, and we're heading to Wolf X as we speak."

"What about Madu? The Federation council?"

Artema's and Crona's eyes flicked to each other. Whatever it was, Rei knew it was bad.

"The Path has attacked the city of Madu and killed the rest of the council."

Rei's heart sank into her stomach. There was no one left to lead. She was just a figurehead, but all eyes would be on her now. "It's another reason I can't leave. Even if it's symbolic, I have to be here. Who else will the Federation rally behind? Yuri?"

Artema sighed.

"Rei?" Bronx poked his head into the room and smiled when he saw her. "I was so worried." He was at her side, embracing her, in moments. She wrapped her arms around him and took in his warmth.

"I'm alright," she whispered into his chest. "I can't walk very well at the moment. But I'm sure I'll feel better by the time we get to Wolf X."

He pulled away and met her eyes. His dark eyes held hers while he cupped her face. Concern was written all over him in a haze of deep red. He worried for her safety, just like the others. Rei didn't doubt it.

"What did Yuri say?" Crona asked.

"He's excited to be a war hero again."

"Oh, he's one of those," muttered Artema while rolling her eyes. "I assume he'll be as much of a control freak as Urius?"

Bronx nodded, his eyes remaining on Rei's face. "I told Manden we would go to Tas'und'eash. The star cluster is not safe for us, and we'll need the Volocio to help us."

Rei opened her mouth to protest and demand why he decided without talking to her, but the words died on her lips. Everyone was right. She couldn't stay much longer. She was so convinced she could handle this, but only now did she realize it was because she already had the support of so many other people: the Federation, the council, Yuri, the Volocio.

She was not equipped to do this alone. Someone needed to take Urius's place. At least Yuri had experience, but he wasn't well liked from what she understood—not in times of peace. That was what the Federation needed. War was coming, and they were terribly outnumbered. Yet there still needed to be a voice of reason.

"You're right. I should have listened to Manden. We go. But not all the Volocio go; some of us need to stay behind. We need to keep the fires burning while I'm gone and keep Praymer's attention here."

Artema once said Rei needed to fulfill a prophecy so that the Volocio army would follow her. That meant tasks and time. Praymer couldn't learn what she was doing; he could never know she had left. "I'll talk to Kaz," Rei continued. "Maybe he can masquerade as me once in a while to let Praymer think I am still here."

Bronx nodded. "That's a good plan. But now I can't get the image of Kaz in one of your costumes out of my head."

Crona laughed. "Neither can I." She pulled Rei in for a hug. "But I will stay with Kaz," she whispered. "Someone has to keep Bernie company after her loss."

Rei hugged her harder. She hadn't even considered Bernadette. She had already lost her parents because of Praymer—and now they'd lost Urius.

She didn't want to be separated from everyone, but the time would come where they would have to do their part in this war. There was a prophecy, after all.

"We need time to prepare," Rei said. "As soon as I do my part, we get ready to scatter."

"And what do we do about Arram?" Artema asked. "Do we leave him to the Dominion?"

Rei thought about what she last said to Arram. She missed him, and it still hurt that he chose Praymer over her. She cared very much what would happen to him, but she had to hope that Praymer wouldn't hurt him. She couldn't save him or Niko when the rest of the star cluster needed her. At least her brothers weren't alone. She had to have faith.

"We have to trust Niko. He wants to save Arram, so let's hope he can get them both out before it's too late."

Artema gave Rei a small smile. "Do you feel better about Niklaryn and Infiernen?"

"Not entirely. I would like to talk with my brother now that I'm calmer. But I had decided long ago that I would trust him. As much as I am still wary of Infiernen, he has our best interests at heart because of Niko. And Niko . . . well . . . he's always been my Niko. But I can't save him like I planned. It was never an option. So I have to help those I can, even if it means running away."

CHAPTER 47

Infiernen was the first to greet Arram when his shuttle docked on Anekris's ship.

"Are you all right?" the Negander asked.

Arram furrowed his eyebrows, unsure why the man would ask. "My sister almost killed me. Had I waited to board the shuttle, I would be dead. Do I look like I'm all right?"

"It was the risk you ran when you arrived in a Dominion ship."

Arram knew the man was right, but he didn't want to admit it out loud.

"I sent her a message telling her I was arriving and in what ship I was arriving, yet she still destroyed it." He lowered his head. "I don't know if talking to her will be enough."

Infiernen grimaced. "That doesn't sound like her."

Arram rolled his eyes. "Ah, yes. I forgot you know Rei so well."

"Whatever Nik knows, I know. So you are correct."

Arram sneered but made sure the Negander didn't see him. He hated that Infiernen was right, in a way. Rei most likely never got the message and Arram just wanted to sulk. Infiernen merely drove home how much Arram didn't know his own sister or even his own brother.

Both men arrived in the ballroom where Anekris paced in front of a throne that had been placed there while Arram was gone. Some of the Ettowa and Bray relatives who remained on the ship chatted happily to the side.

"Well?" asked Anekris, who gestured for Arram to come closer. "What do you want to do?"

"I need to talk to Rei. Going in your ship was a bad idea and only resulted in people dying. I should have remembered her temper."

"I don't know if that's a good idea, Arram," Anekris said, his voice soft. "She's probably on edge at the moment. We should wait and see. She will probably make a statement trying to cover up what she did. Our sensors detected the god king's ship fleeing the planet and we are tailing them as we speak. A battle ensued after they left, and I lost a lot of warriors in the process."

"What do you think?" the sovereign then asked Infiernen.

"I agree, sir. Niklaryn's sister is volatile at best, and as long as we remain calm, we will appear to have the upper hand regardless of her intentions. I think with her actions, you can finally prove that she is the blood empress."

"So you think there will be war?" Anekris's eyes glittered.

"I think so." Infiernen's lips turned up slightly. "The Path had also attacked the Federation, and they killed the council. She will want blood now."

Arram's chest tightened as dread settled. "If only Rei had agreed to ally with you, we could have beaten the Path already." Arram didn't understand why Rei had to be so stubborn and avoid the inevitable. Not only were the council members dead, but his sister's carelessness in fighting the Path caused an innocent Dominion ship to be shot down.

Arram met Infiernen's gaze, which was no longer predatory. His blue eyes were wide, and Arram was no longer sure if it was the Negander who stared back at him or someone else.

"I should get back to the guests." The sovereign readjusted his jacket and patted Infiernen on the shoulder. "Well done," he muttered.

Anekris appeared to straighten his back ever so slightly, his chest puffed out. He then excused himself and joined his other guests, leaving Arram alone with Infiernen.

Arram had to admit, he wanted to understand the Negander. Infiernen was supposed to be their ally yet remained in Anekris's good graces. Arram watched the knight play the game with fascination.

"You should never believe one hundred percent of what the sovereign says." The Negander's voice was lighter. Arram knew at that moment that Niklaryn spoke, even though Infiernen's face remained. "There's a lot more going on under the surface than you know."

"Then tell me. We're allies. We're family."

"We're not family. Niklaryn is your brother. I am not."

Arram's head flinched back. "Then where, pray tell, is my brother?"

The Negander's eyes flitted to the side where the other guests stood. Aurelia's gaze studied both Arram and who appeared to be Infiernen. Arram wasn't sure if she was close enough to overhear, but obviously Niklaryn was. "Nik's still not doing well. Come." His brother spun on his heel and made his way out of the ballroom.

Arram followed closely behind, wanting to find out more. He had not even glimpsed at Niklaryn since Arram yelled and the switch happened. He wanted to know what made the switch happen now.

His brother didn't stop until he found what he was

looking for: the Benoit painting of Micaela. Arram shouldn't have been surprised, it was always about her.

"What are you not telling me?" Arram asked.

Infiernen's piercing blue eyes stared back at Arram's violet ones. Now that Arram knew about his brother's ability with illusion, it was astounding how small tweaks meant the difference between Niklaryn and Infiernen.

"There is plenty that I am not telling you, Arram." Niklaryn was the one who still spoke.

Arram rolled his eyes. "I just want to know where you truly stand."

"Right here."

Arram pressed his lips together. There was no reason for either men to trust each other.

"Nik–" he began.

"Shhh," his brother hissed. "I don't want them to know when I'm around."

"Then why did you show up?"

Niklaryn sighed. "I had to warn you. You have to be careful with Praymer. You can't trust him."

"What about you? You have worked for him for over a decade."

Niklaryn shook his head. "Not me. Infiernen. He took over and took the credit for all those atrocities. He wanted me to remain innocent while he did what he had to in order for us to get close to Praymer."

Arram scoffed. "Infiernen said the same thing to me. I think that's just too convenient."

"Convenient? What's convenient about losing ten years of my life? The last image I saw was attacking Riodan to save Bronx when he was sixteen. The next thing I know, I'm waking up to see my sister on stage and Bronx there again protecting her, but now they're both adults. I have spent the last six months trying to figure out all Infiernen has done in that time."

"Our," Arram snapped.

"Pardon?"

"*Our* sister. We are brothers, so Rei is our sister."

Niklaryn sighed yet held his hands up in surrender. It was clear he didn't want to fight, but Arram still felt the sting. "I know, Arram. I'm sorry. I am just trying to fill in the blanks. I feel horrible that my illness has kept me from knowing you. What can I do to make it up to you?"

"For forgetting about me and leaving me behind?" Honestly, Arram still didn't understand why the idea hurt so much. He had always been told he was orphaned because of his parents' deaths, but even his grandparents knew that he had a brother and sister out there. They had to suspect he was left behind. A little voice reminded him that his abandonment was not a choice. He shouldn't blame Nik for the quick decision of a child. Nik did enough of that. Arram's pain paled in comparison to his brother's guilt. Arram didn't think about the issues that came with having dissociative identity disorder. His brother lost so much time —and not just that decade that Infiernen was running amok, but also those three years their parents were fleeing from Anekris. His anger deflated in that moment. "Nothing. Family is a touchy subject for me, and I lash out too easily. What happened that day is done. Luckily, I was found and raised by our grandparents. Aside from Infiernen chasing me around the star cluster for several years, I was happy and loved."

Niklaryn's shoulder relaxed. "Loved?" His lips pulled into a small smile. "I am grateful that the universe gave people who loved you. You deserve that. You don't deserve what I did to you."

"What you unknowingly did. You were also a kid."

"It still happened."

"I know. But being raised by Sagitan and Virga was worth it."

Niklaryn's eyes grew wide. "Sag-Sagitan Bronto was our grandfather?"

Rei didn't know; Arram shouldn't have been surprised that Niklaryn was also in the dark. Yet, seeing his brother's look of surprise and awe made Arram feel proud. "Yes. He was our mother's father."

Niklaryn scoffed. "Wow. Well, consider me jealous, Arram. What I wouldn't give to have been raised by a man like that."

"He was a good man. Virga was an amazing woman. I know it's unfair to our parents because they died when I was so young, but the Brontos were my parents."

"I am sure they were wonderful parents. I knew they died, but Infiernen has kept a lot of the details from me."

"The Negander killed them. They attacked our town, trying to get both Rei and me. Our grandparents were killed and when another Negander tried to kill me, Rei used her powers for the first time." He remembered seeing her eyes glow white and the bolt of lightning that struck her staff. The god queen making her first glorious appearance. It was the same sized bolt that took down the ship he brought to Gliese VI. He was envious of her power and that her anger toward their grandparents' deaths could manifest in such a way. At the same time, knowing that there was someone who could exact the justice those Negander deserved for their horrendous act was also cathartic for Arram.

"Don't forget these Negander also work for Praymer."

"Many people work for Anekris. You can't pin all the violence of a party on one man. He doesn't want violence, not anymore. He wants peace. He chased us for so many years because he fears Rei will bring his destruction. He wants her as his ally. I know our father and Hotara spent years trying to keep Rei from him, but now that I know why, I'm wondering if it was all worth it. If our father had worked with Anekris, maybe they would still be alive and we would have been a family together."

Niklaryn pressed his lips together. "I don't know. I don't know if it would have worked out that way, but the best we can do is move forward now. I don't want you or Bronx or Rei in the middle of this. I have spent so much of my life trying to protect what's left of my family from whatever destiny has in store for all of you, and I want to protect you too. I may be late, but please know that the reason I stayed behind when the others left was for you. I could have gone with Rei and Artema, but you need someone on your side. You don't know Praymer like Infiernen does, and you need an ally."

Arram's eyes burned. He had been so hurt when Rei turned her back on him. He didn't stop to think of someone else extending a hand. He did so now, and Niklaryn took it. His grip was firm.

A traitorous little voice whispered in his mind, unable to ignore the fact that Bronx was in Niklaryn's list as family. Bronx didn't belong.

"That means a lot, but we aren't kids anymore. We're adults and we need a different sort of help. Maybe you can help me with Rei. If she is still angry with me, maybe she'll talk to you. Perhaps even Bronx will listen to you. She respects both of your opinions, and I worry that Bronx might push Rei before she gets all the facts. My fear is that she will do something rash and plunge us all into war."

Niklaryn shook his head. "I will help you anyway I can. But Arram, I saw Rei after her confrontation with Praymer. There was never going to be peace between them."

CHAPTER 48

It was late in the evening when they arrived on Wolf X. Bronx made sure he was the first off the *Luciernaga*; he wanted a word with his brother.

Yuri had more gray in his dark hair compared to the last time Bronx saw him almost a decade before. But seeing his older half brother was like seeing into the future. His future. They both took after their late father with their almost-black eyes, dark hair, and fair skin. Even before people knew Bronx's name at the Daer Academy, they knew he was a relative of the war hero Yuri Manca.

"Hello, little brother," Yuri purred as Bronx walked down the ramp from the ship.

"Yuri." Bronx gave his brother a tight smile.

"My god king and queen, welcome!" called Yuri with a bow. Bronx saw Rei and Manden out of the corner of his eye, but they remained by the ship. "You want to speak with me before the rest join us?"

"I do." Bronx leaned in close to his brother. "First, I want to thank you. Despite our heated conversation earlier, I am glad we are on the same side on this. That we are fighting on the same team."

"This war is too important to let my feelings for you impede it."

"Then let me give you some brotherly advice." Bronx knew he should let Yuri figure it out for himself, but he couldn't help himself. "When working with Rei, don't assume you can control her. It won't work. Work with her.

You'll get a lot further with her as a team member than as your subordinate. Urius could never get that right."

Yuri narrowed his eyes, and Bronx swore his brother would retort. The man then gave a gentle nod and muttered, "We'll see."

Bronx smiled. "Don't say I didn't warn you." He gave the signal, and Bernie and the rest of the Volocio joined Bronx and his brother.

Yuri received Bernie and the other Volocio with a stiff smile and a stiffer handshake. Bernie and Kaz were equally civil to the once commodore, but neither Artema nor Crona could hide their disdain. A small smile tugged at Bronx's lips at the sight of Crona wagging her finger at the older gentleman.

Manden and Rei were the last to greet Yuri. "I heard about your contribution to the Wolf X's civil war when I first arrived at the star cluster," Manden said, shaking Yuri's hand. "I am looking forward to seeing you in action and leading the troops."

"The honor is mine, God King. I look forward to fighting along with you." Yuri glanced in Rei's direction. "Beside both of you. God Queen, I appreciate you finally making the right decision."

Rei kept her distance from Bronx's brother, her green eyes calculating her next move as she measured Yuri. "It is not a decision I take lightly."

"Nor should you, but had you made it earlier, fewer people would have died."

"Perhaps," Rei said. "I have grossly underestimated the lengths Praymer will go to get what he wants. Even Urius thought Praymer could be reasoned with."

"I wished he was right, but after the first massacre of Yticol thirty years ago, I would have thought losing

Bernadette's parents would have been enough for him to see what you already see."

"At least we are in agreement."

"Indeed." Yuri gave Rei a genuine smile. He clapped his hands and gestured to the two vehicles parked near the landing platform. "So now that you're here, I suggest we go to the Temple of Aladonis where you and I can call the troops for war."

"No." Rei's voice was firm.

Bronx swore his brother's soul left his body. "What?" Yuri asked.

"It's too late tonight. I need a shower, and I would like to sleep in a normal bed after the day we've had. I am sure Kaz would also like to see the holy father in peace. The man did raise Kaz after all."

Yuri blinked several times and scanned the faces of each of the Volocio. "But we should make the announcement as soon as possible."

"I agree, but once we do, Praymer will arrive almost immediately," Bronx said. All eyes turned to him. "Praymer wants both Rei and me, and we need to make sure we have everything prepared before the Dominion comes."

"What does he want with you?" Yuri spat.

"He needs a reaper to keep himself alive. We saved the one he had." Bronx glanced in the direction of the *Lucier-naga* where Ana still waited inside.

"There are more like you?"

Bronx nodded. "As soon as Rei calls for war, she also starts the clock. Praymer will bring everything he has to capture us."

"Then why don't you run?"

Bronx swore he heard concern in his brother's voice. He had thought about running; he had thought about taking Rei and disappearing well before they met Praymer. But Rei felt she had a duty to the people; she was their pillar of hope, and the Federation couldn't afford to lose another Ettowa, not after Nik.

"We will," Rei said. She glanced in Bronx's direction. "But I don't know how much time we will have. The prophecy says I have to declare war, so declare I will. I still don't know if it's a good time to leave, but the Federation needs all the Volocio."

"I agree," Manden said. "All the Volocio. The Volocio army, which we will bring when we can return to our home planet."

Yuri shook his head. "I don't like the idea of you leaving. We don't need more of you. We have beat the Dominion before, against greater odds."

"We'll see," the redhead muttered before gesturing toward his ship. Ana appeared at the hatch and joined the group. Once an introduction was made, Yuri's eyes darted between both reapers. Bronx had told his brother there were more.

They piled into the different vehicles Yuri provided to bring the Volocio to the Temple of Aladonis. It was a beautiful stone fortress on a hill in the middle of the city of Medeina—the capital of the Wolf X.

"After the attack by the Path, the holy father has only been surviving by a thread," said Yuri as their car bounced along the city's cobblestone streets. "We kept that information out of the news, but I figured you would know the truth soon enough. He's not long for this world."

Bronx already knew this. The whisper of death grew stronger as they approached the temple. His former self was the son of a seer. It was only natural Bronx could sense the future like his sister. He knew what awaited him, and his brother's eyes on him indicated that Yuri somehow knew as well.

Once inside the fortress, the group made their way past a large garden near the primary room of worship at the top floor of the fortress. Just beyond it was a small office and bedroom.

The Holy Father of Sancta Sedes was a frail old man, lying in bed surrounded by other monks in white. His face lit up with an enormous smile as Kaz approached. The bedroom was plain with white walls and a painting of the god queen and god king opposite the bed. This brotherhood had always been known to have little interest in material things.

"My boy!" The holy father's voice rasped as he reached for Kaz. "You cannot know the joy it brings me to see you here again."

"I am sorry it took me so long to come back," Kaz said, clasping the man's dry, wrinkled hands.

"The universe seems to have unique plans for you, my son. The gods are wanted elsewhere, but it pleases me to see you all joined here today." The holy father's milky blue eyes scanned the others in the room. His eyes rested on Bronx's face at the end. He had an uneasy feeling, as though the holy father knew his end was coming.

"Oh, thank the gods," the elder whispered. He reached for Kaz, who graciously gave his arm, and the holy father pulled himself to a seated position. "I am ready," he said, his eyes never leaving Bronx's face.

All eyes in the room turned to Bronx. Rei's hand slipped into his and gave it a squeeze. He felt the pull, the need to help the holy father reach the Land of the Dead. This tug was so different from his time with Praymer. Whatever Praymer did was unnatural and painful. This was warm and comforting. This pull to the holy father was peace.

"What does he mean?" Yuri asked.

"He's ready to die." Manden stared distantly in the holy father's direction.

Yuri muttered something in reply, but Bronx didn't hear. He approached the dying elder. The holy father settled into his bed, Kaz on one side and Bronx on the other.

"Could we have some space, please?" Bronx didn't need an audience for this, and the monks hovered a little too closely.

"Please step back." Rei's voice wasn't much louder than his, but it had an edge that did the trick. The monks pulled away from the bed.

Bronx glanced in Kaz's direction. "Do you want to pray with him?"

Kaz nodded and squeezed the holy father's hand while saying a prayer in a low voice.

Bronx took the holy father's free hand in his. The old man's hands were dry, but he didn't focus on that fact. He closed his eyes and sought the tapestry. Every person had a tapestry that weaved through someone's life and came unraveled at the end. Bronx's job was to tug on that tapestry, and as the threads frayed, it released energy, flowing into him like ice in his veins. He opened his eyes in time to see the familiar plume of smoke floating lazily in the air.

The holy father let out a final sigh and died.

The monks around them fell to their knees and chanted a low prayer, Kaz also joining in.

Bronx let go of the holy father's hand and stood. Energy raced through his veins, and he had to find a place to transfer it. The garden outside the place of worship should do it.

He barely registered the others as he walked by. That was normal. A high came with that energy, and he let it carry him toward the garden he saw earlier. He knelt onto the wet earth and dug his fingers in. He took several calming breaths and imagined returning the energy to the earth. The high ebbed and eventually dissipated. Bronx looked up to find Yuri watching him.

"The god queen told me what happens afterward. Where the energy goes."

Bronx knew what he was talking about. After his father died, Bronx stumbled into a tree on the family farm and unknowingly transferred his father's energy just as Yuri ran him off.

"If you are wondering about our father, I'm quite sure what's left of him is in the old tree, the one with the swing." Bronx stood and brushed the dirt from his trousers.

"I know. The tree was dead before, but it bloomed shortly after you left. I never understood how it happened, but now . . ."

Bronx refused to meet his brother's gaze. Instead, he studied the dirt caked under his fingernails. "Well, now you know."

"I think I finally understand what you meant when you said that Praymer wanted you."

Bronx flexed his fingers. He didn't feel like talking to his brother about this topic. He didn't need the man's sympathy.

"What else can you do with that energy? Do you just return it to the universe?" Yuri's eyes bored into Bronx's.

"There's more, but I haven't learned how. Ana wants to teach me."

Yuri rubbed his chin, and Bronx swore he heard the gears turning in his brother's head. "I don't think you should go to the Volocio home world. You should stay here and use your powers to help us beat the Dominion."

Bronx scoffed. It would take more than that to stay here while Rei left to go to Tas'und'eash. But a little voice somewhere in his head told him he may have to stay. Something tickled the edge of his consciousness, warning him he and Rei leaving together was a bad idea—but that's not what bothered him. "What do you think I have been doing this whole time? I have been fighting the Dominion."

"Keeping her bed warm at night, more like."

Bronx lunged to his feet and stood inches from his brother's face. "You know nothing of what we have. You wouldn't know that kind of love if it stood in front of you and gave you the slap you deserve."

Yuri's face remained neutral. "Enlighten me, then."

Bronx's breath quickened. It was none of Yuri's business what he and Rei had, but he couldn't bear to stay silent. "She and I are a team. There's nothing we wouldn't do for each other."

"I doubt that." Yuri's smirk drove Bronx mad.

"I ripped my soul in two to bring her back to life," Bronx said through gritted teeth. "I would do it again in a heartbeat. But it won't come to that because I won't leave her alone again." He grew dizzy and his breathing became rushed. "I left her side once and she died. I did it again and Praymer assaulted her. I won't fail her a third time. I won't." Colors appeared in his vision and his heart thrashed in his chest. "I won't," he whispered. "I can't." His breathing became short and labored.

Yuri grabbed Bronx's arms and gave them a squeeze. "Bronx, I need to you to close your eyes and listen to me."

Bronx barely heard what his brother said. He couldn't breathe.

"Close your eyes, Bronx."

Bronx did as he was told, but the pressure in his chest was too much.

"Now clench your fists, take a deep breath, and hold it."

Something ice cold pressed against Bronx's forehead and the shock made him gasp.

"Just breath." Yuri's voice continued in a calm manner.

Bronx focused on clenching his fists. This continued for several minutes as the icepack slowly warmed until Bronx's heartbeat eventually slowed and his breathing came easily. The colors finally abated, and Bronx pulled the pack from his eyes.

Yuri took the icepack away from Bronx. "I may not know that kind of love, but I know panic attacks." He held up the used pack. "I sometimes need this too." He pressed a button and the pack immediately refroze and he offered it to Bronx.

Bronx took it and placed it back over his eyes.

"I didn't know you did that for her."

"We don't advertise it." The icepack really helped, and Bronx felt more himself with every second.

"You really love her. I guess I should be happy for you."

"I don't really care what you think, Yuri."

"I deserve that."

Bronx pulled the pack away from his eyes and met his brother's gaze. Yuri always gave Bronx a hard look, but now a hint of a smile appeared.

"Bronx, I am not a medical professional, but maybe letting her go can help you confront your anxiety. I may also have my own selfish reasons for wanting you to stay. You are a Daer Knight, and we will need all the help we can get. But your fear for her safety is crippling. It's no wonder I see the two of you together all the time. If you want, I can give you more tips. I wouldn't wish this anxiety on anyone."

Yuri had his own battle experience long before Bronx was even born. Bronx didn't realize that he still carried the scars after all these years. He didn't want that for himself. He needed help, and maybe Yuri was right: Rei could go alone, but he wasn't ready for that. Not yet. He had to stay by her side.

"Thank you, Yuri. I will think about it." He offered the pack back to his brother.

"You keep it. I can get another one."

Bronx held the used pack to his chest. "Again, thank you."

Yuri nodded then walked away, passing Crona, who stood off to a corner and must have observed the whole thing.

"Did my eyes deceive me or did you and Yuri have a moment?" she asked with a large grin.

"We did. Were you here to rescue me from the big bad brother?"

Her grin turned into a chuckle. "I was. But luckily he decided to not be an ass."

"Thanks for coming to my rescue anyway."

"You know I always have your back, brother."

CHAPTER 49

Rei placed a hand on Kaz's shoulder as he wept quietly. The monks had placed a shawl over the late holy father's face before disappearing in a flurry of white robes to begin the next stage: electing a new holy father.

Rei knelt down by Kaz, and Manden also appeared at her cousin's side.

"He's in a better place now," Manden said.

Kaz nodded, but tears continued to stream down his face. "I know. I am so grateful that I could see him one more time, but saying goodbye still hurts."

Rei slipped her hand into his and gave it a squeeze. Her attention drew back to the body of the holy father. This complicated things. The man deserved a proper funeral, but she needed to fulfill the prophecy and declare war, and that would also leave this place open for attack.

"His body should go to Escalante," Bernie said from her place near the door next to Ana. "It's the holiest city in this Volocio religion, and it's on Earth. It'll be well away from any danger."

"Are you suggesting we smuggle the body out?" asked Artema.

"That won't be necessary," Kaz said, wiping his face. "He wanted to be cremated and have his ashes scattered in Escalante." He rose. "We keep it simple."

"What about the funeral? From what I recall, the last holy father had a grand sendoff." Ana fidgeted with a strand of her white hair.

"That holy father was of a more ostentatious order."

Kaz looked at the body. "He didn't want one. We can do a simple one this evening and keep the press out of it until after we get through tomorrow."

Rei gave Kaz a hug. "If you need time to grieve, take it."

He shook his head. "I need to keep busy. I want to take care of this."

Rei hesitated.

"I already mourned his death long ago. I thought when I ran away from the brotherhood, I would never get to see him again." He gave her a tight smile. "Now I have this opportunity, and I want to continue to make him proud, even if I don't become the next holy father. But don't you fret, Crona and I have discussed my masquerading as you. Just bring us that army."

Rei nodded and let Kaz leave, and Ana followed, muttering something about helping him. She briefly scanned the room for Crona, but since she wasn't around, she only assumed that the blonde had gone after Bronx.

Yuri was also unaccounted for, but Rei didn't care about him. She briefly tapped into her bond with Bronx and felt a rush of agitation and a haze of pink, and she had a feeling she knew where the war hero had gone. Bronx had been on edge around his half brother since he first stepped off the *Luciernaga*.

"So what's our next step?" Bernie asked. "You said you wanted a day. What's your plan?"

"I wanted to talk about you," said Rei.

"Me?"

Rei nodded. "Bronx, Artema, Manden, and I will head to Tas'und'eash, even though Kaz will be here masquerading as me. We still need a leader."

"I thought you would have picked Yuri."

Rei scoffed. "I don't pick anyone. But I know you have

always been the Federation's favorite. Even if I said nothing, the truth would become clear soon enough."

"Yuri will not like that," said Manden with a laugh.

"He can kiss my ass," Rei muttered. "When I declare war, I want you by my side, Bernie. I want to make sure this is clear to everyone before I leave." Especially Yuri, but she dared not utter that out loud.

"I am glad you feel that way. I wasn't excited about leaving Yuri to have all the fun." Bernie smirked. "I received a message from Skylar. She, Sariah, and Elmessa are safe. They were there during the attack on the Federation council on Proxima Centauri II. They wanted to know what you have planned."

"I am getting us an army. That's my plan. The rest is up to you. What would you want to do?"

Bernie pulled her wildly curly hair back to tie it. A few golden strands broke free from the hold and fell about her face. Her hazel eyes flitted about as she calculated. "We'll need a new council. We have to start over and plan for the future. We should plan for *a* future." Bernie locked eyes with Manden, then with Artema, then finally with Rei. "I will contact Skylar, and we'll make plans."

Someone cleared their throat, drawing the attention of the four in the room. A monk stood at the door and gestured at the dead body still occupying the room.

The group excused themselves and left.

Manden and Artema followed Bernie to contact Skylar and the others. They asked Rei if she would come to the funeral later.

"I'm not sure," she said. "I need to check on Bronx first, and I wouldn't be surprised if he didn't want to be around the body."

But that wasn't all. Bernie's words kept playing over and

over in her head. *We should plan for a future.* To be honest, she had thought little of what would happen if, by some grace of the gods, they could beat the Dominion and be allowed to live some semblance of a normal life. But she wanted it desperately.

One of the monks directed Rei to the rooms assigned to the Volocio. She found Bronx alone in a bedroom, standing on the balcony with a beautiful view of the city. The sound of traffic and the smells of the nearby restaurants wafted in their direction. A servant had left a pot of tea outside their door, which the couple now enjoyed as the sun descended over the skyline.

"Your brother is devastatingly handsome," Rei said, leaning against the thick stone railing of the balcony.

Bronx furrowed his eyebrows. "Um . . . thank you?"

She giggled. "I mean, he is an utter ass, first and foremost, but he's easy on the eyes. I've seen photos of him before, and they don't do him justice. And to think your mother cheated on him with your father. . . ." She grew quiet and lost in thought. "Patro must have been gorgeous. Do the men in your family just grow more attractive with age?"

Bronx smiled. "By your logic, I was probably ugly as a baby."

"Oh, I'm sure you were a hideous child."

They both laughed. She wanted a way to lessen the tension between them, the tension about their unknown future. Tomorrow she would declare war and Praymer would follow soon after. They would run. The thought ran through her mind more than once. The concern for her own safety paled compared to her fear for Bronx's life. Every time she closed her eyes, she saw the fear in his eyes as he healed Praymer. Once again, Bronx couldn't control his powers. Those very powers that could take away any life were useless against the one man Rei wanted dead.

She watched him as his eyes remained on the city sprawled out in front of them. The sun's dying rays hit his face, and Rei's heart clenched at the sight. She loved him so much, and she would do anything to keep him safe from Praymer.

"You know, I am actually looking forward to having a break from this star cluster," he said finally. "When we go to Tas'und'eash, you get busy winning that crown, and I'll sit around getting used to our soon-to-be lavish lifestyle."

Rei snorted. "I don't want the crown. I don't want to rule, you know that. If I had a choice, I would live in a hut away from all these power-hungry people who just want to use us for their own gain."

Bronx put down his cup of tea and leaned closer to Rei. "And I would gladly live in a hut in the most isolated part of the galaxy with you if it made you happy."

Rei smiled, her heart feeling full. Then her lips turned into a smirk. "Get your own damned hut," she barked with a wink.

Bronx laughed. He took her cup away to set it aside and placed both hands on either side of her, trapping her against the balcony. His eyes darkened as he drew closer. She felt the heat from his lips only a breath away from hers, and she was once again under his spell.

"Okay, fine, we can share the hut," she whispered.

He said nothing but watched her. He waited, waited for her to hint she wanted what he wanted. She gave him a brief smile and tiny nod. He pressed his lips against hers, and she melted into him. He nipped at her bottom lip.

Rei would do whatever it took to make him happy. She would tear the star cluster apart for him.

His hands drifted down her back, and she arched into his caress. He broke the kiss but remained only a hair's breadth away. "We have a big day tomorrow, if you would rather rest."

Rei clicked her tongue. "Don't start something you don't intend to finish. This could be our last time."

He lips hovered above hers, and he cupped her face. His thumb gently stroked her neck. The touch sent a shiver down her spine. "If you insist."

"I do."

Bronx lifted her, and she wrapped her legs around his waist. He only needed a few steps to take her into the bedroom.

Their joining was fast and hard; Rei had him pinned underneath her as she brought him to his end, only to find her release almost immediately after.

"I love you," he said against her lips. Rei wished she could capture it, to find a way to keep that sound forever, this moment forever.

"I love you," she responded, pulling him closer. Her body always loved him without reservation. Every piece of him etched into her soul, her thoughts, her dreams. Even if tomorrow was their last, her love for him would continue beyond that, as something that could not be destroyed.

For several long minutes afterward, they remained here, staring at each other. Bronx tucked a strand of her hair behind her ear. His thumb stroked her cheek. Rei wanted to stay like this forever, but eventually she would need to sleep. She gave him another tender kiss on the lips, readjusting herself off of him and into his arms.

She lay awake that night, too many thoughts running through her head. She had checked her slate at some point and found a message from Manden stating that Dominion ships were already in the atmosphere. She feared she wouldn't be able to even get off the planet. They had to get to Earth's solar system; that's where the wormhole was that would take them to Tas'und'eash.

Soon the sun's rays peeked over the skyline and into their room.

<hr>

BRONX STIRRED. HIS EYES OPENED AND MET REI'S. SHE loved waking up next to him; she never tired of watching him slumber.

"Couldn't sleep?" he asked.

Rei shook her head.

"Same."

They freshened up. There were always clean clothes and costumes in the *Luciernaga,* and once again Rei wore her god-queen costume, staff in hand, as she walked through the temple. Manden wore his god-king costume and stood close to her, Yuri, while Bernie. Bronx, Crona, Kaz, and Artema were several steps behind. Ana stayed in the shadows.

Several monks stood on either side of the hallway and bowed as the Volocio walked past. They mumbled prayers; they were going to need whatever blessing they could get.

The doors opened, letting in the harsh noonday sun, blinding Rei only briefly until she approached the awning at the steps of the temple. Cameras flashed rapidly before her eyes, and several voices called out questions to her, but she ignored them. Today was not a day to answer questions.

Rei's heart raced. Thousands of people gathered before her, pressed against the gate that surrounded the fortress.

She was always nervous before a crowd, but once she started talking, the nervousness usually lessened.

She faced Bronx one last time, and he gave her a smile.

She called Bernie forward to stand with her, Yuri, and Manden. She didn't bother looking at the war hero's reaction; she was more anxious about what she had to say next. Her heart hammered in her chest, threatening to burst.

She gave them her biggest smile before she finally spoke.

"People of the Tyre Star Cluster. Yesterday—a day that will forever burn in my memory—the Federation was suddenly and deliberately attacked by the forces of the Dominion, along with their allies in the Path.

"Until this point, we have been at peace with the Dominion and still in conversation with its sovereign about the upholding of peace in the star cluster. While we may have had our disagreements, I have always felt we could settle them through democracy, through the vote. But I was wrong.

"The attack yesterday not only affected the capital Madu but also the Underground—its location was always a secret, but its existence was not. You know it as one of the first fires of rebellion lit because of your own fight for freedom from the Dominion almost thirty years ago, after the first Yticol Massacre. Your leader, Urius Boyard, lost his life in that attack, among many others on Gliese VI at the hands of a Dominion ship, including the council on Proxima Centauri II by those terrorists of the Path.

"I know you have longed to meet the Dominion on the battlefield again and have waited for me, your god queen, to make the call to arms. I believe life is too precious to rashly start a war and believe we should reconcile differences in more peaceful ways. Yet the Dominion has proven that they have no intentions of respecting life or obtaining peace. They want war, so we will give it to them.

"We will not only defend ourselves, but we will make it very clear that this form of violence shall never again endanger us. I declare that as of yesterday, war lives between the Federation and Dominion."

CHAPTER 50

Arram's jaw dropped when Anekris made the announcement. Rei had declared war. It was all happening too fast. He and Niklaryn were going to work together to stop her. He couldn't believe she was so rash—the Federation was grossly outnumbered. War was suicide.

He stared out the window; Wolf X floated in the stars just out of reach. Naturally, she would declare war on Bronx's home planet. Bronx would have her run to his brother, Yuri. He had the only army available since the Federation council no longer existed to assemble one.

As much as Anekris claimed Rei was dangerous, Bronx and his influence over her was more so. He shouldn't have let his sister go. He realized his mistake now.

"What are you thinking about?" Arram heard Anekris's soft voice before the sovereign appeared at his side.

"I think Rei will do more harm if she continues whatever it is she's doing with the Federation."

"I told you she's dangerous."

"Only because I'm not there to guide her. I should have gone with her or worked harder to convince her to stay. We work better as a team. The minute she and I separated, that reaper finally got what he wanted—a war."

"So you want to divide the two?"

Arram nodded. "It won't happen. They're more dangerous if the other is threatened, especially with their link."

"What link?"

Arram stared at the floating planet before him. He hesitated to divulge more information, but the sparkle in Anekris's blue eyes as he beheld Arram swept away the need to hide anything. "Bronx tore his soul into two for Rei. That's how he brought her back to life. They're bound in ways none of us understand. They are aware of each other, and I have wondered if it extended to their powers, but I haven't seen my sister reap anyone so I can't be sure."

"Interesting." The sovereign's piercing blue eyes sparkled.

"Now what are you thinking about?"

Anekris didn't answer right away. "I wonder if we use the reaper as bait for your sister."

Arram shook his head. "I told you, they're more dangerous when the other is in harm's way. Take him out of the equation, yes. But if you want her to come to us, you can't antagonize her. We can't afford it. It's imperative now more than ever that she joins us. I worry what will happen to her if she stays with the Federation. Maybe we need to do something to bring the other Volocio to us. We always move as a group, and I think she'll follow."

"Of course, of course. Perhaps you should reach out and talk to her first. See if she will join us willingly. If not, we may have to capture her."

"How?"

"You are both matched in power, correct? You can easily overpower her to the point of exhaustion. She won't fight back, not if it meant hurting you."

"To exhaustion? Rei hardly gets tired from her powers anymore. I still get winded when we skirmish."

"But there's something else. Rei can call upon something more powerful when necessary." Anekris tapped a finger on his full lips. "It's what she used to break my ship. Her eyes turn white and she emits an extraordinary burst of energy before she passes out. You have seen this before, correct?"

Arram remembered vividly the first time Rei used her powers. She saved his life when the priest in Ballarat tried to slit his throat and Rei turned him into a charred husk.

"She only uses that much energy when she's cornered." Then the idea came to Arram. It was as clear as day. It was high risk and Rei may never forgive him, but she would not survive the war if she sided with the Federation. He needed her safe; he needed all of them safe.

"Is Nik the only Volocio descendant you have in your employ?" Arram asked.

Anekris's face broke into a big smile. "I am glad you asked. The answer to your question is no, he's not the only one."

"We'll need firepower for my plan to work. We will use others for bait, and we'll need Infiernen to be the messenger."

"You mean Niklaryn?"

Arram's heart skipped a beat. He knew his brother's concern of being noticed masquerading with Infiernen's face.

"Oh, don't act so surprised," Anekris continued. "I know everything that goes on. I know your brother has resurfaced and occasionally spoken to you. You can't trust him. You can't trust either of them."

Arram furrowed his eyebrows. Nik had warned him not to trust Praymer, and now it was the other way around. He knew to take such comments with a grain of salt, but he was intrigued with what Anekris had to say about someone who'd stood at his side for so many years.

"I have known that Infiernen has been a double agent for years. His relationship with Skylar Ettowa has also caught my eye, but I have done nothing because I found it rather amusing how far he would go to prove his unwavering loyalty for me. Hunting Niklaryn's old apprentice and eventually shooting his brother was delightfully unexpected." Anekris stopped and eyed Arram. "No offense. But now that Niklaryn is back in the picture, and Infiernen's attempt on your and the reaper's lives are no longer his concern, I worry that I cannot predict Infiernen's actions as before. Infiernen has done great work for me in regards to infiltrating the Path, and I almost believed he was still on my side. That is, until you noticed it as well. I can't ignore it any longer. In fact, I believe Infiernen and Niklaryn are still playing both sides, but their point of contact is someone else. It is no longer Miss Skylar."

"Who?" This made sense, but he was surprised how nonchalant the sovereign was at acknowledging having been double-crossed and how Infiernen, and by default Niklaryn, had stayed alive for so long.

"Oh come now, you're cleverer than that. Naturally, Niklaryn would turn to his old apprentice. Bronx."

Arram took a step back. "Are you insinuating that my brother has been working with Bronx to make sure Rei started the war?"

"Your brother wants me dead, and the reaper doesn't want to compete for your sister's affections. He knows that you and I are close and will manipulate you to his advantage."

Arram recalled what Nik had said to him. *There was never going to be peace between them.* Bronx said almost the exact same sentence before leaving with Rei, except he made a promise. He promised there would be no peace. Arram growled with frustration once he realized it. He couldn't believe he thought his brother was on his side. Of course Nik wasn't. He was always on Rei's side, or even Bronx's. The reaper had claimed Nik to be akin to a brother, and Niklaryn obviously felt the same way. Arram was once again left to the side.

"Even more reason to include my brother in this plan. But we have to move quickly before your soldiers invade the planet. How long will it take for your faux Volocio warriors to arrive?"

"Quite a number are already on Wolf X."

Arram's attention returned to the floating planet. They had to hurry and get Rei out of danger before the carnage began. He couldn't afford to lose her. She was all the family he had left.

CHAPTER 51

Bronx and Manden watched from their perch on the north tower of the fortress as Dominion ships peeked through the clouds above them. More had been coming over the last few hours, yet none had tried to land. They were waiting for Praymer's last order, but what was he waiting for?

"I thought I would find you here." Ana leaned against the wall behind him. Color had returned to her cheeks, even though she shared the same pallor as him. Her hair remained white, and dark bags hung under her darker eyes. He wondered if they were permanent effects of what Praymer had done to her.

"You look better," Bronx said.

"How do you feel?" Manden asked.

"Like shit," Ana muttered. "I don't think I would survive if Praymer caught me again, but I'm well enough to still do my job."

"That's worrisome." Manden's green eyes glanced in Bronx's direction.

"I was looking for Crona and Kaz. Have you seen them?" Ana asked.

Bronx shook his head. "The fortress is big, but they're around here somewhere."

Ana pressed her lips together and crossed her arms.

"How were you captured?" Bronx asked. He wanted to know how Praymer knew where to find a reaper when he couldn't. Something had to have happened, and he needed to know how to avoid it.

"I was looking for another reaper, Gadreel. He had disappeared some time ago, and I tracked him to Praymer's palace. He died before I could save him and I was captured instead."

"Has Cesar mentioned a talisman to you? Something that belonged to Atrius?"

Ana bit her lip. "He did, but he didn't tell us the details. He knew Praymer was capturing reapers and didn't want us to have too much information in case Praymer could extract it from us."

"Cesar thinks that's how Atrius bound Praymer to Hamastagan and thus kept the sovereign from dying. If we find that, maybe destroying it will sever the link." Bronx couldn't imagine what tool Praymer had been using to prolong his unnatural life. But if there was a chance to kill him and protect Rei, Bronx needed to find out what.

"But none of us know what we're looking for," Ana said.

"They were probably waiting for you, Bronx." Manden cupped his elbow with one hand while tapping his lips with the other. "You are Atrius reincarnate; you may be the only key to recognizing this talisman."

Dread pooled in his stomach as he realized that this was probably what the little voice in his head warned him about. If there was a talisman, it would have to be somewhere in the Tyre Star Cluster, somewhere where Praymer had easy access. Going to Tas'und'eash with Rei wasn't a good idea.

It wasn't the first time he thought about it. Every time she brought up the idea, he remembered Praymer's words: *The two of you are inseparable.* He was right. Praymer would only believe Rei had stayed in the Tyre Star Cluster if Bronx was at her side.

"I need to find Rei." Bronx left the tower, Manden and Ana following close behind. He had to talk to her.

The temple was empty; most of the monks had already fled, taking the cremated remains of the holy father with them.

He didn't see Kaz or Crona as he and the others walked through the empty halls. They were probably in one of the other towers.

His boots clicked on the stone floors as he made his way down to the place of worship, a large room with no windows, lit only by candlelight. The entire fortress had to be more than a thousand years old, but no one wanted to upgrade facilities in the primary room of worship. Everywhere else had modern amenities, but not this room. Nothing should hinder a worshiper's path to the gods. To the Volocio. One of the statues leading into the room was of Atrius, and Bronx made sure to give it a wide berth. He hated seeing artwork that looked like him.

Rei was in the room with Bernie and Yuri. The latter yelled at the god queen, his face red.

"I was not consulted in this decision!"

Rei placed her hands on her hips and stood her ground. "You were going to find pushback from the rest of the Federation anyway. Bernie was always the favorite and was the only reason most of the council put up with Urius in the first place. May he rest in peace."

"We have to work together, Yuri," Bernie said. "No one is going to argue that you are a better leader for our army than I, even though technically I am more decorated than you. However, even you have to agree that you don't have the most likable personality. It's no secret that there's bad blood between you and your brother." Bernie's eyes flicked briefly in Bronx's direction. "Although most believe it is because you blame Bronx for your father's death and not also the sweeping romance between your wife and father that resulted in Bronx being born. We have an opportunity to do something different with the Federation. To bring new life, to take what my uncle did and evolve."

"There was nothing wrong with how Urius led. Look how many planets there are in the Federation now!"

"That's because of us," Bronx said, finally breaking his silence. He had enjoyed watching his brother get dressed down by both Rei and Bernie, but he was ready to step in and join. "People started voting for the Federation again once Rei got on that stage on Trappist V and made her first speech. Those other planets followed suit once the rest of us Volocio joined her."

If looks could kill, Yuri could have murdered Bronx. Yuri's hand clenched as though grasping for a weapon that wasn't there. It wouldn't be the first time the two clashed swords, but Bronx knew he could beat Yuri again if it came to that. Luckily, it didn't.

"Face it, Yuri," Manden said, drawing closer.

Ana said nothing from her post a few steps behind Manden, but the look in her eyes relayed the same message.

"You're outnumbered," the redhead continued. "If you want to play the game with us, you have to work with us as a team. It's the only way we'll have a shot at beating the Dominion."

Yuri's face turned into a sneer, and his gaze returned to Rei, who returned the look with equal fire. Bronx knew he would jump in if necessary, but Rei could take care of herself. Then his brother huffed and left the room, purposefully knocking shoulders with Bronx on the way out.

"We'll try your way for now," Yuri said. "But we'll see if we even survive the day's end."

Bernie gave Bronx a smile that didn't quite reach her eyes. "We should get ready. Manden, Ana, come with me, please. The Daer will be here soon to help."

Soon it was just Rei and Bronx alone, surrounded by candlelight. The soft glow reflected in her green eyes and shone in the copper strands of her dark hair. He remembered Praymer's hand around her neck. He never wanted that to be a possibility again. But the Dominion ships kept coming, and soon she could be backed into a corner. He had to make sure he stood in the way of it.

"I can't go to Tas'und'eash with you."

He felt her heart skip a beat, felt the tightness in her chest. He hated their bond now. He hated feeling how much those words hurt her.

"What's changed?" she whispered.

"Cesar believes that the key to killing Praymer may be an object of Atrius's. Something Praymer can use to keep from dying."

Rei chewed her lip and meandered toward one of the large candelabras. He waited as she thought things through. He wrung his hands, all the while not taking his eyes off of her.

"We can do that together. We will take Praymer down together."

"But being together is the problem."

Rei took a step back. "You're not pulling away from me again, are you?"

Bronx shook his head. "No, definitely not. You talk of Kaz masquerading as you, but you forget one important element to make him believable. Me. Praymer knows we are always together—and that could be our downfall."

Rei sighed. "We tried that. When Kaz tried to be you,

Praymer saw through it and they almost captured you. At least if you come with me to Tas'und'eash, you'll be safe."

He drew closer to her and cupped her face. "But you need time. Artema said there will be tasks you have to do to gain their trust. We can't do that if Praymer knows where we both are and chases us to the Volocio homeworld."

Her lips trembled. "You're right," she whispered. "I just wish it didn't have to be this way."

"I know."

"But what if something happens to you? What if he captures you?"

He smiled. "Then you bring back that army and save me."

She scoffed. A tear traveled down her cheek, and she quickly wiped it away. "Of course. It's so easy."

Bronx's eyes burned. He blinked any possible tears away. "It will be easy. You will be among other Volocio like you, and you can learn to use the fire." He leaned in and pressed his lips against hers. "No one will stand in your way."

"I'll come back a true blood empress." The smile appeared on her lips. He tasted the salt of her tears on his.

They could do this. He would find a way to kill Praymer so when she returned she could smite him on the spot and end the war quickly. They had to do this for their future.

She kissed him again. "But this is not a goodbye. We stay together until there's no choice and I have to leave."

"Agreed. We face today together."

"Together."

They kissed again. His arms wrapped around her frame, clinging to her like a lifeline while her fingers tangled in his hair. He tried to memorize every curve of her body and the scent of her skin. He would have to live off the memory, and he didn't want to miss a single detail.

Someone cleared their throat, and it was Rei who broke the kiss.

"You have a call, God Queen," said a soldier at the entrance to the place of worship.

"Thank you. Send the call to my room," she rasped. She gave Bronx one last look. "I'll be right back."

Bronx turned to look at the statues at the front of the room, not wanting to watch her leave. Soon he would watch her leave for Tas'und'eash, and that would be hard enough. The idea of it left an ache in his chest. He breathed hard and his heart raced.

"There you are!" Artema's voice pulled him out of his head and shocked him out of his anxiety.

Bronx turned and his heart sank when he found Artema wasn't alone. Niklaryn stood at her side.

"What are you doing here?"

"It's begun," said Niklaryn. "Praymer will overrun the city and its citizens unless you meet his demands."

"They sent you as a messenger?" Bronx approached his old mentor. He was surprised to see Nik wearing a Daer uniform, but it would have been the only way he could have entered the fortress.

"I have to go back. I'm worried about Arram, and I can't leave him with Praymer."

Arram was a lost cause, but Bronx dare not utter the words out loud. The Ettowas were always blinded by their family loyalty. Rei was no different.

"What does Praymer want?" He probably knew the answer: him and Rei.

"You know who he wants," said Artema.

"And if we refuse? He sends his army into the city to

take us by force? He is aware of what Rei could do to a ship." He hated the idea of her using the fire, but if she did, he was there to catch her.

"There's more." Bronx noted Artema's voice was just a tick too high, but his eyes remained locked on Nik's.

"He has Kaz and Crona."

CHAPTER 52

Rᴇɪ ᴅɪᴅɴ'ᴛ ᴇxᴘᴇᴄᴛ ᴛᴏ ꜱᴇᴇ Aʀʀᴀᴍ's ꜰᴀᴄᴇ. Sʜᴇ received a blocked message through her slate, and when she transferred it to the nearby screen, relief filled her core.

"I was so worried about you," she gasped as tears formed in her eyes. "I am so sorry I yelled at you earlier. I was—I was not in a good place."

Arram smiled. "I know. We are very much alike—lashing out when angry was never a very good look for us. I miss you too."

Rei chuckled. "Is Praymer treating you all right?"

Arram cocked his head to the side. "Of course. He wouldn't hurt me."

Rei's hand went unconsciously to her neck. The hand mark was no longer there, but the memory of Praymer squeezing her throat remained.

"We have to talk," Arram continued. "I understand you are still wary of Praymer, but declaring war is too much, even for you."

Rei's face grew numb. Her heartbeat increased in rhythm. "What did you expect me to do? He started it."

Arram sighed. "You sound like a child. *He started it.* He wanted an alliance, and you lashed out at him. Is your pride worth more than peace?"

Rei couldn't believe what she was hearing. "His idea of an alliance is that I am still in a legally binding marriage with him. To him, I am Micaela and his property."

Arram rolled his eyes. "I doubt that."

"When I told him no, he attacked me. There's video

proof, and I blasted it for all the Dominion and Federation to see."

Arram furrowed his eyebrows. "I saw that video. I didn't see anything that looked like him attacking you. It's just your word against his."

Rei's eyes stung at the betrayal. She couldn't imagine him seeing what happened to her and saying those words. He truly was in Praymer's thrall.

"He destroyed the Underground," she whispered. "He killed Urius, Alma, Camila, all those people in Yticol."

"Stop lying, Rei!" Arram yelled. "I know it was the Path. I told you defeating them was more important than revenge. Then you felt threatened, you lost control of your powers, you broke that ship in half, and it fell onto the planet. You are too dangerous."

"I broke that ship, yes. I broke it because I woke up in the middle of the night to find Yticol on fire. Bronx and I watched that ship drop bombs onto the lake, flooding the Underground. Kaz, Crona, Artema, and Bernie were the only ones to make it out. Yes, it was stupid of me to destroy the ship, but it landed on something that had already been destroyed. And everyone on that ship deserved their fucking fate."

"I was on that ship!" he cried. "I almost died. I was lucky to have gotten onto a shuttle just as your lightning broke everything apart. I came because I wanted to talk to you, and I almost died because of your fucking temper."

Rei's heart stopped. There was no way she could have known that. The thought of almost killing her brother was too much. White flickered along the edge of her vision. She didn't need the Fire of St. Erasmus to come now. "You brought the ship to the Underground?" she asked, her voice dangerously low. "You are the reason all those people died?"

"Praymer would never attack. He wasn't even on the ship to make the order."

"He would have made the order beforehand, idiot. If you didn't have your head so far up his ass to begin with, you would have known how he is using you."

"I am not the only one being manipulated, sister. I see the strings that the reaper pulls. How he pulls the wool over your eyes."

Rei let out a frustrating scream as her hands burned. She didn't want to unleash the fire, so she threw her slate at the screen and both exploded in a burst of sparks.

"Rei?" Bronx stood in the doorway. "I felt . . . what happened?" He ventured further into the room.

"Arram betrayed us," Rei sobbed. "He brought the ship that destroyed the Underground. Praymer must have manipulated him into giving away the location. He is besotted by Praymer and believes everything that monster says—even over me." The last words choked out. Pain ripped through her chest as she remembered Arram's words. He saw Praymer attack his sister and yet saw nothing wrong. "I don't understand how the truth stares him straight in the face and he refuses to see it."

"Praymer won't let him see it," Niklaryn said, appearing in the doorway.

"Niko?" Rei gasped, falling to her knees. Her brother came to her side and knelt beside her, and she threw her arms around him. She couldn't bear the uncertainty anymore. She couldn't handle staying angry at a brother who had little control over his actions.

After all of her dealings with Infiernen, it was obvious now that they were two different men. Niklaryn would never do what Infiernen was capable of. He was still her Niko. She pulled away and vigorously wiped her face and met Artema's gaze as she also entered the room. Then Rei returned to Niklaryn. "Explain."

"Dante has used his illusion to make sure Arram only sees what Praymer wants. I watched the video of Praymer attacking you, but Dante had his hand on our brother and Arram saw something different. I don't think he realizes what's happening to him. Part of his devotion to Praymer is blindness and emotion, but the sovereign knows how to sow the seeds of doubt to begin with."

"Then why didn't you tell Arram the truth?" asked Bronx.

"I am not exactly high on his trust list. He knows about Infiernen and me, but he still sees me as one man. I have to continue to gain his trust if I am to save him." Niklaryn laid a hand on Rei's cheek. "That's why I can't stay long. I failed to save Arram when we were children and now is my opportunity to make things right. While inside, I can still feed you all information—at least those of you who stay in the star cluster." He gave Rei a kiss on the forehead. "I spent so many years thinking I was protecting you when you didn't need it. You are so strong and you will save us all. That's why I need to focus on our little brother. He needs us now more than ever."

He got up to leave, and Rei's grip on him tightened.

"He's a lost cause, brother. He turned his back on me."

Niklaryn cupped Rei's face in his hands. "Don't lose faith. You never lost it with me."

"That was because I thought you needed saving."

"You didn't need to save me. I've always been where I needed to be: paving the way for you. The star cluster needs you."

Rei nodded. He was right. She still had a duty to help

the star cluster. He was also right about faith. Arram still loved her. There had to be hope for him yet.

"Come with us," she said.

"I can't. Praymer expects me to lead soldiers in a different part of the city. Infiernen and I have to pretend we are still on his side so we can stay close to Arram."

"We should go to Arram. He won't listen to us separately," Rei countered, "but maybe he'll listen to us together. All of us. Where are Kaz and Crona?"

"Praymer has them," Bronx said through gritted teeth.

Rei's eyes remained on her brother's face. "What?"

"That's why Nik came. He came to warn us that Praymer is using your cousin and my sister as bait."

"It's what he did the last time," Artema said. "It's how he lured us for the final battle." She scoffed. "He captured Max, Kaz, and Alexia to lure Mica, Atrius, and myself. He is determined to repeat history."

"But this time we have Manden," Bronx said. "And Bernie, and Ana, and Yuri, and the Federation. We're not doing this alone."

"There was no point in luring us," Rei said. "He knew I wanted to meet him on the battlefield."

"But we can't kill him" Bronx's concern flickered along Rei's vision in a bright green.

"Doesn't mean I don't want to rip off his mechanical arm and beat him with it."

"He wants us in a specific location," Artema said. "He has something planned and wants to maneuver us into place."

"And where are we supposed to go for Kaz and Crona?" Rei asked.

"The port outside the city." Niklaryn pointed out the window toward the other side of the valley where several ships were visible even at this distance. "It's the perfect vantage point."

A horn blew into the distance, followed by another and another. Rei felt it in her core, making her blood run cold. She stood and followed the sound to the balcony. She was vaguely aware of the others behind her. An explosion rocked the ground as the far north wall of the city crumbled and a flood of soldiers poured in.

The invasion had begun.

CHAPTER 53

"Headstrong, stupid woman!" Arram yelled as his screen went black. He rubbed his face. Gods, he loved his sister, but her blindness enraged him.

"That's not very nice, Arram." Crona's voice rang in his head. He spun around and faced her as she sat in the chair he had procured for her before he called his sister. Kaz sat next to her, his nostrils flared and chin held high. The blood red collar around his neck gleamed in the fluorescent lights above them. Arram had never seen his cousin so angry.

"Don't act as though you've never gotten angry at your brother's pigheadedness, Crona. I have heard you call him worse."

"True. But we both know I am perfect and not a hypocrite, Arram. You, on the other hand, are an ass."

He couldn't stand Crona's humor at the moment. "Excuse me?"

"Did you really watch that video of Praymer putting his hands on your sister's neck and calling her a whore and still claim that you saw nothing?"

Arram furrowed his eyebrows. "I have no idea what you're talking about."

The three stared at each other in silence for several agonizing moments. Arram then paced the small shuttle.

It had the same black and green aesthetic that Anekris preferred on the outside of all his ships. There wasn't much space; most of it was taken up by a glass case with vines spilling down from some unseen pot on the back wall.

Anekris preferred keeping live plants on all his ships as it helped with the efficiency of the ship's oxygen tanks.

"You didn't see the video," Kaz said, shaking his head. "Arram, my friend, you are being manipulated."

Arram rolled his eyes. They were the ones trying to manipulate him. Of course they were on his sister's side. The god queen was more important than her brother.

"Why did you bring us here?" Kaz continued as Arram looked out the window of his shuttle to the city down below. Three horns blasted, followed by an explosion. The north wall crumbled like sand, and the soldiers were pouring in. He hoped Infiernen got to them in time to tell them where to go.

"It's for your safety. I wanted you away from the city before the invasion happened." That's what Arram told himself. They were bait, of course, but Arram also didn't want them to die. The Dominion were told not to take prisoners.

"And the others?" Crona asked.

"Let's hope my brother was fast enough to warn them." Nik or Infiernen would warn them. They were always on Rei's side. Arram didn't know who he spoke to when he discussed his plan: Nik or Infiernen. It didn't matter. They were both nothing to him and soon wouldn't be a problem for anyone else.

But he knew his sister and her strength. She would come, and Bronx would not be far behind. He never lost faith in his sister's remarkable abilities.

"Beautiful," Anekris said at Arram's side, watching the soldiers flood into the city. "I always wanted to see this city burn since that nuisance, Yuri, fought my troops on the battlefield all those years ago. They were the first to rebel, but they will be the first forced back into the fold."

"Are the bombs ready?" Arram asked.

Anekris nodded.

The plan was to threaten to bomb the city and drop a few empty shells filled with fireworks to look like explosives just close enough for Rei to easily dispatch them. However, at this distance, she would have no choice but to use that burst of energy. Anekris claimed he would keep Bronx busy while Arram wore his sister out enough for Anekris's army of Volocio descendants to subdue her.

If that wasn't enough, the soldiers with lightning abilities could help take her down.

Arram watched the chaos unfold in the city but noticed silence behind him. "What? No more smartass comments?"

The only response he received was the sound of glass breaking.

Arram's violet eyes flicked in Kaz and Crona's direction, but all he saw was a vine that ripped into his cheek just under his eye. The shock made him lose his footing, and he fell into Anekris's arms. There was no way Manden could arrive so fast, yet when Arram looked again, Kaz and Crona had escaped.

"Find them," growled Anekris, and Arram ran down the ramp.

They didn't get far. Crona and Kaz ran across the landing strip toward the forest on the other side. The trees had enormous trunks at least the width of three people. Quite a few trees stood in the way, but a sharp drop lay on the other side. There was nowhere for them to hide. All they would need to do to escape was for Kaz to make them disappear, but the collar around Kaz's neck made things rather difficult. Still, that didn't explain the vine striking him.

Arram ran after them. "There's nowhere to go!" he yelled, gesturing to the nearby Negander to also follow suit. "It's safer here with me!"

"Fuck off!" Crona cried, drawing closer to the trees.

Arram had to have been hallucinating. He swore the trees reached for Crona as well.

Kaz turned to stand his ground. "Keep going, Crona!" he called to her.

Arram slowed as he drew closer. "Cousin, you're outnumbered. There's no need to fight us."

"I couldn't even if I wanted to." He shrugged. "I have no weapons, and you are using this abomination to keep my gift from me. But at least I can keep you distracted."

"From what?"

"TREE!" cried a Negander before being trampled by a large trunk. Several more of the gargantuan trees reached out of the forest and smashed a few soldiers and at least one Negander who didn't move out of the way fast enough.

Arram's heart leapt in his chest. He didn't understand how that was possible. There, in the middle of the chaos, stood Crona, hands moving in formations that the trees mimicked. It made no sense. She shouldn't have been able to do that.

He dragged a hand through the air to draw sparks and threw a burst at her. It hit her square in the chest, and she fell to her knees, gasping for breath. Two Negander rushed to her side, yanking her to her feet, while a third held a collar and clasped it around her neck.

Arram's attention returned to his cousin. Kaz's blue eyes burned with anger, and the illusion Volocio swung and connected with Arram's jaw. He probably would have struck Arram again, but more Negander grabbed him.

Arram tasted copper but said nothing at first as he drew closer to his cousin.

"You'll thank me later, Kaz," Arram said, finally gesturing for the Negander to take them away. "You'll thank me when we're all together again."

CHAPTER 54

"Are you coming?" Bronx asked Nik, who remained on the balcony. His mentor's blue eyes stared at the columns of smoke rising from various parts of the city.

Explosions shook the ground beneath them, and the smell of smoke and burned flesh filled the air. Bronx continued to watch Niklaryn. They would have to fight their way out of the city, and they were going to need everyone.

Nik didn't answer right away. His eyes stared at the violence before him, and after a moment, he lost focus and blinked slowly.

"Nik," Artema said, gently grabbing her husband's shoulders and giving them a shake. "Don't dissociate. I need you here with me now."

Nik shook his head and met his wife's gaze. Then he nodded. "Yeah. You're right. This may be our last chance to help Arram together."

Bronx took Reï's hand and led her and the others out of the bedroom. They met Bernie and Manden at the little garden outside, the same place where Bronx had transferred the holy father's energy just the night before.

"The Dominion soldiers with several Negander are clustered around the broken wall," Bernie said. "The Daer are already fighting them, but we need to monitor other weak parts of the wall where they might break in."

"Okay, but we have somewhere we have to be," Reï said, gesturing for the others to follow her down the stairs. "Praymer has Crona and Kaz." The group followed Reï through the fortress's hallways, the only sound was the clicking of their shoes on the stone floor.

"How could the Dominion infiltrate and get inside?" Manden asked. He shook his head. "Doesn't matter. Do we know where they are?"

"The port," Nik replied. An explosion shook the ground again and a some of the paintings fell off the walls, clattering to the ground.

Bernie's eyes grew wide when she finally realized Nik was in the group. " Are you back with us, Nik?"

"We're joining forces to help Arram."

Bernie scoffed. "Good luck."

"Can we hurry it up?" Bronx said. He and Rei had already reached the entrance. He didn't want to leave his sister with Praymer any longer than necessary, and the explosions were growing louder. He didn't know how much time they would have until the Dominion reached the fortress.

Artema moved past the group. "Let's go."

Bronx and the others followed suit and met Yuri and Ana with a group of soldiers on the steps of the fortress. Several plumes of smoke had sprung up in different parts of the city. The front gate of the fortress groaned as more and more Dominion soldiers attempted to wrench it open. They were surrounded, the roar of the crowd making it hard for Bronx to even think.

"The eastern tower is down, as well as parts of the wall," Yuri said, watching the area with a scanner. His mouth dropped when he locked eyes with Niklaryn. "So what Praymer said in the video was true. You are alive."

"We have to go to the port," Bronx pleaded. They didn't have time to dwell on Niklaryn.

"Whatever for?" Yuri frowned.

"Praymer has my sister and Kaz. He wants to lure us out of the city."

Yuri chewed on his lip as he debated. "Fine. But monks have taken all the vehicles. We must commandeer one in the city."

"We?" asked Rei.

"I'm coming with you. I promised Bronx I would not let Praymer lay a finger on him."

Bronx wasn't sure he heard that correctly, but the determined look in his brother's eyes suggested that he had.

"So we find transportation." Bernie rammed a new clip into her gun. "How hard can that be?"

Several Dominion soldiers poured through the front gate of the fortress. Several had guns and wasted no time firing. Bronx rushed to the front of the group, his gladius whirling, and the bullets bounced off with little sparks. Artema manipulated the air around the bullets, and she slowed them enough to drop onto the ground.

Manden and Rei were the next to circle around and begin their attack in a flurry of vines and bolts of lightning. Yuri, Bernie, Nik, and Ana finished the stragglers before they moved on.

Bronx was surprised he didn't see any wearing the orange robes of the Path. But he assumed that their purpose was done, and Praymer got what he wanted: Rei and the Volocio on the battlefield.

The group continued through the cobblestone streets of the city. Several of the people tried to flee in a panic. Most had already taken their vehicles, so finding one that was abandoned proved a little more difficult than planned.

An explosion shook the ground beneath them, and a cloud of dust and smoke raced between several buildings toward them. The dirt stung Bronx eyes, and he rubbed them vigorously.

"I found one!" cried Yuri from somewhere in the pandemonium.

Bronx followed the voice, running into Ana on the way. Wind rushed by his ear, clearing the smoke just enough to reveal a Negander in red robes. His hands were raised in a similar position Bronx had seen Artema wield.

"He's controlling the wind," murmured Ana.

The Negander flicked his fingers, and another large gust threw both Ana and Bronx to the ground.

Bronx groaned as he rose. The Negander had already forgotten them and now had his sights on Rei, who was barely visible in the dust cloud.

Bronx had to act fast. He rushed toward the Negander, gladius in hand, and in one motion, planted his blade into the Negander's back. Bronx touched the man's face, and the familiar black smoke appeared before the dead man crumpled with a thud.

Energy coursed through Bronx's veins like ice. This time felt different, as though the ice had less bite than before, or perhaps it was because the energy could manipulate wind like Artema. It didn't matter, the world around sparkled differently, as though he could see each atom in the air.

"Use it!" cried Ana, breaking Bronx's reverie.

He swept a hand to the side, letting the wind take the remaining dust and smoke from the area, and he could see the rest of the group, all covered in a thin layer of dust like himself and Ana.

He found Yuri next to a truck with a large bed in the back, enough to fit all of them. He rushed to join the others and climbed into the back next to Rei. He had to tell her what he saw, what he experienced, but there wasn't a chance as they tore through the city. Rei was busy clearing a path with lightning, and Artema helped. Bronx used what wind he could to keep away the truck that was following, eventually gathering enough energy to throw it to the side.

Once they reached the wall of the city, Bernie motioned for Yuri to stop before she jumped out.

"Where are you going?" Manden asked.

Bernie wiped the dust from her face. "Someone had to stay and fight with the soldiers in the city."

"If things go south," Yuri said, "meet us at the address I gave you."

"Will do!" cried Bernie before following her soldiers back into the city.

Yuri drove with reckless abandon, but Bronx knew they had to hurry. From his view from the bed of the truck, he saw several Dominion fighters appearing from behind the clouds. Not enough Federation fighters arrived to counter them. There wasn't enough to begin with.

A few dared to follow them, but Rei took care of them.

Bronx swore he saw the shadow of an even bigger ship behind a cloud. He prayed they would not have a repeat of the Underground.

The vehicle drove onto the landing strip and whizzed by several parked ships. Several held people trying to board, but there was nowhere to go—the Dominion had taken over the sky. The smell of smoke from the burning city reached them out here. They pulled up to several Dominion ships circled around a few Negander holding Kaz and Crona on the ground, a gun pointed at his sister's head. His blood boiled and his hands itched with need, a need to wrap around the Negander's neck and squeeze the life out of them until that familiar black smoke wafted into the air.

"We're here!" Rei called, taking a step into the camp. "Come out, Arram."

Her brother appeared at the hatch of a nearby shuttle and sauntered down the ramp. A new cut had appeared under his right eye, already scabbing over.

"You should have listened to me, Rei." Arram gave his sister a bitter smile.

"Do you enjoy the view?" Praymer appeared behind Arram and gestured to the battle that raged through the city below. There were more red robes than not. Praymer brought more soldiers than he ever needed. He made his point. "I did this all for you."

"For me?" Rei snarled.

"To show you how futile it is to deny your destiny. Micaela and I were powerful together as allies. Even your brother recognizes the good you and I can do."

Bronx rolled his eyes and took his place next to Rei. Niklaryn also drew close. Arram's eyes turned murderous once he saw his older brother had joined their group.

"That's enough, Praymer," Bronx said. "When are you going to get it through your thick skull? History will not repeat itself because we share some commonalities with our previous selves."

"Yet the two of you found each other. Arram tells me that Rei remembers Micaela's fond memories of me, so there are enough commonalities to prove my point."

Bronx felt Rei's eyes on him. It was true, but Bronx trusted that the universe still gave them free will.

"Anyway, I am bored with this conversation." Praymer offered his hand to Rei. "Darling, I can end my invasion along with the destruction of your friends with a quick word. Your word. Just come home with me and take your place on the right side of history."

Bronx looked at Rei to find her eyes still on him. For a moment, he felt her indecisiveness. He shook his head. She shouldn't sacrifice herself. There were plenty of people in the cluster who would gladly fight this tyranny. It should never have fallen on her shoulders alone.

"No," Rei said, facing Praymer. "I refuse."

"You are so weak, Rei," yelled Arram. "Once again, you let Bronx dictate your opinions. You know you can't win."

"Arram, shut it," Rei snapped. "You still understand nothing."

"I understand he's a threat." Arram lifted hands. Lightning danced between his fingertips. He threw them forward and lightning burst forth toward Bronx, but Rei stepped in front and deflected it.

Arram's gesture had been a signal as several Negander and Dominion soldiers closed in. The other Volocio answered the attack with cries and the clashing of metal.

Rei surged forward toward Arram, leaving Bronx alone.

A glint of steel appeared in the corner of Bronx's eye, and he raised his gladius to counter it. Praymer had used the distraction to attack.

"I agree with Rei. Arram shouldn't be the one to hurt you," said the sovereign with a devilish grin. "I should have that honor."

"No!" cried Yuri, his own broadsword in hand, putting his body between the sovereign and his brother. "If you want Bronx, you must go through me."

CHAPTER 55

"What the fuck, Arram?" Rei yelled, approaching her younger brother. "Why are you doing this?"

"I love you, Rei," Arram said, bringing up more lightning. "But your ego has gotten us into this mess."

"My ego?" Rei's voice was higher than normal. Her surprise quickly turned to anger. "What about yours? You still think I'm not heeding all of your advice, that Bronx must influence me and I am incapable of making my own decisions."

Arram threw lightning at her, which she threw aside with her staff. "What are you doing?" she asked. "Why would you want to hurt me?"

"You know I can't hurt you. But I do have to wear you out and subdue you. You don't understand and you won't listen." He threw another bolt at her.

"Stop it!" she cried.

"Look behind you, Rei! Look at what your carelessness has brought to this city."

Rei turned to find a ship breaking through the clouds above the city of Medeina. It was the same model that dropped bombs on the Underground. She would never forget what she saw.

She turned back to her brother, mouth hanging open. "You wouldn't dare drop bombs on that city."

"I cannot control them. The Dominion is out for blood and will do whatever they want, regardless of what I say." Arram drew closer to her. "But the Federation still follows you. You are the only semblance of actual leadership left. You can tell Yuri and his thugs to stand down and maybe there will be a ceasefire."

Rei rolled her eyes. "It won't work. The Dominion has always wanted war. I had to accept the prophecy. It's the only way to move forward."

She turned back to the ship just as a few bombs fell from the sky. Pressure built in her chest and flashes of white filled her vision. The only way to take out the bombs from this distance was with the fire.

"I got it!" Artema cried, whipping her arms around.

The wind picked up around them, so strong that Rei knelt down to keep from being knocked over. The air above the city turned a slight tinge of green, and the scent of ozone filled Rei's nose. The wind continued to pick up and circled around until a small tornado appeared, throwing the bombs in their direction.

Rei pointed her staff at the approaching bombs and lightning burst forth. The bombs exploded in a burst of color.

"Thanks!" breathed Rei.

Artema gave her a wink and turned her attention to other Negander and Yuri's soldiers, who had also arrived.

"Now!" Arram cried, and a string of warriors surrounded Rei. Then all at once, several bolts of lightning centered on her. She swung her staff to deflect, but some still hit her, knocking her to the ground.

Rei didn't understand how that could have happened. But some small voice reminded her she shouldn't have been surprised. If Praymer had control of Infiernen and Niko, then he had other Volocio working for him in the Dominion. Her heart hammered in her chest, threatening to burst.

"Again," her younger brother cried, and another onslaught knocked the wind out of her.

"Arram, stop!" Niklaryn cried, stepping into the circle and standing in front of Rei. "You don't want to do this. Trust me, I have spent enough time with Praymer to know you don't want Rei to be with him."

"Yet you stayed with him for almost a decade."

"To be close enough to kill him. So Rei could be safe."

"And what about me?" Arram cried. "Who was there to keep me safe when *you* branded me? I am your brother too!" Tears streamed down his face. He wiped his face aggressively, his violet eyes bright against the redness from his tears.

Rei's heart ached at the revelation. She never realized how much the pain of being left behind really hurt, to realize that when given a choice, Niko chose her. It didn't matter that Niko was a child suffering from trauma; Arram's survival meant separation from her and Niko. It meant missing years that could have been spent together.

Praymer knew this. He had to. She couldn't believe Arram came to this conclusion on his own. Or maybe he did, but the sovereign gave her brother the nudge.

Arram threw his own bolt, and when Rei tried to deflect, the lightning slammed into her staff and broke it in half.

Rei stared, dumbfounded. She breathed hard and her hands shook as she let the two pieces fall to the ground. His power should not have done that.

"Take them both," Arram cried.

Then the soldiers threw more lightning at both of them. Rei threw her arms around Niklaryn, just as the lightning struck them.

"Again," Arram said as more lightning burst forth. This

time they didn't stop. Rei tried to hard deflect, but so much energy flew around, she could only absorb. This is what Arram wanted: he wanted her to call the Fire of St. Erasmus because it would burn her out and leave her unconscious. Trapped.

He also wanted Niklaryn dead. There was no going back now.

The lightning grew with intensity around them; she couldn't fight it off forever. She had to act—and fast.

"When I pass out," she whispered to Niko, "get me to safety."

"What are you doing, Rei?" Niko asked.

"Trust me."

She focused on the surrounding energy, like the storm above the Underground, or whatever she called that day in Ballarat. She allowed the energy of each bolt to flow through her, accumulating in her core. She focused on each fragment, like beads on her skin. She focused on everything around her until every atom bent to her will. The fragments of white flickered around the edges of her vision, filling the space until all she saw was white light.

Plasma filled her veins until it replaced her blood, burning away traces of her until she was only a vessel of energy. Electric pulses of every living thing danced around her. She could stop the heart by disrupting one of those pulses.

Her gaze turned to her core, where several branches of light fed into her from those nameless faces throwing lightning at her. She smiled and snapped her fingers. The flow of lightning reversed and blasted into these poor souls. She vaguely heard their screams.

Someone called a name. It might have been her name, but she ignored it. More nameless faces came for her, and with another snap she used their own electricity to combust and burn them from the inside.

She needed to see more connections, see more pulses. She absorbed more current from the air and breathed deep, her lungs filling with fire. Pain pierced at her fingertips, but she ignored it. She needed to stop them, but she couldn't remember who exactly.

Her attention drew to a flood of light from a city, as well as from a large ship floating above. She could make the city burn. There were so many connections, it would be so easy.

The pain flowed from her fingers to her arms. It was harder to ignore now.

Another voice called a name. This voice was stronger, and it tugged at her heart. She followed the voice to the being connected to her. This connection was precious and had to be protected. She followed the bond and met the beautiful being with the deep, dark eyes.

Bronx.

Her focus faltered, and she remembered who she was. Rei was now aware of the pain, the burning pain in her body. She had to let this energy loose, but she could not release all of it. She needed help.

Bronx's hand reached out to her, his voice pleading with her, offering himself to save her from the pain.

Rei answered by reaching across the runway toward Bronx, toward her other half.

Bronx knew he was outmatched. The first time Praymer's sword clashed his gladius, the strength from the sovereign's mechanical arm jarred Bronx down to his very bones.

Yuri attacked from the other side, but Praymer was quicker. The brothers continued their attack, a thrust, a parry, a swing, but Praymer answered every attack with ease. Yuri was slower with his sword but harder with his strikes. Bronx was quicker as he circled and knifed at the sovereign with his gladius, all to no avail. Bronx gritted his teeth and tried to be faster.

Yuri pulled out a gun with his free hand, and Praymer grabbed it with his mechanical, squeezing until it broke into several pieces, all the while kicking the sword from Yuri's hand and dodging Bronx's swing of his gladius.

The sovereign used that same inhuman arm to punch Yuri in the stomach, and the older gentleman fell to his knees, gasping for air. Then he came for Bronx, bringing his sword down with alarming speed. Bronx's heart leapt to his throat as he sidestepped and narrowly avoided the kiss of the Praymer's blade.

Praymer kicked Bronx's gladius away and caught it before rushing at Bronx, faster than any foe he had ever fought before. The mechanical arm found its mark, wrapped tightly around Bronx's neck with a force that slammed him against the side of a nearby shuttle. Stars shone along the edge of his vision from the blow.

Yuri's cry came from somewhere behind, but Praymer held up his arm to stop the soldier in his tracks.

"Come a step closer and I crush his windpipe." Praymer's hand squeezed Bronx's throat a little more.

"You can't kill him," said Yuri, who wandered into Bronx's line of sight. His hands were empty and raised in defeat.

"I won't kill him. I can always hook him to a ventilator. I'll make sure he feels only pain." The sovereign turned to Bronx, his blue eyes bright with what Bronx could only call insanity. Panic rose inside Bronx, and he fought hard to ensure Praymer didn't see it.

"I know all about your bond with my wife," Praymer whispered in Bronx's ear. "I wonder if the bond extends to your powers. It would be fitting if she could heal me like you heal other reapers. If that's the case, I will have no need of you."

"If you take her," Bronx gasped, "I will never stop hunting you."

Praymer shrugged and his hold on Bronx's throat relaxed just enough for him to gasp a lung full of air before tightening again.

"Just because I want to get you out of the way so I can win back my wife doesn't mean I don't have plans for you. I could simply put you to sleep like I did with Atrius."

Praymer's grip tightened again and spots fluttered around Bronx's vision. It had to be oxygen deprivation. There was no way Praymer insinuated that Atrius was actually alive. The sovereign smiled as though he recognized Bronx's confusion.

"Oh yes, I made sure it looked like he died, but he is suffering a fate worse than death. Trapped in his own body for the last two thousand years. I wonder how long you'll last."

Praymer was going to take him no matter what. His heart fluttered from fear and lack of oxygen. Bronx was ready with a retort when he heard screams. The Negander to his left burst into white flames, then another, and another. Praymer's hold on Bronx's throat relaxed, but not enough to where he could escape. Bronx gasped for air again, and his vision finally cleared.

He searched the crowd for Rei and found her in the middle of a ring of white fire, her hand raised as she snapped her fingers. Her eyes were no longer green but as white as the surrounding flames.

Her hands rose toward the ship above Medeina, and a beam of white light burst forth. This time, the ship didn't break in two. Not right away. She slammed enough energy to push the ship far and away before the force broke the ship into thousands of burning pieces, scattering up into the atmosphere.

"Excellent," Praymer said. "Soon she will burn out, and you will have no choice but to watch."

Bronx struggled to get free of the hold; he had to get to Rei. Praymer shoved Bronx's head against the wall again, and his vision filled with stars.

"Rei!" Bronx called before Praymer tightened his hold on Bronx's neck. The Daer reached for Rei, feeling for their bond and only seeing the white light. Rei turned to him, and for a moment he swore her eyes cleared. She reached back for him, her fingers glowing white. He wished he could help her shoulder the burden, help take some of the energy . . . but maybe he could.

Bronx's consciousness waned. He was going to pass out soon, so he used what he had left to call to her, to draw energy like he would any person who was dying. He felt his own breathing slow as did the world around him.

A spark of lightning appeared across his wrist. It seemed like a hallucination until another appeared. He continued to call to Rei, and soon several danced around his hand. Electricity raced through his body, and his heart hammered in his chest as though it would burst. His own vision clouded in white light, but he was still aware enough to grab the mechanical arm and let the lightning flow. The arm short-circuited and opened.

Bronx gasped for air and would have fallen to his knees if the energy from the lightning wasn't already holding him up. He pushed both hands forward, straight toward Praymer's chest. A burst of lightning threw the sovereign against another shuttle on the runway where the sovereign slammed with a sickening crack before crumpling to the ground.

Bronx didn't see any of it. Darkness replaced the white light as his knees bent under him and the ground rose rapidly to meet him.

CHAPTER 57

Arram stared in horror as charred husks were all that remained of the surrounding army. It was just like Ballarat. He could have easily been one of them, but he had been spared. He should probably have been grateful for that. Yet he didn't feel it. He trembled as the reality of how close he came to dying finally settled into his core.

Niklaryn caught Rei once her knees buckled. Anekris had told Arram she would pass out, and yet she remained conscious. In fact, those green eyes zeroed in on Arram's face and her mouth turned into a snarl.

"You!" she cried, stumbling as she approached him. He barely saw her move. His cheek stung when she slapped him. She was always faster than him. "You could have killed me."

Arram's cheek burned from the strike. He lifted a hand to his face to feel its warmth. "You were only supposed to be subdued. Like Ballarat. It's just lightning."

"Is that what Praymer told you? Because he is the only one worth listening to?"

"No, but—"

"I could have died, Arram." Rei's voice broke as she spoke. "When are you going to listen to me when I tell you that Praymer will have me or hurt me? There is no middle ground with that monster, and he's just using you to get to me."

"That's not true. He respects my ideas."

"And I didn't? Who always fought Urius for your ideas

when he was too stupid to listen to you? Or did my loyalty not count because you're not attracted to me?"

"Shut up." He couldn't look at either of his siblings. He felt both pairs of eyes watching him, one blue, the other green. Rei spoke some truth, but to admit that she was right was to accept the fact that he chose the wrong side. Deep down, he knew he was doing the right thing.

He wanted to protect them, especially Rei. The Federation was a lost cause, and the only way they could survive was joining the other team. They could not bring about the change they wanted if they were dead.

"You betrayed us, Arram. You chose him over me. Your sister. Your only true ally. We stick together and you fucking blew it in your attempt to kill me."

Arram furrowed his eyebrows. He didn't understand how his sister was so dramatic. "How could that have killed you? You have used that kind of lightning before."

Rei sighed. Her lips turned down into a frown and her shoulders slumped, making her look smaller. The spark had been quieted. "It's called the Fire of St. Erasmus, and it's dangerous for untrained people like you and me. I have only been lucky so far, and I could have burned from the inside if Bronx hadn't . . ." Her eyes grew wide. Her mouth formed the words of his name, but no sound came out.

She whirled around and ran through the bodies of the burned Negander to Bronx lying on his side in the distance.

Anekris, on the other hand, was nowhere to be found.

His sister screamed, but the reaper appeared to not respond.

Arram was painfully aware that Nik was still at his side. The sun beat down on them, but the angle was just right that he was in his older brother's shadow. It was as though the universe had to remind him of that painful fact. Nik and Rei would always overshadow him.

"I know how charismatic Praymer is," Nik said finally. "But I never thought I would see someone who could look past everything he has done to our family and still think there's good in that man."

Arram shook his head. Nik didn't understand. "Anekris can be kind. You have never tried to see that side of him."

"Praymer is only kind when it's convenient."

Niklaryn then rushed to Rei's side. Ever the loyal brother.

Pain settled in Arram's chest as he watched the other Volocio join Rei from their various places in the battle. Rei had created such a commotion with this so-called fire that the battle died down on the runway. Yet down the valley, explosions continued to shake the city, and more and more smoke rose from the ruins.

There was so much they didn't know about their powers, and he had trusted Anekris to give him the correct information.

He didn't think about how out of the loop he had become. Crona could wield plants, his sister could wield fire, and Bronx . . . Bronx did something to save his sister's life. Perhaps it was at the cost of his own. Arram didn't know.

He had let his sister down with his ignorance. He had let them all down. He thought he was protecting her, but had he been wrong, and if she burned because of him . . . he would never have forgiven himself.

In fact, he couldn't forgive himself. He wanted to go to her, help her, help Bronx. But Niklaryn watched him, his blue eyes hard. The younger brother was not welcome in their little club. He was never welcome; he ensured that when he surrounded his siblings with lightning warriors.

A hot tear rolled down his cheek. He had already gone so far down this path, he should commit to it.

He left to find Anekris.

CHAPTER 58

HE HAD A STRONG HEARTBEAT, AND HIS BREATHING WAS steady. Yet Rei calling Bronx's name produced no response. The fool took some of the fire from her and passed out.

"Is he okay?" Crona asked, coming to Rei's side, a large cut on her cheek bleeding. "Please tell me he's okay."

Rei cupped his face. "I think so. I hope so." She took his hand and held it to her chest, to her own beating heart. "We have to get him out of here. In case the show starts up again."

"He's all right," Ana said. "He just handled energy he wasn't used to." She placed a hand on Rei's shoulder. "I'll make sure it doesn't happen again."

Yuri stumbled toward the group and grabbed his brother's shoulder. Manden took his legs and together they carried Bronx into the back of the vehicle they had commandeered. All around them more Dominion ships descended on the city. They were everywhere. Rei had no idea how they were going to get off the planet. Niklaryn helped Crona and Kaz take off their collars, and they threw them into the vehicle.

"I have a place we can hide," Yuri said. "We will have to wait until things die down. But I can get us away from the city."

Rei scanned the area for Praymer, looking where Bronx had thrown the sovereign with lightning. But he was nowhere to be found. Arram also disappeared. It was just as well. She couldn't bear to look at him right now.

They had to move. It was no longer safe here. Praymer

would keep hunting for her and Bronx, and with Arram's help, he could find them faster.

"We should go," whispered Manden. "Now's the time to go back to our home world and get the Volocio army."

He was right, but it didn't tell her what to do with Bronx. She couldn't leave him, not like this. This was not how she wanted to say goodbye.

"Go," Yuri said. "Go get help. I will take care of the others, and we will find sanctuary until you return."

Rei couldn't take her eyes off Bronx's unconscious form. She had to leave, but her body refused to listen.

"I will take care of my brother." The concern in Yuri's voice was enough to make Rei look at him. Bronx shared so many of the same features as his brother. It was almost like she was looking at him. Almost. It reminded her she wanted to see Bronx reach Yuri's age, and she was doing this to ensure he had a future. She believed he would take care of his brother. It would have to be enough.

"All right," Rei said, looking at Artema and Manden. "Let's go." She turned back to Bronx and gave him a soft kiss on his lips. "I will bring you an army," she whispered. Perhaps he heard.

"I'm coming with you," Niklaryn said. "I can't go back to the Dominion, and I am too recognizable to stay here."

Artema smiled and put her arm around her husband. "Good. We need all the allies we can get for what lies ahead back home."

"Find Felix Royalt," Manden said. "He is the one who helped broadcast the signal to the Dominion. He's another Volocio, and we can trust him."

"Use the scanner," Yuri added. "There's an Alcubierre-Krasnikov tunnel that can lead you straight from Wolf X to Earth. It's barely visible, but I am sure most

Dominion aren't aware of its existence. It should buy you some time."

Rei followed the other three away from the vehicle, but not before she stole one more glance at Bronx and then at Crona, who nodded her approval. The blonde's jaw set with determination.

"When Bronx wakes," Kaz called, except now he looked like Rei. It was slightly unnerving to hear him speak with her voice. "We'll tell him what happened."

"We'll hold the fort," Ana said before getting into the truck next to Yuri.

"Just come back to us," Crona said.

"I will," Rei said.

Yuri had stepped into the driver's seat and started the engine. Its roar was drowned out by the bombs of Medeina being conquered in the valley below.

Rei wanted to jump into the vehicle and return to Bronx's side, but she couldn't. She had known they would separate, but knowing now that he was unaware of what was happening left a dull ache in her heart.

Artema, Niko, and Manden already began their trek to the *Luciernaga* that hid in a far end of the runway. At least that's what Manden claimed. The pitch in his voice hinted that he wasn't sure after what they experienced. He started making plans, but Rei couldn't focus on the words, just that his lips moved and she heard his voice.

Her attention turned to the burning ruins of Medeina below. There was no way they were going to win today. They were always going to run. She could have kicked herself for not having listened to Manden sooner. If she had gone to Tas'und'eash when he first advised, they could have had more of an edge. She hoped Bernie survived and found the others.

"You coming?" Niko had returned to her side and placed a hand on her shoulder.

"Yeah." Yet her feet didn't move. Her heart thundered in her chest, and a little voice inside told her that this was the last time she would see this. She may never see the others again, never see Bronx again.

Niko's hand slipped from her shoulder to her hand, giving it a reassuring squeeze that quelled the voice inside. He tugged gently and her feet finally followed.

The *Luciernaga* appeared unharmed despite the other burning shuttles and ships around them. Manden had set a cloaking device to hide his beloved ship, and it appeared to have worked. Rei assumed the redhead was inside, but Artema waited at the hatch. She gestured for them to hurry, and the roar of the ship's engines emphasized it.

Rei took a deep breath and followed Artema and her brother inside, and the hatch closed behind her.

CHAPTER 59

ARRAM STAGGERED THROUGH THE DESTRUCTION.
Several shuttles burned, both Dominion and Federation
alike. The smell of ash and burning flesh hung in the air.
Although it was nothing compared to what was still
happening in Medeina.

A truck roared by, almost clipping Arram. The tires
screeched into a stop, and Arram met Yuri's gaze from the
driver's seat.

"You tell your master that this isn't the end," Yuri
growled.

Arram had never seen the man up close, but he was
taken aback by how much he looked like his younger
brother. Next to Yuri was a woman with white hair and eyes
that matched Yuri's and Bronx's: dark to the point of black.

Arram's eyes flicked toward the bed in the back where
Rei and Crona stared back. Bronx lay next to them, his eyes
still closed. Crona's aquamarine eyes stared daggers while
Rei's continued to burn with fire. But something was off,
something was different.

"He's not my master," Arram spat.

"Continue to tell yourself that," Yuri said with a scoff
before pressing on the gas and driving away.

Arram stared at the bed of the truck as it continued on
its way. Rei and Crona watched him, flipping him obscene
gestures as they drove away.

A few surviving Dominion soldiers stood nearby, and he
almost commanded them to follow the truck. But he
thought better of it. If his sister was captured now, she

would be even less willing to listen. She needed time to cool off.

Arram hoped that Bronx survived, for his sister's sake, for the star cluster's sake. He never hated Bronx; he simply wished the reaper knew his place. Family always came first. If anything happened to the reaper, there was no telling what Rei would do.

He needed to show mercy. For now.

Eventually he found Anekris being lifted into a shuttle on a hover chair. His mechanical arm was missing, the blackened arm being carried away by another Negander. The sovereign barked orders as more Dominion ships entered the atmosphere. His eyes softened when he saw Arram approach.

"Where's your sister?"

Arram shook his head, feeling numb. "Did you know using the fire could hurt her?"

Anekris gestured for Arram to join him on a shuttle that descended toward them. Many more Dominion ships continued to rain from the sky. They were beginning another attack, and it was time for them to get out of the way.

"As young and untrained as she is, I worried she would come to harm, but I would have made sure she was subdued before she reached that threshold. You didn't answer my questions, Arram. Where's your sister?"

Arram shook his head. "She got away. Bronx helped her through their bond, I think."

"That's where the lightning came from," Anekris muttered to himself. "So you let her get away?"

"The other Volocio were there, and all of your Negander in the vicinity are dead. I could do nothing."

Anekris nodded. "I am disappointed. But it is a minor

setback. For now, send some soldiers to find them and let's clean up this city. It's about time they learn the true value of being part of the Dominion."

Arram hesitated. He was still unsure if he wanted to commit to Anekris or perhaps find Rei and beg forgiveness. But what else was there for him? Rei would make sure they branded him a traitor for what happened to the Underground, even though it was unintentional. He didn't know what awaited him if he continued his friendship with Anekris.

"I have splendid plans for you, Arram. Help me make the star cluster a better place, and there may even be a crown for you."

A crown. There were so many ways that could be interpreted, but it guaranteed a chance in the spotlight and no longer in his siblings' shadows.

"Let's go."

"Sir!" said a Negander, a young woman with hair that matched her red robes. "Sensors pick up the god king's ship has just left the atmosphere."

Anekris met Arram's eyes. Arram then realized what was wrong with seeing the Volocio in the truck. Some were missing.

"Manden has been itching to go back to the Volocio home world this whole time. I guess the coward finally got his wish." Arram assumed the others went with him: Niklaryn, Artema, and Kaz. "I think he's hoping to get the Volocio army."

"Do you think he'll succeed?"

"Not sure. He needed Rei to go with him, but I just saw her with Bronx. She would never leave him. She's too dependent on him and his survival."

"We need to find them and make sure they don't get off

this planet." Anekris's lips pressed together in determination.

"We will." Arram ran a hand through his tousled hair. He watched as the Negander closed the hatch on their shuttle and felt the ground beneath him shift as it lifted off. "They can't get far. We've already captured the capital. The other cities on the planet will fall in line."

CHAPTER 60

The wormhole rippled on screen as the *Luciernaga* approached. It hid behind Jupiter's shadow, and the thought made Rei chuckle. It was only fitting that a "lightning goddess" would find her way home through a doorway behind the planet named for an ancient lightning god. Poetic, really.

Niklaryn and Artema stood in the doorway behind Rei, her brother's arm wrapped tightly around his wife's shoulders. Manden controlled the ship at Rei's side as they reached the wormhole's gravitational pull and their ship picked up speed.

"Just think, Artema," Manden said, "a quick trip and we'll be back home."

The ship groaned around them as they drew closer. Two weeks was not "a quick trip," and Rei wondered if Manden's ancient ship could still withstand the journey.

"She'll hold," Manden said as though reading Rei's anxiety. "Just focus on the goal. First, we'll head to my kingdom so you can get your bearings and you can see Hotara. Then you'll go to Dinay and the real work will begin."

She didn't hear what Manden said after Hotara's name. Rei missed her so much, and the thought of reuniting with the woman who raised her filled her with hope. She already had allies on Tas'und'eash. It should help. She wasn't sure if she could pull it off, but the others were counting on her.

Bronx's safety counted on it.

Her heart ached at the memory of not being able to say

goodbye to him. She hated leaving him in such a vulnerable position, but she trusted Yuri, Crona, and the others to keep him safe. Hopefully, the others would find the way to kill Praymer in the meantime.

She wondered what would happen to her bond with Bronx on the other side of the wormhole. She wondered if the distance would make it weaker, being stretched so thin. She hoped she could still communicate with Bronx if possible. But there was nothing to be done.

The ship shook underneath them and time stretched all around as they ventured further into the wormhole. Rei's heart hammered in her chest, partly from excitement, partly from anxiety. She would get the army, learn to handle the Fire of St. Erasmus, and return to fight the Dominion more powerful than ever. She couldn't wait to get started.

If you're interested in Niklaryn's prequel short story The Knight and the Goddess and sales or new release updates, please subscribe to our newsletter so you don't miss out!

Read Niklaryn's prequel in The Knight and the Goddess (free for newsletter subscribers)

WILL A SIMPLE MAN BE ENOUGH TO PROTECT A GODDESS?

Niklaryn Ettowa only wants two things in life: to avenge his parents' death and to protect his sister, Rei, from the killer still hunting her.

After a decade of training to become a fierce Daer Knight, Niklaryn finally feels he has the experience and skill to protect his sister who's said to be a reincarnated goddess. He tracks Rei to a backwater town on Earth where she's been hiding and sneaks her away from her caretaker.

Niklaryn takes Rei on a pilgrimage to a nearby holy city, But as they travel across the desert, Niklaryn learns how little he knows about his sister and what it will really take to prepare her for her destiny. Will a simple man be enough to protect a goddess?

GLOSSARY

A

Alcubierrre-Krasnikov—the drive used to allow ships to travel through premade tunnels in order to travel faster-than-light.

Alexia—the goddess of time, prophesied to return in **The Second Coming**

Alma Canale—representative for the **Federation** on the planet **Trappist V**.

Ama—the goddess of ice

Ananiel "Ana" Szabo—a reaper

Anekris Praymer—sovereign of the **Dominion**, husband of **Micaela Roya**

Ara'nden—planet capital of the **Dominion**, capital city: Corincancha

Arram Ettowa—reincarnation of **Maximilian Roya**, a lightning **Volocio**

Artema Ettowa—**Niklaryn Ettowa**'s wife, also known as **Tasya**

Atrius Duque—a reaper, lover of **Micaela Roya**, prophesied to return in **The Second Coming**

Aurelia Ettowa—paternal grandmother of **Niklaryn**, **Rei**, and **Arram**

B

Ballarat—town in what was once California, USA. Resting spot enroute to holy city of **Escalante**

Benot—painter, famous painting of the god queen

Bernadette "Bernie" Boyard—soldier of **Federation**, niece to Federation leader, **Urius Boyard**

Bronx Manca—reincarnation of **Atrius Duque**, a reaper

C

Camila Canale—daughter to representative **Alma Canale**

Castelan—one of many official languages of **Tas'und'eash**

Cesar Duque—reaper and father of **Atrius Duque**

Corincancha—capital city of planet **Ara'nden**

Connocillin—preferable antibiotic of both **Dominion** and **Federation**, only grown on planet **Trappist V**

Coronta—purple liqueur produced by **Hotara** in **Ballarat**

Craegus—god of animals

Crona Sandern—reincarnation of **Alexia Vagner**, a time **Volocio/seer**

D

Daer—knight of the **Federation**

Dante Estoro—ally of **Anekris Praymer**, a **Volocio**

Descendents—people with a **Volocio** ancestor. They have longer lives and the ability to manipulate elements—though not as strong as a full **Volocio**

Dinay—**Volocio** empire where **Micaela Roya** was empress on **Tas'und'eash**

Dominion—political party of the **Tyre Star Cluster**

E

Elmessa Ettowa—cousin of **Niklaryn**, **Rei**, **Arram**, **Kaz**, and **Skylar**. Wife to **Sariah**.

Escalante—holy city of the **Volocio** religion, located in the Death Valley of the former United States

Ettowa Starline—biggest producer of the star ships for both **Dominion** and **Federation**

F

Fabrecido—capital and port city of planet **Kepler IV**

Federation—political party of the **Tyre Star Cluster**

Felix Royalt—famous author and historian, ally to **Federation**, a Volocio

Fiamatta—goddess of fire

Fortress of Riodan—fortress where famous **Daer Niklaryn Ettowa** was murdered by **Negander Infiernen Jessar**

Fire of St. Erasmus—a plasmic power only certain lightning **Volocio** can control. Most die when they use too much.

G

Gliese VI—planet in the **Tyre Star Cluster**, home of the **Underground**

Griselda Ettowa—mother of Niklaryn, Rei, and Arram

H

Hamastagan—another name for the Underworld, the Land of the Dead

Holy Father of Sancta Sedes—holy father of **Volocio** religion. Seat of power is the **Temple of Aladonis** in the city of **Medeina** on the planet **Wolf X**

Hotara Quin—bar owner and adopted mother of **Rei Ettowa**, also known as **Tara**, goddess of the earth; wife of **Manden** and queen of **Munda**

I

Iarann—goddess of metal

Ildana Ettowa—mother of **Elmessa**, staunch **Dominion** supporter

Imperator—ancient emperor of the old **Tyre Empire**, **Anekris Praymer** was the "last imperator"

Infiernen Jessar—**Negander** knight of the **Dominion**

Infinity Dogs—**Negander** knights who follow **Infiernen Jessar**

Ixchel—town on the planet **Kepler IV**

J

Jeanh Ettowa—twin brother of **Jenson**, father of **Niklaryn**, **Rei**, and **Arram**

Jenson Ettowa—twin brother of **Jeanh**, father of **Elmessa**

K

Kapetyn II—planet in the **Tyre Star Cluster**, currently going through election cycle

Kazimir "Kaz" Ettowa—reincarnation of **Kazimir Roya**, an illusion **Volocio**

Kazimir Roya—god of illusion, prophesied to return in **The Second Coming**

Kepler IV—planet in the **Tyre Star Cluster**, origin of antibiotic **Connocillin**

L

Lucas Roya—grandfather of **Micaela** and **Maximilian Roya**

Luciernaga—**Manden**'s ship, over 2,000 years old.

M

Madu—capital city of **Federation**, located on the planet **Proxima Centauri II**

Manden Walt—the god king, a plant **Volocio**

Mara—priestess in the Temple of **Tasya** on planet **Kepler IV**

Maximilian Roya—god of lightning, prophesied to return in **The Second Coming**

Medeina—capital city of planet **Wolf X**

Micaela Roya—the god queen, a lightning **Volocio**, prophesied to return in **The Second Coming**

Munda—kingdom on **Tas'und'eash** where **Manden** and **Hotara** rule as king and queen

---

N

Negander—knight of the Dominion

Nenen—god of water

Nexus, the—an intergalactic system of interconnected computer networks within the **Tyre Star Cluster** that communicates between networks and devices

Niklaryn Ettowa—Daer knight for the **Federation**

O

Oksana—grandmother of **Micaela** and **Maximilian Roya**

One True God—main religion of the **Dominion**

P

Path, The—terrorist movement demanding for the prophesied war between the **Dominion** and **Federation**

Patro Manca—father of **Bronx** and **Yuri Manca**

Prox—form of currency in the **Tyre Star Cluster**

Proxima Centauri II—capital planet of the **Federation**, capital city: **Madu**

R

Reapers—**Volocio** who can manipulate energy of living beings

Reina "Rei" Micaela Ettowa—reincarnation of **Micaela Roya**, a lightning **Volocio** and the god queen

Rose House, The—popular restaurant in town of **Yticol** on planet **Gliese VI**

S

Sariah Bray—**Daer** knight, year mate of **Bronx Manca**, wife of **Elmessa Ettowa**

Second Coming, The—a prophecy that states that six of the murdered **Volocio** will return to war against the **Dominion** sovereign

Seer—a **Volocio** that can predict the future

Siba Sandern—mother of **Bronx** and **Crona**

Skylar Ettowa—**Daer** knight, sister to **Kaz Ettowa**

Stars of Saskia—flower native to **Tas'und'eash**. **Seers** use them to amplify their ability to see the future

T

Tara—goddess of the earth

Tas'und'eash—the **Volocio** homeworld

Tasya—goddess of wind, prophesied to return in **The Second Coming**, now known as **Artema Ettowa**

Tau Ceti II—planet in the **Tyre Star Cluster**

Trappist V—planet in the **Tyre Star Cluster**, home of the fungus **Connocillin**

Tyre Empire—ancient name of the current **Tyre Star Cluster**

Tyre Star Cluster—a group of planets split between two political parties: **Dominion** and **Federation**

U

Underground, The—a secret **Federation** base
    Urius Boyard—**Federation** leader

V

Volocio—humans with a longer lifespan and the ability to control the elements, believed to be gods

W

Wolf X—planet in the **Tyre Star Cluster**, home planet of **Bronx**, **Crona**, and **Kaz**
    Wolf X Civil War—civil war between **Dominion** and **Federation** right after **Anekris Praymer** won elections and dissolved the original **Federation** (~26 years before the events of The God Queen)

Y

Yticol—tourist town on the planet **Gliese VI**

    Yticol Massacre—the residence of **Yticol** disappeared, presumed dead. **Anekris Praymer** has been accused of inciting it, yet he denies it. Among the missing: **Bernie**'s parents

ACKNOWLEDGMENTS

It took me two decades to write *The God Queen* and under two years to write *The Last Imperator*.

One of the first people I want to thank is my editor Tiffany White at Writers Untapped - you have made me a better and more confident writer. I was able to have so much fun with the story because of the tools you taught me through *The God Queen*.

To Hannah Jane, Luralee Kiesel, and K. D. Reid for your valuable input in helping make *The Last Imperator* what it is!

Hannah - you have been my absolute life saver! I cannot tell you how important our Skype chats have been and how you've helped me with plot holes, learning about anxiety to help make Bronx's more real, and overall having someone to gush with and talk about all my plans for this world!

My Fellowship: Kirsty, Abbie, Wendy, and Maggie - 2020 has been a crazy year and having our Skype chats have been the balm I have needed. You ladies reminded me to find balance when I could have easily gotten lost in my writing cave.

April - you have been such a great advocate and friend for my work. I can't wait for our future projects together!

My sister, Angie, you have been one of my biggest cheerleaders for *The God Queen* and it pushed me to make sure I gave you the same quality with The Last Imperator.

Meg LaTorre - Thank you again for your patience in

looking at the million book cover ideas for the series as well as your input with marketing. You have given me so many great ideas!

My parents, John and Maria, you have been some of my biggest advocates for my writing and I don't know what I would do without your continued support.

Thorsten, my husband, my love, my partner-in-crime. Thank you for listening to all of my crazy schemes and keeping me grounded and always trying to find ways for me to continue with my passions. I could not have gotten this book done without you and your unconditional love.

ABOUT THE AUTHOR

Mari, a native Hoosier, currently lives in southern Germany where she entertains people with her adventures as an American expat in the Land of Beer and Pretzels on her blog and YouTube channel Adventures of La Mari.com as well as the adventures of her pugs, Abner and Roxy. When she's not writing, Mari cooks, snowboards, dances to the beat of her own drum, reads late into the

Author Photo © **Tobias Vogt**

night, and binge watches Netflix with her husband. *Go to mltishner.com to learn more about the world of the Rebirth Saga.*

tiktok.com/@mltishner

youtube.com/mltishner

instagram.com/mltishner

bsky.app/profile/mltishner.bsky.social

facebook.com/mltishner

SIGN UP FOR OUR NEWSLSETTER TO STAY UPDATED
ON ALL THINGS M. L. TISHNER AND REBIRTH!
SALES, PREORDERS, NEW RELEASES, GIVEAWAYS,
AND MORE!

Subscribe here or go to mltishner.com/newsletter

Find me on my website:
mltishner.com
Subscribe to our newsletter:
mltishner.com/newsletter